# The Dragon
# and
# the Rose

## by

## Gini Rifkin

This is a work of fiction. Names, characters, places, and incidents are either the product of the author's imagination or are used fictitiously, and any resemblance to actual persons living or dead, business establishments, events, or locales, is entirely coincidental.

**The Dragon and the Rose**

Cover Art by *Nicola Martinez*

The Wild Rose Press
PO Box 708
Adams Basin, NY 14410-0706
Visit us at www.thewildrosepress.com

Publishing History
First English Tea Rose Edition, 2009
Print ISBN: 1-60154-500-2

Published in the United States of America

**God above, how he wanted to taste all the
sweetness she offered.**

But Martanzia was a young lady of breeding, and destined for a nunnery. Surely she did not know what heathen longings she kindled in his belly and what pagan thoughts she inspired in his mind.

They intertwined so perfectly, and although layers of fabric separated their bodies and true desires, the softness of her breasts was remarkably evident, and he remembered laying his hand upon her there. That mind altering experience had nearly been both their undoing. Last night it had taken all of the resolve he possessed to keep from picking her up and carrying her away to his room to satisfy her curiosity and his need.

At the recollection, the embers of need flamed anew and he transferred his weight to one leg trying to alleviate the hurtful pleasure that laid low his ability to think clearly. The maneuver drew Martanzia closer, transporting him to a new plateau of desire. She sighed and the tremulous sound reverberated against his mouth. Did Martanzia want him as much as he wanted her? Yes. He could feel it in her touch. That bit of knowledge pleased him beyond measure, even as it brought him to his senses.

He pried her arms loose from around his neck, eased her away from his body, and held her at bay. There was a hunger in Martanzia's eyes and a quickening of her breath and she leaned forward as if to recapture his mouth. Reluctantly he released his hold on her and took a step back.

"Would it disturb you overmuch," she asked, "if I were not here to vex you and disrupt your camp?"

The question took him by surprise. "More than you might know, lady," he admitted under his breath.

## Dedication

In memory of Gary, the man behind all my heroes.
Dedicated to my family and friends—
you not only kept me alive
but gave me a reason to live.
With gratitude and thanks to Amanda Barnett
and The Wild Rose Press.

Prologue
*Castle Lillebonne, Normandy 1088*

Today should have been the most glorious day of his life. But glory and honor were capricious spirits, swayed by the whims of fortune and easily tempted by the will and desire of others.

Cloaked solely in the chill of the new day, Branoc Valtaigne stood alone in his sleeping chamber. Sunlight slipped softly over the windowsill, the promise of warmth clasped tightly in its arms, but he yielded not to the early morning display. Instead, he stared at the gray and black trappings carelessly tossed upon the floor at the foot of his sleeping pallet. Where were the fine blue raiments, he had so carefully laid out the evening before?

He had slept too soundly, falsely reassured by boyish dreams of courage and valour. He had not heard the intruder as the switch had been made. Intruder indeed. Why not make known the villain, for Rathgar Relentes was his name. This was his malevolent way of ruining Branoc's day of achievement. Just another plot to disgrace and embarrass him. This time in front of all those who had gathered to see him pledge his fealty to God, king, and country.

His gaze streaked across the room and snagged upon the shield braced upright against the nearby wall. The fierce black dragon's head glared back at him with an expression that mocked and challenged and for one shameful moment, Branoc was glad that his father was dead and not here to see the name of Valtaigne defiled by a Relentes, their smiling enemy, their foe most benevolent.

Memories of his father kindled thoughts of his mother, and his heart twisted with a new sorrow. She had worked a miracle to provide him with the mazarine blue embroidered under-tunic and emblazoned hauberk. Now those precious gifts were gone. She would not see her young son wear the colors of Valtaigne.

The sound of people, as they congregated for today's event, drifted upward. Still brooding and angry, Branoc stepped to the tower window to observe the guests below. Like a swirling sea of color, they ebbed and flowed across the courtyard. They chattered and laughed their gaiety profane in contrast to the anguish that surrounded his soul.

Hands clenched in frustration, he ground his fists against the rough edge of the window casement. The pain transformed his thoughts from despair to determination. There was no time to remedy his plight. The ritual would begin shortly, and he dare not arrive late. He would be among the first to pledge himself to King William II, even as his father had pledged his loyalty to King William I.

Standing tall, he turned his back to the window slit. His lot had been cast, if not by his own hand then certainly by that of Fate. And now, as before, he was left to gather together the crumbling pieces of his life. Now, as before, he was left to carry out in personal tragedy the promises uttered by others in good faith.

"Damn your eyes, Rathgar," he swore. "A dark knight you have made me, and a dark knight I shall be. From now until Destiny decrees otherwise, I will wear the shade of doom and retribution that you have chosen for me."

Crossing the room he touched the rim of the shield, and studied in more detail the fearsome image depicted upon the painted hide. He did not believe in the existence of dragons, yet he felt an odd sympathy for the hoary worm; a mythical beast both feared and admired. An invincible creature who's memory survived only in the hearts of men and the minds of children. Sad to be only an illusion.

Or perhaps we were all mere illusions. Reflections of what we could be, or what we hoped to be. Truth and illusion. Opposite sides of the same coin. And 'twas the toss of that coin that determined a man's future.

Grabbing up the somber attire, he dressed with pride and care, while visions of Rathgar still dogged his thoughts.

"Before this game is through, old friend, you shall know the fury of the beast you have created, and you shall tremble before his might. I will champion this day," Branoc vowed, "and conquer all of my tomorrows."

"Neither God nor man shall deliver unto this earth a dragon more formidable than the one known as Valtaigne."

## Chapter 1
*The North Sea, July, 1100 A.D.*

A monstrous wave tossed the tiny ship about with disinterested ease, and the windblown sea-spray added another layer of freezing mist to all that it touched. With a hand pale as death, Martanzia Verheire drew her sodden cloak closer about her shivering body. Now she was cold as well as afraid.

Another breaker of grotesque proportions swept the listing craft upward, and for one breathless moment, the boat clung to the frothy crest. Then the unseen pelagic hand relinquished its grip, and the floundering craft careened downward at a riotous angle.

Clawing at the slippery surface, Martanzia fought to remain seated on the heaving deck. Her senses reeled and her stomach rebelled. Never in her wildest dreams had she imagined that sailing from Flanders to England would be such a dreadful ordeal.

Lightning fractured the sky, and thunder spilled through the cracks left behind. The rain could wait no longer. It poured down from above, blurring the dismal panorama, creating a perfect backdrop for the fiery images that blistered and burned in the back of her brain. She could still see Uncle Malbourne, smiling smugly and waving good-bye. 'Twas because of his trickery that she was here. Anger boiled anew, sparring in her belly with the nausea already well entrenched there. She clutched at her stomach, and hunkered down lower on the deck of the small ship. Thoughts of Uncle only made her feel worse.

Another great paw of water tore at the boat. The craft nearly up-ended, flinging Martanzia backward. She slammed against the rough-hewn framework. Pain exploded in her shoulder and speared down her arm. A whimper escaped her lips, and a new and horrifying idea surfaced in her mind and gasped for breath. Would it aid Uncle Malbourne's purpose if she died in the crossing? He was capable of murder...

She seized the knotted hemp that hung from the wooden hull, and braced her body against the strut. She must survive, if for no other reason than to spite him. Besides, she reasoned, even Uncle could not control the weather, and therefore he could not be assured of her demise at sea. If he had wanted her dead, he would have devised a method more certain of success.

But why allow her to live, and cart her off to an English nunnery? Surely, it was more than simply a punishment for her refusal to marry the odious Rathgar Relentes. Only time would reveal at what amusement Uncle played, and only then would she know her part in the game. One thing was most assuredly clear, he did not rescue her from Rathgar's clutches out of pity, yet to be rescued at all must be considered a boon. One day at a time, she reminded herself. That was how she would survive. There was no point in worrying about the future when none might exist.

She hazarded a glance back across the churning waves, and bid a last farewell to Flanders. Having been given no choice, she had left willingly enough, but exile whether self-imposed or otherwise, was a cruel master. It had seen her torn from her home and the graveside vigil of her Mother and Father.

Another upsurge of water hurled the ship closer to its destination and farther away from her home, and like a fist wrought of iron, a heartfelt sob balled painfully in her chest. Then the boat shuddered and skidded sideways, and the bottom seemed to drop out of her stomach.

Stifling a cry of alarm, she searched the faces of the burly crewmen. Their expressions were grim, but they did not appear overly concerned as they rowed like demons and cursed the lashing rain. Apparently, they were accustomed to being mauled by nature, or perhaps they had suffered worse crossings.

Her gaze tumbled sideways, coming to rest upon her traveling companion. Terrified by the onslaught of weather and the battering of the unforgiving sea, her handmaiden wept nonstop. She should have insisted that Ealgith stay behind. Wet to the bone, the girl sat hunched on the foredeck with her arms wrapped around her knees. And like an addlebrained child, she rocked to and fro alternately chanting prayers for deliverance and pleas for mercy.

"Dearest Heavenly Father," Ealgith sobbed, "save us from this watery grave. Do not condemn us to die young like our dear departed mothers." So impassioned were her cries, even the chaos of the howling wind did not obliterate her words.

"Silence that bleating sheep of a woman, or I'll have her throw'd overboard," the captain bellowed from the stern. "We only promised to deliver the one of you to dry land, so it makes no difference to us whether she stays or not. We'll be paid just the same."

Unmindful of the ultimatum, Ealgith continued to wail. Martanzia crawled forward and gathered her friend into her arms. "The girl will be quiet," she promised, not doubting for a moment that this horrible man would make good his threats. Recklessly, she aimed a glare at the captain. Disgusting in both form and manner, his expression held not a hint of pity, nor an ounce of human kindness.

He growled in her general direction then turned his attention to grappling with the steer-board as he shouted orders to his men. The crew scrambled to do his bidding, and the ship heaved to.

"Hush, dear, please," she whispered, and bolstered Ealgith into a more upright position. "We are most assuredly in enough trouble already. Do not antagonize the wretch who governs the ship."

"I'm sorry, Mistress Tanzie," her companion whispered back. The girl's usual smiling blue eyes were red rimmed. Tears streamed down her cheeks to mingle with the rain and sea spray. Her short mop of curly brown hair was thoroughly soaked and flattened against her head.

Casting her own silent plea of hope to the wind, Martanzia hugged her companion close. Then her expression froze and turned wide-eyed as a formidable blast of wind materialized out of nowhere to batter the ship broadside. The pine mast creaked and groaned. Water began to leak into the hull between seams that did not appear to have seen fresh pitch nor tar since the day the boat was built.

"Come, Ealgith," she urged, as she pushed and prodded her friend farther back beneath the frayed and torn canopy erected for their protection. The small cordoned off section acted as their private retreat, and though the men on board had frequently leered and gawked at them, the sanctity of the restricted area had yet to be violated. Now she prayed the fragile shelter would protect them should the mast snap in two or the rigging foul and rip loose.

Her lips near blue, Ealgith shivered and stared transfixed at the water as it accumulated in the bottom of the boat.

"It will not be long now," Tanzie encouraged,

though she had no idea how far they had come. "Soon we shall be safely across the Sleeve, our feet firmly planted upon the English soil. And by nightfall, we shall be warmly ensconced behind the walls of Elstow Abbey."

Ealgith glanced up, her eyes lucid yet wild with fear. "God has forsaken us," she said, barely above a whisper.

"No, Ealgith, He has only glanced away for a moment. But He has given us the strength to endure in His absence. His love and guidance are always with us."

Though her words seemed to comfort Ealgith, Tanzie feared it was Ealgith who spoke the truth.

Like a creature bestowed with a life of its own, sorrow again welled in her chest, making it hard to breath. For a fleeting moment Tanzie wished the emotion would smother her completely, putting an end to her life, calling a halt to an existence which of late seemed pointless and filled only with grief.

Then the pounding wind and driving rain lessened into a fitful squall and disentangling herself from Ealgith, Tanzie grabbed the gunwale and levered upright into a kneeling position. A dark smudge on the horizon heralded their approach to England, and guiding the ship with surprising finesse, the captain brought them about and steered a northerly course along the jagged eastern coastline.

The shore heaved up and down with the rhythm of the ship, a rhythm that pulsed strong and sure like the heartbeat of a huge beast. Her own pulse quickened, and an unexpected sense of anticipation blotted out her fears and sorrow. Something about this land seemed familiar to her.

But that was impossible. She had never before traveled beyond the duchy of Flanders.

No doubt, these feelings were triggered by the

stories she had heard as a child. Her mother, Beorce, had been Saxon born, and she had delighted in recounting the mystical legends and extraordinary tales of her homeland. And marvelous stories they were; all about sorcerers and wondrous beasts and heroes in the making. But those were yarns spun to beguile a little girl. Tanzie didn't believe in them any more. She didn't believe in anything, other than her own will to survive.

Gliding her hand sideways, she grazed her fingertips against the leather pouch stowed in the adjacent niche. Easing the bundle free, she clasped it to her chest and the tension and worry lifted from her mind and body. Concealed within the soft hide wrapping was a stone carving, a Celtic figurine. It was a keepsake from her mother, and it too had come from this craggy isle.

The ancient statue and her father's manuscripts were the only personal possessions from her parent's estate that Tanzie had managed to retain. Disinterested in books, and believing the pagan icon to be worthless, Uncle Malbourne had not given these items a second thought. Of course, he had thought long and hard about the rest of her inheritance. As her legal guardian, he controlled her entire legacy, and would continue to do so, until she was wed.

She grimaced at the irony of it all. Soon to be sequestered at a nunnery, the likelihood of making the acquaintance of a prospective husband now dwindled from doubtful to nonexistent. She was trapped in a netherworld, frozen in time. Uncle Malbourne and his wretched son, Landow, had succeeded in making her life a living hell. Perhaps she would find deliverance from their evil at the convent.

Everything would be different if her parents were still alive. A tear slipped from the corner of her eye, and slid down her cheek. She cuffed it away with the back of her hand. After nine years, she still mourned their loss, and sorrow still remained her constant companion. In her most defenseless moments, it reared its head and renewed the attack, reminding her of what she had lost. As if she could ever forget.

****

The boat shuddered and slowed forward progress. The steer-board tied off, the men rowed the wide-bottomed vessel aground. As it lurched to a halt, they leaped from the ship into knee-deep water, and muscled the craft landward onto the sand.

Two oarsmen tossed the baggage ashore. A third reached up, grabbed Tanzie around the waist, and unceremoniously dragged her over the gunwales. Still clutching the leather wrapped bundle, she managed to secure her footing and gain higher ground. Ealgith, the next item to be deposited onto the wet sand, struggled to her feet and followed in Tanzie's footsteps.

No longer fearful of being cast overboard, Tanzie faced the captain to speak her mind. "After you have escorted us to the convent," she announced, "I shall have no choice but to enlighten the Abbess as to your harsh treatment of us. I am sure that she will demand penance for your unchristian-like behavior."

The captain contorted his face in mock horror. "That be quite a threat," he said, as his men made haste to bale the boat, "and I'd be afeared indeed except for one thing—we ain't your escort."

Hoots of laughter erupted from the crew.

This bit of information left Tanzie stunned. Before she could utter a response, the men pushed off and re-boarded their small craft, leaving her and Ealgith standing alone on the windswept shore bordering a dense forest.

She hurried to the water's edge. "Come back,"

she cried, reaching out to them. "'Twas only an idle threat. I won't report any of you...I promise."

The men laughed all the harder, and quickly rowed away.

Like a frightened child, Ealgith stood at her side and plucked at a piece of wool twist on the shoulder of Tanzie's sodden cloak. "What are we to do now, mistress?"

She turned to face her friend. The other girl's eyes were round as duck eggs reflecting the panic that gripped her as well. "I do not know, Ealgith," she answered truthfully, and glanced around.

Out of the cauldron and into the fire. An unfriendly thicket of trees grew further inland, but the tangle of woods appeared more forbidding than the unprotected shore. They were alone and defenseless in a foreign land. What could be worse?

Her unspoken question was answered by the snapping of a twig, and a rustling in the underbrush. Two surly looking men and a pair of motley young lads materialized from the dark shadows of the forest. Trailing unhappily behind them was a half-starved pony pulling a ramshackle cart occupied by a pinch-faced woman. There was a meanness about the tattered bunch that seized Tanzie's attention. Outlaws looked the same in any country.

Desperately she scanned her surroundings for a place of safety. The trees were too far away, and the beach offered no defensible shelter. As the brutish gang drew nearer, she squared her shoulders and resigned herself to making a stand. Ealgith gave a frightened squeal and fiercely clasped Tanzie. As her own fear won out, Tanzie shut her eyes and held tight to her handmaiden. The half forgotten leather-wrapped bundle was wedged between them.

"We could be makin' better progress if you womens was to open yer eyes," a masculine voice stated. He spoke Saxon, her mother's native tongue.

11

Squinting open one eye and then the other, Tanzie glanced around. Their belongings had been loaded up onto the now unoccupied dray, and the band of wolf-heads seemed to be waiting for them to climb aboard as well.

"Are you here to guide us?" she asked, in halting Saxon.

"If you be Malbourne's property we are."

"How far is it to Elstow Abbey?" she questioned, ignoring the remark that she was her Uncle's possession.

"About one day's travel," answered the shorter man with the broad face. "But it don't matter much seein' as we ain't agoin' there."

"What do you imply?" she asked, and assumed what she hoped was an imperious attitude. "I demand to know where you are taking us."

"Hear that?" the man mimicked. "Her ladyship demands to be knowin' our plans of travel."

Contemptuous laughter rippled through this nasty little group too, resurrecting memories of the insolent men who had manned the boat. Tanzie glared at her new tormentors. "If you do not favor me with an answer," she threatened, "I am prepared to stand here until Yuletide."

The stubborn lot silently glared back at her. Then goaded by the impatience of youth, one of the boys blurted out their destination. "We be on our way to a castle, lady," he informed her, and ducked to avoid having his ears boxed by the larger man.

Tanzie's shoulders slumped in relief. A castle—that sounded reassuring. They would be well protected there and whoever was in charge could quickly set matters aright. "Will we reach there before nightfall?" she asked, eying the darkening sky.

"No, lady," the other lad replied, as he vied for her attention. "We won't even reach there by nightfall tomorrow. The castle be six or seven days journey from here."

"What!" Both Tanzie and Ealgith exclaimed in unison.

"There must be some mistake," Tanzie insisted, directing her words toward the tall man who seemed to be in charge of the ruffians. "You will take us to Elstow, or to wherever King William is in residence. Either will do nicely and we shall compensate you for any inconvenience caused by the apparent confusion."

Surely the king would grant them temporary shelter. William II may be at political odds with Flanders, but she did not see how he could possibly hold her responsible for such a state of affairs. Why his own mother had come from Flanders. And years ago, at a state ceremony in Bruges, Tanzie had been formally introduced to Matilda and William I, the present king's parents. Then, only a ruddy-faced lad, William II had gone grouse hunting with her father. He must remember. He must take them in.

"From what I hear," the man before her sneered, "the king's more likely to open his gates and braies to cherub-faced boys, not women. I don't think he'll be receivin' the likes of you with open arms."

"Then what of Elstow Abbey?" she persisted, ignoring the crude reference regarding rumors that the king harbored a propensity for male companionship. "Uncle promised us sanctuary at the nunnery in Bedfordshire."

Turning florid-faced, the man in charge heaved an exasperated sigh. "I don't know nothin' about no Abbeys or nuns. And it was Malbourne hisself told us to deliver whoever come off that boat to castle Bamburgh in Northumbria."

Heavenly Father, not Northumbria...That seething borderland was a hornet's nest of treason and unrest. The last bit of hope to which she cleaved plummeted to Tanzie's feet. Was this the treachery she had suspected all along? Up until a few years ago, Robert de Mowbray had been the Earl of Northumbria and castellan at Bamburgh. Now the man was sole proprietor of a cell dug so deep beneath the castle at Windsor the worms had higher residence. He was imprisoned so firmly and with no expectation for release, the church had granted de Mowbray's wife annulment and given her permission to remarry.

"Who holds the castle?" she asked, praying against all odds someone with whom she was acquainted had been installed there.

"Word has it a foreign devil named Valtaigne is to be takin' over," the big man spat. "He's another bloody Norman, comes from the same place as the black hearted Mamzer's son who's choking the life out of this country. And that's all the questions," the man added, and roughly jabbed at her shoulder. "Now," he continued, altering his scowl to include Ealgith, "you can come along peaceable like or be trussed up and stuffed in a poke. Either way ye both be goin' up country."

Tanzie's breath caught in her throat, but it was not due to the man's threat. For an instant, it seemed as if the leather draped statue she held quivered in her arms. She glanced up. No one else seemed to have noticed. By the Face, she was losing her reason as well as her temper.

"Well?" the man bullied. "What's it to be?"

She started at his words, then her mind wrapped around a daring idea. If she were to be forced to deal with these misfits, she'd bloody well do it on her own terms. "Since it is Valtaigne we go to meet, by all means let us be on our way. And you had best take good care of us and our belongings. This man does not tolerate the mistreatment of those entrusted to his care."

Grasping her skirt with her free hand, she raised the hem, and made to climb up into the dray. The leader of the outlaws grabbed the stave of the wagon, his extended arm blocking her advance. "How is it you're acquainted with this Norman soldier?" he asked, his eyes narrowed with suspicion.

She shoved at his arm. "All of Normandy, Ponteau, and Flanders has heard of Valtaigne," she declared.

The man frowned.

Did he believe her lie? She had no idea who this Valtaigne might be, and if he was in league with Uncle, she did not wish to know him. Yet, she needed his protection and would rather take her chances reasoning with one of the king's men than with this lot. "There is no man more feared on the continent," she added. "He delights in meting out punishment for disobedience, and trust me, 'tis not a pretty sight."

Ealgith appeared as confused as the outlaws. As she opened her mouth to speak, Tanzie gave her an elbow to the ribs to insure her silence.

The leader remained unmoving. He furrowed his brow and grimaced as if the act of pondering her words was a painful ordeal. She did not think he was in the habit of weighing facts or making decisions.

Suddenly the woman in the group strutted forward, and with dirty and covetous hands, she boldly fingered the embroidered trim on Tanzie's cloak. "I think her ladyship's lying," she challenged.

Their gazes locked.

Tanzie stared her down, and tried to ignore the foul smell that emanated from the filthy woman. "If you value your hand," she warned, "remove it from my person." Beneath her cloak she wrapped her fingers around the hilt of the dagger that hung at her waist. The carved ivory handle bit into her palm with painful reassurance.

The glow of hatred still burning in her eyes, the nasty woman hesitated then retreated. "Let's kill them here and take their goods," she urged, trying to incite her friends to murder. "No one would be the wiser," she wheedled, with the hopeful eye of a vulture, "and 'twould save us a good long trip to the cold north,"

The band of criminals closed-in, panting and bright-eyed.

Was this how her life was to end? But of course, Tanzie thought angrily. It was fitting that her death would be as senseless as her mother and father's. It was fitting that her death would be as pointless as her life had become.

The shorter man snatched up a lock of her hair, and sniffed at it like a dog with a fresh bone. "Don't be killin' them too quick," he advised. "We could have a bit of fun with them first."

She felt light-headed at the thought of this man touching her, and dying suddenly took on new appeal. Ealgith stiffened at her side as if preparing to rise to her defense.

The other outlaw shoved the smaller man aside. "Stand back you fools," he ordered. "Have ye all gone daft? She belongs to Malbourne, and sooner or later he would hear of our misdeed and have our heads for it. The width of the channel is no protection from a man like him. His temper is short and his reach is long. We'll be doing just as we was told and that's the last of it."

Without allowing for further debate, the crimson-faced man strode toward the woods.

The rest of the company grumbled and followed suit.

Tanzie and Ealgith crawled up into the moving cart.

****

The journey proved long and arduous, especially

for Ealgith, as the food was none too plentiful and the girl's appetite was legendary. The outlaws seemed inept at hunting, or rather at poaching, and their meagerly meals often consisted of only dried meat and crusty bread dotted with mold.

The sour wine, however, flowed in abundance. Every morning the men heartily imbibed while they lamented how William Rufus, who held the forests sacred, begrudged them pannage. And as the king had declared himself every man's heir, all the land and what flourished upon it belonged to him. Then, come evening, they cried in their cups and boldly declared how much better off they would be should Edgar Atheling return to England to lead them against the swiving Norman pigs who made their lives such a misery.

On their third evening, following another night of imbibing by the outlaws, Ealgith moved restlessly beside Tanzie in the makeshift bed within the cart. As true darkness engulfed them, an ungodly howling echoed through the woods.

"What was that?" Ealgith whispered fearfully.

"'Tis wolves," Tanzie answered. "They probably follow a roe or a boar. They will have better fare for sup tonight than did we."

The beasts were closer than any wolves she had heard in Flanders, and as the ghostly wailing pierced the night, each unearthly cry sent a new chill down her spine.

Ealgith jumped, and jerked the blanket over her head. "'Twas shortsighted of God to keep me safe from drowning, only to see me used as fodder for English wolves," she sobbed in a muffled voice.

Rigid with fear, Tanzie inched closer to her friend, and her imagination ran wild. Innocent noises seemed to resound with wicked intent, and even the gentle whisper of the breeze upon the grass transformed into wolves passing like gray ghost in the night.

"The others sleep peacefully," she pointed out, trying to sooth her own fears as well as Ealgith's. "Perhaps the wolves are a common occurrence."

"Or perhaps the others are too drunk to notice our peril," Ealgith countered.

As the cries and yowls drifted off into the distance, Tanzie's body sagged back in relief against the hard floor of the cart. "Close your eyes, Ealgith. The wolves move away from our direction." She tried to follow her own advice but long after Ealgith's breathing had deepened, and slowed into a pattern of contented sleep, Tanzie lay awake staring up at the night sky. Cold and dirty and hungry and scared she felt completely abandoned by life.

****

At mid-morning on day five Tanzie requested to speak to the leader of the group. Because the man was as florid faced as the king he professed to hate, she and Ealgith had dubbed him "the Turnip". Tanzie leaned out of the rig to speak to the red-faced man. "Please, may we stop somewhere to bathe?" she asked. "There must be a suitable stream or river nearby."

"No, you can't," he snarled back at her. "We ain't got no time for primpin' and fussin'. Ye can clean up in a day or two when yer gets to the castle."

Well, really. Yet what other response should she have expected from someone whose body appeared as if it had not been touched by water since the last good rain storm. Settling back into the cart she grabbed up the leather wrapped dragon statue, and held it on her lap.

"'Tis shameful, mistress, to see you in such a condition," Ealgith lamented as she knelt beside Tanzie and plaited her hair. "Your clothes are torn and dirty, and your beautiful hair is matted to where I can hardly work with it."

"Yes Ealgith, I know. We could change our apparel but I'm afraid all that would accomplish is the ruination of more of our clothing, the likes of which we lack in number as it is. I'm sorry we are in such a pitiful state."

"'Tis not your fault, lady. It's your wicked Uncle's doing. Will the man never be made to pay for his sins?"

The anger in her maid's voice transcended to her hands, and Tanzie winced as the girl pulled her hair too tightly. Reaching up she patted Ealgith's hand to calm her. "Destiny will see to Uncle. The deeds we do have a way of coming back 'round to either comfort or haunt us, whichever is just. Besides we have more pressing matters with which to concern ourselves."

"Such as what, lady?"

"Well, I for one have been considering what I shall say to Lord Valtaigne when we meet. My anger and dislike for the man grows daily. I look forward to our confrontation with great relish." She could only surmise that this soldier was a cowardly man. Anyone in consort with her unscrupulous Uncle would have to be lacking in decency. "I had hoped to find the Normans made of more honorable substance," she said, "with character able to resist bribery and intrigue such as Malbourne's."

"All men have their price, mistress," Ealgith said, with a giggle. "And 'tis not always money that they covet."

"Oh, Ealgith, your mind is ever on men and what lies beneath the tails of their gambesons."

"Yes, lady," she admitted. "But 'tis better to daydream of love than to acknowledge the bad circumstances that surround us. My schemes are harmless enough."

Unlike Malbourne's, Tanzie thought. What purpose could it serve, to send her to some God forsaken castle on the doorstep of the Scots? She had been trying to second guess her Uncle for many years and usually, she succeeded at foiling his plans. But this time it was beyond her ken.

Finished coaxing Tanzie's hair into a semblance of order, Ealgith eased down beside her on the floor of the dray. Tanzie shifted about to make more room and grimaced as her now-tender bottom smacked against the floor of the cart.

The terrain was merciless but at least they had not been forced to walk, and in truth, the land through which they passed highly appealed to her. The forest abounded with ancient oaks. The air murmured with wisdom and secrets of times past, and even the rough edges of the landscape were softened by bits of cool greenness forestalling the approach of autumn.

Thoughts of her mother again fought for her attention and a startling revelation ran full tilt trough her mind. Before traveling to Flanders, Beorce had lived in Northumbria. Now Fate was sending Tanzie along the same path in reverse, as if she were returning home for her mother. It was a stunning realization, and it gave her an odd sense of purpose. But her musings were cut short as the cart jolted over an unusually deep rut.

The axle groaned in protest, and Tanzie gasped in bruised agony. Thankfully, the boy leading the conveyance was forced to slow their forward progress. The dray settled into a gentle swaying rhythm and before long, the repetitious motion lulled her into sleepy contentment. Caught up in a moment of little girl fancy, she glanced about the forest for signs of the mythical creatures that according to her mother had once existed.

Had the footsteps of her ancestors once echoed through this countryside, the sound of their voices softly fading away amongst the bracken and the trees?

A gentle warmth filled the air. It comforted her like the caress of her mother's hand upon her cheek, and she felt safe and at peace. Then she saw her-the lady in white.

Tanzie sat bolt upright, ignoring the pain that screamed through her stiff sore muscles. "Ealgith, look!" she cried, and pointed off to the left. A woman watched them from the trees. She appeared somehow familiar but was too far away to be seen in detail. She stepped into a small clearing, then raised both hands heavenward as if offering up a prayer.

Ealgith squinted and leaned forward. "What is it, mistress?"

"Over there, the lady dressed in white. Do you not see her?" Tanzie was amazed that Ealgith could miss such a display. Perhaps the woman could help them in their plight? Tanzie waved to attract her attention.

Ealgith peered again in the direction indicated. "I still see nothing, mistress, other than the trees and a sparrow or two."

Tanzie struggled to her feet. "Please, help us," she called. "Oh, do not go," she added, as the lady turned and moved deeper into the weald.

The cart lurched to an abrupt halt.

Tanzie pitched to one side, fell to her hands and knees and skidded along the splintery wood floor. Her words had not kept the woman from disappearing, but they had drawn the attention of the boy leading the wagon.

Annoyance heavy upon his face, the Turnip strode over to see what had caused their delay. "Here, here. What's wrong with ye now? We can't be a stoppin' for yer every whim or it'll be the Nones of September before we reach Bamburgh."

The others drew near, jeering at her for disrupting their progress.

"But I saw someone," Tanzie insisted, "over there." She pointed to the location where the figure had been.

"Well, who was it?" he asked, as if she would possibly have any idea. "There ain't nobody there now. Run over yonder, lad," he ordered with a nod in the direction she indicated. "See if there be signs of somebody."

The older of the two boys sprinted through the underbrush. The Turnip grabbed Tanzie's forearm, and jerked her closer so he could peer into her face. "This had better not be yer idea of amusement," he hissed, "or you'll rue the day ye landed on English soil."

"I already have my regrets as far as coming to your wretched little island," she retorted, and wrestled her arm free. "And 'tis no prank. I saw a woman plain as I see you."

The boy loped back to their side. "There's no one there," he said. "But I found these." He held out two pure white feathers.

"Looks like they be from a white dove," the man said. He took them from the boy and inspected them more closely. "This female you think you seen, what did she look like?"

All eyes turned towards Tanzie, and the band of misfits awaited her reply as if a great deal hinged upon her words.

"She wore a long white gown, girdled in gold," she began. "Her hair was free and long and honey-brown the color of mine. She...she stood proud and tall, her arms raised skyward, as if she prayed to the forest."

A queer look came over the leader's face. "The byrd woman," he muttered and threw the feathers down as if they seared his fingers.

The smaller man gave the sign to ward off the eye of evil, and though they did not seem a religious

22

lot, the Saxons made the sign of the cross over and over as they uttered the word wiccidom and backed away from the cart.

"What is wrong?" Tanzie demanded.

The outlaws huddled together and conversed in hushed tones. Not one of them would answer her question or even glance in her direction.

## Chapter 2
*Northumbria, Castle Bamburgh*

Being the best was a double-edged sword. It merited the most difficult duties as well as the highest honors. Being the best was a solitary tribute. It left no room for error and no time for personal longings. Branoc Valtaigne was the best in any realm.

He sat his black horse like the acclaimed knight he was, and as he waited for the drawbridge to finish its descent, Branoc studied the defenses of castle Bamburgh. The huge crumbling behemoth seemed to glare back at him, defying him to find its weaknesses.

"The west wall needs reinforcing," commented the man on his right, "but the rest of this old Roman stronghold seems militarily sound."

"Upon first glance, Leofric, I must agree," Branoc replied. "With its back to the roiling sea, cutting off invasion from that vantage and the other three sides protected by natural moat or slope of land, it would appear quite safe from frontal attack. Still it is not impervious." He nodded toward Malvoison, the once victorious siege castle that glowered upon the horizon. "The king proved that when he captured Robert de Mowbray not five years past."

As if in protest to their scrutiny, a chink of mortar tore loose from high atop Bamburgh's ancient parapet. The jagged piece scraped and clattered along the side of the wall and hit the ground with a dull thud.

"'Tis a shame the English are not more learned in masonry," Branoc said, gazing at the rubble. "If they had maintained ongoing repairs, we would not be faced with such a great undertaking now. Much work will be needed to restore this relic to its former glory."

He fell silent, and memories of the splendid castle at Lillebonne crept into his thoughts. That gleaming Norman fortress, now so far away, with its lofty spires and verdant land, was more home to him then any place he had ever known. With scarcely an effort, he recalled the scent of briar roses that floated on the breeze there in the summer. He had seen no roses here.

A lone dog barked, shattering his concentration, and the pleasing image of Lillebonne faded from his mind. He refocused his attention and gazed at the ramshackle cottages and tattered huts that dotted the grounds near the castle. Living this close to the Scottish border, he did not blame the townspeople for choosing to dwell well within the shadow of their protector. But the muddy streets and alleyways at his back lay deserted, and Branoc knew his arrival had not gone unnoticed. The silence that greeted him was born of discontent and defiance, not indifference or acceptance.

In truth, even the landscape, swaddled in thick low-lying fog, seemed annoyed at his presence. The hills held not one dash of color for relief. Black, leafless, tree branches, reached up to claw at a sky the same gray hue as his shield. Beyond the village, the terrain was a misty blur, and though near midday, the air remained chilly and damp.

Was the weather here always this dismal? It made little difference. The presence of blazing sunlight might warm his backside, but it would not comfort Branoc's soul nor brighten the world that he chose to perceive in dark lonely hues. Indeed, the somber elements of this dreary domain fit well his mood and his reputation as the dark knight. Yet the truth be known, blue was his favorite color, but that fact like so many others lay hidden in his heart. A warrior could not afford the distraction of fond memories nor the weakness of sentiment. The less other people knew about him, the less likely he was to be hurt by them.

His mount pawed restlessly at the ground, and Branoc experienced a sense of unease.

"I hope Normandy fares well in our absence," he said. "With Duke Robert on crusade, she is like a beautiful woman left behind with few men to protect her and many to take advantage of her. Even the King of France, turns his lustful gaze in her direction."

"The defense of Normandy is no longer your concern," Leofric reminded. "You have served her well. More faithfully than many a man and for more years than should have been expected."

"Yes, and now I shall claim the estate promised to my father so many years ago. I had hoped to be given a parcel on the smiling southern face of this isle, rather than this somber patch on the boney, northern hind-end."

"Tis better than no land at all," Leofric quipped.

"We shall see," Branoc said, "of late, circumstance has become a fickle maiden, demanding more of my patience and stamina with each passing year. What future lies here for us is yet to be told."

The drawbridge down and bolted in place, he urged his horse toward the unfamiliar entrance. The animal warily tossed his head but without hesitation obeyed his master's command.

Branoc felt as if he entered the gaping jaws of a great beast, and gut-instinct told him it would be a long time before the heathery shroud of gloom and mist lifted from his new home. As he passed through the gatehouse, he silently christened the castle *Gray Scorn*.

Dismounting, Branoc traversed the bailey and went directly to the stables. He scrutinized the area with a practiced eye. "'Twould seem sufficient," he said to Leofric as he finished his inspection. "With but a few minor improvements it should serve our needs well."

He turned to address his soldiers who awaited his leave to stable their mounts. "You may proceed," he ordered, "and advise me personally of any concerns."

"Have any of the beasts shown signs of sickness or injury from the journey?" he asked, his friend.

"All appear hearty and strong," the man reassured. "You worry over your mounts like an old lady with her cats. I wish someone cared for me with such concern."

"Transporting horses over water is treacherous at best." Branoc bent to inspect the left fore-hoof of a bay stallion. "There is always need for worry," he said and straightened. "The beasts are unpredictable. I fear they are much like women, easily frightened and remarkably willful."

Leofric raised a brow. "I am all for willful companionship."

Branoc gazed at his friend in wonder. "Does your blood never cool?"

"Well, 'tis not just a matter of one's fire and need," Leofric protested. "I merely enjoy doing what I do best, delighting women...and 'tis also a brave service I perform, for all men who remain in Normandy," he added, with a grin. "Someone must confirm or dispel the notion abounding as to whether Saxon women are made the same as Norman women."

Branoc gave a bark of laughter, and shook his

head. "When your results are tallied, inform me of your final conclusion. I have neither the time nor the inclination to conduct such a study of my own."

An odd feeling of discontent punctuated his mood. He shrugged but the sense of concern lingered. "I believe a great adventure lies before us here," he declared, "but I do not know if it be for good or sorrow."

"Good I trust," Leofric replied. He folded his arms across his chest and casually leaned against the stable door. "Perhaps even great riches and romance awaits us in this foreign land."

"Pray hold your tongue, man," Branoc protested, "lest you curse us with your wishing and longings."

Leofric cast a look of doubt his way.

"Well mayhap I would take the riches if rightly deserved," Branoc admitted, "but foolish liaisons are not my cause. You are the one who thinks of little else but skirts and what lies beneath them, and you are welcome to any and all romance that we may woefully encounter here."

To Branoc women seemed a troublesome and confusing lot, and he certainly was not ready to let one command his heart. For the present, he was content with being faithful to his King, his briar roses and his vows as a knight. Long ago, when he had trained for the priesthood, he had accepted a future devoid of women, and though the hand of Destiny had drastically altered the direction of his career, it had not yet contrived to change his marital status.

Leaving the stables, his longtime companion at his side, Branoc continued his assessment of the castle and grounds.

"I fear something more serious than horses and women bothers you old friend," Leofric observed. "What truly causes such a scowl to rest upon your brow?"

28

Branoc paused in a secluded area near the castle wall then he glanced around to make sure they would not be over heard. "William Rufus bleeds this country dry with taxes," he began, "and the church bleeds it dry with tithing. The people and the land lie near death. I would rather have stayed in Normandy, to live in peace, than be sentenced to govern or contain a people who will resent, nay hate, my authority."

"'Tis a new decade," he added resignedly. "The world is changing but I am not. I have had my fill of the battlefield, yet would still sooner fight a demon than talk it to death and I do not seek to be a councilman or a shire reeve. I have never felt more unsure of the future."

"You are tired from our travels and the responsibilities set upon your shoulders," Leofric pointed out. "Things will look brighter in the light of a new day."

"Perhaps. But I've grown disenchanted with both warring and politics."

"That is why I worry about affairs of the heart, rather than affairs of state. 'Tis a more constant milieu and much safer ground upon which to tread."

"You are right there, my friend." He clapped Leofric on the back. "For no matter how much women try to change, they really only succeed in staying the same."

\*\*\*\*

Branoc stood in the room he had chosen to serve as his council chamber and thoughts swirled through his mind like chaff in the wind. There were many challenges for him at Bamburgh. The grain towers were full, and the mews, bakehouse and forge were still functional, but there was no fresh water within the bailey. Not one single well existed near the keep. It was a situation that caused him much surprise and great concern. And it was a situation that must be remedied.

Then there was the northern border to be defended. He would need a detailed assessment of the area to counter any Scottish attack. He frowned at the heap of manuscripts and charters that cluttered the table before him. He had personally requested the plethora of ancient documents, but now the thought of transcribing the tower of Latin seemed a formidable undertaking. Perhaps, he could find someone to help with the chore, thus freeing him to concentrate all of his efforts on re-enforcing the castle.

Either way, his days at Bamburgh would thankfully not be spent in idleness. He had come to the conclusion that it was better to be granted stewardship of this windswept promontory than to be moldering away in London or Winchester where he would grow soft and complacent with court intrigue his only diversion. And there was also another blessing not to be overlooked. At Bamburgh he was many leagues away from Rathgar Relentes.

He snatched up a book from atop the pile. Then setting the tome aside he roamed about the room coming to pause before a large window. The open casement faced eastward, affording him a clear view of the North Sea and the wild Northumbrian coastline. He savored a deep breath of air. At least he was once again by open water.

The smell of the ocean danced on the wind, and the waves down below crashed upon the rocky shore with a fierceness not seen in Normandy. But the power of the sea neither awed nor intimidated Branoc. He had made his peace with the rivers and great waterways a long time ago. They were forces he sought to live with in harmony rather than conquest.

With boyish interest, he studied the churning breakers, trying to read his future in the dark rolling waves. But all he saw was the cold gray water and a sea raven that cawed back at him in ridicule for his fanciful thinking. Besides, his fate was not his to choose. He was a soldier in the service of the King of England. He would go where he was bidden with loyalty and good faith, and he would defend his liege, if need be to the death.

Then why worry over what he could not change? Could it be that he was getting old? At near thirty years of age his six-foot frame was still lean. The musculature of his broad chest and trim waist was as limber and tight as any younger knight's. Yet, he had to concede that it was now an effort to maintain what before had just come naturally.

He sighed and passed his hand across his eyes. When had he lost the spirit of wanderlust? Having his heritage denied to him for all these years, had left a sharp taste in his mouth, and little enthusiasm in his heart. Or perhaps, Leofric was correct and he was only tired.

Fighting the fatigue that tugged at him, he pulled himself to his full height. He had crossed from Normandy to England, met with William at Bosham and immediately traveled overland to Bamburgh— all within the last six days. 'Twas enough to physically tax the most resilient man or beast.

As the lengthening shadows give way to night, he wondered when the hostage of good faith from Flanders might be arriving. King William Rufus had told him to expect the lad at any time. And guessing that Malbourne's son favored his father, Branoc did not look forward to the association.

"'Tis a woman who comes, not a man."

Branoc tensed at the sound of the unexpected voice, his surprise taking precedence over the prophetic meaning of the words. As he turned, his gaze fell upon a decidedly old and stooped man. His craggy face was framed by long gray hair and beard.

His eyebrows, shaggy gray as well, protruded like a shelf over striking blue eyes.

"What do you here in my private chambers?" Branoc asked. As he awaited an answer, he silently marveled that even the people prowling about in castle Gray Scorn were of that same hue and coloration.

"I've come to serve the new master of the keep," the man replied. A boldness bordering on brazenness emanated from his eyes. "My name is Morcar, but many call me the old one."

"And what service do you profess to offer?" Branoc asked.

"Why the service of enlightenment and understanding, my son."

Though the old man's eyes were lucid and clear, Branoc questioned Morcar's sanity. Then he noticed the odd symbols and runes on the long flowing robe that hung upon the old man's sparse frame. Had the people of Bamburgh sent a sorcerer to spy on their new overseer?

Preoccupied with his duties, Branoc was in no mood for a jest. He was about to order the man out of the castle, but Morcar spoke before the demand could be uttered.

"Do not be so quick to dismiss what you cannot understand. Sending me away will do you more harm than good."

Branoc studied more closely the ancient figure that stood before him so fearlessly. It was as if Morcar had read his thoughts. Perhaps he had underestimated the knowledge housed in that brittle form.

"Stay if you like," Branoc granted, feeling the old man would do as he pleased. "But trouble me not nor confound me with your prattle. Save your spells and charms for the women and children. I need no magic for the tasks before me here."

Morcar muttered several words in a language unknown to Branoc, and the visage of the old man seemed to grow in height and bulk. The air smelled of exotic fragrances, pungent and heady. Everything, save Morcar, blurred before Branoc's eyes. The crystal-gazer's countenance now seemed boundless. It filled the room and the outline of this now imposing figure seemed to sparkle in brilliant array.

With a voice strong and deep, Morcar chided Branoc for his foolishness. "We all have want of magic at some point in our lives, and you will be no exception. Your time comes soon, Branoc Valtaigne, and your need will be great. This I have seen. You would be wise to know me as a friend, rather than an enemy."

The voice of the enchanter echoed around the chamber like thunder bouncing off the wall of a canyon, and Branoc, the Dragon of Normandy, chevalier to the King of England, survivor of more than six campaigns, suddenly felt helpless. Were his arms made of stone, his legs rooted to the floor? He wanted to move but could not, and although he did not fear for his life, he somehow understood that whether he lived or died at that precise moment was a condition that Morcar controlled. Struggling for his freedom, Branoc fought for a decent breath of air.

As the room jolted back to normal, the invisible bonds that held him prisoner lifted. With one hand, he reached for the high-backed chair to steady himself. Shaken by the experience, he sucked in a deep breath and pressed the heel of his other hand against his forehead.

When he lowered his arm and stared at Morcar, the man seemed once more the old and benign hermit.

Had he truly just witnessed some type of transformation? The lingering fierceness in the old one's eyes assured him it was possible. Not being in command of his surroundings was a new feeling for Branoc, and he did not like it overmuch. Such deception and ultimatums usually garnered his anger, but he felt intrigued by the words he had just heard and humbled by the man who had spoken them.

"Preoccupation and mistrust prompted me to recognize only your outer shell," Branoc said. "Perhaps my judgment was hasty. Henceforth, I shall look upon your advice with consideration. Even if I have not the slightest notion as to what you may allude."

"It is often difficult to discern help from hindrance," Morcar admitted, "especially if one is newly arrived. You will trust me in your own time." There was a twinkle now in Morcar's eyes.

"You must admit," Branoc said, "your approach and trappings do not put one at ease."

"When you see me as the old hermit you perceive what I want you to see. When you behold me as the ancient one it is your courage that directs your vision. Few have seen me so clearly and lived, Valtaigne. You are one of the chosen."

One of the chosen? What the devil did that mean? "Perhaps I do not wish to be chosen," Branoc challenged.

"Your wishes are of little consequence. Regardless of personal desire, you will do what needs be done because you are of that kind. Your sort insures the future. Besides, it is too late. It has already begun."

Branoc paced before the windows and felt Morcar's piercing gaze following his every move. "And what exactly is *it* pray tell?"

"Soon you will behold sights and events beyond your understanding. The old ways shall be awakened one more time before they are gone forever. You will also fight the greatest battle of your life, and the good of all men shall be the prize."

Branoc halted abruptly. Legs braced wide and his arms folded across his chest he studied Morcar's inscrutable expression. What in God's holy name was all that suppose to imply? This was exactly why he did not like dealing with conjurers and soothsayers; they always spoke in those damn annoying riddles.

Branoc did not bother to fear this seer who masqueraded as a man, for the power he had felt previously transcended the defenses of common mortals. His main concern was whether the power wielded be demonic or divine.

"With your leave, master Valtaigne, I will retire now," Morcar said. "I am sure you have much to think upon. I reside in the tower if you need me. I am usually there or in the catacombs."

Not awaiting Branoc's permission, the old man turned to leave. Was there now an expression of sly wit in his eyes?

"'Tis a woman who comes, not a man," Morcar repeated as he passed through the doorway. "A beautiful young woman."

Chapter 3

"This be castle Bamburgh?" The Turnip asked the gatehouse guard.

"Aye it is," the sentry replied, in halting Saxon. The foreign words tripped and fell awkwardly from his Norman tongue. "What is it to you?"

"I brung these women here as requested. So's if you could open up and take them in, I'll be on my way."

The unsmiling soldier peered out at them. "I've no orders to admit females. Bamburgh is a military stronghold. 'Twould cause dissension to have such young women around. Minds would turn from duty to beauty, if you gets my meaning."

"Well, I've a delivery for ye then," the Turnip said. "I'll just leave it over there, and you can sort it out at yer leisure." Returning to Tanzie's side, he led the horse-drawn cart away from the guard. "Get down," he snapped. "We done our job. Now you be on yer own."

"I will do no such thing," Tanzie snorted. She was not about to be dumped off at the castle gate like a load of peat. "Fetch Valtaigne to properly receive us. I'll not stir a hair's breadth before he appears."

"Still playing the pampered guest, are ye?" the outlaw mocked. "Valtaigne will be here soon enough, I'm sure. You'll just have to wait for him. That's the way of it in these parts. Now come along and stand down."

"I do not care what traditions you follow here," she said sharply. "Good manners are always good policy. Now clear this matter up quickly, or I shall tell the sentry that you are an outlaw and point out to him where in the woods the rest of your lowly little band doth hide."

The man hesitated, then yielding to her threat, approached the guardhouse to try reasoning with the sentry one more time.

"I applaud your bold words, lady," Ealgith spoke quietly. "You are always so brave when needs be."

"'Tis ire not bravery that spurs me on, Ealgith. I am sorely tired of the treatment we have been shown since first we left Flanders. We have done nothing to warrant such abuse." Fighting her growing impatience and exhaustion, Tanzie forced herself to scrutinize the castle. Her observations failed to improve her disposition. Bamburgh was the most ill-favored, homely, fortification she had ever laid eyes upon. It seemed a forgotten outpost, situated in no-man's land, at the mercy of the fearsome countryside that surrounded it. Of course, first impressions could be misleading.

A second, more in depth consideration, surprisingly tempered her aversion. There was something rather reassuring about the monstrous structure. It seemed lonely, she thought with a pang of sympathy, and she decided she approved of this shored-up old assemblage of dreams and memories. Like some devoted hoary beast, it hunched resolutely on the rugged edge of the world. Scoured by the wind and whipped by the sea, it was an imposing sentinel, yet, there was pride in its scarred edifice and noble arrogance in its dark profile.

As she stared at the castle walls, the setting sun peeked from beneath the canopy of late afternoon clouds. The great expanse of weathered stone before her was suddenly illuminated in dazzling shades of yellow and burnished gold. Then, in a trice, the fiery orb sank below the horizon, and as the comforting display of light disappeared, dusk quickly followed ushering in the chill evening air.

Annoyed at having to endure yet more discomfort, and with the promise of shelter and food waiting, Tanzie was about to try her own hand at arguing with the sentry. Then a company of horsemen materialized on the far hill, and in the face of their approach, all thought fled from her mind.

Shouting and laughing, the warriors rode through the glimmering twilight, advancing toward the castle at a spirited gait. The dogs at their side barked and nipped playfully at the heels of the horses. A slain deer, slung across one man's pommel, declared the men victors in the day's hunt.

One figure, riding more masterfully than the rest, fascinated Tanzie. His hair, windswept and unruly, was black as a raven's plume. It matched the hauberk he wore and the horse that he rode, and she could not take her eyes from him. He laughed and added his voice to the cries of triumph, and for one spellbinding instant, a roguish smile brightened his countenance. Then quick as sheet lightning, the joyful expression was gone, and he was once again a somber study in black.

The mounted men drew closer, the stride of their horses never lessening. The thunder of hoof beats grew louder, pounding in counterpoint to the cadence of the great warhorses' heavy breathing. The ground shook with their approach. So boisterous and terrifying was their advance, for one horrible moment, Tanzie feared the castle under attack. From the corner of her eye, she watched the Turnip abandon them and run for the woods. She was tempted to do the same.

The gates were thrown open, and in a swirling storm of dust and noise, the mounted soldiers clattered over the wooden planking, through the dim passageway and into the bailey. Just as quickly, the big gate swung shut behind them.

Tanzie coughed and fanned the dust from in front of her face.

As the murky air settled, she glanced up to see that one of the men had remained behind. He towered at their side and worked to restrain his eager stallion from following the rest of the men and horses.

By the Saints, it was him, the soldier who wore black and silver. Her breath caught in her throat. He was even more imposing as he glowered down at her.

"What do you here?" The French words were blunt—offering no welcome or introduction. His abrupt demeanor nurtured her ire back into full bloom.

"Do all the people of this northern clime have the manners of simpletons?" she retorted. "I demand to speak to Lord Valtaigne. I am told he is in charge of this ill run riotous abomination." Still seated, her fists clenched in anger, she openly glared at the warrior. "'Tis a poor excuse for a Norman out post," she muttered.

The man's gray eyes changed from curious to dangerous and his mouth tightened. "What business have you with, Valtaigne?"

"I will tell him when he has the decency to address me. I do not wish to speak to his attendant."

"You will speak to me or no one at all," the soldier challenged.

Tanzie crossed her arms and stared straight ahead.

"The decision is yours," he warned when she did not speak. "'Twill be a cold night and a most uncomfortable one if you spend it in your present accommodations."

Over the past several days, Tanzie had been bullied beyond endurance. Even if logic and reason were on this man's side, she refused to back down. Ignoring his presence, she shifted her gaze to the far horizon, and fought not to hug herself for warmth.

"As you wish, lady," he said. "'Tis a pity you will not share the hearth and fire that awaits within. Nor will you savor the fresh venison we have taken. Perhaps your pride will fill your belly and warm your flesh."

He turned and rode toward the castle. The guard jumped to attention and manned the half-gate.

To Tanzie's surprise, Ealgith spoke. "Good sir, please wait. We have come a great distance to meet with Lord Valtaigne. Could you at least advise him that we have arrived?"

"Hush, Ealgith," Tanzie scolded. "I will not give in to this wayward knave." Secretly she thanked Ealgith for overstepping her bounds. She did not truthfully wish to spend another night in this wagon of torture.

The man glanced back over his shoulder, then irritatingly slow, he pivoted his horse and rode back to their side. "And who is it that calls for Valtaigne?" he asked.

"'Tis mistress Martanzia Verheire of Flanders," Ealgith proclaimed. "Third cousin to the late Queen Matilda and faithful servant to the English crown."

"Quite an impressive introduction for so ill-tempered a lady," he acknowledged.

Infuriated by his sarcasm, Tanzie stood up in the unsteady cart. She lifted her hand to slap the man's insolent face, but he seized her arm midair.

A taunting smile crossed his lips and amusement sparkled in his eyes. "Few men are brave enough to accost me so. You are either more fearless than most or more foolish."

As she tried to wrest her arm from his grasp, his lips twitched as if he found her efforts so improbable as to be laughable.

"Release me at once you, you...Norman," she demanded.

Ignoring her irate request, he raised her wrist and shook her arm as if he toyed with a young pup. His simple actions nearly pulled her from her feet, making her fear she might topple from the dray.

"I will gladly set you free," the warrior said, his expression, now serious, "if you promise not to aim any more brutal attacks in my direction."

"I promise," she said through clenched teeth, as a string of less polite words scurried through her thoughts.

Gently he lowered her arm, steadying her, waiting until she was again properly seated before he released his grip on her.

"Not that you have given me any choice," she added in a huff.

He stared at her with an intensity that made her uncomfortable. She felt as if he picked through her thoughts as he weighed her character and graded her mettle. "Not being in control of one's destiny plagues us all, lady."

His words struck a chord, and for an instant, she thought this arrogant man seemed as lonely as the castle that guarded his back. Then the feeling was gone.

A fox yipped in the gathering gloom, and there was a bustle in the hedgerow. The dark knight's attention shifted in the direction of the sound. Then his gaze settled back upon her face. "You may enter the castle," he said. "Valtaigne has yet to turn his back on a fair lady in distress."

"I will be sure to point out to him," she said sweetly, "who it was that so distressed me."

His mouth twitched, as if a smile fought for release upon his lips. But he seemed to fight the impulse and win. He bent down, grabbed the pony's lead and without another word, he turned his horse toward the gatehouse. Tanzie grabbed the slats of the cart as it jerked into motion behind him.

Despite her fury, she studied this man. He was fearsome, yet handsome and most appealing in stature. Broad through the shoulders and narrow in the hips, his strength seemed tempered by agility. He sat his horse as if he were quite at home there, and the powerful destrier obeyed him with but the slightest encouragement, giving the impression that the beast responded out of devotion rather than fear.

Yes, he was a most magnificent and formidable animal—and so was the horse.

They crossed the outer bailey and at the entrance to the great hall eased to a halt. Their escort dismounted in one fluid movement, raw power underlying every motion.

"You are welcome to spend the night," he said and politely assisted both her and Ealgith down from the conveyance. "I will find someone to show you to a room and will personally inform Lord Valtaigne of your presence. No doubt, he will wish to speak with you later this evening."

Once again trapped under this knight's cool regard, Tanzie stood a little taller. Realizing how frightful she must appear, she brushed at her impossibly dirty outer tunic, and patted her tangle of hair.

At her hopeless attempts, his face gentled and the hint of compassion reached all the way to his eyes. "I will have hot water sent to your room as well as food."

Left breathless and speechless by his perusal, Tanzie watched as he led his horse to the stables. Before she could gather her spinning thoughts, a hunched old woman appeared at their side and motioned for them to follow.

The crone deftly collared two passing lads and

set the boys to fetching the trunks and baggage from the cart. Before either could pick it up, Tanzie seized the small bundle that held her statue. She would carry that herself.

Similar to the edifice, the interior of the castle was a patchwork of construction. The original walls, as thick as the height of two men, supported the newer repairs and improvements. Traversing the main floor, they worked their way around to the northern most corner of the structure where they came upon a spiral staircase that served all floors. With one hand on the wall for good measure, Tanzie cautiously followed the old woman up the dark twisting stairwell.

"Ealgith," she whispered, to the girl at her back. "When first we arrived did you see how the sun broke through the clouds to reflect upon the castle walls?"

"Yes, 'twas most brilliant," Ealgith agreed.

"For that one glorious moment it mirrored such welcome and cheer," Tanzie added, "I think I shall call this castle *Shining Hope*. 'Tis the only glimmer of brightness that I have seen so far in our woeful travels. Truly it must be a sign."

"No doubt it is lady," Ealgith replied with little enthusiasm. "But I wouldn't be so sure of what it heralds. The walls will look as black as any others in the dead of night."

Undaunted by Ealgith's pessimism, Tanzie eagerly followed as they were led into a sleeping chamber.

The quarters afforded them were spacious, airy and much more comfortable than the room allotted Tanzie by her miserly Uncle in Flanders. Rich tapestries hung upon the walls and the floor, though not layered with rushes, was clean. Wolf hides and bearskins generously covered the area near the bed and before the open fire pit, and braziers stood along the opposite wall, one on either side of a small table and chair. It would be a comfortable room even as the chill of autumn approached.

The lads piled the luggage in the center of the room. Then the old woman nodded and ushered the boys out the door.

Ealgith lit the candle beside the bed. Tanzie set the dragon statue beside the candle, slipped free of her cloak, and wandered over to the bartizan window. Though softened by the fading light, the panorama was spectacular. The drop was sheer and very long, yet the steadfast roar of the sea drifted up to her on the vortex of a breeze.

Beyond the cliffs and rocky shore, a single dark stone jutted up from the churning water. The rugged monument reared up out of the sea like a tiny fortress. The base appeared stalwart and anchored to the earth's core, but mist curled around the top giving the illusion that the peak soared upward joining with the heavens.

There was something wondrous about the towering monolith. It imparted a sense of great age and remembrance, and even after the darkness of night came to steal away the vision, she continued to stare in the direction of the mysterious pinnacle.

"Mistress?" Ealgith called.

"Yes." Tanzie forced her gaze from the rock.

"The food is here and the hot water too."

"What blessed words those be, Ealgith." Unbinding her hair, Tanzie hurried toward the steaming buckets of water.

After snatching up a large morsel of food popping it into her mouth, Ealgith unlaced the back and sleeves of Tanzie's over-tunic. "Merciful heaven," the girl clucked, "these ain't even fit for the begger's bin." She stripped away the dirty tattered clothing and tossed them to the floor.

"Don't despair. Once we reach the cloister, we

shall no doubt be provided with habits."

"And won't that be a tremendous boon to your meager wardrobe," Ealgith chided. "We must be sure your Uncle does not hear of it, as he may appropriate those as well."

"Now Ealgith. 'Tis wrong to harbor such hatred. Remember one is hurt by one's own anger. It will eat you up inside, and you will become as pitiful as Malbourne."

"If I devoted a lifetime to it, I doubt I could become as cruel and cold as that man," her friend muttered.

"Tis true," Tanzie admitted, "he has achieved a level of malevolence not reached by many."

Naked and shivering she knelt beside the pails of water. Ealgith grabbed up a fur, draped it around her mistress's shoulders, and assisted her in washing her hair and scouring her body.

Clean, contented and swathed in white linen, Tanzie sat before the fire. The tingle of being fresh-scrubbed still lingered on her skin. "You have revived my spirits most heartily," she called to Ealgith, who proceeded with her own ablution. "No easy task, I might add, as I think they did lie very near to death. Now I am ready to face anything or anyone."

"Even Lord Valtaigne?" Ealgith quipped over her shoulder.

Tanzie's exhilaration evaporated as quickly as pond ice. She bolted upright, nearly upsetting the tray of bread and cheese at her side. She had forgotten the appointment. What should she wear to meet their dubious host? She must be strong and confident in his presence and not worried about how she was perceived. After all, one's appearance counted for much when confronting the enemy. Her russet kirtle would do. Of her few costumes, it alone best enhanced her coloring, making her seem older and less vulnerable.

She dressed as if preparing for battle and all the while, she reviewed the statements that she intended to hurl at this man. She wondered what he might look like and what excuse he had devised to explain why she had been brought to Bamburgh rather than Elstow Abbey.

After adjusting an old copper fibula at her shoulder, Tanzie dabbed a precious drop of rose attar on each wrist and at her throat. The fragrance engulfed her, soothing her worries, weaving a charm of strength and confidence around her. How she missed her early morning interludes in the rose garden at the chateau. Caring for the flowers had become a daily ritual, a sacred event that brought her closer to God than any formal ecclesiastical ceremony ever had.

Some would consider such an idea pagan. But, she could not help what thoughts entered her mind. She believed that God was part of all things and that honoring an oak tree or water from a stream was just as edifying as kissing the feet of a golden crucifix or supplicating one's self upon an ornate prie-dieu, whose price could feed an entire village for a winter.

She retrieved a pair of soft leather shoes, slipped them on and laced them tight. She didn't mean to harbor such controversial concepts and when they popped into her head, it created a troublesome conflict. Of course, the precepts of formal religion confounded her as well. The church was far from a haven of peace. Men fought ruthlessly for the holy see of Canterbury, as well as for the throne at Westminster. Anselm and Flambard were in constant defiance of one another and Odo's manipulations, God rest his soul, were legendary. The clergy merely waged their wars more subtly. Yet, in the end their means were just as detrimental to the common good of mankind.

Did Lord Valtaigne wrestle with such concerns? Of course not. That would indicate he had a conscience, and Uncle would never be foolish enough to employ a man encumbered by such a burden. She could not imagine what code of ethics this ogre of a knight might answer to.

Raising the lid of a small inlaid box, Tanzie selected an emerald encrusted dagger and slipped it into the sheath that hung from her girdle. The dirk was just for show of course. If she had any hopes of wounding her new keeper, it would have to be by sharp wit and honed logic.

A few moments later, forced from nervous wandering about the room to apprehensive immobility, she commended herself into a chair and Ealgith's capable hands.

"You appear most lovely, lady," her friend reassured as she combed the last of the tangles from Tanzie's hair. "This Norman will be at your mercy. But," she added as she rummaged about in a nearby trunk, "for the finishing touch we must have some ribbon. And I've a surprise for you, lady."

Ealgith returned to Tanzie's side, proudly bearing a handful of tiny dried flowers. "On our journey north," she explained, "my foraging for food was unsuccessful, but at least I found these."

"Oh, Ealgith, they are lovely. Thank you for your kindness in thinking of me. I wish there was something special I could do for you in return."

"Well," the girl said with a grin, "when you speak to Lord Valtaigne, perhaps you can extract a promise from him assuring we shall continue to be properly fed from now until we reach the nunnery."

Tanzie smiled at her friend's request. If only the procurement of food was their biggest concern.

As Ealgith finished weaving the dried flowers and matching ribbons into Tanzie's long unbound hair, a knock sounded on the chamber door. Without waiting to be told, Ealgith hurried to the portal.

"Who is there?" she asked.

"I am Leofric, come to escort Lady Verheire to her interview with Lord Branoc Valtaigne."

"Branoc," Tanzie repeated softly. So that was his Christian name. Such a noble sounding word to signify a man of such questionable character. She rose from the chair and motioned to Ealgith to open the door.

The man revealed, was easy to look upon and hard to ignore. His smile radiated a charm and optimism that brightened the atmosphere. His dark eyes scanned the room as he waited for permission to come forward.

"You may enter," Tanzie said, pleased with his good manners.

"Do you want for anything?" he asked, striding forth to stand before her. "Pray let me know what your heart desires, and I shall deliver it unto your side." He studied each woman, not rudely, but quite thoroughly. She was not sure, but she thought he winked at Ealgith.

"Thank you for your kind offer, Leofric. So far our every need has been seen to."

"Then if you are ready, Valtaigne awaits you."

"I am ready." Tanzie, picked up the scroll that Uncle had given her in Flanders. "I only hope he is ready for me."

Ushering her down the dim passageway, Leofric did not seem inclined toward conversation.

"How long has Sir Branoc been in residence at Bamburgh?" she asked, attempting to pry some useful information from her escort.

"Long enough to already miss Normandy," Leofric replied noncommittally.

That told her little. Leofric was a good and faithful man. "Are your plans to occupy this stronghold temporary or more definite?" she prodded.

"We will stay until King William Rufus bids us go."

Again, he sidestepped her query. She fell silent, deciding to save her questions for Valtaigne. His answers were the only ones that mattered.

Her escort halted before a forbidding oak door. Tanzie's mouth went dry. Her palms began to sweat and fearful anticipation trampled about in her stomach.

Leofric glanced at her and smiled. "My lord has already eaten well today. I believe you are safe in entering his lair." Rapping loudly, and without waiting for a response, Leofric pushed open the door and led her forward into the council chamber.

Maps, papers and manuscripts, strewn in disarray, covered the entire top of the massive table that sat square in the middle of the room. A large supply of precious candles lay nearby. Evidently, the setting of the sun did not stop the reading and studying that took place within these walls.

From the corner of her eye, she spied an assortment of coffers and trunks. Nestled contentedly along one partition, lids open, they resembled the upturned faces of baby birds, mouths wide, waiting to be fed more papers. Her father would have felt at home in this room.

As her eyes adjusted to the dim lighting, Tanzie detected a man sitting concealed in the far corner. He continued to look outward through the open window, though surely he had heard them enter.

"By your leave, Sir," Leofric announced, "I present Mistress Martanzia Verheire." Leofric disappeared from her side, closing the door on his way out, leaving her to feel small and defenseless in the cavernous room.

She swallowed hard and squared her shoulders

and her heart thudded wildly with expectation as the silent man unfolded from the chair and gained his feet.

Then Tanzie's mouth dropped opened in amazement, and the words of her well-practiced speech took flight. Mutely, she stared up into the face of the same dark knight she had tangled with outside the castle walls. Astonishment turned to anger. She had been played for a fool.

The fire of indignation burned upon her cheeks, as she lifted her chin a degree higher to meet his gaze head on.

God's bones he was a handsome man.

## Chapter 4

"How dare you so deceive me." Animosity crackled in the girl's voice. "Your ill manners are only outdone by your peculiar sense of what is humorous." Hands upon her hips she stood before him, defiant and unafraid. The unwavering glare she aimed at him could not have been more effective had it been flung from a mangonel.

Branoc had not anticipated this reaction to his unplanned jest. He also would not have predicted that his guest would prove to be so comely beneath the road dirt she had worn earlier in the evening.

"I see a respite and hot bath did little to temper your mood."

"And why should my mood be improved?" she retorted. "I have been dragged, unwilling, the entire length of England, to a destination not of my choosing. Then I am left waiting at the front gate of this ancient ruin, only to fall victim to your insults and buffoonery."

She stormed about the room as she spoke. With a ragged sigh, Branoc pulled out a chair and sat down. He might as well be comfortable as she railed against the world and her current circumstances within its bounds.

"You did arrive unannounced at a military garrison," he calmly pointed out. "'Tis a time of great unrest. We are not in the habit of admitting whoever just happens to call at our gate."

"But I must have been expected," she protested, and tossed the parchment she carried onto the table at his side. "'Tis from my Uncle," she declared, "I had thought to be relinquishing this to the Reverend Mother, not an insolent Norman soldier."

His gaze fixed upon her person, he reached sideways to retrieve the scroll. He examined the seal to make sure it had not been tampered with, then quickly unrolled and read the document. The sigh that escaped him now was long and heavy—filled with discontent.

Malbourne had broken his pledge. 'Twas not his son that he sent to Northumbria after all. Branoc reclined in his chair, and the words of the sorcerer rose up like specters in the back of his mind. The old man had been correct. A woman had come in Landow's place.

"You are Malbourne's—niece?" he asked.

"Of course I am. And you needn't pretend to be surprised."

"But I am surprised. 'Twas Malbourne's son, Landow, we were promised. What kind of man sends a female to be hostage?"

"Hostage!" She appeared stunned at the revelation. "You have made a mistake. I am to be remanded over to the nunnery at Elstow Abbey. My journey was to serve no other purpose."

"Then 'twould appear, lady, we have both been deceived."

"I don't understand. Deceived by whom?"

"Count Baldwin is away from Flanders on pilgrimage," Branoc explained. "During his absence, King William II has requested a hostage of good faith." He pointed a finger at the document and then at her. "Your Uncle has volunteered you."

This information reduced her to silence, but he imagined the full meaning of what he had just told her was ruminating in her mind. Carefully, he re-rolled the scroll and set it aside. Then he prepared himself for the forthcoming explosion.

"I shall be no such thing," she declared. "I do not

care what arrangements you made previously with my Uncle. You will send me and my handmaiden, to Elstow. Immediately."

She dictated her demands with the ease of an empress. "'Tis not my fault," she added irritably, "that you men cannot properly arrange your transactions of war and tentative peace. I will not pay the penalty for my uncle's falseness to you, nor for your lack of attention to detail. You should have sent someone to fetch my cousin Landow, instead of waiting for delivery."

Her hands were clenched at her sides, and her full lips were pressed into a stubborn, no-nonsense line. Only the tiny quiver of her chin belied the bravado of her words.

Branoc stretched out his legs, crossed his arms over his chest and studied her. He could not decide if she were a pawn in Malbourne's scheme or a willing participant. Although, her surprise and confusion seemed genuine.

"I cannot allow you to go to a nunnery. Once there, you would be granted sanctuary, leaving William with no hostage at all. Right or wrong, you are the one who was sent to me. And right or wrong, it is here that you shall remain."

"But this is impossible. I will not stand for it."

Branoc gained his feet. "You, lady, do not have a choice in the matter. Only by William's word will I release you."

"Then you must write to him at once," she demanded, as she stormed about once more.

He would write to William when he damn well pleased and not by her command. As he stalked toward her, she spun around and came to a sudden stop. Her hair swirled about her shoulders. Her gaze held his, and the scent of roses momentarily waylaid his senses.

"You are overwrought. Sit down and calm

yourself." He reached for her arm to escort her to a nearby chair, but she snatched her elbow from his grasp and backed away from him.

"Of course I am overwrought" she replied. "I am being held prisoner in a foreign land with no one to champion my cause. My uncle has once again betrayed me, and you are recalcitrant and without honor in the situation. Pray tell me exactly how should I feel?"

He watched her animated display, noticing how the earthy colors she wore infused her skin with a warm glow. The flowers entwined in her hair lent an ethereal aspect to the mantle of gleaming tresses cascading to her waist. She appeared as if she had recently tumbled from a woodland bower. With each movement of her arms, her outer tunic shifted, revealing the curve of her hips and the swell of her breasts hidden beneath her kirtle. And with the blush of anger upon her cheeks, she was all the more alluring.

"I am not pleased with the situation myself," Branoc admitted and ran a hand through his hair. He forced his gaze from her face and concentrated on the leaping flames that burned in the hearth. "There is more than enough trouble in this land to occupy my time without having to worry about the needs and protection of a young woman of good breeding. At least Landow would have been of some use to me." He turned again to face her. "You will no doubt be a daily trial if this is to be your manner."

They stared at one another a silent battle of wills raging between them. Her gaze never wavered, and he admired her courage or perhaps it was simple stubbornness. Then, although, it appeared to cost her much, she relented and sat down. She seemed overwhelmed by all that was happening. Worse yet, he thought she looked about to cry. But when she spoke her tone did not waver.

"What was he to do for you?" she asked.

"Who?" Branoc asked.

"Landow for heaven sakes. Of whom do you think I speak? If I am to remain here even for a short while, I may as well do something useful to pass the time."

"I see," he said, unable to hold back a smile. "Well, Landow was to dirty his hands and bend his back and help with the reconstruction. And if that did not suit his liking, he was to stay out of my way and not cause me care. I doubt either occupation appeals to you."

Her ire did not seem to flare up at his sarcasm. Instead, she carefully studied the room. "Perhaps I could help you here," she offered. "I delight in reading. 'Tis a great enjoyment and sometimes the only solace one has. And maps," she added with enthusiasm, "why they are the stuff that dreams are made of."

Branoc weighed her surprising request. Dare he allow her to see the confidential information he had compiled thus far? What if she were a traitor, a beautiful Judas set down in their midst? What if she were sympathetic toward the Saxons or the Scots or both? Anything could be possible with Malbourne's finger in the pie. To uphold his promise to King William to secure this northern territory he dare not trust anyone, not even the most innocent lamb in the fold.

Still pondering the girl's offer to help, he leaned his hips back against the table and crossed his arms over his chest. "Can you read Latin?" he questioned.

"Yes, quite well. Father insisted I learn it. He believed the greatest knowledge of all lay buried in that language. It holds many of the secrets to the universe."

"And do you like secrets, my lady?" he asked and decided he quite approved of the way her nose ended with just the slightest bit of pertness.

"I'm afraid I am not very good at keeping them," she answered, with an expression that seemed the essence of innocence. She was either truly pure, or extremely artful, he knew not which.

He stared at her pink lips, fascinated by their curve. What words passed them to his ears, truth or lie? Depending upon her allegiance, the time she spent in this room could prove to be his salvation or his undoing. He decided he would allow her limited freedom and keep watch upon her. Eventually, her actions would declare what loyalties dwelled in her heart.

"You may help me if you wish," he conceded. "But your work must be timely and accurate. My own Latin is painfully slow, but sufficient enough, that I will see if you twist the truth in your interpretations. Bear that by your side as you labor."

He studied her hands where they rested in her lap. They were long and tapered and in keeping with the tall, willowy rest of her. He pictured her fingers gently wrapped around a quill. Then he pictured the same hand held high, her fingers tightly gripped about the handle of the dagger she wore at her side. She seemed well suited to either task. He must remember to look past the honey-brown hair and tender form.

Levering himself away from the table, he stood to his full height. "While you are here at Bamburgh," he decreed, "you will obey my orders without question and without hesitation. Your life may depend upon it." He waited for her reaction, but none came. "If you do not obey me," he reiterated, in a cold deliberate tone. "You will be held accountable and afforded the usual punishment, even death if the crime so warrants."

This time her clear hazel eyes widened in alarm. Her nod of acceptance was slow in coming, but she did not protest. Again, he could not help but admire her courage. "Have you any questions?"

"Yes my lord. Why do you fear me?"

"You confuse fear with mistrust, lady. It is my duty to mistrust all. I fear no one."

She canted her head slightly and raised a brow as if she found the last part of his answer bordering on the doubtful.

Suddenly Branoc was angered at having this quandary and this young woman dropped unceremoniously into his lap. He did not need this complication in his life and surely, that is what she would prove to be. Intrigue and rebellion lay smoldering all about him. He needed not someone here to fan the embers of discontent. And he needed not someone whose fair face and lively spirit could prove to be a distraction

"You must be tired." Branoc kept his voice even and without emotion as he walked toward the door. "Leofric awaits to take you to your room."

She seemed surprised by his sudden dismissal. "Yes," she admitted, rising. "I am weary. Being kidnapped and held hostage tends to deplete one's energy." The edge of displeasure had returned to her voice.

Branoc watched her graceful movements as she crossed the room. She seemed so young. How could she be a part of any wrongdoing? He wished upon all that was sacred that she was not. She paused for a moment at the door and glanced back over her shoulder.

"What time do you wish me to begin transcribing tomorrow?"

"Mid-morning will be acceptable."

"Since I shall not be otherwise engaged at that hour, I will see you following tierce."

"And, I suppose, I should be greatly honored by your consideration."

"You may be anything you please," she replied. "You are the lord of the castle."

Without further comment, Mistress Verheire wrenched open the door and swept from the room. The fragrance of flowers lingered in her wake prodding memories of the briar roses of Lillebonne. The unsolicited recollections filled his heart with discontent, and his blood burned hot with a long forgotten craving.

****

Leofric did indeed linger in the passageway, but Tanzie did not speak to him nor wait for him as she hurried toward her room. She walked stiffly, made rigid by her fury.

This whole ordeal was monstrous. Lord Branoc Valtaigne had actually threatened to kill her if she misbehaved. Would he do such a thing or did he merely try to frighten her?

The devil take him.

She refused to guard her every word and action lest it be misinterpreted. She would not so easily capitulate and certainly not be ordered about like one of his soldiers. Handsome he may be, but he was also arrogant, disrespectful and totally lacking in compassion. And most of all he was wrong to keep her here.

How had the events governing her life taken on the aspect of a whirlwind? She knew not, from one moment to the next, where she might be sent or who might be given control of her circumstances. So far, the situation here proved even worse than at home, which brought Uncle to mind. The man was without conscience. She knew Malbourne's overwhelming need to protect Landow would push him to any extreme, but this time he had truly put her in a position most perilous. Again, it occurred to her that perhaps he wished for her demise.

She hurried along the corridor ahead of Leofric,

58

her feet keeping time with the thoughts that careened through her mind. Surely, King William would come to her aid. Then her new warder would not be so smug. In the meantime, she would ferret out all of the information she could from Valtaigne's precious council chamber. She needed further insight as to the conditions and terms of her bondage and with the use of the maps stored there, she might even work out an escape route. It couldn't hurt to be prepared.

"Have you known Sir Branoc long?" Tanzie asked Leofric. She slowed her step that he might catch up to her.

"Nearly all my life."

"And has he always been so arrogant and unreasonable?"

"I do not follow you, lady," he said with a bewildered look.

Refusing to explain the obvious, she once again quickened her steps.

"Most find him to be quite capable and valorous," Leofric defended as he lengthened his stride beside her.

"I am not most," she replied. "And he needs soon realize it."

A vivid image of Lord Valtaigne seared through her mind. In this late part of the evening, an illusive shadow of a beard had shown on his cheeks, adding a look of danger to his strong and angular features. Tall and so sure of himself, he seemed a formidable enemy, an unshakable force. But even the mountains moved during an earthquake, and the calm of the sea could be thwarted by a tempest, and right now, she was angry enough to emulate either force of nature.

Leofric still at her side, they reached her chamber. She opened the door, entered and turned to face her escort. "Thank you for your courtesy tonight," she said, by way of dismissal. Leofric did not seem to hear her. His gaze searched the room at her back, and an appreciative smile enlivened his expression.

Tanzie glanced over her shoulder. Ealgith stood beside the bed, pretending to straighten the already perfect coverings. She wore her best nightrail, one usually reserved for high holy and feast days. Unbuttoned at the neck, near indecently low, it offered a view that was most provocative as she bent to adjust the furs.

Tanzie laid her hand upon Leofric's chest and pushed him backward to accommodate the closing of the door. "For heaven sakes, Ealgith," she said in reprimand. "Could you not stay at Bamburgh for at least one night before you began to torture the hearts of the Normans? This is a military stronghold. You could well unleash emotions here that you would be want to control."

"'Tis cold and lonely in the north, mistress," Ealgith protested. "I only seek comfort and merriment before we are banished to the nunnery."

"The nunnery is not so soon on the horizon. By Uncle's hand, we are held here as hostages of good faith. I do not know when we might be allowed to leave."

"Praise be," Ealgith cheered, as if she had just been granted a stay of execution. "Those good tidings alone will warm me tonight," she added, with a look of contentment. She seemed to care little that they were being held prisoners in a moldy castle on the Scottish border.

"You are not bound to remain here, Ealgith. Our circumstances have greatly changed, and I would not expect you to unquestionably suffer my fate."

"Do not speak of such a separation, lady." A look of panic gripped Ealgith as she rushed to Tanzie's side. "I would never leave you mistress," she declared "not for love nor riches no matter what the tribulation. And if need be I shall die beside you even as my mother died beside yours."

Tanzie nearly wept with relief. Her confinement here would be unbearable without the companionship of her friend. "I believe you would not leave me for wealth, dear Ealgith," she teased, "but I am left somewhat in doubt of your oath in respect to love."

A delightful smile brightened Ealgith's face. "It is my weakness to be sure," she giggled, "that and custard pudding. But come mistress, allow me to comb out your hair and braid it for you. It always comforts you before you retire."

Tanzie prepared for bed then surrendered to Ealgith's ministrations. Her handmaiden's touch was light and gentle, and it felt as if faeries danced in her hair. As the tension eased from her mind and body, she smiled. Uncle had duped Sir Branoc Valtaigne as well as her. 'Twas almost hard to sustain the flame of anger burning in her heart for the unsuspecting man, but not impossible. At least, Sir Branoc had recourse in the matter. As usual, she had none. But she was too tired to think about it tonight. There would be time enough tomorrow to worry over her plight

"I am for bed." A yawn widened her mouth as Ealgith tied off the plait. Tired enough for two people, she stumbled across the room and crawled between the covers. "You must be exhausted as well."

"Yes mistress. Good night mistress," Ealgith called from her pallet by the fire pit.

Tanzie settled into the blessed softness and an image of Branoc again invaded her thoughts. He had appeared a bit pale for a soldier and a man of the sword. It told of missed meals and too many worries. She suspected he spent more time with his books and maps than with sunshine and fresh air. Flopping onto her side, she punched at her pillow and fussed with the coverlet. What cared she for his health and observances? She was not his mother. She must put him from her mind.

Then a new dread reared its head. What if Lord Valtaigne never wrote to King William? No one would ever know that she had been forced to this impasse. What if she were forgotten and held here forever?

Closing her eyes again, she envisioned herself old and gray, locked away in Branoc's council chamber. Feeble of eye and withered of hand, she was made to translate yet another damnable manuscript while hundreds more loomed nearby awaiting her attention.

With a shudder, she opened her eyes and stared at the little Celtic statue that sat upon the bedside table. The horrible vision of being held captive dissolved away and as usual, the presence of the familiar creature calmed her. She patted the dragon upon the head and reached to extinguish the lone candle. Then she hesitated. Was there something different about the little beast? It was impossible of course, only a deception of the wavering light, but he seemed to have grown larger.

****

The waxing moon weighed anchor and sailed free across the starry sky and like waves beneath the prow of the night, the hours slipped away. Then the celestial radiance slanted in through the window, and as the light touched the dragon, his eyes began to glow with a pale reddish hue.

He was finally home.

Chapter 5

It was well past Tierce, mid-morning had long since come and gone, but Tanzie was not about to inconvenience herself by rushing about.

Instead, she lounged in a chair before the window of her room, her feet resting upon a charming little padded footstool, Ealgith had miraculously procured for them. Today the kindhearted sun fought its way through the clouds to console the world, as well as Tanzie's beleaguered spirits.

"'Tis shameful," she said, "to be so tardy my first morning assisting, Lord Valtaigne."

"Most shocking, indeed, lady," Ealgith agreed. "Other hand if you please."

Shifting in the chair Tanzie withdrew her right hand and extended the left, so that Ealgith might pumice and buff the remainder of her miserable collection of ragged fingernails.

"Sir Branoc deserves to await my pleasure," she said, trying to justify her contrary actions. "If he expects us to take all of our meals in the private hall located across the castle from our sleeping chamber, I see no possibility of adhering to the prearranged schedule."

The old hall, where the soldiers ate, was but a short distance from her room. The guard posted there, however, had informed her at breakfast that she and her handmaiden were forbidden entry. Valtaigne had so ordered it. Another rule to follow. Another dictum to inconvenience her life. She drummed the fingers of her right hand upon the arm of the chair.

"Perhaps we ought inquire whether a garde-robe schedule exists," Ealgith suggested with a chuckle. "I would hate to break a precept, or disoblige anyone, by relieving myself at an inopportune moment."

Tanzie smiled at the thought, then countered the proposition. "We'd best leave well enough alone, Ealgith. There might just be such an agenda. It would be wise to tread lightly, until we are more accustomed to this drafty prison of a castle and the man who rules the keep."

With a sidelong glance, she wondered what her handmaiden may have gleaned from the rumor mill. Ealgith's skills extended far beyond mere domestic duties, and although, they had only been here one night, Tanzie was sure her friend had already put her information gathering skills to good use. At the chateau, Ealgith had often been Tanzie's eyes and ears. The girl prided herself on acquiring only the most interesting and reliable gossip. Yet, to indulge in a habit frowned upon by God and man alike always took a bit of absolution in the form of coaxing. In truth, Ealgith relished a good bit of gossip almost as much as she relished a good bit of pixie pie.

"What think you of our host, nay warden?" she asked, by way of introducing the subject.

"Me?" Ealgith said, as if surprised.

"I will treasure your remarks," Tanzie said, reciting the agreed upon phrase meaning she would forever lock away in her heart anything next spoken, thus guarding the words as she would precious jewels.

The ritual embarked upon, Ealgith nodded and scooted her chair closer and though they were alone, she lowered her voice to a whisper. "Despite the brooding expression he wears, Sir Branoc is most strikingly handsome," she said, with a giggle.

"Tell me something other than the obvious," Tanzie chided, in mock annoyance.

Ealgith huffed at having been interrupted; she took her oratories quite seriously. "He ranks high in the opinion of lords and commoners alike," she continued, "and he is known as the Dragon of Normandy."

"That seems a fitting enough title," Tanzie said, under her breath.

"They say he has never broken his oath to another man, nor has he yielded to another man's sword."

"And who are *they,* pray tell?"

"The hearth girl in the kitchen for one," Ealgith said. "I met her this morning. She's the cook's daughter, born and grown in the Vexin and while Walloon takes a terrible beating upon her tongue, and I'm not much better at that low-land speech, we understood one another well enough."

"And where does she get her information?"

"From between the sheets. The young soldier who guards the buttery is smitten with the girl, and when he is a little tight with the mead, he is sometimes a little loose with his tongue. That is all I know so far."

"Admirable indeed for a few hours work," Tanzie admitted. "But you must not seek to gossip, Ealgith," she added, in her best imitation of a reprimand. Since childhood, she and Ealgith had played the game of wayward servant and pompous mistress. "Of course should similar information accidentally come your way, feel free to pass the burden of knowledge from yourself to me." This mummery and game playing, was their way of fighting back at the unbending doctrines that ruled their lives and the unbridled hypocrisy that ruled the world.

Ealgith scooted her chair back. "I will remember your words, lady. And now that your hands are restored to the best of my ability, I must see to the mending of our clothes." She rose to collect her needles and threads.

"And I must keep my appointment with Valtaigne," Tanzie said and rose to her feet. The Dragon of Normandy indeed. And he awaited her in his literary lair. Unable to find another excuse to further delay the inevitable she crossed the room to the door. "Pray avoid calamity while I am gone, Ealgith," she cautioned. Her friend nodded with well-practiced solemnity. Tanzie smiled, slipped from the room, and made her way to the council chamber. How dull life would be if they kept to all the rules.

\*\*\*\*

Sir Branoc glanced up as she entered, his face stern, his gray eyes wary as a raptor's. It seemed impossible, but she believed his mood was even more somber than it had been last evening. Today he wore all black, with not even silver breaking the dark image.

Feeling guilty for having kept him waiting, she offered what she thought to be her most beguiling expression. "I hope tardiness is not a beheading offense," she said sweetly.

"Not yet," Branoc replied. "But new laws are established on a daily basis."

Did a hint of a smile fight for possession of his generous mouth? No, it must have been a ploy of the midday light.

From his position at the head of the table, Branoc studied her from tip to toe. She felt like a bug on the end of a stick.

His unwavering scrutiny made her self-conscious. She straightened her blue tunic and attempted to smooth her hair, which today had a mind of its own. Her discomfort was replaced by irritation, as she decided Sir Branoc did not seem to care one whit that she had arrived late.

"Please be seated," he finally said, "and I will explain the purpose of what we do here."

She slipped silently into the indicated chair and sat facing a mountain of parchments and books. From the corner of her eye she could see Branoc's shadowy countenance as he ambled around the table to stand at her side. In the cool room, she could feel the heat that radiated from his body and the musky man scent of him, captivated her senses-more potent than the most precious of perfumes.

He leaned forward to slide a particularly large volume closer. His arm brushed her shoulder, and the spot where their bodies had so briefly made contact tingled with his unintended touch.

She fidgeted about in her chair, and stared down at the bound manuscript that lay open upon the table, but the words blurred and swam before her eyes as Branoc's presence overwhelmed her. When he stood so close, an odd fluttering riffled through her. It was a strange feeling, as if her stomach had gone light-headed. She concentrated harder on the matter at hand and tried to revive the mistrust and anger that were the full extent of the emotion she should feel for this warrior—a knight who sought darkness in dress and mood. Yet, his indifference toward her was somehow fascinating. And the more somber his expression became, the more she yearned to make him smile. What would it take? she wondered.

Clasping her hands in her lap, she fought for control of her thoughts and willed logic to save her from saying or doing anything foolish.

"If I am to secure this area for William," Branoc began, leaning down at her side, "it is vital that I know as much as possible about the surrounding land and the people who inhabit it." His words reverberated in her ear, sending shock waves through her body. "I would know," he continued, "down to the last basket of eggs and faggot of sticks, what transpires here."

Suddenly the meaning of his words became paramount to the effect they were having upon her heart rate. "Yes," she agreed, "'twould seem much easier to suppress a people with your own private Domesday book at hand." Tanzie had planned to be pleasant today but it galled her to help the Normans, and the words were out of her mouth before she could stop them.

"You are quick to judge what you know little of," Branoc said harshly, as he straightened to his full height beside her. "Furthermore my intentions and motivations are not your concern. If you cannot do my bidding, lady, without constant retort and remark, we are through before we begin."

She swallowed back her rebellious attitude and the other churlish replies that readily came to mind. After all, she reminded herself, she had sought access to this chamber to find a way out of her own predicament. It did her little good to further alienate this man by championing the cause of the Saxons. "I regret my bold remark," she said truthfully. "But it does seem to be the innocent who are generally crushed beneath the heavy ideals of the sovereigns. I do not take well to watching the downtrodden suffer."

"I do not seek to impose suffering," Branoc said quietly. "But know you this," he added, his lips compressed into a hard line. "I will employ whatever means are necessary to insure that the borderlands under my care do not fall into the hands of the rebels or Scots. I do not make the laws that govern this land, but I have sworn allegiance to the man who does." He stared at her as if he tried to read her soul. "Have you any other concerns, lady, before we proceed?"

"Yes," she snapped. "Stop calling me *lady*. It makes me feel like a table or a chair. I have a name, 'tis Martanzia, please use it." She stared up at Branoc.

His brow furrowed and a frown now captured his expression. "As you wish," he agreed. Then as if suspicious of her offer of familiarity, he moved farther away.

"After you have itemized the worth of the land and the people," he began again, in carefully measured tones, "you will compile a reference regarding the terrain. List each river and the time that it is at its highest and lowest. Also indicate all bridges and fords." He paused for a moment as if he feared his orders were too fast and furious for her to follow.

Did he have such little faith in women's abilities?

"Describe what the land is like in each direction surrounding Bamburgh, be it forest, downs, marsh or so forth and make special note of any high ridges or deep ravines."

"A moment, please," she interrupted. "Do you wish to know when a river is at its highest and lowest point during the day or during the season?"

"Hmm, 'tis a good question," he replied, seemingly surprised that she could conceive of one. "List both."

Well that should nicely double her work. She was sorry she had asked. Why did he need this information any way? "Do you anticipate an enemy attack?"

Branoc stiffened. "Perchance," he said, as he strode toward the window.

For several moments, he stood staring out at the view. He seemed almost to have forgotten her presence. She seized the opportunity to peruse more closely the books and scrolls that lay scattered about on the table.

A nearby map caught her attention. Carefully she extended her left arm. Stretched to the limit she snagged the corner of the vellum between the tips of her fingers, and ever so slowly dragged the rendering closer. Carefully taking up the map, she noticed a route marked upon it showing the shortest distance from Bamburgh to Jarrow. That information held promise. If she could escape the castle and reach the old monastery the priests there would give her sanctuary. But that would be but a temporary solution to her problem. She must speak to the king.

Examining the southern most area displayed, she located London, and using the length of her thumb as a reference to scale, tried to figure how many leagues away the royal city might be.

"'Tis nearly three hundred miles to London," Branoc said, from directly behind her. "But at present the king resides at Winchester."

She started, feeling as if she had been caught with her hand in the poor box at church, and the vellum slipped from her grasp. While studying the details, she had neither seen nor heard Branoc move.

"Do you journey to Jarrow?" she blurted, recovering the parchment from her lap more quickly than her composure.

He reached over her shoulder and retrieved the map from her hands. "It is possible," said the voice from behind her.

The man had a frustrating ability to irritate her with the utterance of a very few words. But she too had been accused of being irascible. She could match his skill with half as much effort.

"Will I be allowed to continue my work in your absence?" What an opportunity that would provide. She would have complete freedom to poke about in every nook and cranny of the room.

"Perhaps." Again the answer that was not an answer.

"Have you written yet to King William?" she questioned.

"I will inform you immediately upon the receipt of any correspondence."

"What if an answer arrives while you are away?"

"Then you will have to await my return to learn of the news."

"And if you never return?"

"Mistress Verheire?"

"Yes"

"Please begin your transcriptions."

She bent her head to hide her smile. He hadn't used her given name, but at least he had said "please".

Branoc crossed the room and sat in a chair located as far away from her as possible, and though he tirelessly read his missives and texts, on occasion, she sensed his full attention focused upon her.

Determined to lose herself in the intrigue of her task, Tanzie contemplated a particularly difficult passage. While pondering the words, she idly ran her hands through her hair, combing out the tangles with her fingers. Continuing to read, she gathered the now smooth mass up atop her head. Holding it there, she glanced up to see Branoc staring at her. Time seemed to stop. Their gazes met and locked as if compelled by some magnetism that was new to her as well the laws of the universe.

She lowered her arms and her hair spilled back down over her shoulders like a warm thick cloak. The loose curls tumbled and fell to her waist.

Branoc's expression remained unchanged but a curious light shimmered in his eyes, and the smoldering sparks reflected there ignited a heat in her belly. Had she broken through Branoc's emotional chain mail? Her breath was near stifled by the swell of pleasure that throbbed deep within her. Hesitantly, she offered him a hint of a smile. No reaction. Feeling foolish, she sobered. Her cheeks burned, but the fire stemmed from embarrassment not urgency. Even so, she refused to be the first to look away.

Finally Branoc clenched his jaw and turned his attention back to his reading.

Feeling contrite, she bent once more to her own task and wondered why Branoc so fiercely guarded the man behind the shadows? Was it simple self-preservation? Most likely. But what circumstances of life had driven him to the shield-wall? She could not imagine that he had been born so pensive and mirthless.

****

The last bit of dried fruit and bread long gone Tanzie stared unseeing at the text before her, and her mind began to wander. The afternoon grew old, and early evening shadows washed the room in a soft haze playing false with her vision and her imagination. For one fleeting moment, she pretended the man with whom she sat was a friend, a companion, someone with whom she could share the day's events, as her mother had often done with her father.

Peeking up through her lashes, she covertly watched as Branoc rose to light the candles and cressets. Silently he prowled about the room and as he reached to illuminate the last sconce, his dark hauberk stretched taut across the flexed muscles of his broad shoulders. Her gaze drifted lower to his narrow hips and long legs. His clothes caressed the contours of his body like the knowing hand of a lover, and she envied that soft woolen fabric and fine-spun thread.

Leisurely he traversed the chamber, the

flickering shadows paraded in his wake. He moved with complete assurance as if he knew nothing in the world would dare to cause his step to falter. Yet, he also moved lightly for a man of such obvious strength.

Without a word, he took again to the chair by the hearth and sat openly staring at her.

It was happening again. The atmosphere was cold but a wave of heat spilled over her from head to foot warming her thoughts and curling her toes. This was beyond her ken. Simply watching Branoc walk across the room enthralled her and being pinned beneath his penetrating gaze left her near faint. It was ludicrous, unacceptable, but undeniably exciting. To cover her confusion, she made a show of setting aside the journal upon which she worked. Then she stretched her stiff neck and shoulder muscles. God's truth, her back ached from sitting and her eyes burned from reading, and she wanted something to quench her thirst.

"'Tis a most tiring task this translating and scribing," she said, in hopes Lord Valtaigne would suspend his attack upon the tomes until tomorrow. "No wonder such drudgery is left mostly to monks with the patience of Saints."

"You have worked quite diligently," Branoc admitted. "Why do you not retire for the day?"

Finally, she thought with relief. Yet, she was somewhat disappointed at being dismissed. Except for the location of Jarrow, she had discovered little useful information today, other than the fact that Sir Branoc was much too serious and duty-bound, and London and Winchester seemed a world away.

Not having been left alone for a single moment, she suspected he knew her intent. His intuition was commendable, and she had also noticed something else about Branoc Valtaigne. He showed a genuine respect and reverence for the odd assortment of books and manuscripts. Only in her father had she seen such qualities in a man.

He stood and faced her, his feet braced slightly apart, his hands clasped behind his back. Again, he studied her.

What had he discovered about her today? Did he know that she yearned to realize the texture of his hair, or that she was fascinated by the idea of touching his cheek?

She lowered her gaze to the table, then stood, and with as much grace as possible, made her way to the door. "Same hour on the morrow?" she asked over her shoulder, pretending she had not been late. She had no intentions of beginning tomorrow any earlier than she had today.

"Yes, if it is not an interruption of your busy schedule," he said. "And from now on when you are away from your chamber, I suggest you bind your hair in some manner. When it is down and swirling about it seems to greatly distract you."

"I have worn my hair in such a manner all of my life," she defended, "and never once have I found it a distraction."

"Then consider my suggestion—an order," he clarified.

More rules to follow. She turned to face him. Anger and disappointment flooded in to undermine the burgeoning commiseration she felt toward Branoc. Then with a small burst of triumph, it dawned on her that it was Branoc who was distracted by her appearance. She had tapped into his emotions after all. Small as it may be she pressed home the victory.

"I don't believe the styling of my hair falls under your jurisdiction," she said calmly, as she eased open the door, "and until you can prove otherwise in the royal handbook of hostage-keeping, or whatever it is you men reference in such instances, I shall arrange my coif in the manner that suits my fancy."

With a toss of her head and a shake of the offending tresses, she leisurely strolled from the room, longing to, but not daring to look back.

Chapter 6

Dogs barked, sheep balked, and a logjam of bodies, both four-legged and two-legged, obstructed all movement before the entrance of the high-walled city of Wallingford.

From astride his horse, Rathgar surveyed the chaos of livestock and peasants. "Move these filthy animals aside," he roared, "or by Mithras, I'll have them slaughtered where they stand."

With infuriating efficiency, the wooly sea of curly haired beasts continued to ebb and flow around the mounted patrol. "You rabble are as ignorant as the creatures you tend," Rathgar shouted, his ire mounting with each breath he was forced to take in this putrid little village.

Yet what more should he have expected? As illiterate as these Saxon were, they seemed gifted at slowing the wheels of progress, and interfering with the desires of the king. And had they one whit of common sense among them, they would not need him here to resolve their petty differences.

Rathgar's right hand man maneuvered his horse closer. "What do we here, Rathgar?" he dared to ask. "I was under the impression it was customary for the local shire reeve to arbitrate such mundane matters?"

"Indeed," Rathgar replied. "There is more than meets the eye regarding the king's reason for sending us on this mission. Does it not demonstrate his power, even as it verifies our willingness to be subservient?"

The man at his side seemed to silently mull over

this theory, but Rathgar had seen through the ruse immediately. And in truth, this menial task was a small enough price to pay in order to gain a snippet of favor from William Rufus. He did not trust the king, and obviously the feeling was mutual. Besides, it was not playing the king's game that drove his irritation to new heights. It was the interruption of his prior laid plans that chaffed. He should be in the Cotentin, sealing his pact with Prince Henry, not tilting with sheep and imbeciles. He should be in Flanders, addressing matters of personal import.

Through a red haze of anger, he mentally reviewed the missive he had received from Martanzia's Uncle two weeks ago. He knew each word by heart, had memorized each syllable stating his marriage to Martanzia had been indefinitely postponed. That Flemish peacock must have been in dire straights to risk such a double-cross. But Malbourne's foul deed would not go unpunished, for this treachery not only struck a grievous blow to Rathgar's treasury it had wounded his pride to boot.

Marrying Martanzia had become Rathgar's personal quest. She was his Grail, and he would settle for no other. And so it had been from the first moment he had laid eyes upon her. He did not know what so attracted him to the girl. He had seen females more fair of face and certainly many who were more malleable in spirit. Perhaps it was love. By Lucifer, how was he to know? He had never experienced that emotion in others or in himself. All he knew was that Martanzia was his grand obsession. She was a prize he coveted more dearly than the lands Prince Henry promised. And she was more worthy of his adoration then the ancient gods who had forgotten Man, or the modern God who never tired of persecuting humankind.

He took a deep breath to ease the fury that consumed him anew. He must not become impatient.

Not when he was so close to realizing his dream. He must tread lightly, here and abroad. The current political arena was as deadly as any warring field, and it was prudent to learn the weaknesses of ones opponent before the battle began. There was much unrest in England, not only amongst the Saxons, but amongst the Normans as well. And the three sons of William the Bastard would insure this discontent thrived and grew stronger.

At times, it was difficult to keep the royal feuding straight and one's loyalties up to date. While William, the eldest son, ruled England, Robert, the middle son, now ruled Normandy. And when the brothers were at one another's throat, the Barons and knights who owned land on both sides of the channel could not support one liege without betraying the other. A worrisome situation at best.

And then there was Henry, the youngest brother. He too demanded attention. Of the three royal siblings, young Henry seemed most likely to prevail, and Rathgar planned to be there when he did. Henry had been left with no lands of his own, but he was persistent, a trait that mattered much in the end. He was coldly ruthless, not hot headed like William Rufus. And he was determined, not easily swayed like Robert Curthose.

As he observed the lessening chaos, Rathgar guided his mount off to one side of the dusty road. Reaching the shade of a large oak he slumped a bit in the saddle, thus continuing his reflections in more comfort.

Whether in England or on the continent, the political turmoil that simmered in every pot made for strange hearth companions. It forced men into dark corners, and difficult decisions. When recent circumstances had demanded that he choose between an ineffectual weakling, a depraved tax monger, and a vengeful demon, he had picked the latter. Rathgar understood cruelty. He had grown up in the shadow of it, lived around the memory of it, and had survived in spite of it. Yes, he had chosen Henry. And why not? Only Henry had drawn first breath in England. Only Henry had been born of a duly anointed king. William Rufus and Robert Curthose were matured seed spilled by a mere duke in the inharmonious duchy of Normandy. That would never do. Without pity, society declared the importance of heritage. And while it mattered a great deal which son a father chose to favor, it mattered even more which son a father chose to forsake.

William the Conqueror had abandoned Prince Henry, just as Rathgar's father had abandoned him. Now they would both have their revenge. But Rathgar intended to champion his own cause. He would not bend his sword-arm merely to further another man's coffers. Past loyalty had gained him little, and mercy had gained him less. And while he may have temporarily lost the lands Martanzia had inherited, he'd be damned if he would be denied a piece of the royal English pie; indigestible as it sometimes proved to be.

As his thoughts had come round full circle, he frowned with renewed distaste at the crowd of shabby peasants. They glared back, their brows furrowed with determination, their mouths tight with hatred. At their lack of enthusiasm, he drew his broadsword, and though the Saxons did not understand the language he spoke, they seemed to easily interpret his intent. Behave or behead was a philosophy understood on any shore.

One man in the crowd needled Rathgar's ire. He moved especially slow, his expression one of pure defiance. Rathgar urged his horse forward and gave the villein new incentive by striking him across the back with the flat of his sword. Contemptuous mirth rose from his soldiers as the man fell to his knees and struggled in the mire.

Being a goodwill ambassador was not part of Rathgar's mission.

If it were up to him he would simply banish the Saxon inhabitants and repopulate this troublesome little island with Normans. Then the belligerent English would cease to be a waste of everyone's precious time.

He was amazed that someone had not already implemented such an idea, though the king and the Church had nearly succeeded as they taxed the common man into oblivion. Ranulph Flambard, King William's holy henchman, was a diabolical genius. His specialty was reinterpreting the law of the land, and bending the canons of the church. He was a great asset to William Rufus, and one of the only true friends the king possessed. In the days ahead, this Holy Terror would also bear watching.

With the villagers subdued and the sheep scattered, Rathgar and his men gained entrance to the inner city. Intent on satisfying his creature comforts, he sought a nearby abode of fairly large proportion. At least it seemed large in comparison to the meager huts surrounding it.

"You three men," he ordered, "secure the structure and evict any residents."

The head of the household was soon brought forth kicking and screaming.

"You bloody mamzer," the rotund Saxon sputtered. "What right have you to intrude upon my property? I would have thought you thievin' Normans would have had your belly-full of raiding by now."

As the interpreter translated the words, the man's insults became appallingly clarified.

"Bind his hands and confine him to one of the out buildings," Rathgar commanded, as he dismounted. "You four men stay here with me. The remainder of the patrol may seek shelter and the pursuit of happiness as they so choose."

Irritated by the Saxon's rebellious attitude Rathgar gave his soldiers free rein as he deployed them in search of suitable lodgings. Since all of the men he had chosen for this maneuver were much like himself, the village was sure to be ransacked, the women violated, and the food supplies heartily consumed. What a pity these people never learned.

"Locate the feuding thralls to be judged," Rathgar ordered, and pointed at two of the remaining soldiers. "Then bring them here to await my convenience." The men indicated road off to do his bidding while the other two followed at his side.

Carelessly tracking mud and debris across the main room of the house, Rathgar motioned for the cottage to again be checked and secured. Standing in front of the hearth, he contemplated the small flame that flickered within the chimney-less enclosure.

A scuffling noise sounded at his back. He turned to watch as his men dragged a young woman forward.

"We caught this one trying to flee out the back window," one soldier reported. "She must have been hiding in the cupboard."

They wrestled the thrashing girl across the room, and pushed her to her knees before him.

"What is your name?" Rathgar demanded.

No response.

"Ask her in her own language," he ordered.

Still no response.

Exasperated he reached toward the girl's face with his ungloved hand intent on tipping up her chin, forcing her to look at him. His hand missed the mark. To his surprise, a sudden pain seared through the soft webbing of skin between his thumb and forefinger. The silly bitch had bitten him.

The girl cowered beneath the raised fists of the burly soldiers.

Rathgar stayed their assault, and examined the wound on his hand. He put the injured flesh to his mouth and sucked away the blood and stared down at the girl. She risked death rather than look at him. Compromise did not seem to be an integral part of Saxon logic; it was always all or nothing. They were a stubborn lot he'd give them that. But it would be their downfall.

With the salty metallic flavor still tart upon his tongue, he indicated that she should rise. Impatiently the guards jerked her to her feet.

Circling slowly, he assessed her from every angle. He grasped a lock of her chestnut brown hair, and meshed the long strands between his thumb and fingers. Her tresses were relatively clean. That was a pleasant surprise. Shifting his hand, he fondled the generous curve of her bottom. She stiffened but did not pull away. Coming around full circle, he stood again before her. She would do quite nicely for one night of mindless swiving.

Using his leather clad hand he roughly chucked her under the chin. This time she met his gaze. The color drained from her cheeks, as if he'd cut her throat rather than merely grabbed at it.

"Attacking one of the king's men is a serious offense," he pointed out, not caring if she understood him or not. "I fear you are in great need of being taught a lesson on how to properly please unexpected guests." He reached out and fondled her breasts. The firm flesh filled his palms and spilled beyond the breadth of his fingers. "Perhaps you will understand better the meaning of hospitality once I have personally instructed you on the rules of etiquette."

Desire rose in him, hot and immediate, and he convinced himself that because of the breaking of their marriage agreement he was justified in forsaking his vow of chastity to Martanzia. Why should he continue to suffer the pains of denial? But business before pleasure. He wanted no interruptions later this evening.

"Take her away," he ordered, "but keep her close at hand. I will send for her when this other nonsense has been resolved."

"Come on then lass," one soldier, said and laughed as they led her away. "You'd best rest up now, as you'll get no sleep tonight."

After eating his fill, and consuming a restrained amount of wine, Rathgar allowed the waiting petitioners to be brought forth.

Normally the king would not have been concerned over a civil matter, but the boundary disputes of these two villagers affected William Rufus's forest as well as the beasts who roamed within it, and nothing under the sun was permitted to interfere with the royal hunt.

With the help of his interpreter Rathgar began the proceedings.

"It is my understanding," he said, "that one of you has constructed a hedgerow across the property to hold the other man's sheep and pigs at bay. Unfortunately this obstacle also inhibits the migration of the king's deer."

"In retaliation the other man has restricted the flow of the upper Thames, cutting off water to the first man's property, again disturbing the king's domain." Rathgar leaned back in his chair, and casually studied the two poor fools who stood before him. "Well what have you to say for yourselves?"

Finding the whole matter beneath his concern he did not bother listening to the men's rebuttals. He was amazed at their lack of creativity for neither of them had offered him a bribe. Now they would pay even more dearly.

As his interpreter finished translating their useless appeal Rathgar dispassionately rendered his verdict. "You are both found guilty of interfering with the natural order of the royal forest. You will work together to restore the land to its former state and you are denied pannage until this time next year. In addition you shall each pay a fine of five pence to the local forester who acts in the name of King William II." The men's shoulders slumped a little more with each interpreted word uttered, and their expressions turned from dejected to hopeless.

"If you do not have that amount at liberty," Rathgar added, knowing full well that they did not, "the debt will be exacted from your flesh."

The peasants shrank back in unison. Rathgar favored them with a merciless smile. Their physical punishment on the marrow would be a memorable lesson to the entire village. Besides, a lively whipping always provided good breakfast entertainment.

The two men stood mutely before him, one fidgeting with the cap he held, the other wringing his hands.

"If I am called here again," Rathgar added, "to settle such a dispute between the two of you, you will not only be flogged to my satisfaction you shall each be relieved of your left eye. Some people, I am told, see things much more clearly following such an alteration. Now be gone from my presence before I regret my leniency."

Nearly tripping over one another, the men fled the room.

Rathgar did not dwell upon the underlying quarrel relative to the two peasants. He had fulfilled his obligation to the crown by showing the people of this outcast village that all of England and every man, plant, and animal living upon it's over-taxed, blood-drenched soil belonged to William Rufus.

Odd, he reflected, that the king had declared himself every man's heir, yet he could claim no issue of his own, and according to court gossip he never would. Elbows resting on the arms of the chair, Rathgar was lost in thought. Was it true the king preferred men to women? It was a curious notion. Yet, a man's sexual predilection made no matter to him. He did not care if the cheek that rested beside the king on the royal pillow was soft and rosy or bristled with hair. What he did care about was the fact that William Rufus was more concerned with the pleasures of the flesh and the sport of hunting rather than running a kingdom. Idle amusement was all well and good, but the king was likely to run the country into the ground before Rathgar had a chance to claim a piece of it. That was precisely why he had joined forces with those who wished to see the king's brother, Henry, installed upon the thrown. The country cried out for a real man to lead them, not a vain, capricious cock of the walk who revered neither God nor man nor his own covenants.

But one step at a time. The events to come would fall into place if carefully nudged at the proper moment. Timing was everything, from winning a game of shut the box, to overthrowing a governing force. There was nothing more he could do tonight to appease the whims of the current sovereign, or to hasten the coronation of the next.

"Bring me the wench," Rathgar ordered.

Struggling half-heartedly, the Saxon girl was ushered to his side.

As if resigned to her fate, she seemed less resistant than before. Taking her hand he noticed that her lips were stained with wine, and her eyes appeared bleary. He hoped the guards had not rendered her too compliant, a little resistance always heightened his need.

"Leave us," he said, to his men as he dragged

the girl onto his lap. The aching in his loins returned full force. "Come my sweet," he urged, "there is much I must teach you before the dawn."

He crushed his mouth down upon hers, and yanked open the lacings on the front of her gunna. Arching his hips against her bottom he lost himself to the pleasure of the moment. His tongue penetrated the depths of her mouth, and easily overcoming her useless struggles, he explored the nether region beneath her skirt, thrusting his fingers into warm flesh.

Grunting and panting he pulled away, the taste of her mingling with the smell of desire. "Pleasure me," he commanded. Then remembering she could not understand his words, he pushed her legs to one side, grasped her hand, and wedged it beneath his clothing.

She hesitated only a moment then awkwardly stroked him.

Burning for release, he rutted and strained against her touch, yet nothing brought him fulfillment. He pictured Martanzia, envisioning her draped across the king's dais, her legs spread invitingly as she begged him to take her upon the velvet cushions of the throne. His mind reeled at the concept, and his body screamed for deliverance. But even his wildest imaginings did not lead him to satisfaction.

Frustrated beyond endurance, he shoved the peasant girl away. She fell to the floor, a surprised look upon her face.

"Get out," he yelled, and gestured toward the door.

Clutching at the torn remnants of her bodice, she clamored to her feet and fled from the cottage.

Never before had Rathgar been plagued with this unnamed malady. His heart had taken too seriously his vow to Martanzia, and his body had followed suit. Suffering from unspent desire he gingerly adjusted his braises and outer clothing, then poured a large measure of wine.

It would appear betrayal sabotaged a man on many levels. He must remember to add this night of humiliation to the already long list of Malbourne's offenses.

Like some creature in a cave, Rathgar sat alone in the dim cottage and with a deadly smile, he reviewed the varying forms of retribution he would exact from Malbourne. His request for a personal leave had already been granted. He would be in Flanders within the week.

Draining the contents of the cup, he reached for the flagon and poured out another good measure. The wine bolstered his resentment even as it depleted his humanity, and in the silence of the deserted house, he rose unsteadily to his feet to reaffirm an old covenant with new anger and determination.

"To you, my beloved Martanzia," he declared. "I shall not be spurned. Regardless of the cost, you shall be mine. And you may rest assured, I will avail myself of you and your inheritance until both are exhausted."

He slumped back into his chair, the empty cup dangling from his hand. Then he threw back his head and laughed. The sound snarled in his throat before clawing its way to freedom, but the utterance that severed the silence was cold and brittle. It did not brighten his bleak surroundings, nor warm his sorry soul.

Chapter 7

It was an overcast morn, and having nothing better to do until the appointed hour in the council chamber, Tanzie passed the time by exploring castle Bamburgh.

She had offered to help Ealgith with the mending, but the suggestion had met with loving rejection. Her friend pointing out that while Tanzie's pattern designs were beyond comparison, her actual sewing skills were abominable. 'Twas true of course, yet hard upon one's ego.

Tanzie smiled and fingered the newly embroidered heart and flower that covered the latest threadbare spot in her kirtle. Ealgith was a master with needle and thread and over the years had become adept at refitting their outdated apparel into newer styles. Dear Ealgith, what would she do without her lifelong friend to share this dreaded time of unjust captivity?

Wandering on, Tanzie reached the north wing. Gloom and silence clung to the walls of the dim corridor, and giant cobwebs dangled from the ceiling obliterating the corners. She inched forward. The drab light and limited fresh air rendered the atmosphere damp and cloying, and with each tentative step she took a thick carpet of dust rippled across the floor in a frosty wave. Perhaps she should turn back. This unused section of the castle was probably off limits to her. All the more reason to venture forth, she thought rebelliously.

Her leather slippers whispered softly against the flagged stones, yet in the oppressive stillness the sound echoed riotously. She paused to study her surroundings. This section of the stronghold appeared especially old, bringing to mind the catacombs beneath the cathedral in Bruges. Streaks of water sparkled upon the walls. It flowed downward to soak into hidden cracks and crevices, and although the floor did not appear to slope, Tanzie instinctively felt the path was leading her deeper underground. A great heaviness pressed inward from all sides, and it was as if the meager walls of ancient stonework kept the weight of the entire universe at bay.

She hugged her outer tunic closer for warmth, and moved on.

On her left was a display of pikes and swords crusted with age. Had these armaments belonged to Aethelfrith, the first King of Northumbria? Or were they even more ancient, reflecting Celtic times when the site was known as Din Guyardi? Ruled back then by the Votadini, the tribal stronghold was believed by some to be "Joyous Guard", the legendary castle of Sir Lancelot and Sir Galahad.

A thrill sparkled through her at the idea of such fable and myth being true. But one must rely on fact when seeking truisms, and recorded history stated this royal capitol of Bernicia came into being when King Ida officially established Bamburgh in 547 A.D.

King Ida... Her mother had told her the history of this king. He had ruled the Angles, a fierce race of warriors who expanded Bernicia after conquering the Celts. By the time King Ida's grandson, Aethelfrith, seized control, Northumbria stretched from the River Humber northwards. The inhabitants of Mercia and the Vikings of York challenged the people of Northumbria, yet it remained the strongest Anglo-Saxon province in all of Britain. Until, of course, William the Bastard had landed at Pevensey. The Normans had changed the course of history, and now the Conqueror's son ruled all of England with a hand doubled into a fist of unrestrained might.

As these thoughts tumbling through her mind, she turned her attention to the shield that hung on the right side of the passage. Blackened with age, its true likeness was concealed by the darkness that encased it. Sir Branoc was equally obscure, with his true likeness overshadowed by his somber attire. Would he grace her with an appearance today? Every afternoon for the last four days, she had faithfully made her way to the council chamber, but a guard had supervised her toil, not Branoc. Where was this man who ruled her existence by day and her dreams by night?

Sir Branoc's absence would not have been such a great exasperation had it at least aided her plans for escape. But the one time she had attempted to browse around the hallowed room, the sentinel had reminded her that she was to only work upon the manuscripts set out upon the table. It was not long before her enthusiasm for the undertaking had begun to wane, but her interest in the Dragon of Normandy had grown daily.

How strange that fate had once again seen fit to usher a dragon, unbidden, into her life. A coincidence, no doubt, for her winsome statue and the austere lord of this castle held little in common. To look upon the ancient carving calmed her heart and eased her mind. To look upon Sir Branoc quickened her pulse and sent her thoughts straying down paths that were better left unexplored.

Lost in thought, she rounded the near corner then stopped short. Her scalp prickled with excitement, and she stared in wonder at the unexpected sight revealed. A beautiful tapestry hung at the far end of the hall. Torches set in large sconces flanked the intricate needlework, and the flickering glow seemed to give life and motion to the rendering. In the center of the tapestry a woodland scene was depicted. The encircling border was a ribbon of runic characters.

"Can you interpret the markings?"

At the unexpected voice, Tanzie spun around, and her heart felt as if it dropped to her feet then bounded back up to wedge in her throat.

An old man dressed in robes of emerald green occupied the empty hallway behind her. He stood straight and tall as a well-turned spear, and though lean and spare he looked sturdy as weathered hickory. A shock of gray hair haloed his head and shoulders, and a long beard of similar hue lay upon his chest. He held a staff, black as ebony and even at this distance his expression was formidable.

Her eyes narrowed. Where had he come from? Only her footprints showed in the walkway behind him.

With regal grace, he strolled forward, and the dust he disturbed fell back into place with perfect precision. Not one mote betrayed the path he traversed.

Her gaze darted back to the old man's face. Age and vitality mixed oddly in him and the energy in his movements belied the years etched upon his features. He halted a short distance from her.

"Who are you?" she demanded.

"I am, Morcar," he said with a slight bow. "The land and I have long awaited your coming." He extended his arms in a ceremonial gesture, and his piercing gaze struck her to the quick. "Welcome dragon bearer."

"Dragon bearer..." Had he been to her room? Was the statue safe?

"All is well. The creature is unharmed."

Did he now read her mind? "How do you know of the dragon?" she said, alarm creeping into her voice.

"It is my place to know of the beast," he replied,

91

"and many other wondrous things." His soothing voice brushed across her like a silken veil, and all her attention was fixed upon his words. "I seek only to help you," he added, with a look akin to sympathy.

At his offer of help Tanzie's brain sparked back into action. She cared not what other wondrous things he spoke of but for certes his help she could use. "If you wish to assist me," she said, "aide me in escaping this castle. If that is not the help you offer then please take your leave."

"Why do you wish to depart? You were meant to come here, Martanzia."

Saints above he knew her name. Her pulse skipped a beat then throbbed in her temples. This strange old man was beginning to frighten her. There was something uncommon about him, and by his robes, she thought he must fancy himself a soothsayer or a priest.

Eyes wide she studied this spellbinder more carefully.

Morcar's lips twitched into a smile.

Unable to resist, though she knew that she should, Tanzie yielded to the urge to stare deep into his crystalline blue eyes. They seemed all-knowing and the knowledge reflected within demanded if not veneration at least respect. But a shadow of sadness was present there too, as if his wisdom had been earned at a very great price. No self-pity was to be found, however.

A calmness washed over Tanzie. The beating of her heart diminished and her rapid shallow breathing slowed and deepened. Her fears lifted as if borne away in a swirling mist. It was the same feeling that overtook her when she held the carved dragon.

"Leaving Bamburgh would cause more harm than good for you and for all concerned," Morcar said, and the words became her thoughts. "There is much I would teach you if you would but let me."

Prudence and logic slipped beyond her grasp and for a moment a soporific spell rendered all thoughts of caution impotent. "Teach me about what?" she murmured with enormous effort.

"About the world, and Man's place in it," the old one said, his words warmly wrapped in enthusiasm. "About things that were that will never be again; about things that will be that never were before. We can begin with the tapestry," he suggested not giving her time to ponder the meaning of his words. He crossed the width of the hall and stood before the brightly colored panel. "What does it tell you?" he asked.

Released from Morcar's commanding gaze, Tanzie slumped back against the wall.

After waiting patiently for her to regain her composure he beckoned. She hesitated then cautiously took her place at his side. Though a forbidding force seemed to lurk beneath this stranger's outer image, discussing the art of embroidery sounded harmless enough.

Several of the runic symbols worked into the border appeared familiar to Tanzie. Her mother had scribed similar characters on scraps of vellum when she told of the legends of Northumbria. Her dragon statue also bore such markings. Tanzie reached out and traced the patterns with her hand. Despite the chill in the air the tapestry felt warm as if it had a life of its own. As she scrutinized the central portion of the rendering she discerned the shapes of various creatures ingenuously hidden within the woodland scene.

"I cannot recall the meaning of the symbols," she admitted. "But the animals appear worried. Their brows are furrowed as if a great concern weighs heavily upon them." Glancing at the old man, she paused to see if her interpretations were correct.

"Yes, very good," he encouraged. "Tell me what you feel as well as what you see."

She concentrated harder. "The animals are afraid," she murmured, then wondered how she knew that. "They sense impending doom. Something dreadful awaits them." Her breath caught and held as if she too waited.

"What else?" Morcar prompted.

She shook her head and exhaled slowly. "Nothing," she said. "What does it mean?"

"'Tis one of many possible futures," Morcar replied.

The future? Though the depiction before her was sad, hope spiraled in her heart. Perhaps this old conjurer could be of use after all. "Can you predict what is to be?" she asked eagerly.

"Yes," he said. "And with your help I can even alter the course to be realized."

She started. "My help? I know nothing about such endeavors? I am no magician."

"No. You are the dragon bearer."

The dragon again. It was true she had an affinity for the little carving, but that was because her mother had given it to her. It possessed no power that she was aware of. "What does the little beast have to do with anything? Or for that matter what could I possibly do?"

"Every man, plant, and animal has its purpose. And whether for good or evil they all affect the world, some more seriously than others. That is why the land is changing." Morcar's voice cleaved the air with such authority she did not dare to question the truth of his words. "The ancient ways are fading, and the new ways demand to be born. But like any birth, the passage will be painful. You shall set into motion what has long awaited to transpire. If you have the courage."

"Not me," she contradicted, unwilling to so

94

easily yield to his views and opinions. "I am merely a hostage of good faith. And at present, my courage has been sorely taxed, perhaps to the point of nonexistence. I do not think I am the one you seek."

"We shall see," Morcar replied, smiling at her rebuff. Using the tip of his staff he drew the tapestry aside. A portal lay hidden behind the wall hanging. The door swung inward of its own accord revealing a spiral staircase.

"Come," he invited, motioning her to begin the ascent. "'Tis the way to the tower, a place of knowledge and enlightenment."

She glanced at the stairs then back at Morcar's face. Though his words fired her curiosity the flame did not consume all her good sense. "Why should I trust to follow you?" she asked.

"Why should you not?"

"Because of late my life has been filled with deceit and crossed-purposes, and I see no reason why your motives should be any more honorable than those of my Uncle or Lord Valtaigne."

"Beorce trusted me." Morcar's eyes twinkled lending a hint of softness to his stern expression. "She always found the tower a most interesting place to explore."

Had he known her mother? Though he spoke the words gently, they felt sharp as flint as they pierced the still poorly healed scars of loss and grief. Confusion fought for the upper hand as the fresh pain crowded the air from her chest. "It is not possible," she gritted. "How could you have known my mother?"

"I helped to raise, Beorce," he said, pride evident in his voice." Right here at Bamburgh. What a loving child, full of kindness and sympathy towards all living things."

Tears welled in Tanzie's eyes. "My mother is dead," she said coldly and watched for Morcar's reaction.

His steadfast expression flickered. "I was not granted the opportunity to intercede on her behalf." The brilliance in his blue eyes faded as if regret washed the color from them. "She sacrificed much for what she believed in. And your father sacrificed much because he believed in her. But the greatest reason for Beorce's existence has yet to be realized."

"And what might that be?" Tanzie snapped, angry that this man appeared to know more about her mother than did she.

"Come with me and learn. All will be revealed to you when the time is right."

Folding her arms across her chest she held her ground. "Who are you Morcar? You are not a soldier of this garrison nor a common villager. What is your purpose here? Begin my learning by answering these questions."

"I am the one who waits," he said simply, as if the distinction was both an honor and a tribulation. "I am here to help Man help himself, and I am here to see the prophecy fulfilled."

"What you are," she countered, arms stiff at her sides, "is very persuasive and good at playing on the weaknesses and sympathies of others. I believe you are here to ensure that your own aspirations reach suitable ends, and if necessary to accomplish your goal, you will convince fish to fly and birds to live beneath the waves."

Morcar raised a brow at her outburst then as if unable to refute the harsh assessment of his motives, he shrugged and silently waited for her to decide her next move.

She would go with him of course. And why not? Though Morcar's answers were as obscure as his questions, at least he did not insist she translate them from Latin. And what if he truly had known her mother? She dare not pass up this rare occasion to find out more about her past.

Armed with healthy skepticism she entered the dark stairwell then paused to let her eyes adjust to the dim light. The steps rising before her were worn by many years and many feet and the air rushing down from above held the fragrance of fresh sea breeze mingled with the scent of herbs. What really did lie at the top of the stairs? There was only one way to find out. Raising the hem of her skirt she began the ascent.

Morcar uttered not one word as they climbed, and she heeded his example. She had seen few people since her arrival at Bamburgh, yet she feared "the walls had mice and the mice had ears."

They spiraled round and round, higher and higher. It seemed a stairway to an unearthly province but what awaited heaven or hell? Light filtered around the final turn giving her hope that whatever it might be, their destination was close at hand.

"Wait," Morcar ordered as she reached the landing. "Neither I nor anyone may compel you to enter here. Do you proceed of your own free will?"

She hesitated. How deep were the waters into which she prepared to leap? "What lies beyond the door?" she asked, her mistrust returning in full measure.

"I cannot tell you that. Either you enter now and find out for yourself, or you remain here never to know. But once you pass through that doorway," he cautioned, "Destiny's hand will guide you, and your life will be changed forever. There will be no turning back."

She swallowed hard. Had her mother been faced with this same decision? Had something in that room ultimately led to Beorce's untimely death? Tanzie was afraid. Her mother had been courageous and noble of reason. She would have based her decision on what was best for others not what was safe for herself. Tanzie wished to be equally as brave. She glanced at Morcar and drew comfort and strength from him, or was it false reassurance he offered? It didn't matter, she had to know what was in that room. She had to know why her journey had led her to the birthplace of her mother and to an old Druid priest who lived in a chamber at the top of the world.

She made to step forward but Morcar stayed her advance with his arm. "Say it," he demanded.

"I choose freely," she softly declared, knowing those three words would impact her life as no others she had ever spoken.

Morcar stepped aside.

As she entered the sanctuary at the top of the castle, the sun broke through the clouds. A shower of golden light encompassed her, and she stood in the center of the circular room and smiled without knowing why. A sense of abandon warmed her heart even as the sunshine warmed her body, and with her arms held wide she turned around full circle feeling like a song bird set free from its cage.

The walls and ceiling were constructed of precious glazing offering a spectacular view of the heavens and a commanding view of the earth. Armfuls of fresh flowers and herbs hung from the rafters, and though it was not cold, a fire burned within the hearth and the contents of a cauldron happily bubbled away in the inglenook.

Tanzie felt safe and comfortable here. Nothing seemed ominous or threatening. It reminded her of how home used to feel when her mother and father were still alive.

She glanced around with a more critical eye. The room was a jumble of jars, vials, coffers, and trunks; each filled to overflowing with the familiar and the foreign. The systematic chaos of the chamber invited investigation and like a child at the fair Tanzie hurried from one extraordinary item to the next.

"You flit about like a bee in summer clover," Morcar observed with a chuckle, as he took a seat at the trestle table. "Your mother exhibited much the same fascination."

What joy to think that her mother had stood in this very room breathing the fragrant flower scented ether. She may have touched this basket or that tome; for a moment it seemed as if Beorce were with her now.

Tanzie rushed across the room to stand before Morcar. "Tell me about my mother," she beseeched, "and the dragon statue."

"All in good time," the old man replied as he patted the chair at his side. "All in good time. For now sit you here and we shall begin lessons of another nature. I will teach you about the herbs, and show you how to release the medicinal power locked within their frail leaves and pale blossoms."

Herbs and flowers. Weeds for all she cared. She wanted to know about her mother. She wanted to know about the wondrous things he promised to reveal.

"But knowledge is wondrous," he said. "You well know that."

Her thoughts stopped short and collided. He really could divine what she was thinking. How positively rude to invade another person's private world. Morcar had the potential to be a nosy old bastard.

"I assure you my parents were married," he quipped.

Blushing at being caught harboring such an expletive she quietly took her seat. This alliance with Morcar was going to be more complicated than she had anticipated.

Resigned to her fate, Tanzie watched the old soothsayer reach for the first plant specimen. She wished to earn Morcar's respect and with true interest she tried to commit to memory the information he imparted.

As the day wore on she learned how to make an infusion and a decoction. She discovered the fine difference between a poultice and a fomentation, and she came to understand the burden that accompanied the art of healing.

Interspersed between the flora and rhetoric, Morcar subtly threw in a few theories about the order of the universe and the wisdom of the old ways. Steeped in tradition these ancient teachings stirred a place deep within Tanzie. Her senses felt awakened with a heightened awareness, and as each new mystery was revealed she wished to know more. At times the process seemed a recalling rather than a learning, as if the knowledge already existed within her and was merely waiting for the old Druid's prodding to push it to the forefront of her mind.

Soon, however, the abundance of knowledge confounded her. She continued to pay strict attention to Morcar's words but the more he droned on and on the more overwhelmed she became. Before long the table was littered with books, and piled high with shriveled greenery.

She felt her eyes glaze over.

Morcar abruptly stopped speaking, and stared at her. "It is akin to meeting a room full of strangers," he reassured, "it takes a while after the introductions before they become your friends."

Tanzie did not think a lifetime of familiarity would help her to remember all the plant-lore she had just heard. By now all the leaves appeared the same, and their individual properties totally escaped her.

Doggedly Morcar went to fetch another manuscript. In idleness she picked up a peculiar looking root that lay off to one side. Toying with the strange tuber she smelled it and turned it over and over in her hand. The specimen resembled a doll with sprouting arms and legs. Leaves crowned the top like unruly hair.

"'Tis mandrake," Morcar said as he returned to the table. "I was saving that for another day, but we shall study it now.

"Mandragora vernalis," he said reverently, and gently plucked the root from the palm of her hand. "This plant is much like a human in both form and deed. It can be male or female, and it has the power to heal or kill. Also like a person it is known by many names; Satin's apple, Baaras, the lamp of elves, and even the devil's candle."

"Where does it grow?" she asked.

"The best specimens still come from afar, though it may be found deep in the great forest to the south. But mind you," he added sternly, "the harvesting of this plant is quite dangerous. It should never be attempted by a novice." The hard glint in his eyes drove home his words. "The root may only be gathered at sundown or in the dead of night, and before it is taken from the ground three circles are drawn in the earth around it. The marks must be scribed with a two edged sword that has never drawn blood. This prevents the demons from rising with the root."

Dumfounded Tanzie stared at Morcar. She thought he must be joking, yet he seemed serious as the plague.

"At the exact moment the mandrake leaves the ground," he continued, "a loud shrill trumpet blast must be sounded. This masks the shriek emitted by the uprooted plant. Its sound you see being fatal to the hearer. After that, the root may be used in many forms for many purposes. Even for the spell of life, or the spell of illusion."

Casually Morcar handed the root back to her.

Granting the specimen the respect she would afford a writhing asp, she gingerly set it aside then watched it for a moment as if it might leap upon her with deadly intent.

"The one lesson you must never forget," Morcar said, "is that there is always a price to pay if you use the mandrake or any incantation to alter the thoughts or desires of another. The risk can be horrible, for you, your subject, or both. You must never use those powers out of hate or revenge."

"Then when would I use such knowledge?" she asked.

"Only to save your own life or to help someone you love. Pray promise you will remember this above all else you learn here. Forces once released can be difficult to direct and impossible to banish. Unseen elements, good or bad, relish their freedom just as we do."

Lost in thought, she realized the knowledge Morcar entrusted to her came heavily wrapped in responsibility. Could she shoulder such a burden? Did she even wish too? "But how will I know what to do, and whom to trust? This land is filled with strange people and strange ways."

"Never act in haste," he advised. "Listen to your heart. You have your mother's understanding of nature, and I will teach you what I can of the forces beyond your mortal ways. Armed with these weapons you will endure what has been preordained."

"You make it sound as if I am preparing to do battle."

"But you are little one. You shall battle for the very spirit of England."

"God's teeth," she muttered. What did this old

Druid insinuate? What did it matter? She was trapped. Morcar had said there was no turning back. Or was that only what he wished her to believe. Surely she had some say in the matter. "Perhaps you are but a maddish conjurer and all you have told me is a lie." Even as she spoke the words she knew it was no more than wishful thinking.

"It would make no difference," he said cheerfully. "If you believe what I have told you then for you it is the truth. Either way it's much too late to worry now."

His blithe attitude rankled her emotions and she was nearly overcome with frustration. A fortnight ago, she had been a relatively normal young woman concerned only with eluding Rathgar's lascivious grasp, and Uncle's current ploy. Now she was held prisoner miles from her home, waiting to fulfill a destiny that she did not understand, one that held the possibility of great jeopardy...or worse.

Suddenly an equally appalling thought sprang to mind. What if Morcar sought to involve her in some political intrigue? It had been four years since the last rebellion in Northumbria. Was the time ripe for another uprising? Did treason again seek a foothold along the border? "You don't attempt to overthrow the king do you?" she blurted, in wide-eyed alarm. Merely expressing the idea made her palms sweat.

"The king?" Morcar sputtered. "Heavens no. Though in truth his days are numbered. What I speak of transcends royal decree and even ecclesiastical canon. Kings..." he repeated the word with an equal measure of annoyance and pity. "They always declare themselves the protector of the land, yet not one of them has understood the meaning of such an obligation. Arthur almost grasped the concept, but even he was not ready, or so Merlin concluded, and my cousin does not easily give up the fight."

Her mind reeled at Morcar's reference to his family tree, but she refused to be sidetracked. "If you do not seek to rule a kingdom," she reasoned, "then it must be wealth you covet."

"Don't be absurd," he gently refuted, "I can change base metal into gold." His good-natured scolding led her to suspect he took pleasure in bantering with her. Of course with the future of the England at stake, it was difficult to relax and enjoy the interlude. "It has nothing to do with what I want," he added as if this were a great clue to understanding everything. "It is Man's desire to govern Himself that will bring about the beginning of the end."

"What man?"

"All Men. It is a universal plea. And not the first one uttered. Perhaps it is the natural order of things. Humankind has come of age and will now live or die by its own mistakes."

"You sound less then optimistic."

"As a species, Man has repeatedly made poor choices," Morcar pointed out, "though he is glorious in defending them. I wonder what the world will be like in a thousand years?"

"I thought you could see the future," she challenged.

He shuddered. "I find visualizing a future ruled by men too horrifying to contemplate. What I do know," he added, "is that the abandoned gods will be left to their own dark amusement, and this new God, unified into one being, will still not unify Man. There will be little order in the universe and only the memory of magic. Of course, I could be wrong. That is the one good thing about the unknown, it inspires hope as well as fear."

Morcar glanced up and gave a self-conscious cough as if he were unaccustomed to being caught woolgathering. "We shall stop for the day," he said, ending their discussion. Turning in his chair, he reached to retrieve two manuscripts from a nearby shelf. Both worn volumes boasted Greek titles, De _Materia Medica_ and _Historia Plantarum_. "Take these with you," he suggested, "and promise me you will continue your studies. Practice with the herbs even if I am not here to help you...all except the mandrake, of course."

"I will," she pledged, giving the forbidden root a sidelong glance. Scanning the pages of the first book, she was awed by the information it contained. There were chapters on powders, tinctures, extracts, and poultices, everything she needed to know from Acacia and Althea to Woodruff and Wormwood. Thank the merciful Lord it was all written down.

Lovingly she touched an illumination inside the second book. It was soft and colorful as a butterfly wing. Reading these volumes would make a pleasant change from Branoc's manuscripts. With no sense of guilt, she realized that she had missed her appointed hours in the council room. She hoped her absence had been an inconvenience. Facing another parchment there without Sir Branoc had seemed a dismal prospect. Would he even notice she was absent for one day?

She stood and her stomach grumbled in empty annoyance. "Would you join us for our meals, Morcar?" she offered. "Ealgith and I would gladly welcome your company. We are not permitted to eat in the old hall with the men, and we miss much of what goes on here and of what news passes by."

"I shall try to accommodate your generous invitation," Morcar said. "But do not look for me soon. My days and nights are without order. Some of my concerns demand hours of their own. Besides," he added, "I eat most frugally now, and before long fasting will be necessary."

Tanzie caught a fleeting expression of wistfulness in Morcar's eyes, and a new insight tempered her vision of the old Druid. This maelstrom called Future held him prisoner too. There was no turning back for him either, and it occurred to her that perhaps he risked even more than she.

Gripping the manuscripts, she prepared to take her leave.

"Can you find your way back to your room?" he asked.

"Yes, Morcar. Thank you." Her gaze swept the lofty chamber. Too bad, none of the sorcerer's concoctions could be used to create a decently scented perfume. If she were at home, she could render roses from her garden into an appropriate attar. Her garden...such an innocent delight. Thoughts of Flanders rekindled thoughts of her parents.

"Will you tell me about my mother now?" she asked hopefully. She had been only ten-years-old when Beorce had died, and many of her memories had been lost to youth's exuberance. She yearned to recall those images of her childhood.

Morcar gazed at her thoughtfully, and surprised her by honoring the request. "You are much like her in spirit and form," he said and settled back in his chair. "Though I think you are more wise to the true nature of Man. Beorce bore well the teachings of her people, but she saw only the good in all. You see what is, as well as what should or could be. 'Tis much safer that way."

Morcar smiled and recollections enlivened his features. "You will understand more the longer you are here. The essence of the land will become a part of you, and soon you will feel the energy and learn with your heart as well as your mind."

Her heart was already overly busy she thought

and pictured Branoc. The lord of the castle, so dark and unyielding, was another mystery she wished to unravel. Desperate to know more about Lord Valtaigne and her future at Bamburgh, she boldly asked for personal advice.

"Would you look far enough into the future to tell me if I will ever find true love?" she challenged.

Morcar gave a snort of disdain and rose from his chair. "So now I am a Gypsy, good for only telling the fortunes of the lovelorn. If only we had the entrails of a chicken or some unlucky slave."

Embarrassed Tanzie stared at the floor. Then she felt Morcar's hand upon her downcast head.

"Forgive my ill-humor," he said. "I forget what it is like to be young with heartfelt desires and needs. 'Tis been a long time since love and passion captured my imagination. A very long time indeed. Come, I will tell you what lies ahead."

He stepped forward into a pool of sunlight and folding his hands, he closed his eyes and chanted.

The room remained temperate, yet gooseflesh prickled her arms as a chill streaked through her.

Morcar's eyes snapped opened, but he seemed to look through her rather than at her as he spoke. "One man shall claim you as his wife, but never make you his own. Another shall love you fiercely and daringly, though you be not wed."

He hesitated as if searching for more information. "One man will find the courage to trust in love. Another will redeem his soul by loving with unselfish courage." Morcar smiled. She held her breath both fearing and longing to hear his final words. "Once the prophecy of the land has been fulfilled," he proclaimed, "true love will be yours. Assuming of course that we all survive."

Chapter 8
*Maldegem, Flanders*

Rathgar assaulted the steps two at a time then breached the entrance of the Verheire chateau. Once this shabby manor belonged to him, he would see it updated with all the modern conveniences. After all, it was the 12th century.

Terrified servants scurried from his path, and not waiting to be announced, he stalked his quarry with the determination of a lion. Ah, there was the man he sought, relaxing before the fire in the great hall. "Good eventide, Malbourne. I am so pleased to find you at home."

Malbourne leapt to his feet. Eyes wide with surprise, a mottled flush crept across his cheeks. The man's horrified expression alone made the journey worthwhile.

"Rathgar," Malbourne sputtered, "I did not expect to see you in Flanders."

"Of course not. You are a fool. Only a wise man expects the unexpected." He stripped off his gloves, and crossed the room to stand before the quaking little rabbit. "I've come to see the girl. Where is she?"

"I can explain everything," Malbourne reassured, his face now as white as fine linen. "It was a most unfortunate situation."

"Yes, unfortunate for you. But pray save your excuses. I will see Martanzia first."

Malbourne's expensive robe hung loosely about his sparse mean frame, and he was near bent over beneath the weight of gold jewelry that bedecked his neck.

Rathgar reached out and flicked his finger at one of the finely wrought chains. "You say little," he accused. "I have never before seen you at such a loss for words. Apparently recanting covenants in writing is more to your liking."

Malbourne swallowed hard then made an attempt at smiling, but his lips trembled too much to complete the act. "You must be fatigued from your travels," he said, ignoring Rathgar's remark about the letter of rejection. "Sit. Rest. I will have wine and food brought to you. Nothing but the best. Then we can converse more comfortably."

His host attempted to leave the room but Rathgar blocked his exit. "The refreshments can wait. Where is the girl?"

Malbourne froze. His eyes darted back and forth as if he sought an avenue of escape. Finally, he took a step backward. "By now she should be in Northumbria; at castle Bamburgh to be precise."

Northumbria... By the Saints. And worse yet, at Bamburgh. Valtaigne was in residence there. At first, Rathgar could not comprehend what he was hearing. Then a pocket of rage burst within him spewing poisonous images into his brain. Fury, blind to logic, set free the hateful beast that ever lurked just below the surface of his being. This vengeful creature needed only the slightest excuse to take control, and Malbourne's words had set it free and soaring.

"I hope my ears have heard wrong or by heaven and hell you shall pay even more dearly than I first intended."

Grabbing Malbourne, he shoved the man into a chair then with a snarl he leaned forward and planted one hand on each arm of the bench, neatly trapping Martanzia's uncle in place. Rage momentarily turned to fascination as he watched the pulse that fluttered along the side of Malbourne's throat. One silent cut of the blade would free all the lying venom that coursed through those tortuous veins...an interesting idea but at present not to his advantage.

"Why is she there?" he asked, his voice deadly quiet.

"It was by royal decree," Malbourne declared. "King Philip of France has torn himself away from the feasting table long enough to form an alliance with Flanders and Anjou."

"Yes, yes," Rathgar interrupted. "I am well aware of the current shift of political loyalties on the continent. What does this have to do with Martanzia?"

Malbourne winced as if he endured physical blows rather than angry words. If this treacherous little living pustule didn't give him an answer soon the man would quickly learn the marked difference.

"The agreement was drawn up in the Vexin," Malbourne blustered, "while the king was off quelling Welsh uprisings, and to ensure the protection of Normandy's border William Rufus demanded Flanders provide a good faith hostage. As Count Robert remains with Curthose on the Crusades, the duty of selecting a suitable person fell to the Flemish Council. They chose my son, Landow. After all, he is third cousin to the royal family, though the distinction has brought him nothing but sorrow and tribulation."

"By the Rood," Rathgar fumed. The man did babble like a drunken old sot. "Get to the point or the story shall die with you."

Sweat popped out on Malbourne's forehead. "I fought their decision," he defended, his words now tumbling out in a rush, "but it was not a request, it was a command. At the last moment before departure, Landow fell ill and could not go abroad. I had no choice but to send Martanzia in his stead."

Rathgar hung his head in a brief moment of disbelief. Martanzia truly was in England, in the hands of Valtaigne. Even without effort, his lifelong foe caused him grief. His thoughts turned as crimson as the blood he wished to draw. "We had an arrangement, old man," he menaced, leaning close enough to smell Malbourne's fear. "The girl was mine. How dare you disperse my property so casually?"

"She...she...wanted to go," Malbourne stammered. "Martanzia said she found exile and being a hostage a more agreeable fate than marriage to you. I could not stop her, Relentes. You must believe me, she volunteered."

Rathgar tightened his grip on the arms of the chair and slammed the ornate bench backward up against the wall. "I would not believe you if the Pope did stand here and consecrate your every word. And do not tell me that Martanzia orchestrated this twisted plot of betrayal. You are the one who guides the strings of the puppets within this household." Grabbing Malbourne out of the chair, he tossed him to the floor then drew his broadsword and towered over the quaking man who cowered at his feet. .

"Please, Rathgar, spare me," Malbourne pleaded, as he levered onto his knees, his hands clasped before him like a supplicant of the church. "I will do anything you ask. 'Tis just a misunderstanding. Martanzia will change her mind if so bidden. Surely you can see that killing me is far from your best interest."

"You tempt me sorely," Rathgar thundered, shaking his sword. "It would please me greatly to run this steel through your quivering guts but 'twould not warrant the cleaning of the blade." Sheathing his weapon, he watched in amusement as Malbourne breathed a sigh of relief. The lying little toad actually thought to get off so easily. "'Tis not

111

quite that simple," he said. "I will not kill you, but your betrayal shall not go unpunished."

He seized Malbourne by the wrist, dragged him still kneeling across the room to a heavy-legged table, and forced the man's left hand flat upon the smooth surface. Easing his short sword from its lamb's wool and leather sheath he held the gleaming metal before Malbourne's eyes.

The other man's questioning expression turned to one of terror.

Rathgar laughed at the man's pitiful struggles, and with one lightning-quick stroke of the blade he cut off Malbourne's little finger.

Howling in pain, Malbourne slumped to the floor. Employing the front of his tunic, he bound the maimed appendage halting the flow of spurting blood. With a sob he gazed at the forlorn bit of flesh and bone that still twitched upon the blood-spattered tabletop.

Rathgar cleaned the blade upon Malbourne's velvet-clad shoulder. "I will whittle you away piece by piece for every lie or act of treason you commit," he said, returning the weapon to his side. "Now," he continued, and took to the chair that the other man had previously occupied, "let us begin again."

Deathly pale, Malbourne hugged the injured hand to his chest. He opened his mouth to speak but no intelligible words came out, and jabbering like an idiot, he curled forward and wept.

"Oh, do show some courage, man," Rathgar tormented. "Perhaps you could sell the liberated finger as a holy relic. After it cures a bit I doubt anyone could tell it from St. Peter's."

"You dare add blasphemy to your sins," Malbourne said, forcing the words out through clenched teeth.

Rathgar slammed his fist down upon the arm of the chair. "I will dare much to see my plans to their rightful end," he growled. "You of all people should know that."

Malbourne whimpered in pain, and nodded in defeat.

During the second interrogation Rathgar was able to extract the correct and more precise version of how Martanzia had been forced into going to England, and deceived regarding her destination. He listened in amazement as Malbourne explained how he had sacrificed his niece to protect his son. He was not pleased that Martanzia had chosen what she thought to be life in a convent over a life with him, but it mattered little. She would belong to him soon enough.

With no additional persuasion necessary, Malbourne eagerly offered his assistance, and a fresh plan was promptly conceived. For only a moderate fee, the necessary documents were expertly forged, and one particularly lethal acquisition was procured.

\*\*\*\*

Departing Flanders, Rathgar followed a circuitous route to the Cotentin there to meet briefly with Gilbert and Roger from the House of Clare. The news was good. Prince Henry had grown tired of waiting. The time for action was upon them. Confirmation was expected daily regarding Robert Curthose's return from the Holy wars, and with his arrival would come the renewal of the private feuds that afflicted the three brothers and the lands that they ruled.

Political hell was about to break loose, and Rathgar was being afforded the opportunity to stand as Satan's advocate. He realized he played with fiendish fire, but eyes wide open, he grabbed the opportunity with both hands. No doubt there was more to the Prince's plan than had been revealed, and he had his suspicions as to whom else might be involved in the scheme, but Rathgar didn't ask questions. Nor did he answer them, for he had secrets of his own. He'd been afforded enough information to remain safe, and that was all that mattered.

The pact sealed, and the plans finalized, Rathgar's mission was to incite the northern rebels. This would further divide William Rufus's forces between the Welsh border, the Scottish perimeter, and Normandy. And during the ensuing chaos, Prince Henry would follow in his father's footsteps and conquer the country by southern invasion.

Rathgar smiled, the prospect of revenge always comforted him. And by executing the orders of the future king, his trip to Northumbria served a dual triumph. He would claim a new bride, and repay an old debt.

All he needed was the unwitting help of the current king.

\*\*\*\*

*Winchester, England / The New Forest*

Awaiting permission to speak, Rathgar stood at attention and utilized the opportunity to study William Rufus and his holy counselor, Ranulph Flambard. The two men were a frightening amalgam of sovereign might and ecclesiastical cunning.

"Be brief, Relentes," the king bid him, as he prowled about the royal receiving chamber. "There are wolves reported near Farnham, and we leave for the hunt straight away. The hellish beasts frighten my roes and eat my rabbits," he groused.

"Wolves of another nature threaten your land in the north," Rathgar interjected, hoping the analogy would snag the king's attention. "Rumor has it on the continent that the Saxons are gathering for another uprising, and this time their ranks are swelled by the renegade Scots and ever opportunistic Danes."

114

At this news, the monarch appeared more thoughtful and less agitated. He toyed with the fletching on an arrow then shifted his gaze to the man who ruled the see of Durham. "That is your bailiwick, Ranulph. Have you heard such talk?"

"Nothing serious, your grace," Ranulph Flambard said. "Of course one cannot be too careful where treason is concerned." Like a well thrown javelin, the Bishop aimed a lethal gaze in Rathgar's direction.

Did the words of the holy hell-raiser have a double meaning? Did he know Rathgar's intentions? Impossible. Being self-serving and devious, Flambard no doubted suspected the same in others.

"What says Edgar of Scotland regarding these border raids?" the king inquired.

"He encourages them," Rathgar said. It was a lie of course, but there was no one at court newly returned from Scotland to refute such a charge.

William Rufus's complexion colored to new heights, and his expression turned feral. "Then Edgar has conveniently forgotten who was at his side when he defeated Donald Bane and won the crown. Perhaps he is in need of having his memory refreshed." The king snapped the arrow he held in two and cast the pieces to the floor. "I will not tolerate insurrection nor any man who encourages such."

Rathgar smiled. This time King William did not appear willing to buy peace. That should help implement Prince Henry's plans. Yet, he must not make the danger seem too imminent. "Why not provide me a well-suited force," he suggested, "and I will lead them to the North Country and discern the truth as to what transpires there."

The king's gaze turned contemplative.

"A show of strength, my lord, that is all," Rathgar hastily added. "Periodic movement of our troops is healthy for their survival. It keeps the men alert and our enemies confused."

"Valtaigne is about my business in the North," the king pointed out. "He is worthy of the challenge."

Rathgar's guts tightened into a greasy knot. "Valtaigne is worthy of much," he agreed, the words clawing at his throat. "Yet he is only one man with a small garrison of men."

"The finest men in all of England or Normandy," William Rufus defended.

Rathgar was surprised at this show of fealty. It was common knowledge that the king had little admiration for anyone other than himself, and he would much rather listen to praise than dole it out. Yet, the king respected Branoc and his men and held them in high regard. How had Valtaigne managed such an achievement? Probably more of that "Dragon of Normandy" nonsense perpetuated by the royal court and blown out of proportion by the bards. The same fictitious folly that the ladies on the continent swooned and romanticized over and the same glorified rubbish the men never ceased analyzing and discussing.

Rathgar rued the day he had switched Branoc's blue trappings for black. Instead of proving an embarrassment, the situation had somehow immortalized Valtaigne as the dark and stalwart knight. Well the dragon was far from home now, Rathgar thought, and couched in a realm that cared not for his previous deeds of valor. "If help is not needed," Rathgar pressed, "I shall return quickly with a first hand account of the situation. What could it hurt?"

King William settled his bulky frame into the ornate chair perched upon the dais. "Many of my troops are in the west occupied with quelling the bloody Welsh," he pointed out.

So, the king was aware of the chance he took in

dispersing his men even more sparsely about the kingdom. No use denying the obvious. "I understand your concern," Rathgar agreed, with forced patience, as he waited for William to reason out the situation.

The king leaned sideways to confer with his henchman priest. Ranulph Flambard's gaze remained piercing as a hawk's, and for one terrible moment, Rathgar feared his suggestion was to be rejected.

Then with a shrug and a nod, Flambard acquiesce.

"Very well," William said. "You may seek out Valtaigne. Bishop Flambard will travel with you as far as Durham. When you are at Bamburgh," he added, "see how fares my hostage of peace. 'Twas surprisingly open-minded of Malbourne to send his own son."

A muscled jumped in Rathgar's cheek, and he clenched his jaw in annoyance. He could not tell what provoked his ire more, the inconvenience of traveling under the watchful eye of Ranulph Flambard, or discovering that William was yet unaware of the switch between Landow and Martanzia. Why would Valtaigne keep such news a secret? This latter bit of information did not set well, but as he'd gotten what he'd come for, he saw no reason to place a burr beneath the sovereign's saddle by enlightening the king on the matter.

"I will have written orders drawn up for you," William Rufus continued. "You may leave in two days time, and personally choose the men with whom you will ride. And since your travels will take you afar, I will issue authorization for you to carry the king's warrant. And Relentes," he said, with a far away look in his eyes, "assess the hunting in the area and count the wolves. I may plan a journey there myself. I grow disenchanted with the scenery in the south. The peasants say the forest here is haunted, and I'm beginning to believe they are correct."

"Yes, my liege."

Rathgar bowed his way out of the chamber, dismissing the king's childish fears regarding local superstitions. His thoughts ran in only one direction now. Soon he would taste Martanzia's sweet lips, spiced by the flavor of long anticipated vengeance. Soon he would transform Branoc Valtaigne's world into the living nightmare the man so richly deserved.

Chapter 9

As Branoc ambled across the bailey and headed for the stables, he glanced up at the window of his council chamber.

She won't be there today, he thought with regret. Mistress Verheire had finished translating all of the manuscripts he had left for her. Would she be disappointed at having been relieved of her duties? As of this morning, she should have been informed of the situation.

Why had he sent a soldier to deliver the message rather than going to her himself? Because, he rationalized, he had more important obligation to attend to like preparing for his impending journey. He dragged his hand across the back of his neck. In all honesty, he knew he found Martanzia too compelling. He had kept his distance from the council room during the daylight hours, but as he prowled about there in the night, it oddly pleased him to know that the girl had previously occupied the same space.

He often observed her, clandestinely, of course, making sure that she kept to the rules and stayed out of trouble. Long-range glimpses of the maid did not seem to cloud his logic. It was her nearness that confounded his thinking, and he could ill afford to make an error in judgment where she was concerned.

He grimaced. Again, his life seemed to be getting overly complicated, and he begrudged having these changes thrust upon him with no recourse. His choices were no longer simply black or white, and it annoyed him that his surroundings were suddenly filled with shades of gray, the color that transformed truth to illusion.

Yet, while he did not favor these changes, he could not solely blame Martanzia for the condition. Indeed, thus far her behavior had been without recrimination. It did not suit well that she had spent one entire day with the old Druid. Still, what harm could be caused by a young girl with an undetermined future and an old necromancer who seemed lost in the past? He supposed there were worse ways for her to wile away her time. And except for that one day of mischief, she had dedicated all of her afternoons to laboring at his request. How could he ask more of her?

He thought about the small remaining stack of ledgers and maps still awaiting review, but those documents promised little information valuable to his immediate cause. It seemed pointless to insist she transcribe them. The girl was quick witted enough to realize the task would be a ruse to prevent idleness, and relying on past experience, he doubted she would take kindly to such a notion.

His mouth curved into a half-smile as he recalled the day Lady Martanzia Verheire had arrived unprotected at his castle gate. Dirty, cold, and hungry, she'd still had enough courage left to challenge him, and enough pride left to defy him. And having gained admission to his keep, she had wasted little time in issuing orders of her own. Scarcely unpacked, Martanzia had interviewed the cook to ensure the uneaten trenchers and edible leftover were being given to the needy in the village, and she had shown prudence in her use of firewood and candles. Branoc admired Martanzia's efforts to make the best of her situation, and he appreciated her practicality.

Forcing the smile from his face, he clenched his

jaw and quickened his stride. 'Twould be easy enough to fall victim to this one's charm he thought in alarm. And although the maid did not appear inclined to lead a fellow a merry chase, he did not doubt her ability to put a man through his paces.

He skirted a patch of mud and fought to overcome his preoccupation with such thoughts. Finding this an impossible course of action, he switched tactics and fully indulged his fantasies as he worked at recalling the exact color of her eyes. They were green...no brown..no both, like a velvety forest at dusk, warm and mysterious. And there was intelligence behind her gaze and a sound mind beneath that incredible abundance of willful hair.

But she was so young and innocent—or was she? Mistress Verheire's unannounced appearance as good faith hostage was a brilliant bit of duplicity, but at whom had the deception been aimed, the girl or the king? In the midst of today's political turmoil, plots and deception were as common as blueflies.

Even Prince Henry may have set the scheme in motion. It was common knowledge he sought to undermine his brother's rule. Or, perhaps, Robert Curthose could have arranged the matter prior to leaving for the Holy Land. He was now in the company of the Count of Flanders, the ruler of Martanzia's homeland. The Duke and the Count—there was an alliance of which to be wary. And now their union would be forged by battle glory...the strongest of bonds. King William Rufus had good cause to worry and demand hostages. He had a number of enemies on both sides of the narrow sea.

He wondered if not revealing the identity of the hostage added to the intrigue. The decision concerned him. But William Rufus's court was steeped in treachery and whether real or imagined, the king had been known to react to threats with untold cruelty and violence. If William were aware of the situation, he might feel compelled to retaliate by imprisoning Martanzia without recourse, or God forbid beheading her for treason. Branoc would not risk either happenstance. King William's written orders had been to protect *the hostage*. No names had been scribed. It was only by word of mouth that Branoc had been alerted to expect Landow. Viewed from that vantage, remaining silent was not disobeying the king's edict but rather following it to the letter.

Branoc's conscience did not easily embrace this concept, but it was less unsettling than believing his desire to safeguard Martanzia was prompted by personal need. Or worse yet, prompted by fear of the king's inability to make rational decisions.

Reaching the stables, he ducked beneath the lintel and turned his attention to examining the additional stalls being constructed along the far wall. They were nearly finished, and the other modifications were already completed. His men had done a proper good job of providing for their horses, sparing no amount of labor, and all accomplished with nary a complaint. Of course, any seasoned warrior would put the needs of his mount before his own. Branoc felt the same way about his horses, Strong Oak and Solitaire. They were his most beloved amusements and his greatest investment. In battle he depended upon them for his life. Off the field, he would show them no less loyalty in return.

As he crossed between the mow and the feed bins, he spied Leofric already about the days work.

"Good morn," he called.

Leofric glanced up, smiled a hello, and led Branoc's black stallion forward. "He appears much better today," his friend, called cheerfully.

"Yes," Branoc agreed, studying Solitaire's gate. "Hold him there." Bending down he raised the horse's near forefoot and examined the underside of the hoof. Yesterday the beast had greatly favored the leg, and last eventide this type of prodding had elicited an unmistakable response of pain. Today the horse merely appeared ill-humored at having had his breakfast interrupted.

Branoc straightened, and rubbed the big stallion's muzzle. "Just to be safe, apply the poultices for two more days. I would not see him relapse by rushing the cure."

"I will have Arland tend to it," Leofric promised, as he led the stallion back to his stall. "Have you noticed the handmaiden who travels with your young hostage?" He called over his shoulder. "A tasty bit of Flemish womanhood there to be sure."

"She is not *my* hostage," Branoc, corrected, "but the kings. And your words confirm my first misgivings that it was a mistake to admit either female to the castle. 'Tis bad luck and bad logic."

"But a grand diversion, this royal burden," Leofric added.

Branoc gave a snort of resignation. "At times the wishes of the sovereign are more trying than the demands of any woman. And the powers that govern this land are more shifting than the seas we traveled to come here."

"With travel in mind, do we journey to Jarrow as planned?"

Branoc glanced around the stable. "The horses are eating well and their nerves have settled. We should be ready to leave before weeks end. Oddly enough our Norman steeds respond well to this English clime."

"'Tis the long days of idleness that they respond well too," Leofric returned. "I have begun a daily routine for them to ensure they remain trim and battle ready."

A tingling crept across Branoc's shoulders, and he felt as if someone walked upon his grave. "You are correct in doing so," he agreed, "for sooner or later a battle there shall be."

"Is that hearsay or premonition?" Leofric asked.

"Both," Branoc admitted.

Leofric nodded, accepting without question Branoc's analysis of the conditions that confronted them, and Branoc knew he need not explain further. He and Leofric had known one another since childhood. They fought many a battle, side by side, guarding one another's back. They knew each other's dreams and nightmares and trusted one another's instincts as readily as their own. It was the kind of friendship that transcended continents, and politics, and at times even words. Above all other qualities, Branoc valued this commitment of loyalty. And above all other comrades, he valued Leofric.

"When the repairs are complete," Branoc said, encouragingly, "the fortress will be secure. Except for lack of water by the keep, we should be able to withstand whatever comes our way."

"'Tis hard to believe a concern such as water would be overlooked by the people who occupied this relic before us," Leofric observed. "Was there nothing revealed in the manuscripts or ledgers?"

"Not one word, and the girl has done an exceptional job of compiling the information. Each night I check her work and find nothing lacking, and there has been no mention of a solution to our water problem. We should begin storing a reserve in casks."

"That seems a worthy idea," Leofric agreed. "We could fill them from the stream in the outer bailey and haul them to the keep. Once in place, we could rotate the butts to insure the water remains fresh. I will have the soldiers begin at once. Olaf would be the best man to organize the work."

"Make the arrangements, Leofric, but do not assign Olaf. He is ill of sorts. This morning I found him misty-eyed over a shattered ax head. When questioned he simply claimed it was his favorite then he proceeded to carry on like a wee lad with a broken toy."

Leofric raised a brow. "Not a normal state for the gregarious Norseman," he agreed. "We will begin without him."

Leofric left to arrange for the water detail, and Branoc continued to walk the perimeter of the grounds.

On the leeward side of the castle, he paused to assess the reconstruction. All was going according to schedule. The timber required to reinforce the masonry was to be brought in this morning, and if the weather held, the restoration should be completed by the end of the week.

He gazed at the imposing splendor of the castle wall. It never ceased to amaze him. Even in its present state of partial collapse it towered nearly eighty feet up into the sky, and the rock-strewn land surrounding it plunged downward another thirty to forty feet. The resulting effect inspired lofty imaginings while it reminded him of his own mortality. Yet though the rampart was impressive, would it ever really feel as if it was truly his? For many years, he had sought to acquire property for the house of Valtaigne. It would take time to trust in this dream realized, and perhaps even longer before he could call this place home.

As he surveyed, the area he spied a figure off to the side of the great sloping hill. Mother of God, it was Martanzia. To what endeavor did she now turn her attention? Arms crossed over his chest he lounged against one of the great stones that lay scattered about the area, and silently watched.

It appeared she dug about in the dirt with a sturdy stick. From his present vantage, he could not discern her intent, but he did notice she had once again ignored his request to contain her hair. Caught by the breeze it streamed out behind her like the mane of a lively young mare. Pure as the sun and wild as the wind, the girl seemed almost a part of the elements.

As she stepped to one side, the object of her attention was revealed. It was a forlorn rose bush that fought for existence on the steep rocky ledge. Branoc had noticed the plant himself a few days ago. Apparently, Martanzia held some naive hope of rescuing the bedraggled shrub.

Did she have a passion for roses? Did her heart gladden at the sight of a summer bud bejeweled by morning dew? Did she enjoy the fragrance of roses lingering like the melody of a lark on a warm evening breeze?

Recollections of the dainty briar roses that clung tenaciously to the castle walls at Lillebonne again sprung to mind. He missed their simple beauty, and he appreciated their ability to endure in the most inhospitable of circumstance. Sometimes he too barely clung to existence in the barren world he had created for himself. Yet, to flourish in the worst of conditions insured the greatest chance for survival.

Without meaning to, he pictured Martanzia in a field of flowers, a ringlet of blossoms crowning her head. She would be the fairest rose amongst the bowers. Petals would envy the softness of her skin, and leaves would weep in frustration, unable to replicate the green darkness of her eyes.

With a snort of disgust, he dismissed his fanciful thoughts. He was acting like a smitten young swain. Then a twinge of pity for the girl caught him by surprise. She labored in vain as far as the rosebush was concerned. The puny plant would soon be sacrificed as the workmen with their timber passed through the area. The concerns of war did not recognize beauty nor give quarter to sentiment.

As if summoned by his contemplations, craftsmen, horses, and soldiers crested the far ridge.

Unaccustomed to their trappings, the great destriers stamped their hooves and rebelled against the task of dragging trees. Truly, they were not suited to such work, but they were the only horses available at Bamburgh. One stallion seemed particularly upset. He tossed his head and strained at the tethers and with a great twisting lurch, he broke free of his harness. Bucking and rearing in terror, the roan tried to rid himself of the leather straps that snapped and fluttered at his sides. A workman grabbed at the frightened animal and was promptly knocked to the ground for his effort. The rest of the men fought to keep the other horses in check.

As if pursued by a legion of demons, the roan bolted forward at a gallop. Blindly he tore along the escarpment, heading straight toward Martanzia.

Branoc stepped away from the rocks and cupped his hands to his mouth. "Take heed! Get off of the ridge!" he shouted, then waved. It was no use. The wind carried his words in the wrong direction. She could not hear him.

The charger gained speed with every stride, and as the distance between the horse and the workmen grew greater and greater, the distance between the horse and Martanzia grew smaller.

Branoc grappled up the sheer slope using the bracken as he fought to find purchase on the slippery incline. Dear God how could she not notice the animal's approach? Look up....see the danger...over and over his mind screamed out the warning, as he battled up the side of the cliff that lay between him and the girl he had sworn to protect.

Losing his footing, he backslid halfway down the hill. Rocks gouged his knees and thistles stabbed the palms of his hands. Ignoring the pain, he renewed the treacherous climb realizing all the while, that he would never reach her in time.

****

Tanzie shivered, but it was a sense of foreboding that caused her to shudder not the chill morning air. She straightened and glanced around. The stick she held slid from her fingers, and her lips parted in alarm.

A great roan stallion charged in her direction.

Wild-eyed, the horse emitted a pitiful neigh, and like a Berserker under the full effects of battle frenzy, he raced forward. His withers glistened with flecks of foam, and his teeth flashed white as he gnashed at the leather straps that terrorized him.

She turned to run then through the fog of panic realized that her plant would be crushed to certain death if the steed did not alter his path. As if thinking to protect a child, she pivoted to face the stampeding animal. The slanting light from the morning sun transformed the horse's coat to a shimmering red. The halo of dust that billowed around him became a crimson cloud. The unrelenting beast truly seemed a vision dreamed in hell.

Fear pounded in Tanzie's chest, and the urge to run again assailed her, but she stood her ground refusing to see her tiny rosebush trampled beneath the hoofs of a damnable warhorse.

She waved and yelled trying to redirect the beast, but he responded only to the horror created in his own mind. Unfastening her cloak, she whipped it from her shoulders and waved it back and forth over her head. The billowing fabric seemed to startle the frantic horse, checking his blind panic, giving him something new upon which to focus.

Almost upon her, the great stallion careened to a halt. He reared up on his haunches, his massive front hoofs pawed the air, dirt and pebbles rained down from his muddy, long-haired, fetlocks.

Tanzie cringed and stumbled backwards.

Crashing back down to all-fours, the beast assumed a skittish stance, one huge front hoof tentatively planted on either side of her rose. His head and neck towered above her, and great puffs of hot breath streamed from his flared nostrils to warm her face and chest.

Angry at having been so terrified, and remaining concerned for her precious shrubbery, Tanzie smacked the huge animal on the muzzle with her open palm. "Get away, you silly beast," she ordered.

The horse snorted then sallied backward. His eyes crossed as he studied the end of his nose.

"Are you mad?" Branoc yelled as he rushed to her side. He grabbed the steed's halter and quickly placed himself between her and the stallion.

Tanzie froze. From where had Branoc materialized? She had not noticed him in the area earlier. He breathed in great gasps much like the horse. Apparently, he had been running too.

He glared at her in steely-eyed anger. "You could have been killed," he said, as if the idea had not occurred to her.

"He nearly destroyed my rose bush," she defended her actions. Drawing her cloak back across her shoulders, she gathered it close and curled her fingers into the fabric. Her heart raced out of control, but she did not know if the condition was due to her fear of nearly having been trampled or from the nearness of Sir Branoc.

The lord of the castle stared at her as if seeing her for the first time, and the dark concern in his eyes warmed to a smoldering gray. His breath still came too quickly, but she no longer thought it was from the running.

Under Branoc's scrutiny, a delicious aching that seemed a cross between pain and pleasure radiated from the pit of her stomach to the soles of her feet. Like the urge to sneeze, the feeling teased through her body then quickly dissipated leaving her weak and restless.

"This stallion has survived the cruelest of battles," Branoc said, a hint of amusement now softening his expression, "he has a brave heart and fearless soul. I would never have thought to see him befuddled by the slap of a female's hand."

He gently stroked the horse's neck. The frightened animal trembled beneath Branoc's touch, and Tanzie trembled beneath Branoc's unwavering stare. His whispered words of comfort were for the stallion, but his gaze never left her face, and she wished it were her throat that Branoc touched and her skin that tingled with each caress.

"Your beguiling fury has rendered him into submission," he said, "'tis often the same with a man," he muttered under his breath. "I had best get us—I mean him—out of your range." He led the horse to the workman who had been chasing the runaway.

With Branoc no longer at her side, the wind felt bitter and the sun seemed to dim. When he faced her once again a brooding scowl clouded his features.

"The rose is not worth your life," he declared, coming to stand before her.

"It is to me," she replied stubbornly, "and I insist that you post a guard here until the work on the wall is completed. If you refuse to do so, I will stand here myself to protect it."

"You insist what?" His expression could not hold more surprise had she requested he fling himself from a castle turret. "You are in no position to make demands," he added sternly. "Besides, even if I wished to do so, I could not spare a man for such trifling duty. I am short one of my best knights as it is. Olaf is not well."

"Olaf?" She cringed mentally and tried not to look overly concerned. That was the soldier whom she had treated two days ago for complaints of the ague. Was he not recovered? Had her slight miscalculation made him worse? "What ails him?" she asked.

"Well he seems much improved from his prior malady, but he cries at the least provocation. Olaf, has never been known to do that before."

"Oh," she said, with a smile of relief. "I am sure that will pass."

Over the last few days, Tanzie had made great strides in bettering her skills at curing the sick, but she was far from reaching perfection. When she had originally heard of Olaf's illness, she had concocted a cure and sent it to him, nothing but compassion and good intentions filling her heart. But instead of a potion for a bad stomach, she later discovered that she had given him a draught to help women with their fluxes and cramping. Apparently, it had cured his main affliction, but it had also confounded his male nature.

Since the strapping Norseman otherwise showed good progress, her sympathy for him was short-lived. 'Twas good for men on occasion to experience the world as a woman. A fleeting case of what a man would consider "female hysteria" would not hurt him.

"I regret that your man is not well," she said, "but I will not accept that as a reason to deny my request. I have asked you for little since my arrival here. It is the least that you could do for me."

Made brave by her concern for the plant, Tanzie stared up at Branoc. Abiding by her convictions had often been her downfall, but it had also led to success. She did not easily turn away from adversity, and at this moment, it seemed as if her whole universe revolved around that one tuft of hard dry earth. She would not concede her demands about the flower.

Branoc gazed at her hair. She was glad that she had left it unbound. A wicked urge to toy with a curl streaked through her, but she knew it was best to fight one battle at a time.

Lord Valtaigne remained lost in thought, and his silence maddened her as much as his arguing. "Please make a decision," she said, "I am cold standing in your shadow."

He shook his head. "You are stubborn to a fault, lady."

Still he called her lady, rather than by her given name.

"I will see what can be done," he said, "but until the construction is completed, you are forbidden in this area."

"Why should your compliance require my concession?" she demanded.

"Because you tempt the boundaries of good sense with your request."

She could not readily argue that point, but it seemed worth testing those parameters to save the rosebush. The plant reminded her of home, and it gave testimony that delicate beauty could survive in the most desolate of times and places. The sickly little shrub stood for courage and determination. Wistfully she wondered if it would ever bloom.

Branoc cleared his throat, and his features softened as he glanced down at the plant. "Once it is safe for you to venture again into this area, you may wish to mix eggshells in the soil to strengthen the poor wretch. I will tell cook to save some for you."

Did he jest with her? What could a knight know of nurturing plants? Still, he seemed in earnest. "How do you know of eggshells and rosebushes?" she demanded.

"I am not always out oppressing the conquered," he said, with a crooked smile that made her heart ache.

Suddenly, Tanzie wondered what Branoc enjoyed at his leisure? What amused and captivated him? She could tell he loved horses, and she knew he readily joined the hunt, but those were pleasures to appease the soldier in him. What made happy the man behind the chain mail? What pleased the man who read journals and understood the needs of flowers?

Their gazes intertwined, and for a precious moment, Branoc was no longer a warrior and she no longer a hostage. They were but a man and a woman. Both strangers in a foreign land; both here at someone else's command.

Lost in their own little world, they contemplated one another, and the fragile branches of the rosebush that stood between them, seemed to connect the two of them with a common bond, a common understanding.

Without further worry or concern, Tanzie knew the Dragon of Normandy would protect the fragile rose.

Chapter 10

Holding high the hem of her kirtle, Tanzie stood barefoot upon the windswept shore. She curled her toes in the cool sand and turned her face toward the rare cloudless sky.

Three days had passed since the rose bush incident and while the golden rays of the sun warmed her skin, a fire of another nature warmed her on the inside. Lord Valtaigne had ordered an upturned wagon to be placed over the plant she championed, and his consideration tugged at her heart.

The man was an inexplicable combination of brooding silence and honorable intent, and she feared she was beginning to favor him beyond reason. He was the embodiment of her most ardent dreams. Yet, he was also her watchdog and warden, and the duality of her feelings for Branoc put her mind in a muddle.

Lost to introspection she took no notice of the oncoming wave until the freezing seawater deluged her feet and ankles. As it rose past her knees to mid-thigh, she gave a shriek of surprise and struggled inland. The receding water sucked the shifting sand from beneath her feet hampering her escape and nearly toppling her into the surf.

Laughing at her own folly, she broke free and gained the shelter of the rocky cliffs. Protected from the late morning breeze, she wrung the water from her dripping skirts, and stretched out on the warm smooth pebbles where she could properly celebrate these wonderful hours of leisure.

She most certainly did not miss her labors in the council chamber, but she did miss Branoc. Only twice, since that day on the ridge had she stolen a cherished glimpse of him. Once as he wandered the east parapet, a shadow in the night haloed in the hushed glow of moonlight, and once as he rode out to hunt, a commanding figure, his silver trappings aglow in the burgeoning dawn.

Neither viewing had satisfied her soul. Rather the brief interludes had stirred desires in her that made her all the more restless. Desires like the ones she experienced now. She felt like a starving cotter with Branoc a savory feast just beyond her reach.

Closing her eyes Tanzie recalled the last time she and Branoc had been together and how she had watched him caress the neck of the frightened stallion. Each stroke favored upon the animal had been as gentle as a summer's breeze. Branoc's muscled forearm had flexed lean and hard, no doubt the rest of his form was as equally firm and appealing.

She felt weak at the imagining, and the thought of his powerful hands exploring her naked flesh burst upon her unexpectedly. As a soft achy feeling teased through her midsection, a tantalizing bead of perspiration trickled down between her breasts. Of late, her body seemed to have ideas of its own and a will much more daring and free-spirited then the will that governed her mind. If the two conspired in passion's cause, it would be a magnificent and unstoppable force.

Her eyes snapped open. Since Branoc seemed unmindful of the desire that governed her thoughts, the entire problem was theoretical and one she knew not how to rectify. Mastering the art of flirtation was not on her list of accomplishments. She found coyness and game-playing rather appalling, which left her few skills likely to capture Branoc's attention, let alone his heart.

If only he would make an effort to know her as a person rather than an unexpected annoyance that burdened his day and compounded his duties. Thanks to Uncle Malbourne, Tanzie knew Branoc did not trust the circumstances surrounding her arrival at Bamburgh but that was not her doing. Why could he not see past the incident and give her a chance based upon her own merit? What did he think of her as a person? For that matter, what did he think of women in general?

With a start, she realized these new concerns had replaced her old troubles. She no longer worried about escaping from Bamburgh and seeking shelter at Jarrow or Elstow. In truth, she would be most distressed to leave the castle Branoc governed. She wanted to stay here forever. She did not care what might be happening in the rest of England or for that matter in the rest of the world. Only the here and now seemed important. This was not practical thinking but what cared she for logic, in the face of the heartfelt emotions that beguiled her of late.

"The situation is without hope," she declared angrily, to no one in particular. The sound of her voice startled a small green lizard basking on a nearby rock. Legs pumping and tail thrashing, he charged through the underbrush and took shelter in a shady niche.

"I beg your pardon, Sir Longtail," she laughed, "I did not mean to disturb you." A similar creature timidly appeared beside the first one. This chartreuse specimen was smaller and somehow more feminine, Queen Greenavier no doubt. The pair scurried off together and a bittersweet sadness throbbed in Tanzie's chest. Even a lowly lizard had someone to love. Did her little dragon statue ever yearn for its own kind? A shiver passed through her as she recalled the legend she had run across in one of the tomes she'd been asked to translate. The story told of an ancient time when the jealous stepmother of a Bamburgh princess had turned the young maiden into a laidley, a loathsome worm, who terrorized the countryside all the way to Budle Bay. The tale confirmed the concept that strange and wondrous creatures existed here. Creatures with minds of their own.

Pushing such thoughts aside, she fluffed out her damp skirts, shifted around onto her side, and a smile warmed her expression. She had also read that Aethelfrith had named the castle yonder after his wife Bebba. Eventually, Bebba's Burgh had become Bamburgh, and that was a happy romantic notion and a much more proper musing for such a beautiful day.

Shading her eyes with one hand, she squinted against the glare of the sun. Hunger gnawed at her belly, and the wine she had sampled earlier made her giddy. She wished Ealgith would return from exploring so they might share the rare bounty of food pillaged from the kitchen and bakehouse.

To Tanzie's delight, her friend came running along the beach in her direction. Short of breath, but smiling, Ealgith dropped to her knees on the ground and holding out her apron, proudly displayed the clams she had found.

"Cook promised if I brought some back he'd prepare them for us," she explained. "Will they not be delicious with new potatoes and jasmine? Of course I must find many more, as he will likely appropriate half the count for services rendered."

"Your resourcefulness for finding food never ceases to amaze me." Tanzie grinned and sat up. She had long ago given up trying to solve the mystery as to where all the food went that Ealgith heartily consumed. Suffice it to say, it proved a never-ending challenge to fill the girl's stomach. "Speaking of victuals," Tanzie said, "pray, let us eat. Though the day is but a piglet we must start back before the tide turns and already the afternoon clouds trouble the horizon."

Ealgith set aside the clams, retrieved a little cloth from the basket, and arranged the food and the half empty wine skin upon it. They had sought fresh water to bring along but had been told it was needed to quench the thirst of the horses and soldiers.

Savoring the cheese and crusty bread, Tanzie silently stared at the forbidding rock formation that stood so resolutely a short distance out to sea. With endless appeal, the hulking monolith continued to intrigue her. From down here on the beach it resembled a great somber cathedral. And it seemed to beckon to her although she knew not how to reach the stony temple for the water surrounding it frothed with the promise of whirlpools and swift currents. Wading to it was out of the question and even passage by small boat seemed dangerous and unlikely.

"You're staring after that big old rock again aren't you, mistress?" Ealgith complained. "'Tain't natural the way you watch it so. From the shore, from our window, you're always lookin' at it. For the likes of me I cannot see what attracts you to it."

"You didn't notice?" she asked, in surprise. "It's the same odd color as the dragon statue."

Ealgith's gaze shot to the jagged monolith. "Blessed Lord," she said a piece of cold chicken halfway to her mouth. "Is that where the little beast came from? Is that its...home?"

Tanzie shrugged. "Something connects the dragon to the stone of that I am sure." She brushed the crumbs from her lap and snuggled back in the secure little nest of smooth rocks and soft green foliage. "I had hoped to ask Morcar about the matter, but again I did not see him."

Nibbling at a last bit of food, Ealgith curled up in a nearby nook. "Good," she grumbled, "Wizards, are best avoided."

"Morcar has not mentioned the dragon since the first day that we met," Tanzie continued, ignoring Ealgith's comment. "He seems reluctant to tell me anything about the past. 'All in good time' is all he will say when I ask for more information about mother or the carving. All in good time," she repeated with a yawn.

"Maybe its healthier not to know what's on the mind of a sorcerer," Ealgith again warned.

The girl's fear of Morcar and his powers was not a secret, and Tanzie had tried to reassure her friend as to the old Druid's good intentions, but her efforts had been in vain.

"You should not put much stock in his riddles and predictions," the girl added peevishly.

"Never fear," Tanzie teased, "I shall rely upon you for all pertinent information."

Ealgith smiled as if she were glad to be reinstated as chief gossip gatherer. "I've heard nothing new regarding, Lord Valtaigne," she said, apologetically.

"Well what think you of him based upon what little information we do have?" Tanzie asked.

Ealgith pursed her lips in thought. "He seeks to understand the world beyond everyday things," she said.

"What does that mean?" Tanzie prompted and prayed Ealgith's assessment of the man of whom she was becoming very fond would be a positive one.

"If Sir Branoc were lost in a forest at night," Ealgith explained, "rather than curse the darkness, he would wonder where the moon goes when we cannot see it. In other words, lady, he thinks too much."

But that was an encouraging insight. Tanzie's

father had been a learned man, and he had raised her to question and ponder the mysteries of the world. He had prompted her to challenge what others accepted at face value, and he had bid her be open-minded. *'Truth often comes wrapped in unlikely trappings,'* he would say. She could admire someone who questioned the workings of the universe.

"Leofric is more to my liking," Ealgith said with a gleam in her eye. "He has a most engaging face and seems accustomed to smiling."

Unlike Lord Valtaigne, Tanzie thought. Branoc rarely smiled. For that matter, he seldom allowed any of his emotions to reach his face or to shine through the aura of darkness he so skillfully employed to frighten people away and hold them at bay. He must be a lonely man. Yet, it seemed a condition of his own choosing.

"And," Ealgith added, in a dreamy voice, "Leofric finds pleasure in activities other than thinking and duty."

Tanzie smiled. So 'twas Leofric whom Ealgith went to see when she crept from their sleeping chamber in the middle of the night. Tanzie could only imagine the pleasures to which Ealgith alluded. Pleasures she herself desperately wished to learn about.

"I'm happy for you, Ealgith," she said and meant it.

Ealgith had the good grace to blush before she smiled contentedly.

As the wine they sampled infused Tanzie with a heady glow, Morcar's prophecy of true love shimmered through her mind. Soon her eyelids fluttered and closed. Wrapped in feelings of languid yearning and childish hope, Tanzie's thoughts drifted to a place where only happy memories abided.

\*\*\*\*

Cold and damp surrounded her. She must be dreaming. No! It was real. Tanzie sat bolt upright. The sun was near set, and the dark water had crept dangerously close.

"Ealgith awake," she shouted over the roar of wind and the surf. "We have slept ourselves into trouble. The tide is in and we are trapped."

Ealgith stirred and glanced around in confusion. Then alarm sharpened her expression, and she scrambled to her feet. "This God forsaken land threatens us at every turn," she cried. "Once the shore is covered with water we shall be dashed to bits upon these rocks."

Tanzie jammed her feet into her leather boots. "I am afraid we shall have to climb out," she said. Ealgith's complexion took on an unhealthy green tinge. "I know you fear heights as much as you fear the water," she added, "but we have no choice."

Gaining her feet Tanzie tore strips of cloth from the sleeves and the hem of her tunic. Fighting the wind, she twisted her hair into a knot and secured it with one of the pieces of fabric. She wrapped the other scraps around her hands and encouraged Ealgith to do the same.

"You go first," Tanzie insisted urging her friend upward toward the nearest outcropping. "I shall be close behind should your foot falter." What really crossed Tanzie's mind was the possibility that somewhere between the bottom and the top Ealgith might stop-too frightened to go on. She would not be able to go back for her. This way she would not have to.

Rising water licked at her heels and a bitter wind battered the cove. Groping her way upward into the gathering darkness she felt like a fragile leaf clinging by chance to a crevice.

Sharp stones cut her arms and bruised her legs and only the occasional small bush cushioned the ascent. The climb was more arduous than she had anticipated, and the urge to give up the effort became a temptation.

The dusky peaks of the cliffs that loomed overhead were near lost to the gloaming and glancing down, she tried to mark their progress, a foolish idea. The water beneath churned in a dizzying pattern of foam and fury. The craggy terrain resembled knobby hands and boney arms that seemed to reach for her, offering a stony and fatal embrace should she slip.

Without warning, the support upon which Tanzie stood gave way and the frightful image of falling become a reality. She hugged the cliff, dirt ground into her cheek and mouth and the shelf beneath her feet disappeared. For a breathtaking moment, she dangled out over the precipice then choking back a scream she kicked, and grappled, searching for a foothold. Her arms ached and the muscles in her shoulders burned with the effort of hanging on. Tears blurred her vision. She might not make it to the top, might never know why fate had brought her to the North Country. Her fingers felt raw and it was hard to grip the unyielding surface of the rock. It would be so easy to just let go, to surrender to this new adversity. But then she would never see Branoc again

Branoc...

She spit the dirt from her mouth and swung her legs sideways. Her feet touched a narrow outcropping. Praying it was sturdier than the last she eased her weight down upon the ledge. It held, but she must move on. Arm muscles rebelling and legs shaking she blinked back her tears and sought one treacherous handhold after another. Regrettably, before she reached the end of her quest, she truly did reach the end of her strength.

Ealgith too had stopped just short of the top.

Overhead the clouds roiled thick and dark. Lightning jagged across the sky. Tanzie's fingers and toes grew numb, and her grip slackened. A tentative raindrop struck her on top of the head, and the wind threatened to tear her from her perch. If she and Ealgith did not reach safety before the rain came, they would surely be washed back down the cliff.

"Saints preserve me," Ealgith wailed.

Tanzie braced herself and glanced up expecting to see her friend slipping backward. Instead, she saw the girl's feet disappear over the top of the cliff. Confused, she inched her way over to the spot Ealgith had occupied. Without warning strong hands from above grasped her under the arms and drew her up, up, into the night. Then her feet touched solid ground and she exhaled in relief.

"Thank the Lord you are safe," a male voice whispered.

It was Branoc. How had he found her? She drew closer, coveting his body, seeking his warmth and sheltering embrace. She turned her face upward, leaning her body against the length of him, and she teased his lips with hers as the terror she had just suffered drove her to reckless passion. She wanted to immerse herself in his strength and think only of how lucky she was to be alive.

He accepted her invitation with a hungry roughness that shocked and excited her.

Slipping her arms up around him, she wove her fingers through his hair at the nape of his neck. It was soft as Chinese silk.

She felt a tremor ripple through Branoc, and he crushed her to his chest. The delightful fluttering in Tanzie's stomach erupted into a river of emotion. It flooded her senses and obscured everything around her other than Branoc's touch.

A brilliant flash of lightning lit the night sky, and peals of thunder shattered the magical silence.

Icy rain pelted down in earnest, and the heat of ardor that smoldered between them crystallized into a precious memory. She shivered uncontrollably from the cold and from a delayed reaction to what she had just endured on the cliffs of doom.

Sweeping her off her feet, Branoc cradled her against his chest and tore through the curtain of rain toward the castle.

Sheltered by the darkness Tanzie nuzzled her face in the warm quilted linen that covered his shoulder. Safe in his sure grip, she clung to him with childlike trust. With her cheek pressed close, she listened to the strong even beat of his heart, and marveled at the ease with which he carried her through the night.

Swiftly he bore her to the east portal to the first level receiving room. Leofric ran beside them, Ealgith clasped in his arms.

As they reached the warmth of the hearth, Branoc set her down to stand before him. "You near drove me mad with worry," he said roughly. His sharp angry words pricked at her like steely tipped daggers. "We have searched long and hard for you. I've better ways to while away my evenings."

"Well I did not mean to inconvenience you, my lord," she retorted, the closeness they had shared now crushed beneath the weight of his anger. "It was not done on purpose. Sometimes I forget that we are on unfamiliar soil. It will not happen again."

"No, it will not because you will not go running off to the shore again."

She bristled at his words and made to protest the issuing of yet another edict.

Branoc raised a hand and put two fingers to her lips. "Do not question my decision," he said, and shushed her into silence as if she were an unruly six year old. He lowered his hand to his side, but the anger remained smoldering in his eyes.

What prompted him to such ire? Did he fear so for her safety, or was it his pride that was threatened? If anyone under his care were to be harmed it would be to his failing.

"Of course," she said. "'Twould be a blot on your glorious record should the king's hostage come to harm."

"Why I protect you is my own affair. You will obey me while you are here and you will be more careful in the future. A mere few days ago you were nearly trampled by a horse and now again you tilt with death."

Branoc hesitated as if he wished to say more but didn't. His nostrils flared with every breath he took, and as he stared at her mouth a ruddy hue heightened the color of his cheeks. "Leofric," he ordered, taking a step away from her, "escort the ladies to their chamber. I will see that food is prepared for them after I alert the other men that our doves have returned to the cote."

Tanzie was disappointed at Branoc's quick retreat. Like a well-curried sauce his kisses still stung her lips, and she wanted more of what she had sampled. How was it that one moment this man was hot as forged steel and the next moment cold as a winter's snow? "Thank you for coming to our aid," she said and reached out to gently touch his arm.

Branoc pulled away. "See to them, Leofric," he said and left the room.

Renounced and denied, Tanzie mutely stared after him. Had her kisses not pleased him? His efforts had more than pleased her. She wrapped her arms around herself and tried to recapture Branoc's warmth and nearness, but like a deserted room, she felt empty and forlorn.

Mortified by his rejection and abrupt departure, and desperate for the solace and privacy of her chamber, Tanzie hurried across the hall and ascended the stairs. She sensed the presence of Ealgith and Leofric at her back. Glancing over her shoulder she saw them gazing lovingly at one another, and envy fought with the happiness she felt for them.

"Leofric," she interrupted.

He gave a little cough, and his expression quickly sobered. "Yes lady."

"I rarely see you or Sir Branoc about the castle. How is it that he knew Ealgith and I were in trouble?"

"Master Valtaigne checks upon you frequently," Leofric divulged. "He is always alert as to your safety and comfort. Sometimes unusually so."

Did he really worry over her then? She had not been the object of anyone's concern for many years, and the fantasy of relinquishing her care and safety into the hands of another was rather appealing. Of course, it was more likely that Branoc only watched her to make sure she did not escape from Bamburgh. No doubt, duty dictated his actions not his heart.

At the landing, she turned toward the corridor that led to her room. The fawning and cooing still taking place behind her back. It seemed obvious that Ealgith and Leofric wished to spend the night together. Why force her friend to once again feign sleep only to later listen to her sneak from the room?

"Ealgith," she said, deciding to aid the young lovers in their cause, "I can make my way from here. Why do not the two of you spend some time together?"

Leofric gallantly protested such a suggestion, but Ealgith laughed and dragged him down a side passage.

Alone in the cold hall Tanzie noted the boldness of Leofric's caress as he placed his hand demandingly upon the girl's backside, and she heard the lilt of excitement in Ealgith's voice as the playful couple disappeared around the corner. With a stab of loneliness, she turned away. Then she paused and glanced back. What was it like to surrender body and soul to a man? Her craving to find out obliterated her good manners, and backtracking she sneaked down the hall after the young couple.

The door at the end of a narrow passage stood ajar, and the voices that came from the room assured her that she had found the couple's place of trysting.

With the slightest of touches, she widened the gap for a better view of the chamber. The storage cupboard filled with wool and cloth, dried feathers and down made the perfect nest for loving. Remaining outside the room, she hugged the wall and watched in fascinated wonder.

Leofric gently removed Ealgith's wet clothing, rendering the girl naked as the day she was born. Ealgith did not seem distressed over the matter. She grandly posed before her admirer, her hands on her hips, her small breasts thrust forward.

Leofric studied Ealgith with unabashed appreciation as he hastily removed his own clothing. Then he grabbed her and kissed her hungrily. He feasted upon Ealgith savoring every bit of her. His hands wandered over her naked form, petting, coaxing, pleasing. Then he caressed her backside and held her in place and slowly and rhythmically rubbed his loins against her.

Tanzie recalled the kisses she had just shared with Branoc, his hard form and the feel of his muscled embrace. If only Branoc wanted her as much as Leofric wanted Ealgith. She bit down on her knuckle to stifle a cry of desire, as the throbbing in her stomach dropped lower.

Peeking once again into the cupboard, she beheld Leofric in all his glory.

Long ago, when her mother had ministered to

injured townspeople, Tanzie had caught brief glimpses of the male form. But she had never seen a man rigid and impassioned. Heat cascaded over her, and she whimpered as the lovers slid to the floor.

Leofric kissed and nipped at Ealgith. The girl moaned and twisted beneath his bold touch, then she reached out to fondle him in kind and with a playful growl, Leofric raised up to straddled Ealgith's willing form.

As the two made to draw together in true union, Tanzie came to her senses. Guilt burned in her soul for her own wanting and for the shame of having watched such intimate moments in someone else's life.

Dizzy with emotion she turned to flee down the narrow passageway, but instead collided with a solid form and reeled backward. Startled and confused, she reached out to break her fall and came face to face with Branoc.

Reacting quickly, he grabbed her upper arms preventing her from tripping.

How long had he been watching?

A smile twitched on his lips. "You seem to tumble from one misadventure to another," he said quietly.

She squirmed in his grasp, more from anguish than from a true desire for freedom, but Branoc held firm. He stood so close she could smell the rain-dampened linen of his hauberk, and it reminded her of being carried in his arms.

Moans of pleasure from the storage room assailed her ears and her distress grew tenfold.

Branoc's eyes were veiled, but his lips were parted, as if he too were affected by the urgent lovemaking and lusty sighs.

"Please," she whispered, "you must release me." Embarrassed and humiliated she stared down at the floor.

Without replying, Branoc loosed his grip and shifted his hands to frame her face, forcing her to meet his penetrating gaze. Then in one fluid movement he drew closer and slanted his mouth down on hers.

She closed her eyes and surrendered to the surge of wanting that assailed her. A shiver tingled across her breast and curled in her belly. Then the tingling dropped lower, and as it transformed into a delightful throbbing, it filled her with a need and desire she had never experienced before. She felt as if she were about to faint or float away to an unknown world. A world she wanted to explore more fully.

Branoc eased one hand to the small of her back. Still possessing her mouth, he urged her closer, and settled his other hand possessively upon her linen covered breasts.

As his fingers brushed across the front of her dress, her nipples hardened beneath the stroking of his thumb, and she wished she were naked before him, no clothing to obscure his touch upon her flesh. Her knees grew weak and she clung to him wanting more, needing more. Then his growl of desire, filled with raw masculine intensity, brought her to her senses.

She drew back and stared into his eyes. Her breath came in fits and starts as she fought to recover a shred of dignity and composure. She must return to the shelter her room before she disgraced herself beyond reparation. It was not what she wanted, but it was truly what must be done. Twisting free, she tried to edge around Branoc and the feel of him full and hard against her hip created a thrilling rush of renewed desire.

A lazy smile tugged at his mouth, and his gaze roamed leisurely, provocatively, over her breasts, her throat, her lips. He seemed to be enjoying her discomfort, as if he knew exactly what longings impassioned her body and tempted her soul. Her embarrassment turned to desperation, and she raised a hand to push him aside.

He grasped her forearm.

She uttered a soft mewing cry of pain. His touch ignited the cuts and abrasions she had received during her climb from the beach.

Concern transformed Branoc's expression, and he pushed up her sleeve to inspect her bruised and torn flesh more closely.

"Your wounds seem even more in need of attention than your lips," he said, in a husky voice. "You had best go see to them." Gently he kissed the inside of her wrist.

The sensation of Branoc's lips upon her flesh obscured the pain. No herbal balm could give her more soothing comfort than this man's presence. Oh, that he would continue the treatment and cover every inch of her body with kisses and touching.

Unable to resist, she timidly stroked Branoc's cheek, and the raspy shadow of his beard prickled beneath her fingertips. Like a glorious wild creature trapped under her spell, he stood motionless and allowed her to savor this new intimacy uninterrupted. His mouth was so tempting, so irresistible. She traced a path to it. The softness of his lips made her think this strong knight somehow vulnerable.

Branoc gently nuzzled the tips of her fingers, and the simple gesture dragged her back to reality. She inhaled sharply and reluctantly withdrew her hand. "Please," she whispered, "let me pass." Her words were nearly inaudible and for a moment, she was afraid she had not spoken them aloud.

The desire that burned in Branoc's eyes both tempted and warned her that his emotions were running high, and she fought the urge to reach for the warm embrace that she knew he would offer.

As if realizing her jeopardy, he stepped back and rescued her from her own lusty emotions.

She slipped past and ran down the hall.

"Sweet dreams, my lady," he called after her, his footsteps echoing softly in the opposite direction.

Safely in her room Tanzie stripped naked and crawled beneath the covers of her bed, but tonight the downy comfort felt cold and lonely.

Hidden in the darkness she recalled each thrilling moment of passion, and the merciless hands of memory aroused her body anew. She ran her tongue across her lips; the taste of him still lingered. Heavenly saints above. If Branoc were here, right now, in this very bed, she would surrender to him.

Overcome with fear for her weakness of will, Tanzie turned onto her stomach and tightly clenched her pillow. She must think of something else...anything else. Thoughts of Branoc were foolhardy. Being with a man out of wedlock would ruin any chance she may have left for a good marriage. It was a sin to do what she dared to imagine, and she risked all if she answered temptation's lustful call.

Yet, despite her good intentions, waves of heat raked her body. The wanting became a physical ache, and Tanzie curled into a little ball and hugged herself for comfort.

Hot with need and drunk with yearning, she kicked off her covers and welcomed the coolness of the night. Then the night air won out and a chill overcame her. Forced to retrieve the tangled heap from the floor, she wrestled the covers back into place and willed herself to sleep.

****

All through the night Tanzie tossed and turned. When she slept, smoky gray eyes haunted her dreams, and the memory of Branoc's knowing smile mocked her resolve. And when wakefulness took its turn, she could do naught but pray for strength. In desperation, she reached out to touch the little dragon that stood sentry beside her bed. The smooth cool surface of the carving brought solace to her troubled spirit, but the beast looked different, she thought drowsily. A new fierceness radiated from the creature's face.

## Chapter 11

Last evening, when Branoc had carelessly lost track of Martanzia's whereabouts, he had witnessed the final illuminated corner of his dreary universe suddenly grow dark. Then he'd seen the girl struggling to ascend a cliff that many a man would not challenge, and along with his relief, had come the equally disturbing realization of how easily he had grown accustom to the maid's uplifting presence at castle Gray Scorn.

There was, of course, no logic to these emotions. But then logic seemed to frequently evade him of late, as his present circumstance clearly indicated. Here he sat, lingering in the new hall, idly pushing food about the trencher, when he should be in the company of his men and well on his way to Jarrow. Annoyed with himself, he poked at the last bit of overcooked egg and recriminations howled through his mind like resolute hounds on the hunt.

Then Martanzia and Ealgith burst into the room.

Chattering gaily, the two females advanced toward the table but as they noticed his presence, they fell silent and careened to a halt. For one fleeting moment, Branoc saw the rosy-cheeked morning happiness in Martanzia's face before it faded leaving a more earnest expression.

His spirits soared. This is what had kept him from his planned hour of departure. He had wanted to see her face one more time before he left. God above he wanted to kiss her good-bye and refresh the memory of her in his heart and on his lips. He hungered for her presence like a sweet ethereal feast to sustain his soul on the journey that lay ahead.

"Good morning, my lord." She curtsied and directed her gaze away from his.

During the night, his dreams had been invaded by erotic images of Martanzia warming his bed and a tortured fitful sleep it had been. An ache stabbed at his groin, and he shifted in his chair. The desire had not run its course and seeing her again added new intensity to his discomfort.

The girl remained motionless as a statue and as beautifully carved. In glaring contrast, her moppet-of-a-handmaiden seemed unperturbed by his presence as she gregariously heaped food upon two trenchers.

If only he could restore Martanzia's mood to happiness. Mirth became her sweet face much more than the consternation that now resided upon her brow.

"Is anything wrong?" she finally asked.

There certainly was something wrong he thought surprised by the sudden anger he felt. He was no longer in command of his emotions, a situation beyond comparison for him. A situation to which he refused to succumb. He gained his feet and stepped closer to her and noticed the smudge of darkness that showed beneath her eyes. A half smile pulled at his mouth. Apparently, Martanzia had not slept soundly either. For some reason that thought pleased him.

"I depart today for Jarrow," he said casually, then watched for her reaction. None came other then the slight narrowing of her eyes. "I did not wish to leave until I knew you had fully recuperated from your excitement of last evening."

This comment managed to initiate a response. Fascinated he watched the delicate blush that spread upward from beneath the neckline of her tunic. The warm hue colored her throat and cheeks, and he wondered if the same enticing glow kissed her breasts.

With a measured intake of breath, Martanzia recaptured her composure and looked him straight in the eyes. "I am quite recovered thank you. All effects from my excitement, as you put it, were completely superficial. The entire episode is all but forgotten."

"I was not referring to your being stranded by the tide nor the cuts and bruises upon your arms," he said.

"Nor was I," she replied hotly. The glint of anger flashed in her eyes.

He studied her more closely. Was she remembering the stolen kisses they had shared? The impassioned embraces and bold yet fleeting touches? Was she angry with herself for feeling out of control and drunk with wanting? Good, because that was exactly how he felt. "You would be wise to cease your explorations of unfamiliar territory," he warned.

Her blush deepened. "But how else does one learn of the many wonders of life?" she asked, assuming an exaggerated picture of innocence.

"How else indeed. If you seek personal experience, I will be at your service upon my return."

Her eyes widened at his innuendo. Then an expression of thoughtfulness sharpened her features. "How long will you be gone?" she asked.

"Three or four days." He studied her expression hoping to see an indication that she might miss him, but a look of contemplation and calculation flittered across her features. "Do not attempt to run off in my absence," he said, trying to squelch any wayward plans she may be considering. "The entire garrison has been instructed to look after you. And upon my return," he added cheerfully, "there will be mountains of new documents awaiting your translation."

She stiffened. "Is that where lies your concern?" she asked. "Pity you cannot just preserve my head and hands and do away with the rest of me. It would no doubt be much less troublesome for you." Arms folded across her chest she turned her back to him.

"Less troublesome to be sure," he agreed, easing closer. "But in truth there are other parts of you that I find much more intriguing than the ones you mention."

"You are dangerously impertinent today," she accused over her shoulder. "Is there anything else you wanted before you take your leave?"

A sea of intimate thoughts fought for expression upon his tongue. He longed to tell her that he worried night and day over her safety and comfort, and that she inspired him to dream of a future that held more for him than soldiering and growing old alone. But those were life altering words, once spoken never to be recalled. And there was no place in his life for a woman.

"Take care in my absence," he said quietly.

Her shoulders relaxed but she did not turn to look at him.

"If you need counsel," he added, "seek out the old Druid." By the Faith, why did he place Martanzia into Morcar's custody? Since coming to this North Country, words and ideas seemed to spring forth from his mouth without waiting for direction from his brain. On the other hand, though he did not personally trust the old sorcerer, he somehow knew the conjurer would protect Martanzia at all costs.

As he waited for a response, he wondered if it was hotheaded pride or cold courage that kept Martanzia's back so straight and her shoulders so squared. He suspected she had championed her own causes for much too long, making her headstrong and independent. He yearned to relieve her of that burden, but as a soldier, he had duties that transcended personal needs and emotions.

She peeked at him over one shoulder then quickly glanced away. The gesture set into motion her long tresses. He was secretly pleased that she refused to contain the shining wealth of hair. He enjoyed watching it tumble and sway with abandon, and he enjoyed the come-hither-look it imparted to her otherwise chaste appearance. Besides, he doubted her hair could be bound into submission any more readily than her willful disposition.

He reached toward her silky locks then balled his hand into a fist and slowly lowered his arm back to his side. He should turn and walk away-before it was too late. Before, he followed through with the fanciful idea of kissing Martanzia farewell.

A painfully jagged breath hovered in his chest. How did a man of reason deal with the troubled times, a delusional Druid priest, and a girl that so tested a man's self-control and trust? More questions that knew no answers. No doubt concentrating on his military obligations would be a better use of his time and energy. Besides, he meant nothing to Martanzia. Just now, she had all but dismissed him, as if he were a mere thrall living only to do her bidding.

A cold loneliness settled over him. Then he bristled as a rush of male pride replaced his sentimentality and uncertainty. This was his castle, damn it, not hers. He was in charge here, and he would not be made to feel otherwise.

Grabbing Martanzia, he spun her around to face him, and before she could protest lowered his mouth to capture hers. To his surprise, she wrapped her arms around his neck and kissed him back. With warm lips parted, she enticed him to a more intimate sharing. God above how he wanted to taste all the sweetness she offered. But Martanzia was a young lady of breeding, and destined for a nunnery. Surely she did not know what heathen longings she kindled in his belly and what pagan thoughts she inspired in his mind.

They intertwined so perfectly, and although layers of fabric separated their bodies and true desires, the softness of her breasts was remarkably evident, and he remembered laying his hand upon her there. That mind altering experience had nearly been both their undoing. Last night it had taken all of the resolve he possessed to keep from picking her up and carrying her away to his room to satisfy her curiosity and his need.

At the recollection, the embers of need flamed anew and he transferred his weight to one leg trying to alleviate the hurtful pleasure that laid low his ability to think clearly. The maneuver drew Martanzia closer, transporting him to a new plateau of desire. She sighed and the tremulous sound reverberated against his mouth. Did Martanzia want him as much as he wanted her? Yes. He could feel it in her touch. That bit of knowledge pleased him beyond measure, even as it brought him to his senses.

He pried her arms loose from around his neck, eased her away from his body, and held her at bay. There was a hunger in Martanzia's eyes and a quickening of her breath and she leaned forward as if to recapture his mouth. Reluctantly he released his hold on her and took a step back.

"Would it disturb you overmuch," she asked, "if I were not here to vex you and disrupt your camp?"

The question took him by surprise. "More than you might know, lady," he admitted under his breath. She cocked her head as if weighing the true importance of his honest response.

"Keep you safe until my return." He glanced at Ealgith and did not miss the knowing expression that scurried across her face. "Leofric goes with me," he added, "which should aid you in concentrating all of your efforts on making sure your mistress remains free from folly or worse."

"Yes, my lord," the maid dutifully murmured, but the mocking smile remained in place.

Not daring to look back, he took his leave. At least now, he had an indication as to what urges fired Martanzia's emotions, though he still did not know what truly dwelled within her heart or where her political loyalties might lie.

****

Pulse racing, Tanzie wished to rush after Branoc. Instead, she held her ground and memorized his walk. He had a distinctive stride, straightforward yet easy. And she had noticed before that he rather led with his left as if he were perpetually girded with shield and sword, prepared to fight his way onward regardless of what the day might bring.

He gained exit via the south door, but even as his visage disappeared from her sight, the memory of his touch lingered upon her flesh.

Branoc had kissed her with such passion and had all but admitted he enjoyed having her near. But it was also possible that he sought to win her over merely because he viewed her as an obstacle. The Normans were expert at conquering what stood in their way, and apparently, brute force was not the only weapon wielded. Winning her heart and exposing her inner most thoughts would be a double victory for Branoc. He would uncloak her body as well as her intentions. Or perhaps, like Rathgar, he sought her inheritance and land.

She turned toward the table and glanced at Ealgith. "What is so amusing?" she snapped.

"'Tis the look upon your face, mistress," Ealgith teased, between mouthfuls of smoked herring and eggs. "I think you are falling in love."

"Nonsense," Tanzie protested. "Lord Valtaigne may be handsome, but he also assumes much, and he is as arrogant as ever a man was."

"Is it his arrogance that brings such color to your cheeks?"

Tanzie frowned. Clutching at her gown with one hand and fanning her flushed face with the other, she meandered the length of the sunlit room. Ealgith was correct; it was most definitely not Branoc's arrogance that infused her with heady excitement. It was just—Branoc in general. His semblance, his bearing, that partial smile he always restricted himself to as if his feelings of happiness might crumble and disappear if he ever favored them with a full-fledged grin. It was the evenhanded manner in which he treated his men and his horses, and it was the compassion he had shown for her rose bush. These were the weapons of Branoc Valtaigne, and they held hostage her heart more securely then his castle walls and turrets held hostage her body.

When she was in his arms, it was as if time ceased, as if they were the only two people in the world. Yet, she could see in his eyes that he did not trust her. The soldier in him refused to surrender to the lonely man she detected behind the somber gray and black image he turned toward others. She wanted to break through the dismal gray shroud he wore so proudly and shed light upon his world. But she did not know how, or if he would allow anyone behind his shield-wall.

She scrubbed her hands across her face as if she could wash away the chaotic thoughts that muddied her thinking and clouded her judgment. Mayhap Ealgith could help. Her handmaiden had been charged with keeping her from folly, but that did not mean they could not discuss matters that may be perceived as reckless.

Tanzie made another pass around the room then halted on the opposite side of the table from Ealgith. "I watched you and Leofric last night," she blurted still not believing she had done such a thing. "But only for a few moments," she hastened to add.

Ealgith's mouth dropped open at the revelation. Then she smiled good-naturedly. "Mistress you are getting a much broader education here than ever you would have received at the convent."

"Yes," Tanzie agreed, "but the instructions tend to leave one wanting. I want Branoc to touch me as Leofric touched you. I want him to need me beyond all else."

"But how can it be, lady? That is where I have the advantage over you," Ealgith admitted. "I can enjoy a lusty man when fate brings one my way, with only the church to answer to and not a heartless uncle or the whims of a fickle society."

"Even those considerations are not strong enough to prevent me from thoughts of hazarding all," Tanzie said. "Encircled by his arms, I feel contented and safe. Safe like I have never felt before."

"From the way he looks at you mistress, I do not think 'twould take much effort to capture his heart. It is a shame," she added sympathetically, "that you must cast aside a yearning as mighty as yours."

Taking to the chair Branoc had occupied, Tanzie pictured him naked. The thought of him hard and purposeful as she had seen Leofric made her shiver but not with cold. What did it feel like to caress a man at the height of his desire? What would it feel like to have that needful part of Branoc filling the void inside of her? "Ealgith," she said brazenly, "tell me what it is like to be with a man."

A dreamy expression overtook Ealgith, the fork she held dangled from her hand. "Why, 'tis nearly beyond description," she began. "It's like being breathless with fright only in a good way. Or feeling an aria of joy building inside of you. Silently the feeling grows and grows, faster and deeper, completely overwhelming. Then your body finds its voice and waves of pleasure sing through you. And as the cascading melody softens, the man's release echoes through you as well. It is a taste of heaven," she said and, resumed eating

"But the thought of being naked and defenseless before a man does make me shudder," Tanzie admitted and poked her food. "I do not think I could so expose myself in body or soul."

"It will seem natural enough if it be the right man," Ealgith promised. "A man you can trust with your true being. Even stripped of all finery you will still have your love to sustain you. Love does not judge or belittle. Nothing you do together will be distasteful if both are consenting and fulfilled by it. And if you are lucky," she added, her smile broadening, "the man will seek to pleasure you as much as he expects you to pleasure him."

"It sounds—wonderful," she admitted.

"'Tis good and wholesome to love a man. It keeps you young and it makes a woman feel needed."

"But to relinquish oneself so completely, leaves one without any dominion over the situation. Surely that is a disadvantage," Tanzie insisted.

"Tis just the opposite. When you please a man and kindle his desire, it is you who hold him under a spell. At least for those few delicious hours. Besides," Ealgith smoothed her kirtle across her lap, "our bodies were intended to be shared, not preserved away like dusty old relics of the church. You will feel the same when the man of your dreams makes your blood boil and your thighs ache."

Riotous feelings stirred within Tanzie. It was too late for she had already crossed that stream of desire. Then a wretched thought sprung from a dark corner of her mind. What if she were not the only girl who yearned for Branoc's affections? Was there a maid in Normandy who pined for him in his absence? Or worse yet, did a devoted wife and a gaggle of children await word that they might join him here? This last thought brought her crashing back to the here and now. It had not occurred to her that Branoc might be wed.

"What if he is married?" she whispered, almost afraid to voice the terrible thought.

"I have already worried over that for you, lady," Ealgith reassured. "Leofric swore to me just last evening that Lord Branoc is unencumbered by wife or commitment."

Tanzie's shoulders relaxed. The awful vision of Branoc holding another woman in his arms shattered like ice and fell from her mind in forgotten shards. There was nothing to worry about she thought happily.

"Unfortunately, other than this newly acquired ruin of a castle, he is also without an estate," Ealgith added halfheartedly, as if she regretted being the bearer of bad tidings.

Thrilled at the discovery that Branoc was not married, Tanzie did not dwell upon the fact that he was a near landless knight. A smile tugged at her lips and she pressed her bottom back against the chair. Branoc's firm thighs and narrow hips had only moments before warmed this cold fabric. She wished he were here now and she sat upon his lap. The heat of his body would comfort her as he enfolded her within his embrace. Then, she pictured Branoc standing before her a sword in one hand and a rose in the other.

Longing drizzled through her like warm honey. There must be some way for her to be with Branoc. God would not let her discover such a miracle as love and then deny her the opportunity of experiencing it fully. Then again why not?

God might very well deny her what she wanted most in this world. He had done so before, and it was sinful to be with a man unless they were wed. Sinful yet according to Morcar, it was to be her fate. Or did she ascribe to the words of the old profit merely to suit her needs and alleviate her conscience. It was much easier to pretend her future was immutable, preordained, and unavoidable. Much easier, even if that concept headed her straight down the path to hell.

Tanzie gripped the arms of the chair. She must look beyond herself and shift her concerns to other matters. She leaped to her feet. "Come," she called to a startled Ealgith. "We shall turn our minds to more edifying thoughts. I will get the basket of herbs and we can apply the arts that Morcar bid me practice."

Ealgith stuffed two biscuits down the bodice of her tunic, grabbed a piece of cheese, and reluctantly gained her feet. "Have you studied much since last we tried this?" she asked. "I still do not feel well from the prior concoction you convinced me to drink."

"I am truly sorry about that, Ealgith. Who would think that changing just one ingredient could alter a potion from a cure for one's headache to a cathartic. I fear I do not truly have a knack for this alchemy," she confessed, "but it seems most important to Morcar that I try, and I hate to disappoint him."

"Perhaps you could put your talents to use on the villagers today," Ealgith encouraged. "They need your help most assuredly."

"A generous notion," Tanzie agreed, as they reached the little cupboard where the herbs were stored. "You carry the book and I will take the basket. If I have any doubts as to how to proceed we shall stop and reference the formula."

\*\*\*\*

As the day promised to be pleasantly warm, there was no need for Tanzie and Ealgith to return to their chamber for cloaks and, uninterrupted, they proceeded directly to the main entrance of the castle.

After solemnly vowing to the guard that they would not wander beyond his view, he granted them permission to stand just beyond the castle wall. Alerted by word of mouth, the villeins, soon sought her aid, and although somewhat tentative at first, the peasants seemed glad for her assistance.

In Flanders, Tanzie knew the cotters were generally left to care for themselves. They learned from one another or by trial and error what worked and what did not. And though it was possible to purchase prepared cures and potions at the yearly fair or from a traveling merchant, she surmised that here in the North Country these occasions were far and few between, just as they were uncommon where she grew up.

As she ministered to the people, Tanzie conversed openly with them in Saxon. Encouraged by her knowledge of their language, the townspeople began to speak freely of their frustrations and anger. She could offer them no remedy for the political and emotional suffering they endured, but just listening to their concerns seemed to help heal their heavy hearts.

"King William Rufus is even more cruel than his bastard father," one old man lamented. "He takes our land to pay off his Earls and soldiers. And the Prince Bishop, Flambard, taxes what is left."

"Aye," another man agreed, as Tanzie applied salve to a burn on his arm, "the Normans steal our crops and animals, too. The land is so forsaken from here to Scarborough, we will be lucky to survive the upcoming fall let alone set anything aside for winter."

The air was soon charged with resentment and

anger.

A gray-haired woman with one eye missing stepped forward to add her opinion. "Day after day all across this land we labor to erect his Lordship's castles, the symbol of our own oppression," she pointed out.

Tanzie tried to concentrate on the woman's words and not stare at the scarred indentation where an eye had once resided. What painful ordeal had caused such a transformation? And what unseen scars did they bear on their hearts and souls?

"He even mocks the rules of the church," the old woman continued, "and has set the death penalty back in practice."

"I say he deserves a taste of his own merciless justice," a young man boldly and foolishly declared.

Tanzie glanced around checking to see that no one from the garrison had wandered near enough to hear the zealot's treasonous comment. He could be imprisoned or worse for such talk. Right or wrong, to openly defy the king was to put one's life in jeopardy. Yet, it was difficult not to sympathize with the plight of these bewildered people. The Pope may have ordained William the Conqueror's aggression as well as that of his son, but she could not, nor could she condone insurrection.

"William Rufus treats his hunting dogs better than his subjects," a wispy-haired woman chimed in.

"That's the truth," the man with the burn agreed. "In my brother's shire, a starving lad was hanged for poaching one raw-boned hare. After "justice had been served" the king fed the long-eared animal to his hound."

"A curse upon the black-hearted mamzer," someone called out.

As a heartfelt shout of support followed those anonymous words, an ominous shudder passed through Tanzie. There was a collective darkness gathering. Darkness powerful enough to blight a kingdom or destroy a land. Such opinions must not be allowed to get out of hand. Such thoughts must not be allowed to swallow up the goodness that still abided within these people.

"At least the master here pays and trades fairly for the needs of his men," the old woman declared, trying to ease the tension. "We must be thankful for that."

"Aye," the others assented.

The vassals were referring to Branoc, and it gladdened Tanzie's heart that the locals recognized his evenhanded treatment. She felt pride at their grudging respect.

"And we thank you for caring, mistress," a little girl with a lacerated hand piped up as Tanzie applied a poultice to the festering wound.

With her one good eye, the old woman curiously perused Tanzie. "There was once another like you," she said, "years ago. She too had a kind heart and a gentle hand."

Was it her mother to whom the Saxon crone referred? "Do you remember the girl's name?" Tanzie asked, not caring if she awakened old memories or new curiosities.

"No, child," the woman replied sadly, "not anymore. Like I said, 'tis been many years. She had hair the color of yours though, and kept company with the crystal gazer. Ain't seen her for a long, long time and now the old one only shows up on occasion. Everything's changed you see, in more ways than one. The spirit of England as we know'd it is fading."

With a shake of her head, the woman turned and shuffled away. The other peasants followed in her wake. As they filed past, each politely nodded their thanks.

In the silence that ensued, the words of the old woman swam through Tanzie's mind. "There was once another like you." Had Beorce stood here on this spot, a basket of herbs upon her arm? If so it confirmed the story, Morcar had told her.

A new feeling of oneness with the land wound through Tanzie. Then in her mind's eye she could see a vision clear as rainwater. Her mother had indeed been here, but the weather that day had been bitterly cold. Snow covered the ground, and the wind howled mournfully, forcing her mother to bend against the gale as she hurried to the side of a young peasant girl about to give birth to her first child.

On the fringe of conscious reasoning, Tanzie realized the midday sun still blazed heartily, but the cold she envisioned felt real and she hugged her tunic closer. Then the image was gone.

"Mistress?"

She heard Ealgith's voice, but it sounded as if it echoed up from the bottom of a well.

"Mistress?" the girl called again, "are you ill?"

Tanzie forced herself to focus upon her friend's face. "No, Ealgith. I am well. I just became dizzy for a moment." The chill was replaced by a wave of heat as she once more recognized her surroundings.

"You are most pale, lady," Ealgith noted, concern evident in her tone. "Come sit a spell beneath the tree." She led Tanzie toward an ancient oak.

What had happened? For a moment, she had been privy to a time long ago as viewed through the eyes of her mother, and the short-lived occurrence had depleted her vigor leaving her weak and confused.

Reaching the tree Tanzie tucked one leg beneath her and dropped down upon the great gnarled roots, the rough bark reassuring at her back. The spirit of the oak helped renew her energy, and the episode that had just transpired began to diminish in clarity but not in importance.

She shifted her gaze and studied the sprawling little town, and her heart went out to the villagers. Again, she felt a closeness with the countryside and her mother. This enduring land and these stalwart people had garnered her admiration and respect, and while the peasants might be enemies to William Rufus, they were kindred spirits to her. They were a part of her past and if Morcar were to be believed, a part of her future as well. She ran her hand across the bark of the old tree. Sometimes Northumbria seemed more like home than Flanders.

"Are you feeling better mistress?" Ealgith asked. "Your color has revived."

Tanzie glanced at her friend. "Yes, thank you, I am quite recovered."

"Good," Ealgith replied though she continued to frown.

A gloomy sight to behold, Ealgith sat with one elbow propped upon her knee, and her chin resting in her cupped hand.

"Why the sad face?" Tanzie asked, as she sat up and sorted through the herb packets and potions that lay in disarray at the bottom of her basket.

"I miss Leofric most fiercely, lady," Ealgith lamented.

"But you have just met him. And he has only been gone since the morning. Do you fall in love so easily?" She hoped her friend had a convincing argument as to how this could happen because she felt the same way about Branoc.

"Time and reason are rarely a consideration where matters of the heart are concerned," Ealgith explained wisely. "The first time I tasted bread pudding and hard sauce I knew I would love it forever. 'Tis the same with Leofric."

"And is he different from the other men with whom you have fallen in love?" she prodded.

"To be sure, lady. Leofric favors me regardless of

my station. He is a skillful lover and a kind man. I believe he could keep me contented for all times. Now that is indeed a most remarkable thought," she mused. "'Tis true love to be sure."

Would Leofric and Ealgith eventually marry? Tanzie wondered. She hoped the handsome rascal did not merely toy with Ealgith's growing affection. Yet, how was one to ever know if a passion were true or if another's heart was filled with pure intent?

She stared unseeing at the contents in the wicker. At times, love did make a mockery of life and life of love. And what of her own situation? Being a near landless knight, if Branoc were to ever ask for her hand, Malbourne would never agree to it. Marriage without her Uncle's consent would mean the loss of her home and wealth forever. And her land ensured permanency, where as feelings could grow fickle.

Was she willing to sacrifice all for the love of a man?

Possibly...if that man were Branoc Valtaigne.

## Chapter 12
### On the road to Jarrow

Discontent lay upon the land like a cold unforgiving fog, and it added to the wariness that heightened Branoc's senses.

Last evening, the first night of their journey, he and his soldiers had sought shelter at Brinkburn priory. The reception at the safe-house had been one of restrained hostility, and although they rested in the holy hands of the Lord's servants, they posted guards and slept in turns.

This morning, not even a crust of alms bread had been offered to break their fast, and relying upon their own devices they had consumed snatches of dried meat and wheat cakes while they stowed their gear and mounted up.

Now, as Branoc and his soldiers again broke trail upon the southern road, the eastern sky awakened and took notice of them. Did Martanzia still sleep nestled in her bed, dreaming the dreams of the innocent? Or did she lie awake and plot his downfall, as she waited for the morning sun to warm her cold intentions? Their parting kisses and embraces had surprised, pleased, and confused him. She remained a Janus of darkness and light, and in his warrior's heart, he knew it must be so. But, in the heart of the man simply known as Branoc Valtaigne, he wanted her regardless of circumstance.

Forcing the girl from his thoughts he studied his surroundings. Traveling in unfriendly territory was cause for concern, and the fading shield of darkness that granted him cover, also sheltered the movement of his enemies. In times such as these, even poorly armed Saxon peasants and ill equipped renegade Scots could prove formidable if they came in number and unannounced. And it was anyone's guess when a band of marauding Danes might present themselves for traditional restitution of Danegeld, or perhaps a skirmish just for sport.

As the sun finally crested the horizon, it drove the shadows from the land and from his mind. And when the impressive bravado of the land eased into a stretch of flat open terrain, he gave Solitaire free rein. The steed's courage and endurance came at the price of roguishness and high spirits, characteristics that warranted a good run when possible.

He leaned forward in the saddle as his horse hit full stride. The pounding of the hooves matched the pounding of his heart. It was a primitive litany that called to the wildness in man and beast alike. The landscape softened to a comforting blur, and the wind took his breath away along with his worries. He felt—invincible.

If only this fleeting panacea could be captured and preserved, stored in a cask to be used whenever the world seemed to be asking more of him than he was willing to give. A means of escape to a time and place where a man need only rely upon his common sense, his prowess, and his willingness to fight to the end. None of these qualities seemed to matter any more. Yet, these were the qualities by which he had always lived, and without them he felt adrift.

As the road wound closer to the sea the trail became more convoluted, and he slowed their gait to a canter.

"Do you run to something or from it?" Leofric shouted.

"Is it so obvious?" he replied, reining in his mount to an even slower stride.

"Only to one who knows you well," Leofric

assured. "I have seen you in many a humor," he said, "but never in a state of melancholy. Of late, you rarely smile, and you miss more meals than you take. It must be a woman who troubles you so."

"Do you know if she is betrothed?" Branoc asked and dreaded the answer.

"She who?" Leofric replied, with feigned ignorance.

"You know well of whom I speak," he said, annoyed at his friend's enjoyment of his plight. "Ealgith's mistress."

Leofric frowned at him. "Why do you always call her lady, or she, or Ealgith's mistress? Does the touch of Martanzia's name upon your lips cause you so much pain?"

"No Leofric. 'Tis not pain that stays the word. After a lifetime of warring, pain and I are familiar companions. Such I could easily suffer for her."

"Then what can it be? She is but a girl soft and tender."

"Aye and more able to cause my downfall than the most brutish of giants." He cast a look of consideration at Leofric. "The girl is a foreigner," he continued. "I know not where her allegiance lies, and although she states she was bound for the cloister, she is at Bamburgh and quite possibly part of a most clever plot. Her uncle weaves intrigue in all that he does, and she is of the same blood. How can I be true to my responsibilities when one such as she confounds my heart?"

"'Tis unfair to judge Martanzia by Malbourne's actions," Leofric readily defended. "Has she done or said anything to warrant your suspicions?"

"Except for robbing me of reason, she plays well the blameless maiden. I can find no true fault with her actions." How much easier it would be if Martanzia were a man. He could call her out with his misgivings and fight her on the field. When one fought a woman, the odds were not fair. By their very weakness, they conquered great opposition.

"You worry overmuch," Leofric said. "I for one am glad to see that someone finally breeches the wall that surrounds your heart." Branoc did not miss Leofric's smug expression. "Besides," his friend continued, "in what could she possibly be involved? The people of Northumbria do not cleave to us but then neither is there open rebellion. The Aetheling and his followers remain silent, and aside from a few half-hearted raids, the Scots have kept a grudging peace."

"All will change with the advent and passing of the fall," Branoc predicted. "Come the winter, the Scots will rise in earnest. 'Tis easy to be content in the abundance of the year, but they will not sit calmly starving before the fires of winter.

"War is in the air Leofric. It vibrates with portent upon my sword and shield. Something is brewing and we shall be caught in the middle of it."

"Your premonitions have oft' saved us from ambush," Leofric admitted. "I will not scoff at your concerns. But do not be so quick to dampen the embers of desire that burn in your belly for the lady. At least let her prove herself one way or the other."

"Yes, yes. You are right. A chance she shall have," Branoc agreed thinking himself more the fool for even being concerned. "I do not know why I worry," he added, as they rode along side by side. "I have no grand title to offer the girl, only a newly acquired ruinous old fortress. She could do much better." And probably will, he thought darkly. The image of Martanzia with another man struck him like a blow wielded by a mailed fist. He had no reason to be jealous but he was. Another new emotion with which to reckon.

"You have acquired a goodly amount of riches," Leofric encouraged, "and your standing as the

Dragon of Normandy is worth more than any royal title."

"Not to a woman. They care little for accolades bestowed on the fighting circuit. It is one's standing in society that most females covet."

Leofric shook his head. "On the first day I brought Martanzia to your council chamber, she declared she was not like most women and that you need soon realize it. I see you are still working on that concept."

Branoc scowled. "I realize one thing," he said, "and it frightens me."

What is that?" Leofric prompted.

"It is profoundly simple," he said, feeling rather foolish and at the same time comforted by the thought. "I like to see her smile."

\*\*\*\*

The afternoon shadows grew to full length as the soldiers reached the banks of the Tyne. They crossed at the ford near Newcastle, and as dusk gathered softly over the mist ridden fells, they crested Gosforth hill and beheld Jarrow—-an indistinct blur upon the far horizon.

"I pray this monastery will be more hospitable than the one we sheltered in last eve," Leofric said.

"I am told that it is," Branoc replied, with more hope than faith that it would be so. He supposed the hostility they had suffered last night from the monks at Brinkburn was born of sound reason. Hardrada's Norsemen had desecrated the church and land before the battle of Stamford Bridge, and less than a week later, William the Conqueror's initial patrols had done the same after Hastings. The entire area had been brutalized by both legions, and the years had not eased the painful memories. Now William Rufus's cruel policies stung like salt in the unhealed old wounds. Who could blame the priests for their suspicions, or the people for their bitterness? No doubt, the holy place before them had suffered the same treatment.

As they drew closer Branoc halted his troops in the shelter of a stand of trees. "What a sight to behold," he said, with respect as he observed the monastery.

The priory ruled supreme over the countryside dwarfing the ancient trees and out-buildings that stood beside it. Jarrow was not sprawling nor was it built for comfort or beauty, but it did capture one's attention. Its sheer bulk towered straight up to the heavens, and like the upraised fist of God, it seemed poised and ready to smote all sinners and foreign devils. Here the temple of the Lord was formidable and wondrous in its construction.

The tower bell sang out, beckoning the monks from bending their backs in the fields to bending their knees in the chapel for vespers. It seemed as good a time as any to make their presence known.

Approaching quietly yet boldly, Branoc and his men converged upon the gates of the abbey.

Admitted with surprising hospitality, Branoc politely petitioned for an audience with the Monastic in charge of the religious stronghold. He knew it would be no easy task to liberate Bede's manuscripts from the care of these monks, but one way or another he would have them. Another accurate history of the land and the people would be a great advantage in overseeing the territory. And knowledge of prior battles and founding politics was always insightful.

While his men saw to the horses and took their ease, he was escorted to the leader of the hallowed establishment. As anticipated, the man was not pleased with his request.

"In the name of the Holy Savior, I forbid any possessions to be removed from this monastery." The round-faced Abbot pounded the table at which he sat to emphasize his words. "No foreign jackal," he continued in a most unchristian-like tone, "shall defile the works which this order has protected for over three hundred and fifty years."

"I guarantee their safe return," Branoc promised. "You may make written note of the items yourself your grace, and I give you my personal assurance that they will be kept safe and handled with the greatest consideration. If time permitted, I would read them here. But that is not an option. Truly I understand your concern."

"I hardly think you do," the old man replied sharply. The veins around his wattle of a neck distended even further. "You are just a soldier. How could you possibly know the meaning of what we do here, or what a monk believes in?"

Branoc leaned forward, his hands flat upon the table top, and he returned the holy man's hostile expression with a steely-eyed glare of his own. "I studied your ways for many years," Branoc said quietly. "Being a second son I was originally destined to join the ranks of God rather than the legions of William."

Pausing he recalled that time so long ago, and in looking back it was as if he reviewed someone else's life. He straightened to his full height. It was a stranger's past now, not his own. Was that the reason he felt safe in revealing such personal information? Did he speak of someone who was dead and buried with no hope of resurrection?

He shrugged away the thought. "My brother died of illness, and my father perished in a French dungeon, leaving me with a heritage of broken promises and nonexistent fortunes. I was torn from the side of the Almighty to care for my widowed mother, now also dead from too hard a life and too soft a heart. So do not tell me I am just a soldier and do not tell me that I cannot sympathize with your religious vows."

The Abbot leaned back in his chair, and assumed a less hostile manner, but the battle was not yet won. "You seek these chronicles to further the machinations of war," the older man argued, his words less sharply honed.

"With or without the information, the seeds of destruction lay buried in every corner of this land," Branoc warned. "And they wait only to be nurtured into full bloom. Can you not understand we seek to defend and protect as well as conquer?"

"But King Edgar shows no aggression towards us."

"Neither does he show allegiance. And the Scots are not the only worry. The border seethes with unrest. Once they choose a leader, the mercenaries who gather there will ride south to plunder and kill for far less compelling a reason than loyalty to a king or country. And they will have no concern for the people or the land. They will lay ruin to both for they want neither." He folded his arms across his chest. "If stopping such acts as these are the intention of war, than so be it."

The Abbot fretted and deliberated as he plucked at the sleeve of his habit. "You ask much. These books are sacred to us, created and cared for by monks of this order."

"When trouble comes," Branoc said, in support of his appeal, "your religious affiliation will not save you from the sword. These warriors are born of corruption, intent upon destroying everything in their path. Your manuscripts will become fodder for their fires and truly lost forever."

The old man's mouth hardened into a stubborn line, but there was resignation in his eyes and both men knew there was only one choice. "I must pray tonight upon my decision," he declared.

Branoc lowered his arms to his sides, and

nodded his consent. He admired the monk's tenacity and would not strip the Abbott of his last vestiges of power and control. Morning would be soon enough for the answer he knew was inevitable.

"Thank you for your consideration," Branoc said. "I apologize for any ills you have suffered at the hands of my countrymen. Normans like all people have their share of good and bad. Do not judge us too harshly upon what you have seen so far."

"Until today I would have thought there no salvation for the lot of you. I know you could take the books by force," the monk added thoughtfully, as he stood. "Thank you for at least asking first. Good eventide, Lord Valtaigne." The Abbot left the room appearing older and more worn then when he had entered.

Seized by a compelling restlessness, Branoc lingered in the vestibule. He had ridden hard all day but was no longer tired, and the welcome oblivion of sleep now seemed unlikely. As he studied the brace of Roman spears that hung beside the door of the priory the desire to see Hadrian's Wall gnawed at the back of his mind. Only a few miles away the ancient wonder would be an ideal location for reflection and quietude.

As a child, he had heard about the man-made structure, and the quick glimpse afforded him on the forced march from Winchester to Bamburgh had merely whetted his appetite for a more detailed study of the phenomenon.

Hoping Leofric would assume he was still with the Abbot, he slipped away unseen, and rode northwest with only his thoughts for company.

Several yards from the crumbling wall, Branoc dismounted and skirted the ditch that protected the south face of the aged battlement. At the remnants of a milecastle, he paused. Illuminated by the waxing moon, the site held mystical intrigue as well as military curiosity.

How many Roman soldiers had trod upon this ground, and how many men had commanded armies from this vantage? The little bastion gave enduring credence to the knowledge and skill of those ancient men as well as those mysterious times.

To his right and left the wall seemed limitless as it stretched beyond his field of vision. Some of the sections were in ruin but the local residents had carted away the clutter of fallen stones leaving the illusion of completeness. For over one thousand years, every ruler of this land had feared being attacked from the hinterlands. And nothing had changed. Branoc's enemy would strike from the north as well.

The night wind lamented through the chinks of the battered wall. It drifted across the plains rippling the long grass like waves upon the sea. Relaxing against the cold stones Branoc gathered his woolen cloak near, and wedged his shoulder more comfortably into a moss-covered cleft. As a stray cloud scudded across the face of the waxing moon, the shadows deepened, and the pools of light darkened and disappeared. In the jarring silence, it was easy to imagine the clank of Roman shields and spears, mingled with the muffled voices of long ago warriors.

What had it been like all those centuries past? He supposed a soldier then felt much the same as a soldier did now. Battles were battles and wars were wars. Truth be told, life itself was war. You fought to be born then fought to stay alive. The old gods fought the new God, and the new God fought the devil. He sighed in resignation. Sometimes a man even fought his own soul.

Yet, regardless of the time or place, men harbored the same hopes and fears. They would wish for undisputed victory then pray for forgiveness for the deaths it took to make such a wish come true. He knew without a doubt that all men were plagued and confused by women. That universal hardship transcended time.

Lost in retrospection, thoughts of his father surfaced. His conversation with the monk had revived many memories; recollections that he had locked away and chosen to forget. Haunting images like the expression on his mother's face the day the message had arrived declaring his father a prisoner of the French court.

Sir Owain had been captured by Philip I and held for a ransom that could not be paid. Then his brother had been fatally wounded, and their father was dead too by the time Duke William answered Branoc's appeal to meet the ransom demands. How would his life have been altered if his father had been there to guide and advise him, or his brother had survived to lend a hand? His mother would certainly have been spared the burden of heartbreak and the forsaken dreams that robbed her of her youth and hastened her death.

War and violence had stolen much from Branoc, even his chance to advocate peace and goodness by becoming a priest. But the decisions that governed his life had not been his to make or question. With honor and a clear conscience he could only endeavor to uphold the choices thrust upon him.

As the clouds thinned, and the moon flickered back into existence, a dull glimmer upon the ground caught his eye. He bent to retrieve the object then rubbed it upon his cloak to displace the caked on dirt. It was a ring, small and delicate. Had it once belonged to a fair Roman maiden? Here lay another story lost to the whim and passage of time.

He turned the circlet over and over in his palm, and watched it shimmer in the moonlight. How could anything so fragile have been wrought by the clumsy efforts of Man? The golden band was daintily engraved with a pattern of wild roses, and as he studied the ring, thoughts of Martanzia tiptoed into his mind.

He could not think of roses without seeing her face, and he could not picture her face without recognizing the hunger in his soul. No woman had ever affected him thus. He had found pleasure with his share of ladies, as fortune had allowed, but those instances were passing encounters, lustful excursions without expectation or promise. By mutual agreement, he had never sought a permanent liaison and neither had any of the women. But now a new emptiness gnawed at his belly, and 'twas not food that would appease this appetite. The ache was loneliness, the kind only a man could suffer and a woman could cure.

He balled his hand into a fist, and the ring dug into his palm. Even a lone wolf dreamed of a warm lair and a gentle touch. But a fiery beast guarded his heart protecting it from pain and sorrow and most assuredly from love, the greatest instigator of both. And this tireless creature would not be easily overcome. After all, the faithful sentinel was there at his bidding, and it had served him well for many a year. He had never opened his heart to a woman. He had never challenged the beast. Until now, there had never been any reason to do so.

He should leave well enough alone.

\*\*\*\*

The old Abbot stood beside the stable door. The dull glow of early dawn intensified his worried expression as he watched the soldiers carefully load the last of the Venerable Bede's one hundred and sixty manuscripts.

Branoc had decided upon the original Latin version. The Saxon translation commissioned by King Alfred had also been available, but he felt the

Latin would be the more accurate and trustworthy of the two. Martanzia could translate the Latin rendering, and he had no reason to believe she was familiar with the Saxon tongue.

"By the respect you grant these tomes," the Abbot conceded, "I know they are in good hands. God be with you and hasten your return."

"I am in your debt," Branoc said, pleased that a grudging truce had been reached between himself and the religious man.

"The relics will be safe at Bamburgh, and the knowledge within them used for the good. On that you may rely."

The monk nodded. The contingent of men took to the saddle, and as they filed past, the hooded man blessed each one with the sign of the cross.

As the miles stretched behind them a rare flicker of optimism stirred deep within Branoc. He touched the little ring that lay safely nestled in the leather pouch tied at his waist.

He had dreamed of Martanzia last night, and he had come to terms with a new decision this morning. For Martanzia he would face the dragon. For Martanzia he would make a new arrangement with the dutiful beast that guarded his heart.

Chapter 13
*Castle Bamburgh*

The taper guttered and threatened to go out.

"Ealgith, another candle, please," Tanzie glanced up from the book that lay open in her lap.

The evening waned, she should really go to bed, but she found such joy in studying the manuscripts left to her by her father. Uncle Malbourne had called them "the fortunes of a fool" and perhaps he was correct, yet to her they were a treasure worth more than any hoard of gold. Each time she immersed herself in their pages she learned something new. During those moments, it was as if her father were still alive, teaching her, guiding her, showing her the wondrous possibilities of the world.

"Do you never tire of reading mistress?" Ealgith rose to fetch another taper. "Lord Valtaigne has temporarily suspended your drudgery, but the old Druid bids you spend all day at it, and you choose the same chore to while away your leisure."

Tanzie lovingly ran her hand across the leather bond chronicle. "Oh but this is different. This is by choice and never boring. I truly wish you would allow me to teach you your letters Ealgith. Then you would understand."

Her friend frowned as she lit a fresh candle off the one that sputtered and pushed it in the holder. "Does that book tell you where to procure more food or how to win the heart of a man?"

"No," Tanzie admitted, with a chuckle "not the Treatise of Alexander the Great. But I am sure there is a tome somewhere relegated to the two subjects most dear to your heart."

"When you find such a book," Ealgith said, "I will defer to your kind offer. Until then," she added, moving closer to the hearth, "I've carding and spinning that needs attention, and my dreams of Leofric are as enlightening as any story ever written."

"I would not doubt you there," Tanzie agreed.

Ealgith hummed and set the spindle to twirling, and Tanzie returned her attention to her book, but before she could read another sentence a calamity of noise reverberated through the lower level of the castle.

She glanced up and met Ealgith's quizzical expression.

Branoc was to be gone for at least one more day, perhaps two. Had he returned ahead of schedule? Not bothering to mark the page, she snapped the text closed, set the chronicle aside, and heart pounding ran to the stairway, Ealgith at her heels. Would it be too bold of her to go down to welcome him home? Pausing on the landing, she leaned over the stairwell trying to identify the voices.

Something was wrong. It was not Branoc's voice she heard, and the words being spoken were filled with ire.

The commotion increased until one voice resounded with a ring of familiarity.

"Merciful Lord," she whispered, and grasped Ealgith's arm for support. "It is Rathgar." Her mouth turned dry as winter straw, and it was near impossible to swallow. "What would he be doing here?"

"If he is up to his usual behavior, lady, he is causing trouble."

Tanzie put a finger to her lips to indicate silence then strained forward listening intently to Rathgar's words.

"You will obey orders, not give them," he decreed. "Since Valtaigne is not here, nor his second in command, it should be obvious that I am the highest ranking soldier present. I am therefore in charge of this castle."

Sounds of discontent broke out again amongst the housecarles.

"Let him pass," the captain of the guards ordered above the din, the dislike obvious in his voice. "We are obliged to recognize your rank and the king's warrant you carry, but let it be noted that we do so under duress. If you need assistance my liege," the man added, "do not hesitate to ask. I have many battletested men available at the ready."

"I will take your surly offer for the warning that it is," Rathgar replied. "Now show me to a decent room, and inform the hostage from Flanders that I will send for her directly."

Tanzie cringed. Holy Mother of God he knew she was here.

"Why should she obey you?" one man blessedly spoke up in her defense. "She ain't of the king's army."

"She will obey me," Rathgar replied, "because she is my wife."

There was a mind-shattering moment of silence then a true uproar began.

Tanzie's knees nearly buckled beneath her. His wife! It was madness. She stood motionless as if turned to alabaster. A cold sweat broke out on her forehead, and for the first time in her life she felt she might truly faint.

Footsteps echoed in their direction. "Hurry mistress," Ealgith warned, urging Tanzie back the way they had come. "We must not be found upon the stairs."

Dazed she followed Ealgith to their room.

"How can he say you are wed, lady?" Ealgith

asked, as she ushered her inside and closed the door.

"I do not know. But whether Rathgar acts alone or in league with Uncle, he weaves a spider's web of intrigue that binds me ever tighter into danger."

"I will fetch the old one, mistress. Lord Valtaigne said to trust him, and perhaps for once this spellbinder can do you some good."

"Yes Ealgith. Go. And make haste. You must return with Morcar before they take me to Rathgar."

The girl hurried from the room.

Tanzie slumped down onto a chair. How could Rathgar declare her his wife? She had signed no documents stating such. If only Branoc were here. He would save her from this nightmare. He would defend her, if for no other reason than that she was under his protection. Gaining her feet she drifted aimlessly about the room wringing her hands in worry.

Married to Rathgar? She cringed at the thought. With his penetrating dark eyes and strong commanding features Lord Relentes was handsome enough, in a forbidding sort of way, and when he had first visited the chateau in Flanders, she had found him broodingly attractive. His aura of darkness had been a fascination, and the mysterious air about him had been somehow exciting. But in time, his true nature had overshadowed all else. He was unforgiving in battle and miserable at rest, never seeming to find happiness in any undertaking. It had not taken long for stories of his cruelty to reach her ears. Rathgar did not give quarter, not to his enemies or his friends. In some circles, this was a highly admired trait, but it frightened Tanzie. And although Rathgar had never mistreated her, she had begun to feel threatened in his presence. Later when she discovered he plotted with Uncle to force her into marriage, all fascination and seduction had disappeared, and she wanted nothing further to do with him.

Now she must confront Rathgar face-to-face. Alone. But she had truth on her side, surely that would count for something. He could not prove his outrageous claim. She had nothing to fear.

A knock on the door made her jump. Hoping it was Morcar she rushed to open it, but 'twas a young squire that was revealed.

"I am sent to inform you, lady, that Rathgar Relentes awaits the pleasure of your company."

Feeling dizzy again Tanzie clung to the door.

The boy stared up at her with concern.

"I am sorry to so distress you lady. If you prefer I will tell him that you decline his offer. All of us men here will uphold your decision."

She smiled at the way he included himself with the *men*. He was scarcely more than a child. "My thanks to you and the others for the noble gesture." She was tempted to accept their offer of protection, but feared it would lead to bloodshed between Rathgar's men and the soldiers of the garrison. Her conscience could not bear that burden.

She took a deep breath and adjusted her kirtle. "I am ready. You may take me to him." She might as well get their meeting over with.

"Are you sure, lady?" the boy questioned. "He seems most foul tempered and disagreeable," he added and gazed at her in wonder as if impressed with her courage.

She touched the boy's cheek. It was as soft as a girl's with no sign yet of a beard. "What is your name, lad?"

"Nimble Jack they call me. I am sure footed on the crenelles and can also juggle and tumble."

"Well Jack. Let us proceed. With you at my side I shall not be afraid."

The boy puffed out his chest and stood a little taller. Full of pride and innocence, he led her into

Rathgar's waiting clutches.

"Thank you for your assistance young Jack," she said as he halted before the appointed door. "Will you do one more thing for me?"

"Aye, lady, anything," he said, with adoration in his eyes.

"Tell my handmaiden where I am. Find her quickly Jack, much may depend upon it."

"I will not fail you," he called, as he ran off to do her bidding.

Tanzie raised her hand to knock, but the door opened before she could lay her knuckles to the wood. She shrank back at the sight of the odd little man who stood before her. Small in stature and of a wiry build, he gazed back at her with rheumy blue eyes suspicious and watchful.

"Enter mistress if you must," he said, in a most unfriendly tone. "Master will be with you shortly."

He scurried off to one side, leaving her standing in the doorway. She resisted the urge to turn and run and instead leaned forward to cautiously peer into the room.

Rathgar stepped from the nearby shadows.

She gasped in surprise as he seized her by the elbow and drew her further into the dimly lit room.

"Leave us, Wiglaf," Rathgar ordered the servant. "You won't be needed any more tonight."

Scowling and muttering, the little man obeyed without question.

Striking out with his foot, Rathgar propelled the door closed, scarcely giving his servant sufficient time to clear the portal before it slammed shut.

At the abrupt sound Tanzie stiffened, then she searched Rathgar's face trying to discern his mood.

He captured her hand and raised it to his lips. "Ah, Martanzia. You are more beautiful than ever." His eyes narrowed as he inspected her with a bold and daring gaze. She felt like merchandise newly arrived. "How fare thee?"

Doubting he cared what her response might be, she didn't bother to answer. And as he did not seem inclined to release her, she wrested her hand from his grasp.

He gave a snort of amusement, and an arrogant smile took resident upon his mouth.

Tonight Rathgar's eyes seemed near black rather than brown, the plains of his cheekbones more chiseled, and in the muted light, he appeared almost boyishly handsome. An admirable mask, covering sinister workings she reminded herself.

"Why are you here?" she asked trying the direct approach.

A sly expression crossed his face. "Where else should a husband be but at his wife's side?"

He dared to tell the lie even to her face. "I will never be your wife, Rathgar."

"According to this, my dear, you already are."

He picked up a document from a nearby table and thrust it under her nose. A new anger filled her as she read the lies it professed.

"'Tis a falsehood, a forgery." She grabbed for the paper, but Rathgar snatched it away before she could liberate it from his hand.

"Call it what you will wife. It was witnessed by your dear Uncle, as well as the Bishop of Ghent. Only the Papal seal could make it more binding. No one will refute its authenticity."

She held her ground and countered. "I have not signed it," she declared, enjoying a brief moment of triumph.

"Of course you have. Right here." He pointed to a line in the middle of the paper and teased her by holding the document close enough for her to see her name but far enough away that she could not set her hands upon it.

"I did not scribe that. I will deny everything."

"After tonight it won't matter. By morning, you shall be my wife in the truest sense of the word. No one else will want you, and I will have this official document to back up my claim."

Rathgar's words struck her mute. She stood there and stared at him disbelieving that he would make good the threat he had just calmly issued.

"I know what makes you so unhappy," he said at her silence. With the document tucked securely under his arm, he once more stepped to the table to retrieve a small package. "A bride must have a ring."

He returned to her side and opened the box to reveal the most ostentatious and ponderous gold ring she had ever seen. It dripped with jewels and filigree, and she could not even guess at its weight.

She glanced down at her hand. She had always pictured something delicate and tasteful residing upon her finger. Something with simple charm that exemplified the pure and true devotion she would feel for the man she married.

She hid her hand behind her back, thus refusing the gift.

Rathgar frowned and for a moment actually seemed hurt by her rejection. He clenched his jaw, and the muscle jumped along his cheek. "You are the one thing in this world that I desire Martanzia." By the stillness of his voice and the intensity of emotion that flamed in his eyes, she actually believed Rathgar told the truth. "And you are the one thing in this world that I cannot, nay will not, live without."

"But I do not love you Rathgar. I will never come to you willingly."

He snapped the box shut. "I don't need love," he said. Hardness edged his voice as if he feared that expressing need for anything, especially love, would somehow make him less of a man. "Once I awaken the passion deep within you," he added, his voice again filled with arrogance, "you will not only come to me willingly, but beg for my attention."

The meaning of his words froze her heart. He truly did mean to take her by force. Had he lost all conscience and sense of honor? "But Uncle gave me a choice, an alternative to wedding you," she said, trying to reason with him.

"Your Uncle lied about that, just as he lied about sending you to a convent. You should know by now that he cannot be trusted."

Rathgar tossed the document he still held and the ring box upon the nearby bed. "Few marriages are based upon love Martanzia. You will want for nothing. Is that not enough to begin our union? Let me prove my good intentions to you."

"Yes," she agreed, "prove your good intentions, let me go and tear up the document."

"That would be foolishness, not good intentions, and although I may be many things, I am not a foolish man." His gaze traveled the length of her, as he untied the twisted fabric belt that girdled his tunic. "Nor am I a patient man. The time for talk is over."

She turned and ran for the door, but before she could open it wide enough to allow for her freedom Rathgar slammed it shut.

He laughed at her foiled attempt and trapped her between the length of his body and the door she faced. "Next to your property 'tis your spirit I admire most," he said.

Bracing a forearm on either side of her, he bent to kiss the nape of her neck. She had nowhere to turn. He pressed so forcefully against her she could not take a full breath. His hips made rude contact with her backside, and she felt his desire growing ever greater.

"Rathgar," she begged over her shoulder, her cheek pressed flat against the cold wood, "please do not do this. You are a Christian and a knight. You are sworn to protect women—- not abuse them."

"Tis not abuse I seek to deliver, Martanzia, but pleasure. The choice is yours." He relaxed slightly, awaiting her reply.

Shifting her hand, she slipped her dagger free from its sheath and twisted around to face him. Closing her eyes tight, she struck out with the blade.

Rathgar blocked the thrust and grabbed her wrist with such force, her fingers went numb. The blade dropped to the floor with a forlorn clank. He kicked it aside and dragged her away from the door and toward the bed.

"I am sorry that is your answer," he said meanly with a curl of his lip. "The outcome shall be the same. I have kept my vow of chastity to you for far too long. I will not be denied tonight."

A loud rapping at the door echoed through the room bringing Tanzie hope and Rathgar heightened anger. He halted dead in his tracks and turned to face the portal. "Who dares to disturb me while I am with my wife?" he shouted.

"Tis only me, Morcar, with a wedding gift for Lord and Lady Relentes."

Tanzie groaned at the old man's words. What was he doing? Had he lost his senses? She needed his help not his felicitations.

"You see my pet," Rathgar said, with a smug look and a jerk of her wrist. "We are already acknowledged as the happy couple."

Roughly, he released her arm. "Do not try to run or elicit help," he warned and shook his finger in her face. "You will pay dearly, later, for any such actions you commit now."

Rathgar opened the door.

Morcar entered, sure and powerful, appearing anything but demented. His claret colored robes swirled around him as he came to a halt before her, and his spirit filled the room.

The controlled expression on Rathgar's face faltered.

"I made this especially for you," the sorcerer said, as he pressed a skin of wine and two cups into Rathgar's hands. "You may find it more to your liking than will your new bride."

Rathgar set the cups aside and uncorked the wine. He sniffed the brew as if he suspected that it might be poisoned. Then a strange look of complacency came over him. "Thank you for your thoughtfulness," he said, with an unusual degree of civility.

Tanzie marveled at the peaceful transformation that affected Rathgar. She opened her mouth to speak, but Morcar gave a shake of his head and then smiled like a cat in the creamery. Without a by your leave, he turned and left the room, closing the door on his way out.

Rathgar sucked in a great lung-full of air as if he had been holding his breath, and he shrugged his shoulders as if to shake away a gossamer web of unease. "A toast, Martanzia," he declared and poured out two measures of wine and handed her a cup. "To the first of many such evenings of carnal delight."

Again, he sniffed the wine, and the same manifestation of contentment crossed his face. Without hesitation, he downed near the whole cupful.

Tanzie peered into the goblet she held. The contents were foul and muddy. She gagged at the wretched odor that rose from the liquid and could not bring herself to drink of it. In amazement, she watched as Rathgar poured himself yet another portion. This too he quickly consumed.

Suddenly a familiar aroma caught her attention. The wine contained mandrake. Morcar had risked much for her. He mingled the spell of illusion with the intoxication of the grape. She smiled and set the chalice aside.

"That is more the expression I was hoping to see upon your face," Rathgar said, misinterpreting the reason for her change in mood. He tossed his goblet to the floor, framed her face with his hands and kissed her.

Seeking release, she pried at his fingers, but he held fast and forced his tongue between her lips. Her senses rebelled. When Branoc kissed her, she saw stars and moonbeams. Rathgar's touch smothered her in a dark panic that no light could penetrate.

He eased his grip and straightened to stare down at her face. There was a wild needful look in his eyes, and she feared there was nothing she could do to prevent him from having his way with her. Yet, she must try.

Twisting free, she sidled backwards until her thighs met the edge of the bed. Abruptly she sat down. She hazarded a sideways glance at the ring box and marriage document now within her grasp. If only she could secure the document and make her escape.

As she contemplated her next move, Rathgar stood boldly before her and began to undress. His expression was one of swagger and expectation as if he waited for her to comment on the prowess of his form. With growing alarm, she prayed the potion in the wine would soon take effect. Rathgar was already down to his gipon and braies, and the bulge below his waistline proclaimed his readiness. Evidently, mandrake did not have an adverse effect on the male's desire for coupling.

"I feared this union would never take place," he said in a husky voice.

Her gaze snapped to his face.

His mouth twisted into a leer, and hot absolute need shone in his eyes with an intensity that seemed to border on madness.

She shrank away and scooted further back on the bed, and although fully clothed, she suddenly felt naked. Rathgar stared at her breasts, then his attention slid lower to the top of her thighs. She glanced down and clutched at her tunic with both hands.

Why wasn't the potion working? Rathgar's unwavering study was so fevered, she could almost feel its consequence upon her flesh. She cringed and wished she could shrink away to nothing.

An animal-like growl rumbled in Rathgar's chest, and with despair, Tanzie realized that her maiden voyage into the uncharted boundaries of lovemaking would be far from what she had imagined. What should be given freely and experienced with tenderness would be brutally taken by force. How could Rathgar do this? Tears ran down Tanzie's cheeks as her cherished dream of romance and love slowly bled to death beneath the sharp sword of reality.

Rathgar stepped closer and reached for her, his breath coming quick and harsh. Then his smile faded, and his eyes glazed over. He passed his hand in front of his face as if to clear his vision.

"What treachery is this?" he bellowed, weaving back and forth. Without another word, he pitched forward onto the bed. Unmoving, he lay face down beside her.

His color was so dusky, Martanzia thought him dead. She angled his head to one side and gingerly placed her hand by his mouth and nose. A faint bit of breath warmed her fingers and a brief moment of disappointment chilled her heart. Then she felt guilty for harboring such a hope.

Easing into a more upright position, she silently gave thanks to Morcar for coming to her aid. Rathgar would be asleep for many hours with only lusty dreams to satisfy his rutting urges. She had been delivered from harms way. At least for tonight. But what of tomorrow and the next day and the next? She must retrieve the forged marriage certificate. The one that now lay crushed beneath his inert form.

Timidly she prodded Rathgar in the ribs. No response. More boldly, she put her shoulder into it and tried to roll him over. His dead weight was too much for her to move.

"Even unconscious you curse me with your obstinacy," she muttered and strained once more at the task.

"You wicked, wicked girl. What have you done to master?"

With a small yelp, she jumped back away from Rathgar. Her heart skipped a beat at the sound of the voice. Had Rathgar awakened already? He appeared to still sleep. Someone else must have spoken.

She glanced around, saw the open doorway, and spotted the sallow little man who had allowed her entrance earlier. Had he returned unseen to spy upon them? The thought made her queasy, and she repented once again for having briefly watched Ealgith and Leofric.

The man scurried forward. His face was contorted with concern, and he blanched at the sight of Rathgar's near naked unmoving form. "What have you done?" he repeated fiercely.

"Nothing" she declared. "Sir Rathgar's evening meal did not mix well with the wine he drank. I am sure he will recover."

"He looks most ill," the little man fretted. "Wiglaf knew you would not be good for master," he accused in a whining tone. "Leave us alone. We don't want you here."

He waved his hands at her as if he shooed away

a gaggle of geese then he tried to rearrange Rathgar into a more natural position upon the bed. His efforts proved as fruitless as hers had been. The knight's bulk was too much even for the servant to move alone.

"Wiglaf," she began, trying to befriend the man, "my name is Martanzia." He straightened and stared at her with frightened and suspicious eyes.

"Let me help you," she offered. "Together we can make Lord Relentes more comfortable."

After a moment of consideration, he nodded in agreement and waited for her to position herself on the far side of Rathgar. In unison, they pulled and tugged and twisted until the unconscious man was properly arranged on the bed. As the precious parchment she sought slipped free, she grabbed it up and leapt to the floor.

"Stop thief," Wiglaf cried out, "bring back master's property."

His voice faded away behind her as she hurtled through the doorway and sprinted down the empty hall. She did not break stride until she reached the safety of her chamber. Shoving the great door shut with enough force to splinter a portcullis, she leaned back against the sturdy wood and tried to catch her breath.

Tanzie stared at the document, then her gaze darted around the room. The forged license must be hidden or destroyed. The hearth and braziers were cold thus eliminating the option of quickly burning the wretched scroll. Fiercely she twisted and tore at the parchment but it resisted her attempt to rip it into shreds.

Footsteps sounded in the hall...just outside her room. Franticly she sought a suitable hiding place. Panicked, she rushed to the dragon statue and jammed the document beneath it. The door opened, and Ealgith burst into the room as if she'd been flung from a catapult.

"Oh lady you are safe," she cried, as she rushed to Tanzie's side.

"Thank heaven it is you." Tanzie's body waxed weak with relief.

"Did Morcar come to help you?"

"Yes, Ealgith, he came to me. At present I am free from Rathgar's fie intentions. And I have the document that proclaims us man and wife. Now we must destroy it."

"Where is it?" Ealgith asked.

"There," she said and pointed toward the figurine.

"Well that won't do mistress. The edges are sticking out all 'round the thing. 'Tis plain as day to see."

"I know Ealgith. Fright drove me to put it there when I heard your approach. We must search for a more suitable place of concealment."

"Perhaps we could weight it down and throw it into the moat," Ealgith suggested.

"And as the tide goes out we run the chance that it will be discovered. I am afraid that is too risky."

Tanzie grasped the dragon to lift it and recover the document, but the dragon would not move. She shoved and pushed with all her might but nothing worked. Even the combined effort of both girls could not budge the obstinate beast nor could they move the stand upon which the dragon rested.

"Oh lady," Ealgith wailed, "this ain't natural." She turned to spit then remembered where she was and simply gave the sign to ward off evil.

"Ealgith," Tanzie reprimanded, "stop that."

"Extreme circumstances warrant extreme measures," the girl defended. "There are spirits in this northern wilderness that only recognize the old ways. I don't need to be a wizard to know that, and we had best protect ourselves in whatever manner necessary."

Tanzie didn't argue. She too believed that ancient forces prowled this windswept countryside. It was as if Northumbria existed in a separate time and place, with its own set of rules and its own brand of truth and illusion. What could it hurt if Ealgith honored local practices? She was tempted to do the same.

With a nod, she silently acknowledged Ealgith's logic then turned her thoughts to the problem at hand and poked once more at the carved dragon. Still it would not budge. "Apparently the choice of hiding places has been decided for us," she reasoned. "The damning parchment will stay where it is, at least for now, and hopefully Rathgar will be elsewhere if and when the little creature decides to relinquish its hold."

Maintaining a good distance from the Celtic statue, Ealgith lit the cressets and then kindled a fire.

Deep in thought, Tanzie absently wandered the room. No matter what Rathgar proclaimed or threatened, she would never willingly submit to him, and without the signed statement, he would find little support for his foul intentions. But what if Branoc found the document? She dragged her hands through her tangle of hair and smoothed the disheveled locks back from her brow. He was already reluctant to trust her, to see Rathgar's lie signed and sealed would give sanction to the misgivings he already fostered. Branoc must never see the writ.

She hugged herself, glanced around and thought how silly she was to think that Branoc would ever find cause to be in her chamber. Of course, she had ended up in Rathgar's room, a situation equally as unimaginable. She shuddered. Rathgar had very nearly robbed her of the most precious thing she owned, her virginity.

What would it be like to surrender this treasure to a man like Branoc? With him, she would not be afraid to learn the secrets of love. She trusted him. He still held her here by force, 'twas true, yet he had never promised otherwise. And except for their first meeting outside the castle walls, he had never played her false. Her heart warmed at the memory of that day. Upon reflection, she could see the humor in that encounter, though she would never admit it to Branoc.

It seemed so very long ago.

Pausing to stand before the open casement, Tanzie rested her elbows on the cool stone of the windowsill and cradled her head in her hands. Branoc held her captive but pretended not to want her, and Rathgar would go to any lengths to force her to his side.

She knew not whether to laugh or cry.

She stared up at the moon. The silvery crescent blazed brightly in the night sky as if all were right with the world. Did Branoc watch the same heavenly display?

Tanzie yearned for him, and sinful and foolish though it may be, she no longer cared what promises might or might not accompany his touch. She wanted him fully, unconditionally. He was the only vision of happiness that survived in her soul. He was lord of castle Shining Hope and master of her heart.

Chapter 14

A layer of road dust clung to Branoc like a custom-made hauberk. He could taste it in his mouth and feel it in his eyes. He scrubbed the back of his sleeve across his brow, the action grinding the fine grit into his skin as it wiped away the sweat.

His muscles ached from too many hours on horseback, and his bones threatened to pierce through his flesh where buttocks met saddle. But he dare not slacken the urgency with which they rode. A premonition cold and foul haunted him, and its persistence had prompted the forced march back to Bamburgh. They had ridden most of the night and all of this morning, yet he ignored the rumbling of his empty stomach and drove himself and his men all the harder.

The sun arced toward midday as castle Bamburgh came into view. The image gave Branoc and the horse he rode one last surge of energy. Solitaire ran unchecked seeking the comfort of his stall and proper feed. Branoc wanted only to see Martanzia and to make sure she was safe.

The thought that harm had befallen her had tormented him since last evening. Surrounded by the restless voice of the forest and the answering snores of his men as they slept, he had wandered alone through the makeshift camp. As he stared up at the moon, an old demon endowed with new strength had dragged its talons across his heart. Fear had beset him. Not the heady hot-blooded anxiety one felt before a battle or tournament. That feeling came from risking one's own mortality. This was different. This was the cruel realization of the mortality of someone other than himself, someone for whom he cared deeply.

Because he could not alter the forces that governed his world or the hand of Fate that affected other peoples' lives, the omen of dread had left him crazed with worry and reckless with frustration. And now, as the mounted patrol thundered over the drawbridge, through the gate and into the bailey, he prepared to confront the object of his unnamed distress.

Reaching the main entrance, Branoc reined in his horse. The stallion slid to a halt, dust and pebbles churned in their wake. Dismounting he tossed the reins to a startled Leofric, and ignoring the baffled expression on his friend's face, he entered the fortress.

Something was wrong. The castle hounds did not bound forward to greet him, rather they were skittish and ill at ease as they hung back in the shadows with their tails between their legs.

A bellowing and cursing echoed down from above, and the grip of foreboding tightened around his innards. Sword drawn, he bounded up the spiral stairs two at a time, and as the stairway wound to the right he instinctively transferred the weapon to his left hand.

Reaching the landing, he recognized the voice that savaged the serenity of his keep. It belonged to Rathgar Relentes, and the disturbance he heard came from Martanzia's room.

All manner of horrible pictures cluttered his mind as he burst into the chamber, and legs braced, he shifted his weapon back to his favored side as his gaze swept the room.

Martanzia's hair fell in disarray, and her clothes were crushed and twisted. "More spells and witchery," Rathgar shouted, as he shook her by the shoulders. He was dressed casually, armed only with a short sword. "After drinking that wretched brew last night, I'm in no mood this morning to consume your tales of nonsense. Give up the document or you will find I am the great tyrant you profess me to be."

Branoc's gaze slipped sideways.

Ealgith cowered in the corner nursing a swollen bleeding lip. No one else occupied the room.

"Release her Relentes and explain your presence here."

Rathgar stiffened and glanced over his shoulder. His expression of surprise quickly transformed to a glare of hatred. Shoving Martanzia aside, he turned to face Branoc.

The girl stood open mouthed rubbing her arms where Rathgar had gripped her. Then as if coming to her senses, she stumbled toward him, hands outstretched, relief shining in her eyes.

Branoc's heart lurched.

The little fool. Her unthinking action placed her between his blade and Rathgar. Branoc grabbed her arm and jerked her behind his back.

"Speak Relentes or feel the bite of this." He raised his sword level with Rathgar's chest.

"There is no need for violence, Valtaigne." Rathgar eyed the weapon. "'Tis just a lovers quarrel, and none of your concern."

A lovers quarrel...Branoc felt the spark of jealousy turn his blood to fire. "I'm making it my concern." he growled. "Now tell your story quickly and choose your words well." He shifted his blade to the other man's throat hoping its presence would cut down on the lies that generally issued forth there.

"William sent me," Rathgar began, "to see if you needed help. You are very far from reinforcements, and the border you guard is long and fraught with enemies."

"'Twould seem today the castle also holds its share of enemies," Branoc replied. He doubted Rathgar had come to Northumbria for so noble a reason as to aid a comrade. There was a more devious play unfolding here, and he would know the story in detail.

"Go on," he prompted, "I have not yet heard why you were attacking a woman who is under my protection."

"I was not attacking Martanzia, I was simply trying to reason with her. She can be most willful." Rathgar raised a brow in nonchalance and casually brushed a nonexistent piece of lint from the sleeve of his tunic. "I sometimes question my choice in wives."

For a moment, Branoc's mind went blank as if his brain refused to conceive what he had just heard. How could Martanzia be Rathgar's wife? He glanced down at her. She opened her mouth to speak, but he ignored her sputtering and returned his attention to Rathgar.

"Explain," he said with dead calm.

"Martanzia and I were married this last spring," Rathgar said, "but duty has kept me from her side, and I thought her still in Flanders. Imagine my surprise to find my dear wife had been sent here by her unscrupulous Uncle to stand as hostage. She will of course return with me to court."

"'Tis a lie Branoc," Martanzia declared, her voice shook with emotion. She placed a hand on his back, and twisting her fingers in the cloth of his tunic clung to him like a frightened kitten. "I chose the nunnery at Elstow over Rathgar's bed. Now he seeks revenge for his injured pride and stifled lust. The prior marriage agreement no longer exists and was never fulfilled."

"She is the one who lies Valtaigne. I have the document to prove our union. She will warm my bed this night and leave with me in the morning."

Martanzia blanched. Branoc wanted to comfort and reassure her, but he knew not who lied most or more skillfully. In addition to her unannounced arrival and nefarious family ties, she was now associated with Rathgar. What could speak worse for her? "Show me the paper," he said.

"I cannot," Rathgar admitted, "the contrary little minx has hidden it beneath this damnable statue. I can neither move it aside nor lift it to retrieve the document."

Branoc studied the carving. Something protruded from beneath the base but not enough showed to prove what the deed stood for. Without shifting his gaze from Rathgar, he set the girl aside, walked over to the small wooden stand and nudged the image. This was most peculiar. It would not yield. He glanced at Martanzia for an explanation. She shook her head and shrugged her shoulders.

"Is it true, lady?" Branoc asked, forcing the question from lips that felt frozen with dread. "Does this record show you are wed?"

"Yes, but..."

"You see," Rathgar smoothly interjected. "We are man and wife. She cannot deny it just as she denied me nothing on the night we were wed." His grin turned wolfish. "A tigress in bed she is. Wanton and lustful especially after what I have taught her."

Martanzia flew at Rathgar and pummeled his chest with her clenched fists. "You lying knave. I did no such thing. You shame me by your words. Take it back. Tell him it is not so."

Rathgar grasped her wrists one in each hand staving off her attack. "Do you care so much what this man thinks of you Martanzia?" he asked. At her silence, an expression of enlightenment dawned upon Rathgar's face. "So Valtaigne," he smirked, "you are no longer in love with only your horses. Will nothing ever change? Again, we seek the same prize, but this time I have beaten you to the victory and a sweet one it was over and over again. Each time I am with her only heightens my appetite for more."

The color drained from Martanzia's face.

The picture conjured by Rathgar's words burned an agonizing image deep into Branoc's mind. Quelling the urge for more impetuous action, he carefully laid the edge of his sword at the side of the other man's neck. "If you value keeping your head, Relentes, you will let her go—now."

Rathgar leaned forward, quickly kissed Martanzia before releasing his hold on her.

She stumbled backward.

With a curse, Branoc caught her around the waist. Using his weapon to hold Rathgar at bay, he dragged Martanzia backward toward the door.

Rathgar roared with laughter. "A sweet victory indeed," he taunted.

Martanzia's arms and legs flailed out again in a renewed attack at the man who declared himself her husband then she stopped struggling and sagged against Branoc's hip. He did not free her but rather tightened his grip about her fragile form.

The thought of Rathgar touching the body he held close sickened him, and in his mind he saw them together, the joining of his worst nightmare and his brightest dream. Suddenly he realized that it was love and not mere desire he felt for Martanzia and the life-altering aspect of that revelation took him off guard.

But whom, if either, should he believe in this impasse? He could not trust Rathgar. That was a known fact. And since they could not retrieve the certificate, the dilemma was reduced to Rathgar's word against Martanzia's. He wanted to, needed to, believe in her.

"You leave today Relentes," he said, "before sundown. Tell the king all is secure here and thank

him for his concern. Help such as yours I do not
need."

"You ungrateful swine," Rathgar sneered. "Is
that how you treat one of the sovereign's men?"

"You are your own man, not William's. And
those who follow you are disloyal by association. You
will prepare for immediate departure."

Rathgar bristled at the insult then seemed to
regain control of his anger. "As you wish Valtaigne.
My wife shall of course come with me."

Martanzia gasped and stiffened.

"The girl will stay with me until this can be
sorted out. Whether or not she is your wife does not
change the fact that she is the king's hostage." He
tightened his grip on the weapon, and Rathgar's eyes
flicker at the slight movement. "Need I point out,
that you and your men are out numbered here?"

Rathgar's expression darkened. "You have won
the day Valtaigne, but not the field. This is not over.
You will come to rue this decision."

"Do not test my patience with your petty taunts
and goading," Branoc warned. "We are no longer
children at play. The stakes are much higher now.
Losing could be fatal."

"You are so right, old friend," Rathgar said, a
feral gleam brightened his eyes. "This time we fight
to the bitter end. Guard well the prize Valtaigne, the
games have only just begun." He stared
meaningfully at Martanzia then strode from the
room.

Branoc lowered his sword. His old companion
had too easily given up the fight. It made Branoc
wonder what other scurrilous plans simmered in the
demented caldron of Rathgar's mind.

Martanzia twisted in the circle of his arm and
snuggled against his chest, and all rational thought
deserted him as she gazed upon him with an
expression of dewy-eyed gratitude. "I prayed you

would come to save me," she murmured.

His pulse quickened. What was he to do with her? He wanted her as he had never before wanted a woman. Yet, she confounded him with her seemingly obvious innocence and vexed him with her questionable associations. He should not touch her by either account.

Releasing Martanzia, he expected her to pull away. But as he sheathed his weapon, she clung to him, stood on her tiptoes, and kissed his cheek. The fragrance of roses weakened his resolve and gazing into her eyes, he was lost. He forgot Rathgar, and felt only the warmth of her body against his. He glided his hands lightly up and down her back and felt her tiny ribs expand and contract beneath his fingertips. She was as delicate as the flowery perfume that clung to her warm skin.

He drew her near and their lips met. Tentatively she followed his lead, her tongue playing with his, first softly then more boldly. Pulse bounding he tightened his embrace, and wished by all that was holy that life was as simple as his need for her. If only there was just the two of them—at least for a little while.

No longer tired, he eased back against the table that stood in the center of her chamber, and gathered Martanzia against his chest. Her body relaxed and flowed over his. He nuzzled her neck and nipped at her ear. A sweet low moan escaped her as he wedged his thigh between her legs and slowly pressed against her.

Her warm breath teased his neck creating waves of pleasure that washed downward and surged through his midsection. Boldly he covered her breast with his hand. This time she didn't shy away, but pressed her supple flesh against his palm.

He wished to strip the clothes from Martanzia's body and take her here upon the table. She could not know what she unleashed in him. Or did she? Was Rathgar truthful when he said they had been together? Did she know exactly the game at which she played? He needed to hear her denial one more time.

He drew back and studied her upturned face. "Did you lay with Rathgar as he said you did?" His breath was ragged and the words come out more harshly than intended.

The mist of desire that softened Martanzia's forest green eyes dissolved away and storm clouds moved in. "You dare to ask such a thing?" she sputtered and strained away from him. "His touch repulses me. Just now, I have tasted of you with a passion I have never known before. Do you suspect that I feel this way about every man who happens along? First Rathgar, then you, whomever seems advantageous at the moment?" She shoved at his chest and wrested free of his embrace.

"Leave," she ordered. Hurrying across the room to the open door, she grabbed it as if seeking support.

Branoc was confused. It had seemed a fair enough question to him. He had just rescued her from the clutches of his lifelong foe, and he thought he cared greatly for her. Didn't he have the right to know what if anything had transpired between her and Rathgar?

"Now," Martanzia added, her voice carrying an equal measure of hurt and anger.

Levering away from the table he made his way toward her, resisting the urge to reach down and adjust the uncomfortable fullness that plagued him between his legs.

After a few steps, he halted and glanced up, hoping to further their discussion, but in the face of Martanzia's murderous expression he continued on. He did not remember the last time he had seen a female so angered. He thought if she had been armed, she would have challenged him to a fight.

He crossed the threshold and turned to look back at her, but all he saw was the great oaken panel as it slammed shut. How had he gone so quickly from Martanzia's warm presence, to the cold loneliness of the deserted hallway?

He smacked his open palm against the wall, then cursing women, he readjusted his sword and himself and headed toward the battlements to make sure Rathgar followed his orders to leave. As he walked a feeling of vulnerability shadowed his steps, not because his former friend had renewed his claim as his current enemy, but because his own emotions had betrayed him more readily than Rathgar.

Chapter 15

Blending with the shadows, Branoc walked the allure then he paused beside a merlon and peered over the castle wall. The chink of bridles and the clatter of hooves upon cobbled stone echoed upward, the sound clamorous in the still evening air.

As they took their leave, Rathgar and his men moved at their leisure. Branoc cared not one whit that they lingered in a childish attempt to annoy him. But he was concerned with the sneering self-assurance and lack of respect they demonstrated before a company of men who greatly outnumbered their own.

Dusk was easing into night before the column of mounted soldiers finally filed out through the barbican. The fanfare of their passing quickly died away on the southbound road, and their images were swallowed up by the impending darkness. The dust they stirred settled back upon the ground disavowing any trace of their coming or going, and save for the bitter gall that churned in Branoc's stomach, it was almost as if they had never been.

He glanced up and studied the sky, and one by one, the constellations appeared. Regardless of a man's predicament, the world carried on without the slightest hesitation. The sun set at its appointed time, the stars came out perfectly aligned, storms brewed and rivers ran toward the sea. Nothing altered the laws of the universe. It was somehow reassuring.

If only life could be so ordered. But every time Branoc believed the path to his future to be straight and plainly marked, the road suddenly forked and no matter which branch he followed the decision always greatly altered the course of his existence. And rarely for the good.

The only constancy in the world was change, and no one escaped its touch. Even Rathgar had changed and obviously not for the better. When they were young, there had been a brief period of camaraderie between them. But now he was a man obsessed with revenge and self aggrandizement . His offenses were becoming more daring, and they involved other people as he nurtured chaos and courted deception. Yet, it was not an inherited trait. Rathgar's father, Sigvald, had been honorable and true to the pledge of comradeship, while Rathgar knew not the meaning of friendship or fealty. Sigvald, now gone to his final reward, had taken Branoc in as apprentice and sponsored him in his pursuit of becoming first a priest and then a chevalier. Without Sigvald, Branoc would never have achieved knighthood, and he never would have salvaged the name of Valtaigne. These deep-rooted feelings of allegiance died hard, but time and circumstance forced him to realize that while he owed the name Relentes much he owed Rathgar nothing.

As he prowled the ramparts, Branoc's mind was seized by a turmoil that nothing would pacify. Each time he felt sure of his decision regarding Martanzia, something new reared its ugly head to throw him once more into the pit of indecision, and there he wrestled with questions and concerns that could alter his life forever.

She had not answered yea or nay to his query regarding Rathgar. Was her refusal to speak a confirmation that the act had been committed? Visions of Martanzia naked and in the arms of Rathgar tormented his mind. He could see her twisting with pleasure beneath the rutting loins of the man he now called enemy.

He covered his face with his hands. Such images were madness and would only lead to more suffering in the private hell he so willingly constructed for himself. He lowered his arms to his sides.

Martanzia and his craving for her unsettled him greatly, and he was angry at his inability to conquer and control his desires. With such ease she enchanted him but to what ends? By the Rood, why did he care what she had or had not done? He didn't need the girl. He didn't need anyone. So it had always been and so it would continue to be.

Swept along by a tide of bitter emotion he finally abandoned the parapet and wended his way through the sleeping castle to the inner bailey and the stable. At the door, he whistled softly to alert his warhorses of his approach. The black destrier still needed rest. He would take the dapple gray. Strong Oak could use the exercise.

Accouterments applied he led the great horse to the dimly lit postern gate at the west end of the castle. At his approach the sentry snapped to attention.

"Stand and declare yourself."

"Tis I, Lord Valtaigne. I go for a short ride upon the moors."

"Would you like an escort, sir?" the soldier asked, concern plainly evident in his voice and expression.

"No, do not bother the men and do not be alarmed. I shall not go far." Without waiting for a response, Branoc swung into the saddle, and the young guard opened the gate.

Eager as his master the horse bounded away into the welcome obscurity of the night. The moonlight that frosted the land with a dull silver glow blended with the color of his mount, and

Branoc felt as if he rode a fleeting gray shadow. His cloak billowed out behind him, and he charged the silent plain seeking solace in the freedom of his flight. The cold night wind numbed his face and mind and blessedly froze his thoughts into unmoving images of black and white. But he couldn't outrun the frustration and uncertainty that pressed down on him with the fury of a thunderhead.

Miles passed beneath the charger's unflagging hoofs before he reined Strong Oak into a trot. Suddenly, Branoc laughed full and loud. "Look at us Strong Oak." He halted the animal. "Into many a fearful battle we have leapt with never a thought of retreat, yet here we are running full tilt from a mere slip of a woman. A woman just beyond girlhood, so small I could crush her with nary an effort. A woman so fragile you could trod upon her and not even know it."

He stroked Strong Oak's arched neck and warmed his hand in the horse's mane. "We have never been known for cowardice old boy. We must return and face the truth whatever it may be." The horse tossed his head as if in agreement, and Branoc circled him back toward Bamburgh.

Maybe admitting the truth would set him free. He could not expect more from Martanzia than he was willing to give of himself. He was changing too.

Taking note of his surroundings, he realized that in his search for answers he had ridden much further then intended and was beyond the area that had already been reconnoitered.

A dark weald loomed nearby. It was the perfect haven of concealment for someone amassing a mercenary army, and the murky depths seemed ripe with the promise of intrigue and rebellion. The remainder of the terrain, however, was more amiable consisting mostly of plains with only a few hillocks and no visible fens. Small patches of trees and thickets dotted the open land. Tomorrow he would come back with a small detail of men to assess the region by the light of day.

He touched his heels to the horse's flanks, but Strong Oak snorted and danced to the right. As a shuffling sounded in the underbrush, Branoc drew his sword and braced for the attack.

Out of the gloom, a man on horseback charged at full gallop.

Leaning low in the saddle, Branoc dodged the main thrust of the javelin, but the sharp deadly tip of the spear grazed his left forearm. He clenched his teeth ignoring the burning pain and prepared for a second man's advance.

His full weight behind his sword, Branoc executed a cross-slash that quickly dispatched his new opponent. Mortally injured, his attacker clutched at a gaping belly wound and toppled from his horse.

The first man circled back but kept his distance and rather than repeat the assault he called a signal into the night. The woods came alive as armed men materialized from the darkness.

As they drew near Branoc eyed them with curiosity as well as concern. Something about the group seemed familiar. They wore the colors of William. It was Rathgar's force. But that was impossible. He had seen them ride out from the castle hours ago and their direction had been due south. They should be halfway to Alnwick by now.

As the warriors closed ranks, forming a circle around him, Branoc chastised himself for his foolishness. By the Saints, how had he let this happen? Strong Oak pawed the ground then pivoted on his haunches affording him a sweeping view of the soldiers and the deadly spears they carried. Each shining tip was poised for action, and he was the central target.

Trapped like a red deer ringed by hounds, he relaxed his arm and let the great sword, he yearned to wield, hang harmlessly at his side.

"It's a wise man who knows his limitations," Rathgar mocked as he joined his men.

"Traveling a bit far off the beaten path aren't you, Relentes?"

"You are no longer in a position to be asking questions Valtaigne," Rathgar said. "It's a different sensation being on the other end of the blade is it not? Almost a naked feeling, like being caught with one's braies down, as they say here."

Branoc studied Rathgar. Here was the treachery he had suspected—nay expected.

"Tie his hands and blindfold him before you bring him to camp," Rathgar ordered. "And do be careful. Valtaigne is a worthy adversary as the body of our dead comrade does attest."

Rathgar guided his horse over the fallen soldier as if he merely crossed a downed tree limb. Then he disappeared into the forest.

A young man advanced and grabbed the sword from Branoc's hand and the dirk from his belt. Branoc ran his hand over the empty scabbard. Without the reassuring weight, he felt off balance as if he had given up a part of himself.

Two more soldiers came forward. They snatched Strong Oak's reins and attempted to wrestle Branoc's arms behind his back. Unwilling to give up without a fight, he thrust out with his shoulder, momentarily, foiling their intent.

The two retreated, regrouped, and came at him again.

"This time don't move," the first soldier warned and poked Branoc in the ribs with his own commandeered weapon.

Recognizing no logical alternative, he submitted to their rough treatment. The coarse hemp tore at the flesh of his wrists, and his arms felt as if they were being twisted from his shoulder sockets. When the men finished, he wrested free of their grasp. His show of anger earned him another jab of the sword, the seriousness of the blow cushioned by the leather hauberk he wore.

"I said hold still," the young soldier repeated.

"You are brave when the one you fight is unarmed and trussed." Branoc watched without emotion as the soldier raised the tip of the sword from his ribs to the left side of his face.

With one flick of the blade, the point cut into Branoc's unprotected cheek. Blood flowed from the gash, wet, and warm against his cool skin, but he did not react to the pain nor to the anger that coiled in his chest. He thoroughly studied the soldier, silently committing him to memory, silently promising to repay the man for such personal attention.

The young soldier's gaze wavered, and he lowered the sword and glanced away as if he regretted his rash action.

A blindfold of coarse material was secured over Branoc's eyes and even the comforting glimmer of moonlight and stars disappeared, plunging him into a world of total darkness. He swallowed the panic that rose in the back of his throat. How incredible that a mere scrap of cloth could render a grown man so helpless. Now, he had no more defenses than a wee babe.

They led Strong Oak for at least a mile, maybe more. Coming to a halt, they dragged him from his horse and cast him down upon the ground.

Branoc spit dirt from his mouth and struggled to his knees as the blindfold was yanked from his eyes. Glancing up, the first thing he saw was Rathgar. Like a king, he sat upon a dilapidated high-backed chair. A stone, shoved under one leg of the decrepit throne, kept the bench steady, his scraggly-haired servant waited in attendance.

"Welcome to my little corner of the realm," Rathgar said cheerfully, a self-satisfied expression livened his face.

Ignoring the greeting Branoc surveyed his surroundings.

The deteriorated walls of an ancient castle lay scattered all around, and a dense forest ringed the crumbling stronghold. A modicum of time and effort seemed to have been devoted to the partial restoration of the ruin, and it seemed reasonable to assume Rathgar had fortified the area prior to his arrival at Bamburgh.

The stockpiles of wood and supplies indicated that this was not a chance destination, and the military nature of the camp implied Rathgar intended to use the position as a command post. Several Saxons openly fraternized with the Norman soldiers, and three men in Scottish apparel stood silently but confidently off to the left.

"You are ensconced here quite nicely Relentes," Branoc said. "But you only rule the long forgotten rubble of former kings."

Rathgar laughed. "With you on your knees before me, that is enough. At least for the moment.."

Though his arms were still bound behind his back, Branoc gained his feet. He'd be damned if he would kneel before this man. "Betrayal hangs upon these rotting walls like ghostly tapestries. Why are you here, Rathgar? As baneful as some of your past behavior has been, you have never disgraced yourself by being unfaithful to your liege."

"Do not worry over my merit Valtaigne. You would be better served to worry about your own valour."

"Do you never tire of scheming and plotting?" Branoc asked. "Think what you could accomplish if you put your talents to good use."

"And think what you could accomplish if you put your talents in league with mine." Rathgar lounged back more comfortably. "We are both mighty warriors, Branoc, forged from the same iron. But we are on opposite sides of the coin each pointing in a different direction." Gripping the arms of the chair, he leaned forward. "Thus it has always been, yet still you do not understand."

Branoc understood all too well. Rathgar thrived upon corruption. The suffering of others nourished his lost soul, just as grace and goodness sustained those pure of heart.

"Abandon whatever ill conceived notion has brought you here and return to William straight away," Branoc advised. "It is not too late to change your path, but soon there will be no turning back."

"I am happy with the direction I follow and with my life as it is." Rathgar relaxed back in his chair a smile upon his face. "Why must you forever seek to redeem me? In my eyes, you are just as pitiful lost in your dreams of chivalry."

"At least I still have dreams. Your destiny is a void of darkness where only nightmares survive."

"I grow bored with this conversation," Rathgar declared, his voice edged with anger. "It is all too similar to the ones we have had so many times before. Take him away," he ordered. "Shackle him to yon tree that I might gaze upon him; the Dragon of Normandy, rendered helpless as an old woman."

Branoc did not waste his energy struggling, but instead schooled his expression to stony indifference as they led him to the oak and clamped the well-worn leg iron around his ankle.

When he was alone he tugged against the chain that ran from his foot to the tree, but no weak link did he find. Hands still tied behind his back, he sat on a fallen log, and realized a new sympathy for the trained bear he had once seen at the fair.

The aroma of roasting venison billowed through the air thick as smoke. His stomach growled, and his mouth watered but as time passed, he realized the smell of food was all they were likely to offer him. It didn't matter. For the moment, gaining his freedom was more important, and as the soldiers ate he took the opportunity to work at the ropes that bound his wrists.

Half drunk with mead the men were a noisy lot. Again, they showed no fear of discovery, which confirmed Branoc's belief that the local Saxons and the marauding Scots considered them allies rather than enemies. At Rathgar's approach Branoc stilled his movements.

"Come to torment me while I am so captive an audience?" he asked and stood.

"Captive is the key word Valtaigne. You have saved us much trouble by so conveniently coming to us. Bamburgh should fall all the more easily."

"You cannot take a castle with this handful of men."

"I have no such intentions," Rathgar said in the tones of a braggart. "In the next few days hundreds more will join me."

"More Scots and Saxons I'll wager," Branoc said.

"Yes, among others. And all are thirsty for blood and hungry for the spoils of war." Rathgar took a step closer, and his cold dark eyes warmed as if in anticipation of the carnage. "We shall lay waste to this land the likes of which has never been seen before. Neither man, nor beast, nor seedling will remain in our wake."

Shocked by such a revelation Branoc peered closely at Rathgar and willed there to be some humanity or compassion where he knew none existed. "What could you possibly gain by such destruction? You need not the bounty. Is it just for the sport?"

"That is a bonus, of course, but no it is not just for the sport. I do it for you old friend. You are the one who will be credited with the horrible death and devastation that shall be wrought. Your body will be found on the side of the enemy with incriminating evidence upon your person. After that, no one will ever again sing your praises. You will be dead, but your name will live on in dishonor for all eternity."

Branoc was stunned. Hundreds of innocent people were going to die because Rathgar wanted retribution? "If you wish revenge meet me in personal combat," Branoc suggested. "Would that not be more to your liking?" He nodded over his shoulder. "Untie my hands and remove this chain. Or are you afraid?"

"Save your breath, Valtaigne. I'll not fall prey to contrived challenges and dares. Your death is not enough for me, or I would fulfill that longing right now. You must be discredited in the eyes of the king and all you hold dear. Only then will I be satisfied."

With remorse, Branoc studied the face of his childhood friend. They were forgotten comrades with a memory for each other's strengths and weaknesses. "You could have been my best friend, but you chose instead to be my worst enemy. Why did this happen Rathgar?"

"Why... Because being your best friend meant having to stand in the shadow of your nauseating goodness and honorable ways." Hate radiated from Rathgar like shimmering heat around a glowing ember. "I needed to best you, not be your best friend," he snarled. "Whether facing a chess board or the field of battle, you always came out on top, wielding a sword to victory as you spouted scripture and debated philosophy. Christened by the court as the Duke's Champion; immortalized by women as the compassionate warrior. The one who dared to show mercy to his enemies and deference for the roses that grew in the chinks of the castle wall. Even my father was taken in by your noble countenance. He often praised you above me, his own son. Our friendship ended the day you stole my father's love. Now you and I can only be rivals."

For one fleeting moment Branoc thought he saw regret in Rathgar's eyes, then the expression disappeared and a calculated slyness contorted his captor's face. "Soon I will have everything I ever wanted, as well as the one thing you desire."

With a burst of rage, Branoc realized Rathgar's hideous plan offered a clear path to Martanzia. She would be at his mercy. A snarl reverberated deep in his throat, and he lunged forward only to have his advance cut short by the chain around his leg.

"The girl is worth fighting for, eh?" Rathgar asked with a cunning smile. "Red roses pale in contrast to her lips and her eyes are greener than the finest emeralds. Perhaps I can arrange for her to be present when your body is found. She will hate you for killing so many helpless people. I doubt she will shed a single tear for your passing."

Branoc pictured his own grave, with no one in attendance but his trusted friend Leofric. 'Twas a small image but it carried a monumental sadness.

"The truth be known," Rathgar continued, "I sometimes think the girl's sympathies lie with the rebel Saxons. She certainly shows no fealty toward the Normans and she reads far too many books to think logically." He took a sip of wine from the chalice he carried, and his smile deteriorated into a sneer. "Of course as my wife, she will bend to my cause both in my bed and out of it. I will think of you as I pleasure myself upon her." He made crude thrusting motions with his hips.

Branoc glanced away and reminded himself that he had yet to see proof showing the two were truly married. Rathgar insinuated much but he had long been a master at twisting the truth. And as far as Martanzia conspiring with the Saxons, he had yet to see evidence of that either. He was not about to convict her on Rathgar's word.

"Nothing to say Valtaigne?" Rathgar prodded. "You never were any fun. You have always been much too serious."

Branoc kept silent disallowing Rathgar the pleasure of hearing the retorts that whirled through his brain.

"Until the morrow then. I do hope you find one of those tree roots to your comfort tonight." He sauntered away then halted and turned. "Where are my manners? Do have some wine before you slumber." Rathgar tossed the contents of the silver goblet at Branoc's feet, splashing him with wine and mud.

At the affront, Branoc had an impulse to kick out at Rathgar as if they were still children ridiculing one another on the training field. But he remained rigidly immobile, again realizing that a lack of response was his most penetrating weapon. The smirk on Rathgar's face faded slightly, and as he walked off into the darkness his derisive laughter lacked enthusiasm.

Branoc shuffled back and forth to stave off the cold, and the memories of his youth shadowed his steps like the heavy chain that dragged along behind him. He, Rathgar, and Leofric had grown up at one another's side. Together they had shared the same experiences and the same lessons of life. He had thought that they also shared the same dreams and purpose. Yet, Rathgar had grown to manhood twisted and cruel, blinded by his ambition and his need to dominate those around him.

Rathgar always sought the upper hand, and he never accepted defeat nor did he learn from it. Instead, he fed upon it like ravens feeding upon fallen warriors. His failures became a part of him. They festered in his belly and poisoned his mind. They made Rathgar's heart hunger for revenge.

A shiver twisted through Branoc. Rathgar's plan of destruction chilled his soul as completely as the night air chilled his flesh. This abominable scheme was lunacy. He must escape and defend the land that had been entrusted unto him. And more importantly, he had to protect Martanzia.

Martanzia...By heaven, denying his feelings for her had led him to rash action resulting in his present dismal situation. Yet, he was not ready to openly declare his love for her. Not yet.

The emotions assailing him when he thought of Martanzia left him floundering. Generally, he trusted instinct and logic in all matters, but those methods were debatable when one dealt with decisions of the heart. Instinct could be confused with need and logic overshadowed by hope. And none of it would matter if he did not gain his freedom.

In an attempt to loosen the hemp bindings, Branoc slouched down onto a log, leaned back, and plunged his wrists into the bucket of freezing water his abductors had provided. The fetid liquid, cold as death, was already coated with a scum of ice. His hands turned numb, his fingers useless, and he clenched his jaw to prevent his teeth from chattering. But he kept at it.

Periodically he worked his wrists back and forth against the bindings, and little by little, they loosened. The pain wrought by his actions, eventually transcended the numbing effect of the cold water, and when he glanced over his shoulder at the bucket, he saw the contents were now dark with his blood. Still he repeated the agonizing process of soaking and twisting.

With a grimace of success he pulled free, threw

the ropes down and shoved his near frozen hands beneath his clothes and up under his arms. His icy fingers met the warm skin of his sides, and he gasped and sucked in a great breath. Slowly his fingers returned to life and the bleeding of his wrists lessened.

Once his fingers were supple enough to obey his commands he worked at freeing his leg.

The circle of iron, carelessly bolted over his soft boot, had a rusty hinge. With concerted effort, surely the weakened fitting would give way. He untied the cross-garter on his lower leg and shoved the lacings and flexible leather down through the manacle and off of his foot. Feeling along the inside of the footwear, he located the small dagger that was concealed within a hidden sheath.

Levering the wedge of steel against the hinge he cracked apart the rusty metal. The iron dug painfully into his hands as the manacle bent sharply, but the gap widened enough to slip his naked foot through the opening.

Replacing his boot, he secreted away the dagger and glanced around for signs that his movements had been detected. Arrogant and cocksure of himself, Rathgar had not assigned men to guard the inner circle of the camp, and to Branoc's good fortune, all remained quiet.

Like a wolf on the hunt, he chose his steps carefully and reaching the first floor of the ruins, he located his broadsword and short sword among the pile of weapons that stood in the corner. Now to locate Strong Oak. But the horse wasn't amongst those tied off east of camp. He saw the animal nowhere.

Unable to delay any longer, he decided to take one of the other mounts. He crept up behind the sentry who guarded the perimeter and the horses and using the pommel of his broad sword knocked him senseless. As he crouched beside the still form, he recognized the unconscious man as the young soldier who had drawn his blood earlier.

Retrieving the knife from his belt Branoc held the weapon to the man's throat. The blade gleamed menacingly. Jaw clenched he shifted his hand and with a whisper of a movement sent the sharp edge slicing through soft yielding flesh. The soldier now bore a cut on his left cheek to resemble Branoc's.

"Bear this scar that in the future you shall remember to fight with honor." He touched the matching deeper wound on his own face. The cut no longer bled but it throbbed with annoying persistence.

Gaining his feet, he studied the horses. The best of the lot turned out to be Rathgar's horse. It seemed a fitting enough choice. He bridled the animal but did not dare waste precious minutes to rig a saddle. Leading the stallion quietly along the picket line, he untied the other horses as he passed hoping they would eventually wander off. Then at the outer rim of the camp he eased astride and rode into the night.

Beyond hearing range of the sleeping men, Branoc turned the animal in a south-easterly direction and kicked him into a gallop. With the moon down and the night dark as pitch, he pushed his luck as much as he dared.

He was sure Rathgar was camped at Yeavering. He'd seen the ancient fortress marked upon the maps in the council chamber, yet he could not get his bearing.

The lay of the land changed radically, hindering Branoc's progress. The flat expanse to his left now became a rocky ridge. It jutted upward, higher and higher, until it rose up beside him like the wall of a castle. The path seemed unfamiliar, had he taken a wrong turn?

On his right, the ground abruptly dropped away.

A black abyss loomed where the land had been, and only a ribbon of slippery shale remained to serve as a path. Darker than the night, the grim chasm seemed to be holding its breath waiting for one misstep, waiting to swallow up both him and the horse for all eternity.

Routed by their unexpected approach, a large hare leaped from the bracken and bounded criss-cross down the path before them. Branoc's mount reared in fright, bucking and teetering precariously on the narrow ledge.

Ill-mannered and nervous, the beast would not turn nor would it go forward, and although the furry little creature that had caused the distress was long gone, the frightened horse worked itself into a frenzy.

Branoc slid to the ground intent on leading the animal to safety. Positioned between the horse and the rocky wall he tried to inch forward, but the powerful destrier sidestepped and pinned him against the rugged embankment. Jagged stone bit into Branoc's side, and his ribs felt crushed. His head slammed backward against the rocks almost knocking him senseless. He couldn't breathe, and the darkness that now threatened his world seemed to come from within.

Losing his footing, he slipped beneath the pounding hoofs and thrashing legs of the terrified warhorse, and a new barrage of pain shot through his body as he crawled and rolled from side to side. Then the battering ceased and, for a long bone-chilling moment, a pitiful neighing rang out. It ended abruptly, followed by the sound of cascading rock. Grim silence followed.

The poor beast must have fallen over the edge.

Branoc struggled to sit upright.

Then he waved his hand in front of his face but saw nothing.

He looked toward the sky, seeking the familiar pattern of the stars, but there was no celestial comfort to be found.

God help him; he was blind.

Chapter 16
*Bamburgh Castle*

"Then we shall search in a new direction," Leofric ordered. "Olaf, assemble more men and fresh horses. We leave immediately."

The early morning fog swirled around Tanzie's ankles and cold dark fear swirled through her mind as she waited near the stable door for an opportunity to speak with Leofric. Branoc remained missing, and the castle was fraught with tall tales regarding his disappearance. She stifled a sob. The last words she had spoken to him had been words of anger, and now guilt rivaled her sorrow as she reviewed the argument repeatedly. So trivial in retrospect. So meaningless in the true scheme of things.

Leofric glanced up, caught sight of her and strode in her direction.

As he drew near, she opened her mouth to speak, but her words were drowned out by the hoof beats of an approaching horse. Was it Branoc, or someone who brought word of him?

She turned to watch as the riderless, gray stallion tore past her and danced to a halt in front of the watering trough. Lathered and sweat streaked, the nervous animal crab-stepped sideways, when one of the men reached out to grip his bridle.

Tanzie's apprehension doubled. She rubbed her hands to warm them, but they were not nearly as cold as the dread that filled her heart. "Leofric is that Branoc's mount?"

Cradling her elbow, Leofric led her away from the stable. "Lady Martanzia, what are you doing here?" The expression on his face gave her little comfort.

She dug in her heels, and jerked free of his grip. "Answer me," she demanded. "Is that his horse?"

Leofric hesitated. "Yes," he finally confirmed. "I would have wished to spare you that revelation. It does not inspire optimism."

"Then he is out there alone and on foot?" A huge weight was added to the burden of worry she already carried. "Oh Leofric. You must find him, you must."

"I swear upon all that is holy, that I will. We depart shortly to begin the search anew."

She reached for his arm seeking human warmth as well as solid support. "But what happened to him Leofric? Where can he be?"

"No one knows. Last evening he willingly left the castle, declaring he went only for a short ride. He has often done so before. But this time..."

Lifting her arm, she buried her face in the sleeve of her tunic and tried to hide the tears she could not stop.

Taking her hand Leofric urged her arm back to her side. "Do not lose hope," he said gently. "I will notify you as soon as something has been discovered."

"Thank you. He has faith in you and so do I."

While she did not doubt Leofric's loyalty or determination, the task before him was great. "It would be a tremendous boon if we knew which direction he had taken," she said, giving voice to the obvious.

"Search for him in the west, northwest. He cannot see the trail upon which to return."

Tanzie and Leofric jerked to attention at the unexpected voice.

It was Morcar. His approach had been silent as a cat's.

"What do you know of this old man?" Leofric

asked harshly. His eyes turned dangerous as he glared at the conjurer. "If you have caused Valtaigne to suffer, sorcerer or not, you shall bear the consequences."

Morcar raised a brow as if amused by the threat. "You are brave indeed and a true friend to Master Branoc. But I am part of the answer not the problem. He takes refuge near free running water. If you reach him quickly he will live."

"Leofric," Tanzie begged, "listen to Morcar's counsel. It may be Branoc's only chance."

"Tis the direction we were to try next anyway," Leofric conceded. "We shall go northwest." He cast another scowl at the sorcerer then joined the search party waiting in the outer bailey.

"You are sure he is alive?" she asked when they were alone. "And that he will return to us?"

"He will live," the old Druid repeated.

But what if Morcar were wrong? What if Branoc lay dying, never to know that he was all that stood between her and a world she no longer cared to face alone.

Covering her ears with her hands, Tanzie tried to quiet her thoughts. Of late, the world around her seemed to buzz and hum with a pulsing rhythm. It unsettled her. And now her concern for Branoc's safety added to these sensations, her emotions dangerously close to being out of control.

"What is happening?" She wrung her hands. "There is a quickening all about. It whispers on the wind and sings through the trees."

"Do not fear it little one," Morcar comforted and put his arm around her shoulder. "All is as it should be. The land remembers and the time draws nigh."

****

Branoc awakened with a start. Where was he? What had happened?

Sunlight warmed his face and assured him that

it was daytime, but he could not see the brightness. He reached out with both hands groping the empty air and a hot sick feeling jolted through his body and mind. It hadn't been a nightmare—he was blind.

With a grimace, he sat up. Every bone and muscle in his body cried out in agonizing response to his movements. It felt as if a horse had trampled him and if memory served, one had.

He took a deep breath and instantly regretted the action. Pain shot through his ribs. Nausea and dizziness passed over him in waves, and he feared he might lose consciousness again. Hunched forward he braced his sides with his arms and fought for air.

As the misery in his chest subsided, the agony pounding in his brain increased. Gingerly he touched his face. Save for the cut on his cheek there were no wounds near his eyes. The damning blindness and misery must be from a blow to the head. Hopefully the condition would soon right itself, for without sight he was at the mercy of all he encountered...man, animal or element.

Assessing the rest of his injuries, he discovered a deep wound on his thigh. He could fit two fingers in the gash but the congealed mass that covered it indicated the blood had already clotted. He tore a piece of cloth from his under tunic and tied it into place over the wound to protect the area from dirt and further injury. Then as he leaned back on one elbow to catch his breath something stirred in the brush.

Muscles tensed he wrapped his fingers around the hilt of his sword. An eternity seemed to pass as he strained to hear what he could not see. Gut feeling told him it was an animal. When he had proper vision Branoc feared no man or creature on earth, but as he blindly lay waiting to be pounced upon, his heart was in his throat, and he was harangued by visions of sharp claws and wicked teeth.

The leaves rustled and branches snapped. The beast was nearly upon him. A snuffling sound and a discontented growl marked the intruder as a badger. Not quite the hoary creature he had envisaged. Feeling sheepish, he relaxed and slid the partially drawn sword back into its sheath. The slight movement was enough to alert the animal, and it lumbered off into the gorse. With a shudder he tried not to think what would happen if he crossed paths with a wolf or a wild boar.

What now? He must rely upon his warrior's instinct. Leofric was sure to be searching for him. His rescue would be forthcoming. But in this offshoot of the trail, he could easily be missed. The first thing he must do was backtrack to a more accessible area.

Assuming it was morning Branoc altered his position until he felt the warmth of the sun upon his shoulders. As he crawled westward on his hands and knees, his great sword dragged in the dirt beside him, and his cloak conspired to tangle his movements. How pitiful it felt to be reduced to such a posture.

Keeping to the right side of the trail, he felt his way along the cliff and experienced a moment of pity for the horse that had gone over the side. Then he thought of Strong Oak, and prayed the animal was safe. Branoc had helped to foal that stallion. Had watched him gambol through spring meadows and grow into an admirable steed. It was his fault that Strong Oak had been put in a position of peril, and it would be his fault should the animal come to harm. He shouldn't have ridden so far from the castle.

Every few yards he halted to listen to the sounds beyond his own ragged breathing. Rathgar and his men were sure to be searching for him as well. He could ill afford to clash with them again.

The gurgle of a quick flowing stream up ahead

caught his attention. He held his throbbing head in his hands and forced himself to concentrate. Slowly and painfully, a murky recollection surfaced. He remembered crossing a small brook last night. He was heading in the right direction.

He licked his dry lips and inched his way toward the enticing sound. Before long, he felt the dampness in the earth upon which he crawled and the pebbles that lined the creek bed. Carefully he eased his way forward and the cool water lapped over his fingers.

After quenching his thirst, he washed his face, arms, and hands, and using a strip of cloth from his cloak, he soaked the fabric in the icy stream and held the pad to the large goose egg on the back of his head. He repeated the application until the swelling went down and the pain subsided from mind crushing to simply unbearable.

A hawk screeched overhead, alerting him to the vulnerability of his position. He should move further upstream away from the ford.

Stumbling over jagged stones and tangled heaps of driftwood, he half-walked and half-crawled along the edge of the water. He had never felt so at odds with nature. Tree branches tore at his clothes and grabbed at his hair. The forested area seemed alive with unfriendly hands hindering his every move, and the breeze that fluttered through the trees sounded like the taunting laughs of a paying crowd.

Blindly he swatted at an insect that bit his cheek. In the process, he scratched the back of his hand on the tendril of a nearby thorn bush. He lurched forward, crashed into a large downed tree and dropped to the ground beside it. Disheartened and exhausted he lay where he fell for a moment, before seeking shelter along the length of the gnarled trunk.

Like a wounded animal, he burrowed into the soft grass and flaky layers of dry rotted wood that accumulated along the bark covered bastion. Stretching out on his side, he reached down and checked his thigh. Warm, sticky wetness met his touch. Re-enforcing the compress with another piece of cloth, he tightened the strip that held it in place.

He dragged leaves and brush over his body and closed his eyes. He needed to rest just for a short while. He was so tired.

**** 

The shrill whinny of a horse jerked him back to full attention, and the hair at the nape of his neck bristled.

Several men approached on horseback, but were they friend or foe? Should he hunker down lower or stand up and call for help? What if it was Leofric?

The jingle of horse trappings and the clink of light armor mingled with the scrunch of leather as some of the men dismounted. A swishing sound whispered all around him. They were searching the tall grass.

"There be nothin' doon this a way."

Branoc jumped. The sound of the man's voice was within spitting distance, and his Scottish burr suggested he belonged to Rathgar's patrol.

He gripped the hilt of his short sword and pressed back into the dirt. Spiders and grubs wriggled on his forearms and neck and seemingly on every inch of his exposed flesh. The act of remaining motionless became a torture. A bead of sweat ran down his side adding to the crawly sensation. It felt as if his entire body teemed with writhing creeping bugs.

A pointy knot in the tree dug into his back, and a leaf from a nearby reed alternately stabbed and tickled his nose. Soon the muscles in his thighs and calves began to cramp with the strain of lying so still.

A branch snapped on his left, then his right.

They were all around him. Did they close in upon him even now? He squinted shut his useless eyes and took a slow deep breath. Blindness stripped a man of reason as well as sight. He did not know his enemies' location, yet he had a dreadful urge to stand and fight. The cry to battle clawed for release at the back of his throat, and he wished to lash out wildly at everything, anything. It was all he could do to remain unmoving.

Gradually the sounds died away.

He remained still, a while longer, to be sure they were indeed gone, then shoved the underbrush from atop his body and gulped in great breaths of fresh cool air. Sitting up he eased his cramped muscles and swatted away the bugs and mealy-worms. As he debated on whether to stay put or move on, the decision was rendered moot, and he sensed he was not alone.

As he freed his dagger, someone grabbed his wrists. They wrenched his arms wide and pushed him backward, and the full weight of a man crushed him painfully to the ground.

"Call St. Cuthbert's honor, and I will set you free."

It was Leofric, bidding him give-in as when they were children. The solace of those words brought a lump to Branoc's throat. "St Cuthbert's," he said in a hoarse whisper as the dagger slipped from his hand and he sagged back against the dirt.

Leofric rolled to the side. "Sorry to accost you so, but you acted as if you could not see me and you did grasp your knife most seriously. I feared you would do me harm before you knew who I was."

Leofric eased Branoc upright. "What has happened to your sight and for that matter the rest of you?"

"I had a slight riding accident," Branoc said dryly, "during the course of which I struck my head and can no longer see, though the pain is much less now. How goes your day my friend?"

He heard Leofric's snort of laughter and felt his hand upon his shoulder. "At least your humor has survived, unscathed, and once we have you back at Bamburgh we shall see to the parts of you that were less fortunate."

"Have you seen Strong Oak?" Branoc asked.

"Yes. He is safe. He returned to the stables this morning. The sight of him without a rider and in a panic did not bolster our spirits. I cannot believe he would cause you such injury and then abandon you."

"Twas not Strong Oak that I rode when the fall occurred," he explained. "The horse belonged to Rathgar. He is here, Leofric, along the northern boundary. He devises plans for death and destruction that leap beyond the imagination. Did you not see him or his band of men just now?"

"We saw no one as we approached. Why would Rathgar wander these woods?"

"'Tis a long story. I will tell you the details on the way back to the castle. How many men are with you?"

"Only four. We split up into small groups to cover more ground in our search. You were well hidden. I would not have seen you had not the old Druid advised me to search near the water."

"Morcar? Well I am not truly surprised," Branoc said. "The enchanter always seems near at hand when trouble is afoot. And though I appreciate aid from any quarter, I am concerned that the sorcerer's assistance is ultimately good only for the sorcerer."

Leofric grunted in agreement and helped Branoc to his feet.

"All is well at Bamburgh?" Branoc asked, as a vision of Martanzia crowded out his other thoughts.

"Yes. Is there cause to worry otherwise?"

"If Rathgar has his way there will be."

Branoc swayed to one side then fought to remain upright. "Thank you for coming for me, Leofric." His voice was thick with emotion.

"It was for selfish reasons," Leofric jibed, "you are the only one who lets me win at chess."

Branoc allowed his comrade to lead him through the bracken. Each step was a jarring misery that sent pain shooting through his body in a hundred different directions. His head ached incessantly and nausea again gripped his stomach. Only with help was he able to haul himself into the saddle.

Leofric mounted to ride double at his back.

In the middle of explaining Rathgar's intentions, Branoc fell silent and slumped back against his friend. He was too tired to speak, and secure in the knowledge that Leofric would see him safely back to Bamburgh, he surrendered to the cold oblivion he had fought against all morning.

****

Tanzie hurried to Branoc's room.

He was back and he was alive. But Holy Savior he was blind. Why did good news always arrive cloaked in bad?

At his chamber door, she hesitated. The thought of seeing Branoc incapacitated made her afraid. She did not know if she had the courage to face what waited beyond the portal.

Footsteps echoed in the hall.

She glanced over her shoulder, grateful it was Morcar who strode in her direction. He toted a small coffer of medicines under one arm, and in his other hand, he carried an ancient vessel containing sacred water.

"We must not delay," he said, "Sir Branoc has great need of our assistance. Think only of him and you shall persevere with good grace and dignity," he added, as if sensing her hesitation. Then the old Druid stepped around her and entered the room.

She followed on his heels, but nothing could have prepared her for what she saw. Her breath caught in her throat, and she gasped in alarm. Branoc appeared worse than she had imagined. His color was much too pale—like a morning sky in winter, and the covers moved imperceptibly so shallow did he breathe. A red slash upon his cheek stood out in livid contrast to his pallor, and as she forced herself to his bedside, she wondered what other wounds he suffered.

As a warrior, Branoc, had always seemed so invincible, his strength and energy limitless. To see the mortal side of him and to know that he could be taken from her by the whim of fortune or the will of God, struck her with the fierceness of a physical blow.

She pressed her fingers to his wrist and felt for the life sign. "Morcar," she beckoned, "you must do something quickly his pulse is weak and much too slow."

"An injury to the head is most likely the cause," the old Druid said taking charge. "We must examine him thoroughly before beginning any treatments."

Morcar set aside his curatives and ordered clean linen to be brought to the chamber. Then he dismissed everyone from the room save for Tanzie. Even Leofric left quietly not arguing with the authority in the sorcerer's voice.

Branoc's torn leather hauberk lay in a heap on the floor bedside the bed. His boots, hose and braises, kept it company.

"Remove the remainder of his clothing," Morcar instructed as he drew back the covers. "And bathe his wounds with the water touched by the blue stones."

Branoc wore only his linen shirt, the sleeves of which were ripped to shreds from the sharp hoofs that had caused his injuries. Blood had leaked through the fabric in many areas, and caked on and hardened, the life giving fluid now melded the cloth to the oozing scrapes and deep slashes. Using a sharp knife, she cut away the shirt leaving the bits behind that would need to be soaked free from his many wounds.

Her gaze traveled the length of his naked body. Even bloodied and bruised he was magnificent. Her cheeks burned, and she covered his hips with a small towel.

She added aloe and betony to a bowl of precious Salisbury rainwater, and then gently and thoroughly cleansed every battle-scared inch of him. A loving tenderness of a special nature guided her hands, and a caring deep and pure sustained her as she saturated the scraps of cloth still adhered to his flesh. He never made a sound as she peeled away the last of the small pieces.

Morcar oversaw her efforts as she stitched the laceration on Branoc's thigh. She had helped her mother do this before, but as the needle pierced the flesh of one close to her heart, it set her hand to shaking and her mind to worrying. Intensified by her ministrations fresh blood flowed from the gash. It hindered her work and frightened her, but she remembered there was less chance of infection if a wound bled freely. Once properly stitched they would bind the site and restrict the flow.

"An admirable job," Morcar praised, as she finished the last stitch and then applied a poultice of cobwebs and tree moss. "We will burn the incense while he rests, and you must entreat him to take water and nourishment. Give the other remedies as I have instructed. He will live," Morcar reassured her again.

"But will he see?" she questioned. No one took kindly to a world of darkness. But how much worse would it be for a warrior such as Branoc?

"If his faith is strong enough."

"His faith in what?" she asked, unsure of the old Druid's meaning.

"His faith in you," Morcar said and left the room.

Tanzie eased down onto the chair at Branoc's bedside. She was willing to sit vigil night and day for as long as it might take to nurse him back to health. But if his recovery depended upon his faith in her, he would have to heal himself.

She reached for his wrist and felt his pulse. The beat came more quickly and was stronger, and Branoc seemed less troubled and restless. Holding a wet cloth to his lips, she was encouraged that he responded to the moisture. As he licked at the water, his tongue touched her fingers.

Tanzie lightly traced the edge of his lips with the tip of the cloth.

He angled his head in her direction.

Hope flickered into life, and she willed him to return to consciousness, but the weakness that beset his body defied her appeal even as it mocked the strength locked within his form.

Setting the cloth aside, she stood and tucked the covers more closely about him. She smoothed the damp hair away from his brow and glided the back of her fingers along the line of his jaw.

The deep cut on his cheek would leave a scar, marring the near unscathed face she thought so handsome. His other new injuries would have to fight for a place of honor amongst the already healed wounds she had seen while bathing him. He carried many painful badges of courage.

Sitting again at his side, she cradled his large hand in hers and softly stroked the back of it. Had Branoc ever known gentleness? A warrior's lot was often a hard one, filled only with cruel realities.

What had his life been like thus far? She glanced around and studied his place of refuge. The chamber was quite similar to her own but larger. The huge bed dwarfed one side of the room while trunks and coffers of varying size cluttered the floor near the far wall. The table held books and documents.

Even at his leisure he worked.

Against the wall by the door, his gray shield stood in readiness. She stared at the design it bore. How did a man come to choose a black dragon as his symbol? Or had the beast chosen him?

Narrowing her gaze, she caught sight of something bright and colorful tied to a ring on the rim of the shield. Gaining her feet, she crossed the room. Did Branoc carry a ribbon or scarf from some fair damsel? Stepping nearer she discovered the cloth was a small tattered piece of embroidery. The fabric was very old and faded, and the design woven within was that of a flower. A rose to be exact.

The dragon and the rose, a scaly fright of immutable strength tempered by the simple beauty of a flower. The fine needlework must be important to Branoc. A man did not frivolously attach an item to the shield that protected his life and proclaimed his reputation.

An ember popped in the nearby hearth, breaking in upon her thoughts. The embroidery slipped through her fingers, and she turned to stir the fire and add a log. The wood burned quickly in this drafty room and very little stood in readiness.

Hurrying to the door she gained the attention of the young serving boy who waited in attendance. Speaking in Saxon, the lad's tongue, she requested more firewood.

Returning to Branoc's side, she was surprised to find him awake his eyes open and staring, his mouth set in a grim line.

"Tis I Martanzia," she said, to let him know who approached.

"Where am I?" he demanded.

"In your bed chamber at Bamburgh."

"Leave me," he ordered his words frosted with ire.

She was taken aback by his request and the tone of his voice. "I am sorry that our last meeting ended in harsh words," she quickly apologized, thinking this the reason for his coldness and anger.

"Your words affect me neither one way nor another. 'Tis the language in which you speak them that interests me."

"I do not understand," she said. He made no response. She wanted to pursue the point but thought the better of it. "Regaining your sight is all that matters now," she added quietly.

"Yes 'tis quite a disadvantage to be without clear vision but my hearing does not fail me. Bring me Leofric. I will have someone trustworthy at my side."

"But you are safe now," she said again, not understanding his agitation.

"Safe? I would prefer Leofric." The weight of his words trampled her spirit.

"But Morcar bid me watch over you," she argued. "He has instructed me in what to look for and what medicine to give you."

"I need someone to care for me whose choices are clear," he said. "I need no Saxon-speaking wench tending me."

So that was it. He had overheard her conversation with the boy. "What are you suggesting?" she protested. "I know Saxon by chance, 'twas my mother's tongue, and I think only of what is best for you. Here take the potion that Morcar left. It is in the cup that I press to your hand."

Though she suspected Branoc must be frightened by his blindness, she did not understand why he lashed out at her so cruelly. "Please," she urged, suppressing her frustration, "drink the potion. It will help to remedy your condition."

"Death would also cure me of my ills," he said, roughly pushing her hand away. "What truly does this contain?"

"You think I try to poison you?" she asked in disbelief, her compassion consumed by her anger. "Does madness beset you as well as blindness?"

Branoc was silent. He faced straight ahead and refused to turn his head in her direction.

"I will taste it first," she offered.

"And how will I know that you swallow the same liquid that you so kindly offer to me?"

"Oh blessed Saints above," she said. "If that is how you feel I will fetch Leofric. Your suspicions wound my soul as deeply as any mark you have sustained upon your flesh."

Without waiting for a reply, Tanzie slammed the goblet down upon the side table and stalked toward the door. Branoc's moan stopped her short. She turned back toward the bed. He sat up, hunched forward, and dug his clenched fists into his eyes. The obvious pain he suffer wrenched at her heart, and she quickly returned to his side.

"Branoc what is it?"

"'Tis my eyes. They burn as two hot coals. For all their uselessness they make themselves heartily known."

"Morcar said if the pain affected your eyes as opposed to your head you should take this at once." She attempted to place a cake of crushed herbs in his hand. "It does not taste pleasant," she warned, "but he insisted that you consume it without delay."

Again, Branoc hesitated. His resistance was maddening.

"If I had wished for your demise," she pointed out, in a precise clipped tone, "I could easily have smothered you while you lay here weak as a lamb...or I could have slipped with the needle that I used to sew your flesh. You already bled profusely; one more good cut of the vein would have done you in nicely. Now, I beg of you, take this medicine."

Branoc's hand closed over her wrist. His grip was so painful she almost dropped the herbal packet. Then he seemed to come to a resolution and relaxed his fingers.

Taking advantage of his change of heart, she quickly placed the herbs in his palm and stood ready with the water.

After gagging down the restorative, he flopped back against the pillows seemingly once more completely spent.

Not wishing to annoy him further with her presence she moved toward the door.

"Please," Branoc said, "do not go. Even when I possess all of my faculties trust does not come easily to me. Now I am even more wary."

She hesitated then took a step closer. "I am still here," she reassured.

"You have done little to encourage my faith in you," he said moodily. "You are associated with Rathgar and now I find you speak the language of the conquered. And," he continued in an even more accusing tone, "for all that I have heard regarding your reason for being here, I still believe that you follow a calling you have yet to explain to me. A calling somehow linked to the old Druid."

Overwhelmed by his suspicions Tanzie didn't know what to say. Should she recount to him what little Morcar had revealed to her? Would it help her cause or reassure Branoc to tell him her mother once lived at this castle or that the dragon statue in her room had been carved from the great standing stone that faced the North Sea as if it kept vigil?

"I too play the game of caution," she said, "and unanswered questions do not appeal to me any more than they appeal to you. But please you must believe me when I say that you are the last person I wish to hurt. At this moment, I cannot tell you any more than that. I can only beseech you to have faith in me."

She gently grasped Branoc's hand and held it to her cheek. "You are the one shining hope in my life," she whispered.

Shifting his hand, Branoc caressed her face. Pure happiness engulfed her as his fingertips played across her skin. Then with a start, she fully realized what she had just quietly blurted out. She should not have revealed her feelings, not when Branoc still doubted her so.

But she loved him and that was all that should really matter. For one overwhelming moment Tanzie wished to crawl upon the bed and lay beside Branoc, to comfort him and kiss away his pain and fear, to cradle his body next to hers. She wanted to do so but dared not. It was unfair of her to heap urgent and deep emotions upon Branoc when he was without vision and not thinking properly. There would be time later to bare her soul. She would be reasoning more clearly then too and be better able to shoulder the consequences of her words and actions.

Still cradling his hand, she lowered it to the bedside. "I must tell Morcar that you have awakened."

A scowl erased the expression of tenderness from Branoc's face. He seemed confused or annoyed by her sudden change in attitude. He could not possibly be more bewildered than she.

"Would you still have me summon Leofric?" she asked forcing her voice to a normal pitch.

"Yes," he replied solemnly. Then his lips thinned into a hard line of resolve. "With or without sight," he said, fiercely, "I have men to lead and battle plans to prepare."

Chapter 17
*Yeavering, west of Bamburgh*

Damn his eyes. Valtaigne had the luck of a cat.
Rathgar threw his gauntlets down and stalked about
the dusty ruins. His nemesis had not only escaped,
he had added to the affront by taking his best horse.
He should have hamstrung the blackguard.

He glanced up as the soldier in command of the
last search patrol returned to camp. The man
hurried forward then appeared hesitant. The news
must be bad.

"Any sign of our quarry?"

"No sir. It would seem that he made good his
flight."

"Then waste no more time in the hunt," he
ordered. "Prepare for battle. Valtaigne's escape has
not altered the inevitable. We will still be victorious,
and he shall still meet his final destiny."

Dismissing the soldier, Rathgar wandered about
his chamber while his mind wandered the corridors
of possibilities. His own future would be determined
in the coming days as well and should things go
awry he would surely be charged with treason and
executed. Prince Henry would, of course, disavow
any knowledge of his existence. And although his old
acquaintance, Wat Tirel, was somehow involved in
this twisted plot, the lord of Poix would be lucky to
save himself, let alone offer succor to anyone else.
There would be no help from the house of Clare. But
Rathgar would not fail. He dare not.

"Wiglaf," he thundered. "Wiglaf you useless twit
get thee here."

"Yes, master. Here I am. What needs you master?" Wiglaf scurried through the dilapidated halls of Yeavering, his sparse blond hair flittering around his head like a tarnished halo.

"You indentured idiot, where have you been? You are ever underfoot when naught needs be done, and when you are required you are nowhere to be found."

"Well..I...ah."

"Never mind," Rathgar interrupted. "Pray just listen. We engage in battle within the week. See that my gear is oiled and polished. As usual I shall whet my sword and dagger myself."

"Yes, master." The servant bobbed his head in obedience. "Why do we fight along side the Scots," he dared to ask, "instead of against them?"

"Do not strain yourself worrying about military strategy, Wiglaf. That is my concern. Just see that we are ready to depart before dawn five days hence. Oh," he added nonchalantly, "since no one is to remain behind at the ruins, you will come along as my standard bearer."

Rathgar could not suppress his laughter as he watched the little man's washed out countenance fade to horrified white. "Well get on with something," he chastised, turning toward the table where his shield and war corselet lay. "You are more likely to die of a beating for your stupidity than of any wound accidentally sustained in battle."

Wiglaf moaned. "Why could I not have been sold to a rich widow?" he wailed. "An old lady who wants only to stay at home safe in her keep."

Rathgar's amusement increased as Wiglaf headed for the midden. The thought of being in the thick of it had evidently made the little man ill with urgency. In truth, his plans did not include taking the quaking little mouse past the edge of the weald, but torturing Wiglaf's mind offered such convenient entertainment.

Wiglaf had come to Rathgar by chance, as payment for a debt, and since that day five years ago, the poor beggar had proved to be worth his weight in gold. Rathgar viewed his servant as a sporting dog, useful when needed and ignored the rest of the time. And just like a dog, despite the rough treatment that Rathgar doled out, the little man cared for Rathgar with a fierce and unconditional loyalty.

At first, he had disliked the servant's unusual attention, for he seemed overly affectionate in his manner. But Wiglaf never overstepped the boundaries between their station and nature, and now Rathgar was accustomed to the man's doting ways. Now he relied upon being catered to with such enthusiasm.

Their relationship could not be called a friendship, but Wiglaf was a faithful companion and they had endured much together. And he was a distraction against the loneliness that often beset Rathgar. The loneliness that had followed him since childhood.

Turning his attention to his field armor, he inspected every ring on his hauberk, assessing the tempered metal and supple leather for weakness and wear. As he finished testing the grip of his shield, Wiglaf scurried back into the area.

"Master?"

"What is it now?"

"You said earlier that you wished your hair cut. Would this be a suitable time?"

"There is no suitable time for your hacking away at ones scalp, but do so if you must. You may as well shave me too, so the blood letting is done all at once."

Rathgar sat down for his grooming. He closed his eyes and realized how tired he was. Fulfilling one's self-proclaimed destiny could be exhausting work. But the rewards would be worth the effort, and other than Branoc's escape things appeared to be shaping up nicely.

The Scottish troops were all assembled. Half were trained soldiers, the others mercenaries. The Saxon rebels were nearly all accounted for and surprisingly well outfitted. They waited only for word that Prince Henry, the would-be king, was nearing the coast of England, poised for the attack. Timing is what would be important. As Prince Henry's men came ashore in the south, Rathgar would create the turmoil he had been instructed to unleash in the north. He knew the diversion was merely an aside, and that a far more devious plot to overthrow king William Rufus was afoot, but it was wise not to be too closely involved in a feud between brothers. There would be time later to ingratiate himself into Henry's inner circle, much later, after the final outcome was revealed and he knew which way the wind blew.

"God's teeth," he swore as Wiglaf nicked his neck with the blade. He slapped the man's hand away wondering why he endured this accursed Norman custom. Perhaps he should just let his beard and hair grow long like the Saxons.

"Be careful you fool," he shouted. "I will be weak as a man after leeching if you keep at me thus."

As footsteps sounded, Rathgar glanced up. Canty McPherson the leader of the Scots sauntered his way. The towering redheaded man cut an imposing figure.

"Rathgar," he began, without waiting to be recognized, "my men are restless. They demand to know the battle plan—now. They do not wish to wait for the rest of your stragglers to join us."

He stared up at the man. How surprised Canty would be if he knew the real reason for the delay.

Rathgar grabbed the towel out of Wiglaf's hand. "Leave us," he ordered, as he sat up and wiped the shorn hair from his shoulders. Irritably he pressed the cloth to his neck, staunching the blood that still oozed from the fresh wound. Under the guise of activity, he organized his thoughts. It was a complicated affair working both sides of the standard.

"I will give you a quick dissertation on the matter," he conceded, and stood to face the big Scotsman. "But the details will follow only after all are assembled.

"We will approach Bamburgh from the northwest, coming straight out of the forest. A swift overwhelming attack would best suit our needs, but if the repairs on the west wall have been completed the castle will be near impregnable. Then we must take it by siege."

"But that could take months," Canty complained, "the men must return home soon for the last harvest."

"It will take but a few days at the most. The keep is without fresh water, and the stored supply has been fouled with inheritance powder. When the dead are piled like faggots of wood in the bailey, the living will beg to come out."

A smile crept across Canty McPherson's face. "Arsenic poison! You are without boundary in your wickedness, Rathgar. I am glad we are on the same side. How soon after we are in possession of the stronghold before the bounty is dispersed and my men can head back to the north?"

"It should take but another day after we breech the walls. All of Valtaigne's men must be killed," Rathgar added. "There is to be no quarter except for the girl. She must be protected at all costs. If harm befalls her," he warned and took a step closer to Canty, "there will be hell to pay and I will collect it."

"What if the girl drinks the poison?"

"A risk of course," Rathgar agreed. "But I've ensured that a few barrels of clean water have been stored in her room. Being too valorous to take water from the mouths of thirsty peasants, she will no doubt use only that."

"How does all this aid your purpose Rathgar?"

"My purpose is my concern. Just follow orders and you will receive the spoils of war and the gold that was promised. I only want the girl. 'Tis quite simple really."

"It is always quite simple until it becomes complicated," Canty said testily. "Do not cross me on this Rathgar or you shall lie moldering beside Valtaigne."

"You have my word," Rathgar pledged. "You shall receive your just rewards."

A contented glow came to the greedy man's eyes before he turned and walked away. Rathgar intended Canty McPherson and several other Scots to die after Bamburgh had been taken. It would enhance the authenticity of the fight and support the assumption that the Scots had collaborated with Valtaigne. It would also cut down on witnesses.

Everyone had to make sacrifices for the good of the whole. Some, like Canty, were destined to sacrifice more than others.

Deciding to forego the shaving of his beard, Rathgar threw down the towel, grabbed up his sword and shield, and made ready to visit the practice field. It had been several days since he had vigorously trained. He could not afford to become complacent with the skills that insured his survival.

Besides, to fight was his nature as well as his occupation. He loved the feeling of power that came with the physical or mental conquering of an opponent. Winning was what mattered most. But there was one man who could claim to be his better, and Rathgar had lived with that disgrace long enough. Soon he would have his revenge on Branoc and the hand of the only woman he had ever wanted.

Lost in thought he fastened his gauntlets. Why, he wondered, had Martanzia not accepted his offer of marriage? Her refusal had wounded him more deeply than he would admit to any living soul. Perhaps in time, a bond could have formed between them, but she would not even afford him a chance.

Although it came as a shock, he realized in his own way he truly did love the girl. Martanzia was the only fair thing in his life; the only noble purpose to which he had ever aspired. He had not lived a Christian life. He took what he wanted with no remorse, no guilt, no concern for others. At times, it worried him to think that he would have to someday answer to God for his deeds but that was why he needed Martanzia. She was not only necessary for his future, she must save him from his past. She was his redemption. Hopefully, once Bamburgh fell, the world would view him as a hero, and Valtaigne would be remembered as a traitor. Then Martanzia would change her mind and come to him eagerly enough.

Warming to his cleverness, he smiled and recalled the lies he had fed Valtaigne about sleeping with Martanzia. In this busy world of warring and politics, one must stop along the way and savor such recollections.

Yes, the telling of those tales had given him great pleasure. He hoped Branoc had suffered an equal measure of pain at the hearing of them.

As thoughts of anticipated victory filled his mind, he wondered when the deadly surprise so ingeniously conceived and hidden would take its toll.

"Wiglaf," he called.

The servant hurried forward swiping at his watery eyes with the sleeve of his tunic. "Yes, master. I am here."

"Tell me once again," Rathgar ordered, "the manner in which you distributed the white powder at the castle."

Chapter 18

"Holy Mother of God," Leofric repeated for the third time, as Branoc finished fleshing out the details of what they were about to face in battle. "Rathgar has gone beyond all reason. He seeks to ruin the entire North Country for the sake of a personal vendetta?"

"At the very least," Branoc said. "He must be stopped. This stubborn land has found a place in my heart and I would see it survive. Besides," he added, "the people living here have suffered enough. We can at least attempt to uphold our honor by protecting what we have conquered."

"Once again," Leofric pointed out, "you fight for the underdog. The Dragon of Normandy, champion of the common man and his common causes. Rathgar knows how you think and will use this to his advantage."

"Yes," Branoc agreed. "Then we shall both know what to expect." He supposed nothing could change what was preordained. But there was one concern that must be addressed, one thing he must plan for. "Promise me this, should the worst come to pass you will see to the girl."

"Your vision will return and you shall look after her yourself."

Branoc didn't respond. He hadn't been referring to his blindness but rather to his death. As the true meaning of his words became clear, he heard Leofric's sharp intake of breath.

"You plan to join the men in battle," Leofric said, his voice incredulous.

"I am their leader. There is no other way."

"You are blind, no one expects this of you."

"I expect it of myself," Branoc replied. "Now give me your word that you will see to her," he repeated.

"Aye 'tis a promise," Leofric reassured. "But I still think you mad. You will be more of a hindrance than an asset on the field."

"Thank you for serving up your honest opinion with no treacle or tears. Now help me to stand. This lying abed only makes me worse. I become weaker the longer I am down."

With Leofric's help, Branoc gained his feet, and resisting the urge to wave his hands out in front of his face, he forced his aching body forward one agonizing step at a time. "If the truth be known," he confided, "I see a tiny glimmer of light. But 'tis the smallest of improvements and it seems to come and go on a whim of its own. I cannot abide this helplessness much longer," he added, not masking his frustration.

"Small progress is better than none," Leofric encouraged. "What did Martanzia say about your improvement?"

"I have not told the girl," he admitted. "She will only give me another dose of the noxious brew she so cheerfully whips up with the old Druid."

"Does she dote upon you then?" Leofric asked, as he continued to guide Branoc in his unsteady ambling about the room.

"Too much I fear. I am unsettled when she hovers about, yet I dislike even more the feeling of loneliness when she is not at my side."

"Whether you wish it or not," Leofric said, "you are in the throes of it my friend. Have you determined where her allegiance lies?"

"No, and some days I do not even care. That is what frightens me the most. Her presence blinds my logic more completely than this injury blinds my eyes. I cherish and rue her nearness all at the same time. Never before has my heart been so forlorn nor my reason so clouded."

He took a deep breath and forced himself to stand a little straighter. "And you may wipe that crooked grin from your face," he said with annoyance. "I need not two eyes that see clearly to tell me what expression you wear."

"I laugh with you not at you. Did you think to live your entire lifetime without finally meeting your match?"

"No. I just did not expect to find someone so extraordinary in the midst of such chaos.

King William resides at Winchester until after Lammas," he added, as the seriousness of their plight once more gripped his thoughts. "But the rider we have sent to alert him of our circumstances will not reach him in time to be of any help to us.

"I realize that," Leofric acknowledged as they turned to make a third pass across the room. "That is the reason we rally the villagers. Most show unusual enthusiasm in coming to our aid, not only because they fear the Scots, but I believe in large part it is due to your honesty and lenient treatment. With their support our chances should be fair."

"Fair perhaps but not good. The blood of the pure will be shed before this is over. I regret that most of all. But Rathgar will not settle for personal combat. He denied my challenge at his camp and he leaves no other recourse." Branoc gripped his friend's arm more tightly. "What have I done, Leofric, that Rathgar should bear me such hatred?"

"You have done nothing. The offenses are in his mind, nurtured by years of bitterness. Now only he has the power to reclaim his soul."

"So it is with each of us I suppose. Yet being held accountable for one's own salvation as well as one's own happiness does not make the furrow any easier to plow."

"No but at least one does not have to look far for the responsible party. What think you Rathgar's tactics will be?"

"I anticipate that he will stay hidden throughout the conflict," Branoc said, "controlling events from afar. When he has what he wants, he will blame the attack on the Scots and Saxons. Then according to what he divulged at Yeavering, I shall be found dead having met my demise in some disgraceful attempt at saving myself at the sacrifice of the castle and the land."

"And," Leofric put in, "true to form, Rathgar will claim to have come along just in time to see all but save none."

"Yes most likely. But there is one thing I cannot reason. Rathgar must know that the west wall is near repaired, thus making us impervious to attack. And though Malvoison stands ready for his use, he possesses neither the time nor the patience necessary for a long drawn-out siege. He has some plan in mind to force us to battle or surrender. A plan, yet to be revealed."

"You had best worry over this puzzlement in bed," Leofric advised. "The wound on your leg begins to seep a bit."

Leofric settled him back against the pillows, and he was glad for the excuse to rest. If just this small amount of effort tired him, how could he lead an army to battle?

"Be at ease," Leofric said, as if noticing the weariness that consumed Branoc. "Healing takes its own time and its own course." Leofric gripped his arm in a show of camaraderie. "I will report back to you later."

Blindly Branoc reached out to return the reassuring pressure. "I have learned one thing through this ordeal. True friendship is the greatest bounty that God put on this earth."

"Then we are both rich men," Leofric said and took his leave.

Alone with his thoughts, Branoc tried to think of all the good things in his life for which he should be thankful. The list seemed absurdly short at present. Passing his hand back and forth before his eyes, he tried to focus upon his fingers. An illusive shadow was all that he saw. Healing indeed took time but his was running out.

A timid knock sounded upon his door. "Enter," he called and quickly lowered his arm.

Delicate footsteps whispered toward him.

"Back so soon to check upon me, lady?"

"How did you know it was me?" Martanzia asked suspiciously.

"The sweet smell of roses announced you," he replied. A sudden urge to tell her of his love for the briar rose streaked through him, but he feared she would think ill of a man who nurtured such delicate thoughts.

"You seem stronger," she said brightly. He marveled that she could muster such enthusiasm in the face of how he must appear. "I have brought your food tonight, and stand ready to aid you in eating it," she continued. "'Tis stew, I believe, highly seasoned and lightly poisoned. Just the way you like it."

He choked back the bark of laughter sparked by her sarcasm. "Then by all means, do not delay in serving it up."

Seeing her as if through a haze, he watched as she put the tray aside and arrange the items neatly upon it. He blinked several times, his vision had improved yet another slight measure, enough for him to see her form, enough to almost make out her features.

"Do you wish me to feed you or would you like to try for yourself?"

Branoc had relied upon no one other than himself since the day he had earned his spurs, and it had been humbling enough to have Leofric helping him these last few days. He was loath to display his vulnerability in front of a woman as independence was often a man's only defense against a female.

"I am not one to be waited upon," he said gruffly.

Sitting straighter, he stretched out his legs and remained motionless as she placed the tray on his lap. He reached out, then quickly snatched back his hand as it came into contact with the hot food. "Damn," he muttered and grudgingly submitted to her as she wiped off his fingers. Irritated, he waved her away and fumbled about trying to find a dagger. As he nearly upset the tray, she grabbed both his hands stilling their futile movements.

"You suffer from enough wounds already," she said, her words tinged with humor. In a blur, he saw her remove the knife from the tray. "Perhaps if I tear the bread and set the food upon it, you could manage the pieces by hand."

"Yes...all right." As she readied the food, he shifted trying to make himself more comfortable, and a pain shot through his ribs and thigh. He could not suppress the groan that escaped his lips.

"Do you need something for pain?"

"No. Truly I am much better." His stomach churned at the thought of downing another herbal cure. "Save your skills for what is to come," he added through clenched teeth as he adjusted his position again.

"Yes even at best it will be terrible," she said distractedly as if her mind were far away.

"How do you know this?"

Only he and Leofric knew the scope of the battle about to be fought. Had she listened at the door, or did she have some prior knowledge of Rathgar's plans?

"Morcar told me. He knew of the trouble even before you returned to us. Of course he has given me no details," she hastened to add. "But he sees the future better than I can remember my past. At times it must be a burden for him to know what is to be."

There was sympathy in her voice. How close had she become with the old man? Their alliance brought concerns of another nature. He feared she could be hurt or led astray by following the sorcerer's schemes and prophecies. Of course, she could also be hurt because of his selfishness in holding her here. He had never written to William about her being sent to stand as hostage in place of her cousin Landow.

At first, he had refrained, because he had wanted to be sure of her intent and he had feared the king's reaction. Later he had delayed, because the idea that she might disappear from his life had seemed too dismal a prospect to bear. Now it was too late. He could not spare the men to escort her to the king, and a letter written at this time would be pointless.

"I have a confession to make." Branoc, forced the words out before he could change his mind. "I never wrote to William about your being here." He waited for her explosion of anger but none came.

"Yes, I suspected as much," she said with surprising calm. "It does not matter. I could not leave Bamburgh now even if I wanted to, at least not with a clear conscience."

"Why would you not leave if given the chance?"

"Because, as you are so fond of pointing out, I have a purpose here just like you."

Another vague revelation.

"Purpose wears many a surcoat. As commander of this outpost I have the right to demand an explanation of your last statement." He set the food he held back on the tray and waited for her reply.

"You have a right to demand such," she agreed, "and I have the right to refuse your demand. We fight for the same cause. Is that not reassurance enough for you?

"Perhaps for now," he conceded. "But that does not change your circumstance. Remaining here puts you in danger. If I had written the letter you would be safely away from Northumbria and Rathgar's schemes."

"You have already saved me from Rathgar, and as for other danger I seem to have been born to it." Her voice sounded wry, but he did not think she found the situation amusing. Over the short time he had known Martanzia she seemed to have blossomed from budding girlhood to flowering womanhood. She retained the wild spirit he had first admired in her countenance, but it now seemed tempered with patience. A virtue he was lacking of late.

She struck a flint to light a taper, and as the tiny flame sprang to life, he involuntarily squinted and drew back.

"You can see," she cried, the disbelief obvious in her voice. "Why did you not tell me?"

"Do not over-excite yourself lady. I can see but a little, and I did not inform you because I do not wish any more treatments tonight."

"But it may be the treatments that are making you better. Please take the next cure. Morcar said it should be given as soon as you gained any sight at all. I am to mix this powder with water or ale and you are to drink it straight away."

He remained silent.

"Do you still see me as your enemy?" she asked.

Branoc heard the disappointment, nay sorrow, in her voice. He peered at her and tried to discern if her chin quivered with the same emotion that colored her words. He needed to trust her, needed someone with whom to share his soul, and he wanted it to be Martanzia. "Mix the foul concoction. I am at your mercy, unable to defend myself against so sad and soft a voice as yours."

She gave a little murmur as she removed the tray, and he pictured a hint of a smile upon her lips.

He heard the clink of metal against metal as she stirred the drink, then tightly he clasped the cup that she handed him. After sniffing the contents, he downed the lot of it. "'Twas not nearly as bad as your previous offerings," he admitted.

Her fingertips brushed his as she retrieved the cup.

He grabbed her wrist with his free hand and held her at his side. "Thank you for helping me."

The empty goblet slipped from her fingers falling with a forgotten whisper onto the bed.

He swallowed hard and searched his mind and heart for the right words. He wanted to say more, knew he should say more, but the language of love did not come easily to a warrior. He tugged on Martanzia's arm until she sat at his side, and he cradled her hand in both of his marveling at its smallness.

He traced a pattern upon her palm, and as his hand slid across hers the sensation of smoothness tingled upon his fingertips. He imagined the rest of her equally as soft and with a great need to hold and be held, he reached to pull her down upon the bed. His pulse pounded harder as she offered no resistance.

Carefully he gathered her into his arms, forcing himself to embrace her gently. He did not dare grip her with all the fierceness and passion that raged in his blood.

She nestled against his shoulder, a pure and simple act, but the tiny movement overwhelmed him and he wanted to believe in love, he wanted to confide in her, he wanted to share his inner most feelings with her. It would take all the courage he possessed to love Martanzia freely the way she deserved to be loved. He stroked her hair. He wanted her more than he had ever wanted any woman or any victory. And just as he had always found the courage to fight his battles with honor and valour, he would fight and win Martanzia's love and never let her go.

His senses reeled at the magnitude of his resolve. Then he feared something beside his lady's nearness caused the heady unsettling feeling.

He pushed her away.

A searing pain rent his stomach, and the agony of it near made him lose consciousness.

"Branoc," Martanzia cried. "What is wrong?"

He felt her hands first upon his shoulders then stroking his cheeks as she sought to ease his thrashing.

Another pain gripped him.

"I must fetch Morcar." Her footsteps retreated from the bed.

God above! She had poisoned him after all. His body began to shake beyond his control. First, he felt hot then cold. He could not think, he could not catch his breath.

Suddenly his vision cleared but the world revealed to him spun crazily out of control, and he felt no joy at being able to see. Good eyesight would be of little consequence to a dead man. Another spasm of misery tore through him. He gripped the covers in his hands, twisted and pulled at the fabric. He was dying.

"Martanzia," he cried out.

The single word echoed off the four walls. He gasped for breath and fell back upon the bed. It was the first time her name had passed his lips aloud.

Had the wench ensured it would also be the last?

Chapter 19

Morcar was nowhere to be found, and Tanzie knew not where to begin as she fought to save Branoc's life.

What had given him this relapse? She was sure she had administered the powder exactly as Morcar had instructed. Yet, he grew steadily weaker, and the possibility that she may have done something wrong haunted her with vicious intensity. She clenched her hands in anguish. She loved Branoc, would do anything for him, anything. Yet fear forced her to do nothing other than monitor his pulse and wipe his brow.

He was gravely ill, his color ashen, and the breath that came from his nostrils was weak and irregular in nature.

A shadow fell across the bed. She started and glanced up. Leofric was at her side. He studied Branoc then scowled down at her. "What happened?" he demanded. "Just a short while ago he seemed much improved."

"Truly I do not know," she answered. "You must believe me. I would not hurt him, not even if it meant my life."

"It might come to that," Leofric threatened. He stepped to the head of the bed to lift the lid on one of Branoc's eyes. Only whiteness met their inspection. His eyes were rolled back. "Can you not help him?"

"I think he needs mandrake," she whispered, "'tis the most powerful of Druid's cures."

"You think," Leofric said. "You must be sure. He will not survive a miscalculation."

"I know that," she cried. "I cannot find Morcar. I'm doing the best I can without him." Tears streamed down her cheeks. Angrily she cuffed them away with the back of her hand.

"Branoc and I are as brothers," Leofric said, his voice now slightly more forgiving. "We have always faced life's challenges together, and I feel helpless now as he battles alone against death."

"I do not know what so afflicted him," she confessed. "My logic falters in seeking a cure when I do not know the cause of his illness."

"Tis your faith in yourself that falters not your logic," Leofric replied. "It is too late to worry about what made him ill. He is dying Martanzia. Trust to your heart. You are the only one who can save him."

Branoc's breathing had become raspy, and a circle of white ringed his mouth. Her fingers shook as she touched his hand. Morcar's warning about working with the root gnawed at the back of her mind. She was afraid to cast the spell of life. But Leofric was correct. She must do something before it was too late. Morcar had said she could use the magic of the plants to save someone she loved, and no greater love had ever existed than the one she held for Branoc. "I will need a few moments to prepare for the ritual."

Leofric gave her a nod of encouragement.

She ran to the tower and then to her room. As she entered, Ealgith leaped to her feet and rushed forward to meet her. "How fares Lord Valtaigne?" she asked, and helped Tanzie set aside the items gathered from Morcar's chamber.

"He is failing," she said, tearing at her clothes. "Fill the tub Ealgith I must bathe. Thank the Lord you thought to store extra water in our room."

"I did not request the barrels lady and the water is ice cold."

"No matter," she said, dismissing Ealgith's

words without a second thought, "the cleansing rites must be performed. Casting the spell of life is risky at best and any deviation from the prescribed procedure could be deadly."

Ealgith's eyes grew wide, and this time she did not hesitate to spit on the floor. Then as bidden, she began to fill the little tub. "Does the old wizard know you attempt such a dangerous undertaking?"

"I cannot find Morcar," Tanzie replied, as she added sea salt, nettle, and yellow dock to the water. "Many hours have passed since I have seen him, though he promised to be gone only for a short time."

"Well, therein waits the trouble," Ealgith muttered, as she picked Tanzie's discarded clothes up off the floor. "Time to a sorcerer is a thing to be cheated or mastered. For them, time does not recognize the sands in the hour glass nor the marks upon the candle."

"But Morcar would not lie to me or do anything to harm me. I am sure of that."

"He does little to help you either," Ealgith boldly pointed out.

Tanzie's doubts and fear doubled. A shiver coursed through her body, and like a living creature, goose bumps skittered across her naked flesh. What she was about to attempt could prove fatal to her. But Branoc's death was more to be feared than her own demise.

Reaching for Ealgith's proffered hand she stepped into the tub, gritted her teeth, and quickly sank down into the water. By the Saints, it was freezing. She hugged herself for warmth and her breath caught in her throat. "LLLeave me now, Ealgith," she stuttered, "and pray that a hasty ablution is as purifying as one performed at leisure."

Ealgith did not move, her expression all but shouting, *You are acting crazy, lady, and should not be left alone.*

"Please," Tanzie said, shuddering with the cold. "I don't have time to argue about this. You must go. The words and ceremony are ancient and secret. And the ritual is dangerous for anyone involved."

The other girl's expression now turned to one of pure alarm.

"I beg you," she pleaded. "I carry enough burdens already without adding the safety of my dearest friend to the lot."

At those words, Ealgith managed a weak smile. "Tis your safety needs worrying about, lady," she said. "Tonight you throw yourself into the path of the gods. Beware they do not tread upon you too heartily." Gently placing the robe Tanzie had brought from the tower beside the tub, Ealgith crossed the room. "I'll be near at hand should you need anything," she promised and disappeared out the door.

What I need, Tanzie thought as she sat shivering in the fading light, is courage and that can only be found within myself.

Cupping the water over her body, she sang the Celtic chant of purification. Her flesh began to tingle but not with the cold. In truth, her skin felt hot, almost glowing. A great weariness raced through her then it seemed to spiral upward straight out of her, leaving all of her senses filled with a heightened awareness.

When she climbed from the tub, she felt agile as a deer and farsighted as a hawk. Following the edict not to dry with a towel, she donned only the chaste white robe and collected the other articles of use. Everything she touched seemed new and vibrant, the textures deeper the colors brighter.

Using three candles of red beeswax and one of orange, she prepared a small altar facing north. Her hands felt clumsy with urgency as she dressed the candles with oil and consecrated them with hurried words and desperate prayers.

She longed to return to Branoc's room, but forcing herself to concentrate on the task at hand, she lit the tapers and incense. The ritual had begun. The scented smoke wafted upward and a palpable silence gripped the room.

*Strength to the strong to help the weak.*
*Strength to the weak to rejoin the strong.*
*Seek out the poison and turn it upon itself.*
*Take what energy be needed from me*
*to exorcise the evil that dwells in him.*
*I ask only to save another*
*and nothing for myself.*
*Strength to the strong to help the weak.*
*Strength to the weak to rejoin the strong.*

With a sure hand, she grasped the mandrake plant and using Morcar's dagger, the one with the handle made of pure crystal, she scraped off enough of the root to cover the bottom of a small earthen cup. Adding hot water from the tiny kettle on the hearth, she steeped the shavings to the count of ten, three times over. Then she poured off the liquid into a silver chalice.

Clutching the chalice, book, and dagger, she left the room and hurried to Branoc's chamber. Ealgith, waiting in the hall, followed in her wake.

"Branoc," she said as she reached his side, "Tis I Martanzia."

He appeared no better, but to her surprise opened his eyes and stared at her. His gaze was wild and frenzied like a trapped animal, and her renewed hope quickly turned to despair.

"Tell me why?" he asked, in a voice of pure agony. Then he closed his eyes, and his head sagged back upon the pillow.

She glanced at Leofric. He shrugged his shoulders not understanding Branoc's meaning either.

"Please Branoc drink of this. It is the spell of life. It will renew your body and spirit."

He rolled his head from side to side. "No, no, no," he shouted as if possessed by a delirium.

She leaned closer.

His eyes flew open, and he stared directly into hers. "Why did you try to kill me?" he asked and grabbed at the front of her robe.

Frantically she glanced at Leofric then back at Branoc. "I do not know what made you ill," she said. He pushed her away.

She stumbled backward almost upsetting the contents of the goblet. There must be some way to prove her love. Someway to prove her intentions were honorable. She handed the chalice to Leofric and resumed her place at the bedside. "Here," she said, and wrapped Branoc's cold fingers around the handle the dagger she carried. Then she wrenched open the neck of the robe and leaned forward until the tip of the knife touched the gentle swell at the top of her left breast. "If the draught should make you worse you will still have a final moment to plunge this blade into my heart. I would be better off dead," she cried, "than alive without you."

Branoc canted his head and squinted his eyes as if trying to focus. His expression remained shadowed with doubt, but he finally nodded for her to proceed, and she knew he was reaching beyond logic, beyond every instinct of self-preservation and all because he wanted to believe in her. He was risking his life for what he felt in his heart. He was putting all his faith in her.

Motioning Leofric to hand her the chalice, she spilled a precious drop of the infusion upon the floor to appease the gods then held the cup out to Branoc.

His fingers tightened around the dagger. He reached for the goblet with his other hand and with his gaze locked upon her face, he swallowed the mandrake.

She chanted the final spell and waited with great expectation. Branoc stiffened as if in the throws of a seizure. The blade of the dagger pierced her skin, but she neither moved nor made a sound. Three beads of scarlet fell from the cut, splashing like liquid rubies onto the white linen robe she wore.

Ealgith gasped and made to step forward, but Leofric grabbed her and held her in place.

Why wasn't the spell working?

Branoc did not breathe and his lips were a fearful shade of purple. Tanzie wished to feel his pulse but she dare not move or touch him. The pain where the knife cut into her flesh increased. This was the end. Her life would soon be over, and she would never know the soft caress of Branoc's hands upon her body. She would only know the cruel twist of the knife as the man she loved sent the blade deep into her chest.

Her heart beat wildly only inches beneath the deadly point of the dagger. What irony. Just as she had found something wonderful to live for, she would not live at all. She closed her eyes and waited for death.

Suddenly Branoc relaxed. Tanzie opened her eyes to see him slumped back upon the bed. He dropped the dagger and took in a great breath. Color rushed back into his cheeks, and the hand that she grasped now felt warm.

"You have done it," Leofric said, as he and Ealgith rushed forward.

Tanzie watched Branoc closely, fighting back the joy that she feared to acknowledge. What if his recovery were only temporary? But as Branoc continued to improve, she too breathed a sigh of relief. Then she began to shake. A ripple of nausea swept through her. Leofric reached to steady her.

"I must go," she mumbled and rising she

stumbled toward the door.

"I will help you mistress," Ealgith offered.

"No," Tanzie protested and gently pushed the girl away. "I would be alone." She felt stifled almost smothered. She could not breathe, wanted no one near her. In a fog, she staggered down the hall all the while praying that using the mandrake root had been the proper thing to do.

Pausing she sagged against the wall for support. Suddenly thoughts of her mother pricked at her mind. Tears clouded her vision and wet her cheeks. She was terrified by the loneliness that swept over her. No one in this world loved her as she longed to be loved. She was an orphan both physically and emotionally, and no consolation existed that could comfort her. How profoundly sad it was to wander this earth with no one to care for and no one to care for her.

She resisted the urge to slump to the floor, and forcing herself back into motion, she headed toward her sleeping chamber. As if drunk on mead, she lurched and weaved across the hall. When would this weakness pass? Did the energy ebb from her body in proportion to the strength that infused Branoc's? That thought was of some consolation.

She halted again to catch her breath. She felt old, almost ancient and empty like a withered husk, so hollow and fragile she could blow away and be carried on the wind for miles and miles. Exhausted, her body refused to obey her commands, and her mind reeled with a collage of images. She felt tall as a tree and thin as a cloud. She was stretching out becoming invisible, becoming one with the universe.

The light in the passageway grew dim, fuzzy, and little dots danced before her eyes. She was floating, falling, fainting....

Sinewy arms caught her before she hit the floor. "You've had a busy day little one."

The familiar voice was gruff, tinged with pride, and as gray gossamer hair brushed across her face, she felt as if she were in the arms of a mighty Archangel. She felt warm and safe, even as the darkness closed in all around her.

****

Tanzie opened her eyes. She was in bed in her chamber. Morcar dozed in the chair at her side. A fire crackled in the hearth, and the fragrance of herbs and incense filled the air. She had not been abandoned after all.

Half awake she smiled, and out of habit she grabbed at the nearby dragon statue. No longer bound to the table, it came freely to her and she cradled it in her arms. The document that had been tucked beneath the creature slipped silently to the floor. In the back of her mind she knew that this was a most curious thing and she recalled that the record was of great importance. Then she was once more overwhelmed by fatigued and try as she might she was unable to remember what the deed stood for or why it had been placed there.

Chapter 20

Three days had come and gone since **Tanzie** had dared to employ the mandrake root, and two days had passed since castle Bamburgh had come under siege. In all this time, she had not seen **Branoc**, but Ealgith kept her apprised of his recovery. At first Tanzie had been too ill to care, but with her own return to good health her yearning for Lord Valtaigne also gained new strength.

This morning she stood before the window of the west solar and wondered at the sudden change in the weather. Overnight the last vestiges of summer had fled, and a brisk autumn had descended upon them. Fog prowled amongst the trees and crept over the hillside and the sky, layered with thick clouds, pressed down from above as if seeking friendly commiseration from the roiling haze below.

Would such weather help or hinder Branoc's cause? The dreary veil all but hid the line of enemy soldiers who watched from afar. With unexpected patience, they bided their time and with the finesse of gray ghosts, they wavered in and out of view, stark illusions of impending doom.

The sentries, stationed at the far outposts, had seen the horde of Scots and rebels advancing and there had been ample time to warn the villagers to safety. Outnumbered many times over, most of the villeins had come to the stronghold seeking protection. But those who trusted neither the Scots nor the Normans had fled to the woods to take their chances on their own. As another day of defensive tactics began at Bamburgh, Tanzie wondered which group of townspeople had shown the most wisdom.

Footsteps sounded at her back. She turned to face the open doorway and was surprised to see Branoc enter. He paused to observe her then strode forward. He appeared fatigued but otherwise healthy. Tanzie knew his responsibilities demanded long hours, but she guessed that the frustration of the situation took its toll upon him even more readily than the lack of sleep.

"I could not come to you sooner," he said.

"We have all been busy," she acknowledged. "You most of all I would imagine."

"Leofric tells me you risked much to heal me." Wariness still lurked in his voice and caution shimmered in his eyes. The statement was matter of fact. No hint of a thank you, no apology for doubting her intentions, then or now.

"Are you quite recovered, lady?" he added with what seemed true concern. "You appear flushed."

By the Rood, the man was obtuse. 'Twas his nearness that inspired her cheeks to flame with color, and her stomach to churn, and her palms to feel damp. How could he not be aware of the affect he had upon her?

"Sometimes," she muttered under her breath, "you are so thick-headed I wonder if you devote practice to the art."

"I beg your pardon, lady," Branoc said, and took a step closer. "I did not hear your last remark..

"I am well," she answered more distinctly. "Please, do not concern yourself. I would do it again without hesitation." Was the devotion she felt for him audible in her words? "I am thankful that you are alive and your vision has been restored." 'Twas a pity, she thought, that he could not see her as clearly as he once again saw the rest of the world.

Their gazes locked, and she searched his face even as he searched hers, perhaps, for answers that did not exist. What more could she do to certify herself and her actions? Every time she thought the seed of trust had begun to take root in Branoc's soul, something new cropped up to kill the fragile growth. Then the look in his eyes was rendered barren once again, and the little faith he granted her quickly withered away to nothing as if it had never existed.

Branoc did not speak nor move.

She could not bear the damning silence. "Several soldiers and cotters are also beset with illness," she said, her voice a little too loud. "Their symptoms are remarkably similar to yours."

Last evening she had helped Morcar nurse the poor wretches. But the old Druid had taken over administering the cure. Using the mandrake root did not seem to affect him adversely. Somehow, he was able to cast the spell of life with no illness or loss of strength.

"No one knows what causes this sickness?" Branoc asked.

"Tis arsenic," Morcar declared as he swept into the room. Anger thundered across his face and retribution flashed in his eyes. "It is in the water."

She stared at him stunned by his announcement. "All the barrels of water are tainted?" she questioned.

"Yes, except for what little was already stored in the rooms for individual use. But there is more. The poison was also mixed in my vials of medicine. That is what made you so ill, Valtaigne. You would have died had Martanzia not used the mandrake. She showed great courage in her choice of action."

Relief flooded her senses. Branoc's suffering had not been caused by an error on her part. She glanced at him, and for a moment his expression seemed almost joyful. Then it turned serious again.

"All will recover?" he asked the wizard.

"Yes," Morcar assured. "Those who drank of the

foul liquid have been given the cure whether they show signs of sickness or not. Even some of the horses had to be treated. I regret that three people died before we could discover what was wrong. One was just a child."

"It was not your fault," Tanzie defended, as she gently touched the old Druid's arm. "But now," she added, and lowered her hand limply back to her side, "we are without safe drinking water."

Branoc prowled about the room. Then he halted, his gaze locked upon Morcar's face. "If you are a sorcerer why did you not foresee this treachery?"

Morcar shrugged, seemingly unperturbed by Branoc's accusing tone. "The gods show me what they will and while they may on occasion show concern for Mankind, on the whole the plight of mortals does not often worry them."

Branoc gave a snort of derision. "At least you answer honestly, crystal gazer."

"Do not take their lack of interest personally," Morcar added. "I too am often at their mercy."

"That knowledge brings me some comfort," Branoc said.

As they stood in silence, the pitiful lowing of cattle and the helpless cry of a baby could be heard. How could they withstand this hardship? Soon they would be thirsty to the point of dire distress, and the wailing would fill the air with true urgency. If only they knew what the castle was like when first constructed.

"There must have been a well or an underground spring here in times past," Branoc said echoing her thoughts.

"Personally I know that neither existed at Bamburgh in the last three hundred years," Morcar said. "I lived elsewhere before that time, and the castle was already in use for many years before I arrived."

Branoc's eyes narrowed. "Your statement gives one pause," he said, challenging the old man's remark.

"Yes I am sure that it does," Morcar replied, "but it is the truth."

Branoc raked his fingers through his hair, and took again to pacing. "There must have been water," he muttered, "there must have been. Without it neither the Romans nor King Ida would have selected this sight for building such a fortress."

"Perhaps the manuscripts from Jarrow could aid us," she suggested.

"It is possible," Branoc said. "From what little I have read there are detailed accounts of every stronghold that Bede visited. He most likely came here at some point in his travels. Of late I have not had much time for reading."

She too had neglected the transcribing, yet maybe it was not too late to help. "I know you have not a single sentry to spare, but would you allow me, without a chaperone, to search for the information in your council chamber?"

Branoc studied her face intently and this time she saw hope reflected in his. The seed of trust that fought for life between them seemed to have finally settled upon fertile soil.

"Yes," he replied, "and gratefully so."

Her heart soared and she stood transfixed by this new revelation.

"Go child," Morcar interceded and ushered her toward the door. "We need the water now. The two of you can stand and stare at one another later."

As she hurried down the hall, her prior anger at Branoc's wavering attitude dissolved. He was newly recovered from his journey to Death's door, and he shouldered much responsibility. She must consider these things and not judge him so harshly. And her recent weakness and present exhaustion no doubt jaded her own mood as well.

On the other hand, she must not be too easily taken in by his lone-wolf demeanor and the soulful expression in his eyes. She allowed his opinion of her to carry too much weight. Her spirit lived or died by it and to allow another person so much power and influence over her was dangerous. Yet, she could not help wishing to please Branoc, wishing to be found intriguing and desirable in his eyes. He had reordered her life. He was the center of her universe, and all her thoughts and actions circled around him. But was she prepared to relinquish the rest of the world for Branoc? If he truly loved her, she would not need anything else.

At the council chamber, she raised her hand to push open the door then hesitated. She stood there unmoving and recalled the first time she had entered this room. It seemed like only yesterday, as well as a lifetime ago. A remembrance of how Branoc had looked that day was so vivid in her mind she almost expected to see him standing in the room as she entered. But the dimly lit chamber was cold and inhospitable and it seemed to dare her to find the secrets that it sheltered.

She stepped to the table. Her gaze traveled over the huge mound of new manuscripts, and her hope for a quick solution faded. Finding the one passage pertinent to their needs could take hours or days.

Sorting through the chronicles, she isolated the volumes that covered the time prior to Morcar's arrival at the castle. Mercia, Lindsey, Wessex, where was Northumbria? Continuing well into the afternoon she painstakingly examined each ancient text but 'twas all to no avail.

Disappointed she stepped to the window and stretched her aching muscles. Her neck and shoulders felt numb, as if they were carved of wood. She had failed dismally. Branoc would think her ineffectual at best and a traitor at worst. Exasperated she flopped down into a chair only to leap back to her feet as something remarkably uncomfortable prodded her backside. A lone manuscript was wedged against the back of the seat. Half buried behind the cushion, it had slipped unseen from the table and lodged there. It was the correct volume.

She seized the tome and frantically flipped through the various sections. There it was—the heading she sought. *Northumberland: ruled by King Ida. In 559, he built himself a great castle at Bamburgh. The walls are eleven feet thick on one side and nine feet thick on the other three...*yes, yes, but what about the water...*built on a perpendicular rock, one side has a drop of over one hundred and fifty feet...the structure used both masonry and timber...a stone floor supported by arches...*praise be, this was it. *A most curious feature of this castle is the draw-well located in the vaulted cellar by the outdoor kitchens. A marvel of man's ingenuity, it is near one hundred and forty five feet deep.*

Clasping the book in her arms, she hurried from the council chamber and ran through the halls. Where was Branoc? When last she had seen him, he had been wearing his fighting gear. He was probably in the bailey with his men. After a brief search, she spied him near the granary.

"Branoc," she cried and waved to attract his attention.

He stood with Leofric and two other men, and even at this distance, she could see he appeared so very tired. His stance beleaguered, concern pulled at the corners of his mouth.

"Branoc," she said breathlessly, as she reached his side. "Look upon this." She handed him Bede's manuscript. He read the passage indicated and gave her thoughtful consideration. Then a smile more precious to her than the water they sought, washed the concern from his face.

"Martanzia you have saved the day."

He shoved the book into Leofric's hands and in front of all present lifted her up off her feet and hugged her to his chest.

Inhaling sharply, she gasped in delight as he cradled her close and spun around. She clung to him and laid her cheek against his shoulder. Laughter reverberated in his chest, as he whirled them about faster and faster. The images of the people who had gathered to watch them swam before her in a cockeyed blur.

Her soul smiled. But all too soon, the wild ride ended.

Branoc relaxed his arms, and she slid down the front of his body. Dizzy she swayed against him, and he placed a hand on each of her shoulders to steady them both. Leaning forward, he kissed her cheek.

She covered the spot his lips had touched with the tips of her fingers.

Ribald comments and howls of encouragement rang out from the nearby soldiers and peasants. As the intimate and inspired suggestions became clear to her, she shifted her hand to cover her mouth.

"Come quickly," Branoc said, with a grin that bordered upon a complete smile, "lest I fall victim to their goading and advice." He gripped her elbow and guided her along, and she lengthened her stride to match his.

Branoc issued orders to the men that they passsed, and though Tanzie was aware that a multitude of people followed at their backs she had eyes only for the man at her side.

As they reached their destination, a murmur of disappointment rippled through the crowd. The specified area lay in ruins, piled high with rubble. It resembled anything but a kitchen and cellar. No wonder the well had not previously been discovered.

Undaunted, the soldiers began tearing at the debris, hacking at the centuries of overgrowth that bound it into place. They labored heartily, their vigor and pent up energy directed toward the new-found barrier rather than against their true enemies Rathgar, the Scots, and the rebels.

Encouraged by the people who ringed their field of endeavor, the men persevered in their Herculean effort. Finally on the near side the outline of a stone well became visible, and before long only one formidable slab of masonry remained between the people and the water. But even the combined efforts of the peasants and the soldiers could not budge the massive object from atop the well. They tied ropes around it and employed the brute strength of the destriers but to no avail. As their likelihood of success took a downward spiral, Morcar appeared at their side.

"I don't suppose the gods would be interested in lending a hand at this point," Branoc said to the sorcerer.

"Tis not the gods' help you need," Morcar said cheerfully, "but a fulcrum, the principle of which is rather magical in itself."

Using the tip of his staff he sketched the device in the dust of the alleyway. The men quickly grasped the concept and ran to collect the necessary articles. They returned with several sturdy logs and one very large anvil. Unhinging a nearby door, they laid it beside the well and six men muscled the anvil atop the smooth working surface.

The tip of the largest log was forced into the crevice beneath the slab of masonry and leaning the log back against the anvil, several soldiers pushed down on the free-end levering the ponderous obstacle upward. Time after time, they heaved in unison, muscles bulging, and faces darkening with their efforts. Men at the ready, wedged smaller logs into the slowly widening gap.

Suddenly the ponderous masonry tilted and with a last mighty struggle, the soldiers sent the great piece of rubble sliding sideways to the ground.

Mute with anticipation Tanzie watched as the dust cleared and the well was completely revealed. Using many ropes tied together, a wooden pail was lowered into the gaping dark hole. It hit the bottom with a splash eliciting a cheer from the crowd. The water retrieved was muddied but usable.

Morcar stepped forward and stared transfixed at the contents of the bucket, and though all manner of chaos broke loose around the enchanter, he seemed to have eyes only for the dull glimmer of light reflected in the water.

Not dwelling on Morcar's odd preoccupation, Tanzie studied Branoc.

He reached for her hand and enfolded it in both of his. "Again I am in your debt, Martanzia. Thank you."

Dirty and sweat streaked he stood beside her. The wound on his left cheek still angry and highly visible marred his visage, yet as Branoc smiled just for her, she thought his the most perfect face ever fashioned by the Creator.

Chapter 21

Branoc stood alone in his council chamber and watched the light retreating from a petulant sky. The day was done but their troubles had just begun. Thinking to taunt their enemy, one young soldier had foolishly shouted down from the wall that they had found water and discovered the inheritance powder. Now, realizing his plans for a quick siege had been foiled, Rathgar had issued a new ultimatum.

Leofric entered, and Branoc watched without comment as his friend set a wooden platter containing several slices of course bread upon the table. "The last of the Lammas loaves," Leofric explained.

Branoc nodded in understanding. In times of trouble people clung to the old ways, and though it was the fifth of August and the cross-quarter day had come and gone, the Saxons had sought comfort in performing the rituals of old.

"All is well about the castle?" he asked.

"As well as can be expected," Leofric assured. "Only those you specified know of the new missive. The rest are happy in their ignorance of what is to come."

"Tis for the best," he agreed.

"You do not truly expect Rathgar to meet us in fair combat," Leofric said.

"No, and yet I dare not ignore his invitation to open battle. It is the one chance we have to free the villagers he holds captive."

"He uses them as bait," Leofric said, the disgust

evident in his voice. "And we are not assured that the villeins will be released as promised or even if they still live."

"You speak rightly. But not to try would be worse than defeat. We can only proceed with our eyes open, and our defenses ready and hope for the best."

Leofric grudgingly agreed, then idly strolled about the room. He picked up a map and without glancing at it set it aside. He fidgeted with a quill, sighed, and ambled about some more.

Branoc knew the restless feeling that consumed his friend. He felt it as well. Waiting for the attack was oft times worse than the actual battle. "You should be with Ealgith she will take your mind off your worries."

Leofric grinned. "And what about you? You should tell Martanzia of your feelings for her."

"Perhaps I will speak with her later. First, I must write to the king. Although, the letter will arrive too late to change tomorrow's outcome, he shall be given an honest account of what transpires here."

Morcar materialized at the open door. "It will be a waste of your time," he declared. "William Rufus is dead."

Branoc started, then strode to the portal. Glancing quickly up and down the hallway, he ushered Morcar inside and closed the door. "What rumor is this?"

"Tis fact not rumor," the old Druid claimed.

"You have received a communication?"

"In a manner of speaking."

Branoc waited silently for Morcar to continue. "I saw these things in calm water," the spellbinder explained. "The king died at noon three days ago. Shot with an arrow, he was the royal game taken in the hunt."

"The country without a king," Leofric said and paled. "Chaos will be next in line to rule this county."

"More likely Duke Robert or Prince Henry," Branoc said. "Who was responsible for loosing the arrow?"

"That I did not see," Morcar admitted. "I fear the name of the assassin is a secret that will be buried along with the king."

A chilling thought vied for Branoc's attention. "Is it possible," he asked in wonder, "that Rathgar's purpose here is political as well as personal?"

"To be party to a scheme connected with the murder of a king is beyond belief even for Rathgar," Leofric said. "Yet one must admit the timing is suspiciously coincidental."

"Yes," Branoc agreed. "The royal forces are spread thin across England. The Welsh continue to rebel along the western border, the Danes worry the eastern coast, and now under guise of loyalty our old friend is raising hell in the North Country. The sparsely protected south would be an open invitation for invasion by Prince Henry."

"And history repeats itself," Leofric put in. "The three sons of William the Conqueror have vied for the English crown since 1087. Now the competition has been narrowed down to the remaining two brothers."

Branoc feared this shocking development gave rise to a whole new set of questions and considerations. Duke Robert was recently returned from pilgrimage, along with his traveling companion the Count of Flanders. Where did this leave Martanzia, the Flemish good faith hostage?

"With no sovereign to answer to," Leofric said, breaking in upon Branoc's thoughts, "Relentes will dare even more treachery as he lays waste to the land."

"I doubt he will be aware of the king's death prior to the battle," Morcar pointed out. "Unless he employs his own magicians, which I seriously doubt as I have felt no such power in his camp. A hoary star did fling itself across the heavens three nights past, always a portent of great change and royal upheaval. But there are many lands and many kings, if he saw the comet he would not necessarily assume William's reign to be in jeopardy."

"Why did you wait until today to tell me of this?" Branoc asked gruffly.

"The star was but a prelude to the revelation I had today. I felt compelled to take my time with the interpretation. I knew its meaning would have far reaching consequences."

Branoc scrubbed his hand across his face. Three tailed comets and the visions of a wizard. This was a curious way to organize a campaign. Yet, Morcar, of late, had been of much use, and Leofric had ever been faithful, he was thankful for their presence. He could think of no better men to have at his side or to watch his back.

As they passed the time in silence, another missive arrived. This one added to his woes and concerns of a more personal nature

****

Tanzie sighed. The long hot bath had been a totally selfish indulgence. But as there was more than enough water available now and as she had been the one to find the cherished prize, what better reward?

Having soaked the evening hours away, she now sat beside her bed on the little padded footstool. Wearing nothing but her robe, she combed out her hair and mulled over the day's events.

Ealgith had gone to seek Leofric, and Tanzie reveled in the solitude, only the cheerful sound of logs crackling in the fire pit to break the silence.

Then an unexpected knock at the door sent her calm scurrying for cover.

"Who is there?" she asked, lowering her arms and abandoning the brush in her lap.

"Tis Branoc, lady. May I speak with you?"

The tone of Branoc's voice sounded forced, and he addressed her again as "lady". The closeness of their shared victory over finding water had not long prevailed, and like a thief in the night dejection stole her mood of contentment.

"Yes, you may enter," she called and wondered what he might want from her at this late hour. Remaining seated, she twisted around to face the portal. The motion caused her wrap to gape at the neckline. Quickly she reached up to adjust the fabric.

Branoc entered closing the door at his back. She was in trouble again. She could tell by the look of consternation upon his features.

"What is wrong?" she asked, not sure she wished to hear the answer.

"We have received word from the enemy forces. They know we have found water thus thwarting their plans for a siege of short duration. And a new demand has been issued." He studied her as if he tried to peel away her being, layer by layer. "They have issued a challenge to meet us in a pitched battle tomorrow morning."

"And if you do not agree?" she asked.

"They will hang the peasants they have captured and they will carry out their threats to destroy not merely this shire but all of the North Country. The land, the livestock, everything. And although clouds have threatened, there has been no rain for several days, the grass will burn like tinder and it will leap beyond control."

She was stunned by this development yet confounded as to how she might help. "Is there something I can do? Is it your eyes?" she questioned, with alarmed. Panic twisted through her at the thought that Branoc might again lose his sight.

"My eyes have healed completely. I see very clearly indeed." Branoc's gaze lingered on the front of her robe, then he gave a little cough and turned away.

She glanced down and saw the reason why. With each quick breath she took the cleavage of her breasts boldly peeked out through the misaligned edges of her robe. She clutched at the wayward opening. Could Branoc tell she wore nothing beneath the thin wrapper?

"There is more," he added. His gaze returned to her face and pinned her in place. "A second missive is newly arrived. One person has been granted safe passage from the castle."

"Who?" she asked, furious that someone would be afforded shelter by the enemy.

Branoc stood a little taller. "It is you mistress Verheire." The anguish in his voice tore at her heart, even as the implications of his words fired her temper.

"Me. By whose word?" she demanded. "I did not request such consideration."

"The words are written by the Scots, but the message is from Rathgar."

"Well I refuse to leave." She reached for and tightly gripped the hairbrush that lay in her lap. Why did Branoc continue to stare at her so strangely? "Surely you do not expect that I would abandon my post anymore than you would yours."

"I am not sure what you would or would not do lady. Your purpose here is obscure, and this missive suggests you consort with the enemy."

Tanzie felt small and defenseless as she sat in near nakedness. Branoc's doubts were not unreasonable. If they applied to someone else, she would be suspicious of such circumstances.

He stepped closer-towering above her.

She curled her toes into the fur of the wolf hides that lay scattered at her feet and nearly fell over backwards gazing up into his face. What could she tell him? He still nurtured the same old doubts, and she could offer him no new reassurances.

"I told you before," she began, "nothing I have done or will do is designed to hurt you or your cause." His face remained unreadable giving no sign of his feelings. "I wish with all my heart that you would believe in me," she said in desperation.

"I have tried," he whispered. An expression of sadness melted the coldness from his eyes. "But I know first hand that a relationship with Rathgar is a dubious honor at best."

"I have no relationship with Rathgar," she reiterated. Anger rose in her chest fighting for dominance over the life breath housed there. "What is it you want of me?" she dared to ask. At her own words, a flash of heat sizzled through her body, and a mixture of fear and longing burned deep in her belly. Branoc held the power of life and death over her. As commander of this castle, he could demand anything of her. The indecent wish that he would petition her to make love to him careened through her mind. "What do you want?" she repeated softly.

"I want peace in this realm," Branoc said, "and I want Rathgar to end this madness before it is too late. But most of all," he added closing his eyes for a moment, "I want you not to remind me of the roses of Lillebonne."

Branoc's last words made no sense to Tanzie, yet the sentiment they construed touched her heart.

The fire crackled and a small shower of sparks leaped and flared. For one brief moment, the gray trappings Branoc wore encircled him in an aura of silver. Did he desire companionship and the joy of being loved as much as she? He stood before her a mighty warrior, bold and unafraid, glorious and complete in face and form. Yet as on that first day when she had met Branoc outside the mighty walls of Bamburgh Castle, she thought he seemed a lonely man.

"We may all die tomorrow," he said without emotion.

His statement did not appear to cause him fear. Had he faced death so often that the prospect had become mundane? Or was death not the adversary? Maybe dying with unfulfilled yearnings was the true enemy. She could at least spare them both that dismal fate.

She reached out and took Branoc's hand. "Perhaps my lord, we had best make the most of tonight."

## Chapter 22

Branoc withdrew his hand from hers.

Tanzie's breath caught in her throat. He didn't want her, didn't long for her with the same desperate yearning she harbored for him. She felt like a fool.

Or was she wrong? To her surprise, he reached out and slid the hairbrush from her other hand, and a wave of desire tantalized her senses as the silver handle slipped through her fingers.

Shifting his stance Branoc stood at her back. Tentative and awkward as a child or a man not familiar with such notions, he gently brushed her hair. Wonder and disbelief cosseted her. It made her feel special that he would perform such a service for her. She sat straighter then feared to move lest she break this spell of fantasy and find him gone.

Branoc swept her hair to one side exposing the nape of her neck. Drawing his thumb back and forth across the vulnerable skin, he knelt behind her. The hairbrush fell to the fur-covered floor, and his lips lightly touched the place his fingers had caressed. So fragile were the kisses, Tanzie again wondered if she dreamed them. She closed her eyes knowing this was the moment for which she had waited a lifetime. Right or wrong was no longer a consideration. What dwelled in her heart and soul told her to reach out to this man. It told her to accept his offer of comfort and intimacy.

Branoc encircled her with his arms and hugged her back against his chest. Cold air washed over her, as the top of her gown parted to expose her breasts and the bottom edges of fabric separated to reveal her thighs. She was afraid of what was happening, but there was reassurance in Branoc's unyielding form, and when he shifted one hand to the open slash of neckline, she knew all was lost. The possessiveness in his touch made her want to belong to him in every sense, and her mind surrendered as well as her body.

"Your robe is the color of a summer sky," he whispered as he released the closure at her waist. "I am partial to blue," he added, as if it were a great secret.

Branoc edged the garment off her shoulders, and they slid to the floor beside her bed, their gazes locked in riotous need as they fell into one another's arms.

The tickle of wolf skins grazed her naked body and wild sensations captured her imagination. Remembering what Ealgith had told her about love sustaining her, and recalling what she had seen the two lovers enjoy, Tanzie shrugged free of the last folds of her robe and the last shreds of her inhibitions.

"You are more beautiful than the most perfect rose," he said softly, reassuring her that she had not been found wanting. He tugged his tunic off over his head and tossed it aside, and in one sure motion he loosened his braies and removed them along with the soft boots that he wore. Now he was free of all clothing as well.

Face to face, and once more in his embrace, she felt small, yet protected, and the warmth of him gave her confidence, inviting her to press even closer.

Tentatively she ran her hand over the crisp black hair that lightly covered his chest. Her fingers brushed across one nipple and at his twinge of delight, she began to tease him, petting first one side then the other. Made bold by his enjoyment she kissed the places her fingers had just excited. A fluttering of heat rippled through Tanzie as Branoc's hard male body pressed boldly against hers.

He gathered a handful of her hair and drew it forward breathing deep of its fragrance as he nuzzled her neck. She closed her eyes and he tightened his grip upon her tresses. Then holding her at his mercy, Branoc whispered a kiss upon her lips and seduced her willingly into submission.

His touch took her breath away and charged her with fire. He eased his tongue between her lips and his hand between her thighs. Breathing faster she reveled in these new sensations.

This was wrong! The words tore through her mind. This was wonderful! The excitement raced through her body. Surely Branoc must love her to please her so.

He teased her body touching her in places she had never even touched herself. Shock waves of pleasure rippled upward from where his fingers explored and excited her sensitive skin. Then a different sensation of rapture speared deep inside of her until she thought she could bear no more. When Branoc drew back, she swallowed a cry of disappointment. She wanted more of the ecstasy that he created.

Taking her hand, he guided it forward and placed it upon his body as if asking her to please him in kind. And as he pushed against her, encouraging her touch, she marveled at the hard hewn fullness that lay in her palm. Realizing the full dimensions of his prowess, she doubted he took second place to many.

Caressing Branoc increased her own desire and she wished to more eagerly fondle the part of him that so fascinated her, yet she also feared to hurt him. As if sensing her hesitation, he wrapped his hand around hers, directing her movements then he gave her uncensored touch free reign.

Captivated, she explored every inch of him. He lay back and shuddered as she dared to slide her hand downward to the soft vulnerable gathering of skin between his legs. Suddenly, as if nearing some breaking point, Branoc roughly drew her astride his thighs.

She steadied herself, one hand on either side of his broad chest and gazed down at him. His head was tilted back in the throes of pleasure and she memorized the plains of his cheeks and the curve of his jaw.

Angling his head to one side Branoc studied her face and slowly pressed his hips up against her straddled form.

A heightened desire wound through her and she shook her hair back from her shoulders, exposing her breasts. Eyes wide with delight Branoc urged her down to kiss her lips then he lifted her hips and guided himself to enter her.

Pain tore at Tanzie, driving her back to reality. Branoc hesitated but he did not retreat. He kissed away the unbidden tears that wet her cheeks as he breached her resistance, gaining full possession of her body and capturing the attention of all her senses.

Slowly, he moved inside of her and the pain was erased by a wild craving. A primitive rhythm pounded in her brain as she clung to Branoc, matching his ardor, immersing herself in the beauty of their two beings tangled as one.

On all levels of existence she felt united with Branoc and she trusted him completely as they climbed a mountain of emotion that led her to the brink of an unknown precipice. In the face of the gentle fury that consumed them as one, she dared to want more, wanted it all, wanted to feel this way forever.

Branoc stiffened and raised upward, driving into her deeper and harder as he clasped her tightly to his chest and forced the air from her lungs. Bucking beneath her he sent her over the edge, the rough grinding friction of their bodies the final catalyst. She felt his release and cried out as hot unstoppable pleasure convulsed through her body from head to toe. She felt as if she were turned inside out and Branoc touched every hidden fiber of her being. Her mind exploded into a thousand pieces then a shower of blinding rapture rained down upon her.

Branoc's shoulders sagged back against the floor.

Happily exhausted, she lay atop him rising and falling with each ragged breath he took. He smoothed her hair and patted her bottom. A flicker of remembered ecstasy still quivered and pulsed where they remained joined as one and with her cheek against his chest Tanzie smiled with near stupefied satisfaction.

Surely even heaven could not be more pleasing than this.

Then she heard a rustling sound like that of parchment and for no reason that she could discern, Branoc lay very still. She wondered what he was about, but her newfound bliss out-weighed her curiosity. All she wanted was more of the pleasurable sensation that he had offered. But his movements were now stilted, and there seemed a detached aloofness about him that she could no longer ignore. Had she done something wrong?

"Branoc what is the matter?" she asked, her head nestled against his chest.

Receiving no answer, she levered upward, and gazed into his eyes, expecting to see love in their silvery depths, but instead she saw a haunting sadness. "You still do not trust me," she said in amazement. "I would not so give myself to you if there were anything but love and loyalty in my heart."

He held his silence.

Feeling used and embarrassed, betrayed by her own body and by his, she reared back and tumbled to the hard cold floor at his side. "What has cooled your need so quickly?" she cried in disbelief. "Was this simply an idle amusement before tomorrow's battle?"

"I heard no pleas of resistance," he said bluntly.

He was right, and she could not look at him. Shame caressed her naked flesh with a cold hand. She grabbed for her abandoned robe and the part of him he had so willing given of himself ran down her thigh, no doubt along with the blood that marked her as changed forever.

Clutching the twisted fabric to her chest, she scooted away from Branoc and painfully landed atop the forgotten hairbrush. As she retrieved the boar's bristles from beneath her unprotected backside, the silver handle gleamed in the waning light like the blade of a knife. Branoc grabbed her wrist as if he thought she meant to attack him.

She twisted against his unrelenting hold. "What would you do if you found I really was your enemy?" she challenged. "Would you give me over with nary a second thought?"

"I pray daily to the heavenly Father that I will never have to make such a decision," he answered evenly and released her arm. The glow in his eyes did not match the coldness of his words, yet with a shock she believed he might choose duty over love. How could he kiss her and threaten her life with the same tempting lips. She stared at his hands. They had touched her intimately, yet he would use them to choke the life from her body.

In stunned silence, she watched as he roughly pulled on his clothes and gained his feet.

He was a cold-hearted bastard, a warrior first and foremost. No, her heart argued, there had been warmth in Branoc's touch, and the light of passion had shown in his eyes not the gleam of victory that comes from conquering an enemy or a woman's body.

Branoc leaned down and gathered her into his arms. Ignoring her sputtering protests, he picked her up with seemingly little effort and held her over the bed. She tumbled from his grasp and landed in a heap.

Before she could evade him, he framed her face with his hands and kissed long and deep and none too gentle. "Time will tell where we stand with one another," he said, his mouth only inches from her own. He was so close she could see herself reflected in the black centers of his eyes. "No secrets will survive tomorrow."

He stared at her with a near tortured expression then reached down beside the bed to retrieve something from beneath it. "We will settle this when next we meet, Martanzia."

He handed her a document. "Good night, my lady."

Confused and hurt, she lay unmoving in the oppressive silence. This could not be happening. She felt desecrated by Branoc's loving. He had made her wild with unbridled lust, his lips and hands coaxing her until she was ready to give him everything, anything.

She had trusted him, given body and soul to him. Now he cruelly dismissed her. His betrayal was brutal. Even Uncle's treachery had not cut her as deeply.

She glanced at the deed that rested in her lap and recalled the rustle of parchment she had heard while lying in the warmth of Branoc's embrace.

This is what had caused her newfound ecstasy to turn so quickly to sorrow and anger.

Tears blurred her vision as she stared at the marriage certificate that declared her Rathgar's wife.

According to this, it was Branoc who had been betrayed.

Chapter 23

*One man shall love you fiercely and daringly although you be not wed...*Morcar's prophecy ran circles round Tanzie's brain. *Another shall claim you as wife, but never make you his own.*

She was afraid to sleep, afraid to dream, afraid to even think. Her coupling with Branoc had been an astonishing communion of body and soul. And despite his quick departure, it had been the most incredible occurrence of her life. It could also have been the most dangerous as it determined her future and not necessarily for the better. She had given him her most valuable possession.

Guilt now crept up the backstairs of her mind. She had broken the precepts of the church as well as those of society. Yet, at the time, honoring the love in her heart had been all that had seemed important. It still did. How could something that felt so right be so wrong? Didn't the laws of love and nature deserve some degree of importance in the governing of the world?

She threw back the covers and leapt from the bed. She should confess her sin, but there was no priest at Bamburgh and hadn't been for years. Donning a muslin nightrail she drew her cloak about her shoulders, jammed her feet into sheepskin slippers, and headed for the parapets.

She would have to settle for her own council, and cold fresh air—lots of it.

As she reached the allure, she discovered the night was surprisingly warm. Or was it just that her body was still infused with the ruddy afterglow of loving Branoc?

A sob lodged in her throat. She laid her cheek against the cool stone of the merlon. Was it yearning or remorse that burned hot upon her skin? It made no difference. Whatever the cause, she loved Branoc, and would never be happy with another.

Or perhaps she lamented needlessly. Other than Branoc's unspoken reference to her liaison with Rathgar, there had been no mention of marriage or a future together. Yet, need and hunger had burned within those penetrating eyes of gray. Even so, he had left her quickly enough after finding the false document. Left without granting her an opportunity to explain or defend herself.

Had Branoc's leaving been as painful for him as it had been for her? Was he angry with himself for having breached her maidenhead without being wed, or ashamed thinking he had lain with another man's wife. Honor and duty appeared to be a commanding force in Branoc's life. He would always choose the most worthy path, even if it were also the most difficult to follow.

"You are up late little one."

Tanzie's heart lurched. She would never become accustomed to Morcar's silent tread and unannounced appearances.

Turning she faced the old dream spinner then shifted uneasily beneath his scrutiny. She was sure he could tell just by looking that she and Branoc had been together.

As if by his command the clouds thinned and the illumination of a near full moon poured down from above. Remembering that the wizard could interpret her thoughts she silently recited the formula for a posset to cure colic in children.

Morcar raised a curious brow. "Why are you wandering about up here?" he asked.

An urge to protect Branoc and what they had

shared reared up within her. She did not wish to discuss the moments of intimate joy that had been theirs alone. It was as if by speaking of the interlude the event might somehow lose its enchantment. Besides, she thought rebelliously, Morcar never bothered to answer her questions, why should she answer his? "You are the sorcerer," she replied crossly, "look to your own prophecies."

"Yes they seem to be coming true one after another" he said with an astute smile. "What you have done will not alter what is to come or what you must do."

He knew...Embarrassed she turned away.

"Never be ashamed of loving," the wizard said, with a compassion she had rarely heard in his voice. "Love is the last remnant of true magic mortals will be allowed to possess. They do not always use it wisely or often enough, but despite mistreatment, the sentiment endures. Love is the most powerful emotion in the universe."

"Love can also cause the most profound pain and unhappiness," she said, meeting his gaze.

"The risk is great with anything worthwhile," he agreed. "The world was designed in opposition to itself. Opposite colors, opposite directions, opposite choices, opposite feelings. How would we measure one without the other? How would we experience the height of joy without the depths of sorrow?"

"There is truth in what you say, but I wish it were not so."

"Be careful what you wish for," he warned. "That is where Mankind made the most serious mistake. That was the beginning of the end."

"I don't understand"

"No you do not," he admitted, "and it is time that you did. Come." Leading the way he escorted her away from the edge of the windswept parapet to an unused guard shelter, a mere nook housing a rickety bench and a niche for a candle lantern.

Morcar lowered himself to the precarious perch, and for the first time since they had met Tanzie thought the old Druid appeared physically drained, bearing the aches and pains of a mortal man rather than the undaunted energy of a sorcerer.

"Sit down," he suggested. "We have much to discuss. I had hoped that there would be another way, but I'm afraid all will be lost without you." A hint of a smile softened his expression.

Her heart skipped a beat as she took her place at Morcar's side. She had long anticipated this moment, yet it was disturbing to know he deigned to offer these revelations out of dire necessity.

She pondered the sky as she waited for him to begin. A white dove flew through the inky darkness. Tanzie could not see the bird clearly, but there was no mistaking the unique creaking sound made by the motion of its wings in flight. How unusual for such a bird to be out and about in the dead of night.

"Have you guessed who she is?" Morcar asked, as he too watched the dove disappear.

The question puzzled her. "I don't understand."

"The lady in white. Do you know who she is? I believe you saw her when first you arrived in England."

"Oh yes," she said, recalling the experience that now seemed so long ago. "But I only saw her from afar, and no one enlightened me as to her identity."

"She is Beorce, your mother."

Morcar's words stunned her to silence. Then a detailed image of her mother crystallized in Tanzie's mind, and she remembered the shape of Beorce's hands, the way her smile radiated from her eyes as well as her lips. She heard the tune her mother used to hum while she sewed and the lilt of her voice as she spoke of her homeland.

Could it be so? Surely, it was false hope that

sprung so readily to life. It was a lie, her higher thoughts warned. It was madness. Her eyes narrowed, and her expression hardened. "I was only a child at the time Morcar but I saw her. She was dead. They were all dead. You are cruel to suggest otherwise." Even as she said the words, a part of her wanted to believe in what the old Druid insinuated. She was willing to embrace any philosophy if it meant being again with her mother.

Morcar remained silent letting her work through the idea.

What would he gain by such a lie she wondered? What if he told the truth? "Where is she? Tanzie cried, half rising from the seat. "I must go to her. Why did you not tell me before?"

"I feared the knowledge might put you or your mother in danger," he confessed holding her back. "I only do so now because I have no other choice."

"But if she is alive..." Tanzie whispered.

"Not in the manner that you wish for," he quickly amended. "Beorce's spirit survives on the fragile edge of existence. The lady in white is the form she takes only on rare occasions. It is an illusion that she cannot maintain for long periods of time, and one which only a few are blessed to see. The dove-woman exists, but the being you knew as your mother truly is gone."

Tanzie sank back down upon the bench. Again, she thought of the person she had seen in the woods. Morcar was correct. The lady had resembled her mother, but not exactly. Her face lacked the true essence of what made Beorce special, what made Beorce her mother. The image seemed hollow and without substance.

The vision in her mind of the lady in white dissolved away like the snows of spring. Then anger and bewilderment set in. She clutched Morcar's arm and lifted her gaze to stare into his eyes. "How did this come to pass? Please, tell me. I demand to know."

"Yes you shall have the whole story from beginning to end. But the most important element you must understand is that your mother's spirit was one with this ancient land." He paused again allowing his words to find a home in her consciousness. "In fleeing Northumbria those many years ago your mother severed that ethereal connection. Her exile to Flanders meant more than losing her homeland—it meant losing her soul."

Losing her soul? Other than by the Pope's edict, was such a thing possible? Tanzie was sickened by the implications of such a horrible thought. But how could such a dreadful destiny befall anyone as kind and caring as her mother. "I don't understand. Why would she be condemned to such a terrible fate?"

"It is a story that begins long ago," he said, with a sad smile, "all the way back to the first memory of time. An era when the Keepers watched over Man and this eminent land. It also begins with the ending of dragons. Man never did understand dragons or real magic," he muttered.

Dragons and magic? "Morcar," she said, as she grabbed his arm and held on tight, "just tell me about my mother."

"I am child," he insisted, "but that means telling you of the dragons. It must start there."

She wanted to scream with impatience, but the tone in Morcar's voice warned he would not be hurried or swayed from the direction in which he had chosen to enlighten her. Praying for endurance she sought to maintain a civil tongue and not fidget.

"I miss them you know," he mused, "the dragons and the unicorns."

God's teeth. Had she forced herself to wait quietly only to hear childish nonsense? "How can you miss what has never been?" she demanded. "Such creatures are but dreams and nightmares."

"No you are wrong, I have seen them," he said, and his eyes glowed with love for what he remembered. "You are the one who must accept them on blind faith."

"They never were," she insisted angrily.

"I saw them, they existed and things just don't exist that never were."

"Dragons?"

"Yes."

"And unicorns?"

"Yes."

"Then where are they now?" she challenged. "Did we kill them all?" The off-hand question silenced Morcar, and she knew her statement had hit near to the mark.

"Something like that," he said, the sorrow unmistakable in his voice. "Man wished them away. He grew tired of sharing the land with the dragons, so he begged to be relieved of the scaly affliction." Morcar spoke of the occurrence with such easy reference she nearly believed that he told her the truth.

"But weren't the people justified in their request?" she asked, playing along in hopes of speeding up the story. "Weren't the monsters a scourge and a terrible danger?"

"In some ways yes," Morcar conceded. "But they did not pillage with foul intent. They were just— being dragons. A few species were near hospitable. Something could have been arranged." He added the last with clear regret and a good bit of anger. "But," he continued with a sigh, "Man doth be a silly creature. He spends half his life wishing for things that should not be, and if perchance a miracle does occur and his dreams are realized, he rues the day it happened."

"Did Mankind wish the unicorns to leave as

well?"

"Oh no. Man did love the unicorns, as much as he did hate the dragons." An expression of peacefulness and joy warmed Morcar's features. Just thinking of the mystical creatures seemed to smooth away his lines of age. "It was almost painful to gaze upon the unicorns, so great was their enchantment. They brought prosperity to the land. Crops thrived where they passed, and game abounded in the forests where they dwelt. No one ever wished the unicorns to leave."

Dragons and unicorns. Could it be possible? In her father's manuscripts, she had read of cameleopards and oliphants and other equally unimaginable creatures. And the cathedral in Bruges had ramparts carved with the images of creatures so odious they made her dragon statue appear fair of face.

Morcar gained his feet, seemingly lost in thought. She felt the urge to prompt him, to hasten him onward to the part of the story that told of her mother, but she quelled the impulse knowing he would only speak of his own accord and in his own time.

"Man repeatedly begged the Keepers to destroy the dragons," he said. "No matter the cost. Eventually the ancient ones could no longer abide the pitiful repetitious pleas of the humans. The dragons were to be killed." The old Druid ceased all motion, and his last words were stolen by the wind. Then he spoke in a voice that left her wide eyed. "On a dark eve in October, Samhain to be exact, the Keepers sorrowfully prepared to grant man's persistent request. But the dragons begged for mercy promising to aid the humans at some future time if they were not made to perish now. The kindhearted Keepers showed compassion, and on that blessed night when the veils between all worlds grow thin, they created for the dragons a gate to another existence. The beasts passed safely through the rift to live forever in a separate time and place. Even the relics of the dragons already dead crossed over to the other side. Only their memory was to remain on earth."

The old wizard stood to his full height, and anger glinted in his eyes. "Man was overjoyed and prideful at having caused the exodus," he said, "then came the day of reckoning. One does not demand that the realm be rid of dragons without paying a price. And this time the price be the loss of the unicorns. Every trace of them passed over as well. The earth could not bear one creature without the other. Man had to give up the best to be saved from the worst."

As if troubled by the loss of long ago the heavens darkened. A chill wind swept the walkway and licked at Tanzie's ankles. She shivered and drew back further into the sheltering nook. "Could they not come back to us now?" she asked hopefully.

Morcar slashed his hand through the air as if severing the connection between the two worlds. "Never," he said, and the one word he spoke resounded through the night as if it were filled with all the pain and regret that the Keepers must have felt in honoring that final and irrevocable request. "What is done, is done for all time."

Tanzie thought of the Keepers and felt sympathy toward them. She was intrigued by the idea of such beings, but for all their wonder and enchantment, their lot seemed a sad one. "Who were the Keepers, Morcar? You have never spoken of them before."

"You are a Keeper," he said.

She started, then tried not to panic at his words. Again, she had blindly followed the wizard down the path of knowledge, only to be left teetering on the dangerous edge of another new revelation.

"Your mother, Beorce, was a Keeper as well," he added, "and her mother and her mother's mother and so on back to the beginning of existence. That is what I have been trying to explain to you."

"Keepers are the chosen ones; mortals with the gift of understanding the secrets of the world. Their knowledge has been passed down from mother to daughter through many generations."

Tanzie clawed through the rubble of confusion that Morcar's story built around her. His answers always led to more questions and a whirlwind of them dizzied her mind. "Are you a Keeper too?"

"No. I am the one who waits. I transcend the Keepers helping them to endure."

"But for what do you wait?" she dared to ask, then wondered if she might be better off not knowing.

"In the beginning," Morcar said, "the Keepers of the land were to show Man the path to inner wisdom and mercy, qualities he has yet to master. Later their mission became the protection of the last dragon until his release."

"But you said all the dragons were gone forever," she reminded.

"One remains turned to stone. He waits to fulfill the promise to help England. After that he too shall pass through the gate and be gone forever."

Tanzie leaned forward. "Tis my dragon isn't it? And the great rock is that the gate?"

"Very good," Morcar praised. "You have reasoned well. Now the two must be joined and my wait will be over."

Tanzie sat in stunned silence, unwilling to accept what she had just heard, yet in the wee small hours before dawn Morcar's story seemed increasingly credible and it answered many questions. Vanquishing the last bit of skepticism that her logic fought to maintain, she forced herself to accept the possibility that such beasts may once have existed. Glimpses of foreign places and unknown individuals seemed to flash through her mind. They were like memories from a lifetime other than her own, and as she opened her mind to the idea, a gentle humming filled the air. The sound could be felt as well as heard. It surrounded her and stirred a place deep within her. It was unlike anything she had ever felt before, even tonight with Branoc. It was as if a flower bloomed inside of her. But how could any of this be true? Dragons and unicorns, her mother a wandering spirit, and herself a Keeper. Yet, Morcar had no reason to lie to her. Besides, if he were to make up a story he could most certainly concoct a more credible tale than this.

Perhaps latent forces truly did sleep within her. "Morcar," she pointed out, "other than what you have taught me I was never schooled in the way of the Keepers. I am like the dragon frozen in time unable to unlock any power that I might possess. Unable to follow the ancient call that guided my ancestors through history and me to this island."

"What you know will be enough. And what you do not know matters little now. You are the final one. After you there will be no more Keepers."

Why would she be the last? Was she destined to die before bearing a daughter to carry on the history of her people? Or was it simply that the world was coming to an end? She little fancied either choice.

"By releasing the dragon," Morcar explained, "you will help the beast to fulfill his promise to save Man, and you will deliver Bamburgh and the spirit of these humans into a new era. Right or wrong, Mankind has grown beyond wanting help such as ours. And after tomorrow, for better or worse, Man will rule his own destiny. The ways of the Keepers will disappear along with the last dragon."

"But what about my mother? Why is she cursed to wander in this ether between the living and the dead?"

"When the unicorns were taken from the earth," he said, "mortal Man could not abide the pain of separation. The people became angry, forsaking the Keepers and threatening their very existence. At the time, a girl named Ori was the youngest and strongest of the Keepers and the most likely to prevail. The last dragon, turned to stone, was entrusted into her care, and the other Keepers sacrificed themselves to ensure her survival. She was endowed with their combined knowledge as the others faded into oblivion. It was then her destiny, and that of her direct descendents, to honor the promise and protect the dragon from harm."

Tanzie gazed into Morcar's eyes, but it was as if he no longer saw her. Did he look within himself and relive that time lost to the ages. Finally he spoke.

"Young Ori realized there were men who would try to bend the dragon's power to serve malevolence, so she kept the little creature safe by disappearing from sight and hiding here in the North Country. Through Ori's descendants, generation after generation, the dragon and the divine teachings of the Keepers were passed on, mother to daughter. Eventually the little beast came to Beorce and finally to you and had there been time, you would have been instructed in the rituals as well."

Tanzie felt light-headed as if recollections spanning one thousand years tugged at her mind in as many directions. "If it was safe here," she asked, "why did my mother leave Northumbria? She was gentle and kind and we had such a short time together."

Morcar straightened to his full height and his expression hardened. "Unbeknownst to all," he said, "one other Keeper had survived. He was miserly and full of spite, and to save himself he was allied against even the last of his own kind. He was corrupt and self-serving, and he had found the secret of prolonged life. He survived through the ages searching for the dragon and after many centuries, this depraved one discovered the statue's hiding place here at Bamburgh. In my absence, he came for the icon and your mother. She had no choice but to flee, thus seeking refuge beyond these shores."

"But leaving Northumbria, and going to Flanders, came at a great sacrifice to Beorce. Although her body remained strong, her soul began to fade as soon as she went beyond the soil of her beloved homeland. Her only comfort was knowing that the malevolent Keeper would not risk the same fate in following. She was as happy as she could be with her chosen destiny. Your father loved her very much and she had you, the joy of her life."

Eyes now lucid Morcar glanced at her. He had come back from wherever his mind had been wandering, and with a wistful smile, he once more took his place beside her on the bench. "The baneful Keeper grew more and more embittered, wanting, always wanting what he could never have. And when William the Bastard invaded this kingdom, the fate of this wretched one was sealed. He lost his lands and the last of his ill-gotten fortune. Everything that mattered to him was gone. Desperate, and fueled by greed and the need for power, he decided to take the risk and go in search of your mother. But he wanted the dragon to save himself not England."

"Defying the curse of leaving, he too journeyed to Flanders to claim the statue. Your mother, your father, and Ealgith's mother defended the beast, and they forfeited their own mortal lives to defeat and eliminate this desperate Keeper. I could not change their fate or postpone their hour of tragic glory, but I kept the promise I had made to your mother. I gave her the means to restore her soul."

"In the final moment before she gave up her last physical breath, the essence of Beorce was transformed into a dove."

Tanzie dug her fingernails into the palms of her hands. Tears wet her cheeks. "Does she feel pain in her present form?" she asked through trembling lips.

"Only weariness," Morcar assured her. "As a dove she was able to leave Flanders and pass the boundaries to return home. Now she awaits the requiem and honor that are rightfully her reward. When the last dragon flies once more, the restoration of her soul will be complete. For a brief moment she will be as you remember her, and for all eternity she will rest in peace, her spirit renewed and forever joined with that of your father's."

Suddenly Tanzie resented this foreign land. Its secrets had survived at the terrible loss of three people she loved. "But what difference did it make?" she accused hotly. "Why wasn't the dragon used back then? Maybe they all died for nothing." The harsh words spilled from her lips, bitter as the juice of unripe berries.

"Your mother made the correct choice," Morcar said, without hesitation. He cradled his arm around Tanzie's shoulders and held her protectively. "At that time no one was powerful enough to control the dragon. Beorce had been too long from the land, and the depraved Keeper could only begat evil. Released without guidance, the beast would have forgotten the vow to help. He would have sought only retaliation for his kind. Truly it was not the time."

"And now is?"

"Yes. Now is the time," Morcar reassured. "A horror comes unleashed by one who seeks revenge. Even he does not realize that once set free, the destruction will be worse than the combination of all hardships that have thus far come to pass."

"From this northern border to the narrow sea, fires will rise up to devour the land. The blood of the immaculate will run through the fens like a thick red river. If this ancient power is allowed to gain a foothold in the north it will spawn death and uprisings all across the country. Lawlessness will reign, in a country that has no king. The destruction and the suffering will continue for months, perhaps years, until finally there will be no one left on this island who remembers how it once was."

"And worst of all," he added with a visible shudder, "Bamburgh will be destroyed. This must never happen, for it is the seat of Mankind's spirit in this realm."

Tanzie found Morcar's words too overwhelming to visualize. As if understanding her dilemma the old man placed his hand across her forehead and bid her close her eyes. At his touch she was endowed with the ability to see through his mind's eye, the mind of an enchanter, where the completed past and the possible future could be seen as readily as the fleeting present.

The images that filled her mind reduced her to sorrow as they reminded her of the tapestry that covered the doorway to Morcar's tower. She could feel the pain of the land and the animals and the people. She heard the wailing of the victims and smelled their burning flesh. The agony that filled the hearts of every living creature of the North Country writhed within her.

She pulled away, unable to endure the pain of what she saw.

Morcar was correct.

The time of the dragon was nigh.

Chapter 24

The morning broke cold and dismal. A suitable enough atmosphere Branoc thought as he rode out through the main portal of the castle. Fighting and killing in sunny weather was incongruous. When men died in battle, it was only fitting that the heavens should weep.

He road beyond the barbican, and as the great fortress towered up behind him he recalled the day of his arrival. His opinion of the stoic citadel had changed. The bright spirit of Martanzia now tempered the forbidding demeanor of Castle Gray Scorn. In the midst of the unrest and intrigue that plagued Branoc and the land, this stronghold had become a haven of possibilities and a refuge for his dreams.

Dreams of Martanzia...

The memory of her touch, her taste, her fragrance assailed him like a pelting of arrows. He could scarcely remember his life before her appearance. Or rather, he chose not to. And he dare not contemplate what his existence would be like if he were to lose her. It preyed upon his mind. A condition that today he could ill afford. He must concentrate on the battle ahead, rather than last night's pleasurable skirmish.

Urging Solitaire toward the odd assemblage of men, Branoc issued last minute orders as he reviewed the ranks of ragtag townspeople and trained warriors.

The stallion, black as the grim task at hand, pawed at the ground and snorted with impatience.

At least his warhorse was eager for battle. Then a sense of being watched gnawed at his back. Turning in the saddle, he saw a lone figure at the open window of Morcar's tower. The person stood too far away to see clearly, but the abundance of light brown hair that fluttered about the head and shoulders like a pennon told him it was Martanzia.

Who did she champion as she watched from afar? In his heart, he knew the answer. The unique bond he had felt for her last evening had allayed his lingering doubts regarding her loyalties. Yet, for now, he dare not dwell upon the passion and love Martanzia inspired in him. Those feelings were newborn and fragile and to keep them hidden was to also keep them safe.

He turned again to face the day, and the delicate piece of fabric tied to his shield fluttered in the breeze, momentarily snagging his attention. The rose design had been embroidered by his mother, but now the flowers held a new significance for him. They made him think of the future as well as the past. Or perhaps he had ruined all his tomorrows with Martanzia by wanting her too much last evening?

Like a forgotten ember fanned by the winds of an unsettled conscience, anger flared in his belly. It leapt to life of its own volition, and the fury rendered was for the unforgiving hand of Destiny. He had given in to his desire for the girl. And even if he were to die today 'twas no excuse for ravishing her last night. He also felt shame for leaving her so quickly. He had been afraid to stay because in truth he never wished to leave her side.

He wanted to please and protect Martanzia. He wanted to know her joys and sorrows and share in both. He wanted to hold her during a winter storm and swim with her on a lazy summer afternoon. All this in spite of the document he had found at her bedside.

Desolation had come with that discovery. He believed Martanzia's denial of marriage to Rathgar, yet seeing the certificate with the official seal upon it had struck him a blow that pierced a part of him he had thought long dead. It had wounded the secret place in his heart that he had dared to open up to her.

With a growl of discontent, he turned to face his men.

Regardless of Martanzia's marital circumstance, his actions had been wrong. Last night he had taken her unmarried. It was a sin, yet one he would dare to commit again. He yearned for Martanzia, and it was her image that filled his mind as he faced this day of possible death.

Death for himself and his men. But for whom did they risk their lives? Another question that sorely plagued him. If William II was no longer king, then he and his soldiers were not obliged to fight. And if no one could confirm who wore the crown or who held the keys to the treasury his men were released from their sworn oath of fealty. But not from their oath to God and country, he thought. That was why they would fight today. For honor, for valour, for the life of the land that their fathers had conquered, and for the safety of the villagers who looked to them for protection. He needed no king to tell him this.

Solitaire tossed his head and sidestepped along the row of men. Upturned faces flashed before Branoc. His soldiers hardened and ready. The peasants fearful yet trusting.

A new resolve quickened deep within Branoc, and he pledged a vow to the future. The universe might be sinking in anarchy and taking him with it, but he would damn well save this corner of the kingdom. And if he managed to live through this day and safeguard this land from the destruction that threatened it, he would tell Martanzia he loved her and the rest of the world could go its own way. Somehow, they would endure. Somehow, they would prevail in this wild North Country. Yes, to hell with the rest of the world, they would survive and they would do it together.

With renewed vigor and hope, he nudged Solitaire into a proud canter, signaling his troops to the ready, he led them beyond the village to the edge of the near glen.

Reminiscent of the Roman legions, his men were deployed in a three-winged formation, each wedge an independent force containing foot soldiers, archers, and mounted knights. Leofric would take the right unit, Olaf, the left, while he commanded the center.

They moved forward in unison. The thick fog boiled and frothed along the ground giving way in the face of their advance only to close ranks at their backs. Angling toward the east, Branoc sought the slight rise of land between the hedgerows and the forest. It was a small enough advantage, he thought as they took up their positions, but one he dare not overlook.

On his word, the men fanned out into formation.

Then they waited.

A silence fell on the wild wood and time seemed suspended. Where were the Scots and rebels? Where was Rathgar?

A dull glimmer in the woods broke the monotony. The first fire broke out on the right. A detachment of Leofric's men galloped toward the outskirts of the village to investigate. They rousted the enemy soldiers responsible for setting the blaze, but quick as March hares the mercenaries retreated to the safety of the woods. The flames, moving as rapidly as the men who had given them life, scurried from one thatched roof to another.

The second fire erupted on the left. The third, located directly in front of them, followed closely upon the heels of the second. Smoke billowed from all landward directions and added to the impenetrable fog that masked the movements of his enemy. With the castle and ocean at his back Branoc had little room to maneuver.

The sinister silhouette of an archer flickered between the far trees and an arrow hummed through the air. On Branoc's left, a soldier screamed and crumpled to the ground. Another man fell on his right.

"To the shields," he ordered.

Well schooled in combat, his men were already forming a shield-wall, and as prearranged, his archers returned the barrage. But the enemy soldiers slinked to and fro behind the curtain of smoke, and their arrows rained down from afar like a freak hail storm.

Branoc saw neither hide nor hair of the villagers being held captive, and it soon became obvious that he never would. He did not command enough men to route the enemy soldiers as they remained hidden like the wolfs-heads that they were, and with a curse, he ordered the retreat. They must regroup and devise a new strategy, one employing tactics equal to the treachery they faced. But it was difficult to prepare for a battle that had no purpose save total decimation led by an enemy lacking in integrity?

Rathgar had lost all valour. He fought like a common thief not a knight.

****

Standing at the window her heart in her throat Tanzie watched the scene unfolding before her.

Dark and forbidding of form, Branoc had ridden out dressed completely in black. He had seemed invincible as he sat the ebony stallion so proudly. He had seemed as fierce as the dragon etched upon his shield. But he was just a man, and she feared for his life. Feared this day would bring more challenges to him than any warrior should be called upon to face.

Now as he signaled his men to return to the castle, she cheered Branoc's wisdom. To beat the devil at his own game you must play by his rules, and other than their deadly arrows, she had seen no sign of the enemy.

Evidently, Branoc had nurtured a lingering hope that his old friend possessed a last shred of morality. But chivalry did not inspire such a man as Rathgar, and it did not serve Branoc well to live by a strict code of black and white, not when he found himself wrapped literally and figuratively in a world of gray.

Such crossed purposes and extenuating circumstances tarnished the hue of every situation. Perhaps Branoc needed a new color in his life, one that she could provide. He needed to change with the times and the times were changing rapidly.

Silently she watched as the villagers funneled in through the barbican. The regular foot soldiers and house-carles quickly followed, and mounted knights and archers brought up the rear. As Branoc and the last of his men gained sanctuary the portcullis rumbled into place securing the castle's protective embrace. A she-wolf of a fortress, Bamburgh would guard well her cubs. But nothing could save the surrounding countryside.

A shiver passed through Tanzie like a ghost as she studied the horizon. Fires burned in every corner of the shire and it was with despair that she witnessed the spreading of the wanton destruction they had so hoped to avoid. For as far as the eye could see the land glowed red like the ramparts of hell. Terror had become a living entity, and its plaintive howl pierced the billowing smoke as it harbingered the advent of death.

The future as she had seen it through Morcar's eyes was fast becoming a reality, and looming darkly in the back of Tanzie's mind was the dreadful realization that Sir Branoc Valtaigne would never give up the fight. If necessary, he would single-handedly try to alter that future.

Chapter 25

Rathgar set aside the ledger he studied and listened to the sudden absence of noise. Something was amiss. It was too quiet. Only moments ago the makeshift camp on the edge of the weald had been humming with the sounds of his soldiers as they squabbled over plunder taken in the village and celebrated what fools they'd made of their enemy this morning.

As the flap of Rathgar's tent was unceremoniously jerked aside, he suddenly understood the reason for the silence. The Bishop of Durham ducked through the opening. The very sight of the man was enough to stifle a multitude of magpies.

Today, however, Ranulph Flambard was pale as oat straw. Rathgar had never seen the holy man in such an obvious state of alarm. Still, the man remained annoyingly imperious.

"The king is dead," Flambard declared, without so much as a simple greeting. "Killed to be precise."

Rathgar started at the news. Could it be true? He had seen the many-tailed comet blaze across the heavens four days past, and had hoped it heralded the fall of a kingship, but Prince Henry had mentioned usurping a crown, not murdering a monarch.

Gaining his feet he stepped around Flambard, secured the tent flap and turned to face the man of God. "Surely you are mistaken?"

"Tis the truth Relentes." Tears glistened in the Bishop's eyes. He made no attempt to conceal them.

"Wil Rou was hunting in the New Forest in a glen near Brokenhurst. But rather than a stag 'twas him they found with an arrow in his chest. My poor Wil. What a terrible end," he near choked upon the words forced out around his sorrow. "The hunting party deserted him, left him unattended to lie in the dirt where he fell. A charcoal-burner found him and conveyed his lifeless form to Winchester. Can you imagine the royal corpse transported in the back of a filthy peasant's cart, as if the king were no more than a worthless mound of moldering peat." Flambard's voice trailed off, and he shook his head in grief.

Rathgar wandered within the small confines of the tent. Already he felt trapped by this new change in circumstance. He was not particularly saddened by the death of William Rufus, nor was he squeamish about killing off his sworn enemies, but he was greatly angered that Prince Henry may have involved him in the murder of a sovereign. "How did you come by this information?"

"A runner from Winchester brought word to the monks at Rochester. A friend visiting there brought the message north by ship. The winds were favorable and he made good time."

"And whom do they say is responsible?"

"They blame Wat Tirel."

"Based upon what evidence?" Rathgar asked, finding this revelation even more beyond his ken. Tirel was an opportunistic scoundrel who backed Henry's machinations, but to murder a king... It was difficult to imagine Wat committing such an act of treason and violence.

"Walter was a member of the king's personal vanguard that day," the Bishop said. "And the deadly arrow was similar to those Walter carried."

"And you believe this to be true?"

"I do not know. Innocent or not, like any sane

324

man accused of killing a king, Tirel has fled across the sea."

Rathgar could not argue with that logic, the same idea had just occurred to him. But Tirel could seek shelter at the house of Clare, a long time friend to the lords of Poix. Rathgar had no such sanctuary waiting for him. "Who now wears the crown?" he demanded.

Flambard shrugged. "The messenger stated that Prince Henry was at Brokenhurst but Curthose's whereabouts are unknown. He too could have been near at hand. Heaven knows what may have transpired over these last few days. Regardless of which brother now lays claim to the crown," Ranulph said, "they will come for me."

"Yes," Rathgar agreed, "I dare say they will. The gentry and commoners alike will seek your head for the oppression they have suffered at your hands. You have taxed all men heavily and often. Now it is your turn to pay."

Flambard's features sharpened, and the feral look Rathgar had come to know and mistrust gnawed its way through the man's expression of sorrow. Apparently, grief did not long outweigh the Bishop's instinct for self-preservation. "I've come to you for protection Relentes."

"Me? How amazing. Why would your welfare concern me?"

Having regained his old confidence and self-assurance Flambard smiled slyly and gave a sweeping gesture as if to include the camp outside the tent. "You are not here defending the border. I suspected you had ulterior motives when first you sought the king's blessing for this little excursion. Yet what could it hurt I thought. But I misinterpreted your intent and underestimated the ambition that burns within you. I thought you merely out for personal gain. I can respect that in a man or at least accept it. And as your schemes did not interfere with my little patch of the domain, I encouraged the king to let you have your way. Now I see you were part of a greater plot. One that involved the death of my friend. While William Rufus looked to the north where you insinuated trouble did lie, the real enemy came from the south."

"Don't be absurd. I had no prior knowledge of such treachery. Besides, making threats is no longer a weapon in your armory. To whom would you tell your tales, and why would they believe you?"

"Revered or not, when a king is murdered his brothers are expected to mete out retribution. And whether or not Curthose or Beauclerk engineered this plot they will seek a scapegoat to throw suspicion in a new direction. If in accomplishing that task they are fortuitous enough to also silence a witness or two, why all the better for them."

Damn his eyes, Flambard was correct. Rathgar had planned to do the same thing to Canty McPherson and for much less reward than the crown of England. Prince Henry would not hesitate to do the same to him. And if the good Bishop became Henry's prisoner, the pious partridge would sing like a golden lark and offer up any man for sacrifice to ease his own plight. It was better to be allied with Flambard rather than pitted against him.

Besides, a new plan was definitely wanting. This morning's activities at Bamburgh had been for his personal amusement. Rathgar smiled at the memory of Branoc turning tail and riding back to the castle. But gaining access to the stronghold would require good fortune and finesse rather than brute strength and frontal attack. It was worth hearing the priest's strategy.

"If I did consent to afford you protection, what advantage would that render to me?" Rathgar asked.

Flambard's shoulders relaxed as if he knew the

game had already been won. "I understand the good faith hostage from Flanders turned out to be a beautiful woman rather than a truculent lad."

The abrupt change in the direction of the conversation put Rathgar on guard. His concern and surprise must have shown in his expression.

"Little transpires in this northern clime without my knowledge," Flambard said, with more than a hint of pride. "Do not be alarmed," he added, "I was glad to learn such duplicity and unrest was alive and well at Bamburgh castle. An ancient force is sheltered there. It is very old and no doubt pagan. It opposes me. It opposes the church. It was not so prevalent when de Mowbry ran things, but since Valtaigne has come to protect the land, it has grown ever stronger. And following the arrival of the girl and the return of the Druid it has become intolerable.

"It must be stopped," he ordered, with the assuredness of an emperor. "I have battled the contrary precepts of Anselm and the Pontiff himself to secure my position at Durham and regardless of what the future holds for me, I shall not see the county under my ecclesiastical protection burned to the ground nor torn from the teachings of the true God."

Rathgar pondered this most revealing insight. Flambard was a living, breathing dichotomy. For many a year the pious henchman had sanctioned the immoral and notorious conduct displayed by William II and his court. Yet, he feared the survival of a mere remnant of ancient belief as it gasped a dying breath on the Godforsaken borderlands. The man was addled by his own overblown sense of power and self-righteousness. An association with him could easily become a liability. Still, he must not act in haste. With the death of William Rufus, there existed only one more chance to fulfill his plans of revenge before a new king came to power and new policies became law.

"How does your battle of wills with the gods of old concern me?" Rathgar demanded. "I have come to fight a real enemy, not some figment of your imagination. And time is running out."

"Yes time is of the essence. But we shall only remain here long enough to capture that hedonistic crystal gazer and liberate the girl as hostage," Flambard promised.

"And how do you propose to accomplish this miraculous achievement?" Rathgar asked.

"You and I shall go to the castle alone. If we carry orders sanctioned by William we can simply walk in and by royal decree demand custody of the hostage and the old Druid. Valtaigne is a stickler for abiding by the law and it will be his downfall."

"Where are these orders to come from, and what if Valtaigne is already aware of King William's demise?"

"I've told no one other than you of the king's death, and I have already drawn up the documents. They are signed, sealed, and waiting for delivery."

Rathgar was properly impressed that Flambard carried the royal seal. He was also properly suspicious. It appeared the Bishop had everything neatly planned. It made Rathgar nervous. He had already been dangerously manipulated in Prince Henry's contrivance to take over the throne, he was not about to play the same part in Flambard's schemes. On the other hand, it was a more fortuitous plan then the new one he had devised. Last evening, after *interrogating* several villagers, he had learned of a long forgotten passageway that led to the catacombs beneath the castle. Entering by this ancient portal would be a risky venture at best and not to the Scot's liking. If there were another way to achieve his ends, he would welcome it. "And what services do you seek from me and my men?" he asked.

"Once we have the girl and this gray bearded heretic, we shall need protection as we travel north through Scotland. Your mercenaries will be just as happy receiving compensation for simply escorting us across their homeland as for bleeding to death here on the battlefield."

He hated to admit it, but Flambard's proposal made sense. "Where do we go from there?" he prodded. "I do not relish the idea of spending a winter in the frozen back county of a foreign land."

"Nor do I," Flambard admitted. "I have special plans for the Druid, he won't be with us long. And before the snow flies we shall set sail for Flanders. The girl's uncle owes me a favor or two, and with her in tow he will have no choice but to give us sanctuary."

Rathgar gave a snort of laughter. So, Malbourne and Flambard had prior dealings with one another. Here was no surprise. The two wore garments cut from the same licentious cloth, the only difference being that one man had fashioned his attire into robes of political intrigue and the other into an unholy chasuble.

As Rathgar pondered the arrangement, an idea came to him that made Flambard's invitation virtually irresistible. "I will agree to all you have said on one condition."

"And that is?"

"Once we have the girl and are safely underway you shall perform the marriage rite between the two of us."

"Of course if she is willing."

"Willing or not," he amended. "Those are my terms."

He could almost see the wheels of deliberation turning in Ranulph's brain. Again, the man balked at bending a trivial precept of the church. He had broken many more serious ones for his own gain, including the fathering of an illegitimate son back in Normandy. Were the old man's sins finally coming back to haunt him? Were they piling up to such a degree he feared to commit even one more?

"Well?" Rathgar prompted impatiently.

"Agreed," said the Bishop. "But in the future do not press me on issues of the church or try changing our plans behind my back."

Rathgar smiled and nodded. He would not dream of changing their plans. Adding to them of course was a different matter entirely. He was not about to abandon his original objective to disgrace Branoc in the eyes of the world. Somehow, he would find an opportunity to do so prior to killing Valtaigne.

## Chapter 26

Fear widened Ealgith's eyes even as it forced her voice up an octave. "Please, mistress, do not go. What you plan is beyond brave or even foolhardy—it is martyrdom. Let the wizard take your place. This is exactly the kind of danger and misadventure his kind were born to meddle in."

Tanzie grabbed at the cloak that Ealgith held and fought to wrest it from her grasp. "Morcar cannot help me," she answered, between clenched teeth. "He prepares for what is to come after my part is done. And disaster will befall all of us if the dragon is not delivered to the gate." She yanked again on the woolen fabric, but gained no advantage.

The chapel bell sounded Sext. The noon hour approached. There was no time left to worry over the cloak.

Releasing her hold on the garment, she sent Ealgith stumbling backward into the table. Her friend's earthy exclamation ringing in her ears, Tanzie hurried to a nearby trunk, rummaged through its contents and produced a pair of sturdy little boots. Leaning against the wall, she tugged off her thin slippers and replaced them with the more serviceable footwear. Then she retrieved the dragon statue from the stand beside her bed and carefully tucked him into a leather bag.

Ealgith still clasped the cape to her chest, her face puckered in a look of defiance.

"If you will not help me, Ealgith, at least do not hinder me by telling anyone where I have gone." Tanzie stepped to the door and reached for the latch.

"You know I have no choice in the matter."

"Oh lady," Ealgith relented, "I am with you." She hurried forward and offered up the heavy cloak. "The first time I saw that horrid rock I knew it would cause me worry or worse," she groused and quickly donned her own warm clothing.

"God will watch over us," Tanzie reassured, then wondered why He should.

"Tis probably what your mother and mine thought before they met their doom," Ealgith muttered, as she cross gartered her boots. The extent of her agitation was reflected in the jerking motion of her hands. Gaining her feet, she ruthlessly tied a shawl around her shoulders and stood scowling and ready to depart.

Tanzie smiled and gave Ealgith a quick hug. Then she opened the door and peeked out. The passage was empty. She slipped from the room and ran for the backstairs. Ealgith followed so closely on her heels she nearly tripped them both.

Reaching the ground level hallway Tanzie paused to listen. A detachment of soldiers were passing through to the makeshift barracks. She drew back in alarm. No one was allowed to leave the castle. If she were found dressed for the out of doors she would surely be detained and questioned, and there was no time to spare for such an interrogation.

Impatiently she waited for the heavy footfalls of the men to fade away. When the sound of the peasants going about their daily chores was all that remained, she stepped forward, skirted the milling throng and crossed the hall.

So silently did Ealgith scurry along in her wake Tanzie glanced back to make sure she followed. She needn't have worried. Her friend never broke stride, even as she grabbed two handfuls of dried fruit off a tray being taken to the larder.

Gaining the north wing, they entered the dim

and silent corridor. Tanzie led the way to the tapestry that concealed the door to Morcar's tower. Drawing aside the wall hanging, she pushed open the portal.

"A secret passage," Ealgith gasped in amazement. "Who lives up there?"

"'Tis the sorcerer's domain. But do not trouble over it," she added, as Ealgith retreated a step. "Our path lies elsewhere." She pointed to the stairway on the opposite side of the small landing. The steps descended into the darkness. Tanzie had yet to explore the alternate passageway leading to the catacombs.

The torch in the wall sconce flickered. She twisted it free and held it high. "Close the door Ealgith and follow me. Time is wasting."

The stairs were dank and crumbling. Something scurried along before them in the darkness. It sounded like a rat, its tiny nails clicking and scraping along the uneven stonework floor. Tanzie had trouble catching her breath. The air was oppressive, but the feeling of breathlessness was as much from fear as from the fetid atmosphere.

Hurrying down the last few steps, she paused and glanced around. The cavernous room at the bottom of the stairway was of wondrous proportion. Lit only by the flickering light of her torch the walls seemed to expand and contract with a life of their own. She felt as if she were trapped in the belly of a great beast. Standing in the bowels of the castle, she supposed the analogy was appropriate enough. A myriad of tunnels branched off from the main room, one of which supposedly led beneath the bailey to the jagged shoreline and the North Sea.

"Which path do we take Mistress?" Ealgith asked, as she peered over Tanzie's shoulder.

"Morcar promised he would mark the proper course for us," she said and glanced around. "There.

That is the way we are to follow." She pointed to the one tunnel that was illuminated by a strange glow that came from neither sconce nor torch. The light simply seemed to hover in the air.

"Oh, lady, that ain't natural," Ealgith claimed.

As they inched forward, the light moved as well, always advancing ahead of them, stopping when they stopped and proceeding at a rate akin to their own. Ealgith was correct, this wasn't natural and though their path was brightened by this glimmering radiance, Tanzie's misgivings remained shrouded in darkness.

At the end of the passageway, a more natural brightness seeped around the edges of an iron-clad door. They had reached the portal near the east sally port. Using their combined strength they were able to force the door open and claw their way through the twisted foliage that waited beyond the portal. The ancient exit was ravaged by time and hidden by centuries of gnarled growth. It boasted no guard. In truth, she would be surprised if anyone knew of its existence

Smothering the torch in the sand, Tanzie climbed a small rise to get her bearings. A noise sounded at her back. She spun around and scanned the surrounding landscape. She saw no one lurking in the scrub that clung to the hillside yet the sensation that someone followed would not be dispelled.

Cradling the statue more securely, she fingered the hilt of her dagger. At whatever cost she must deliver the dragon to the stony cathedral that awaited its icon.

With Ealgith still at her side, she wended her way amongst the craggy terrain and over the shifting sand. Reaching the water's edge, she paused and her shoulders sagged in defeat. It was impossible. Windswept waves crashed upon the shore and pummeled the jagged base of the monolith. She had thought perhaps if the tide were out and the water were calm, she might wade to the towering stone, but seeing it again firsthand she realized it was out of the question. Still Morcar had promised the prophecy would be fulfilled.

At a loss as to what to do next, she stood as motionless as the statue she carried. The words to a Christian prayer she had learned as a child tumbled through her mind. Then guilt overtook her thoughts, and in light of what she prepared to do, she wondered if the God she had honored in her youth would find her plea for assistance blasphemous.

She cast her eyes heavenward. This day of reckoning would recall ancient prophesies, tenets, and doctrines, ones that roamed the earth long before Christ was born, yet surely nothing existed before the time of God the creator. Was it possible that the path of all religions and philosophies lead to the same destination? It would be the universal parody if God turned out to be whatever we conceived Him to be. Each of us correct no matter the image honored.

Her gaze slid from the heavens and came to rest on the pinnacle of rock. Whoever was in charge of the universe, she thought angrily, she needed help and she needed it now.

Suddenly the wind died as if the world held its breath, and she knew her appeal was about to be answered. A rumbling emanated from deep within the earth. The ground before her trembled then heaved upward and the water eddied aside revealing a narrow strip of land that led from the shore to the dark monolith.

"Oh Heavenly Saints preserve us," Ealgith lamented.

Not dwelling upon what would happen should the newly formed ribbon of wet terrain disappear as quickly as it had arisen, Tanzie took a deep breath to steady her nerves and made to step forward. But a hand clamped down upon her shoulder halting her advance.

"What have you done?"

It was Branoc's voice. Someone *had* been following them. She glanced up and studied his face, and though his eyes were troubled, they were also wide with amazement.

"Nothing—yet," she answered. Branoc's expression turned grim, and her resolve faltered. "I only wished to save us," she added weakly.

"Where is Morcar?" Branoc asked and glanced around. "No doubt he had a hand in this disruption of common sense and the natural order of things."

"He has yet to appear," she said, "though he promised to be here when needed."

"Again," Branoc declared with grave concern, "the wishes of a woman and the promises of a prophet. Why do I not feel more at ease with this combined effort of experts?"

"But I must return the carving to the rock," she defended, as she pulled back the cover to reveal the dragon.

He stared at the statue she held. "According to whom?" he growled, "the old Druid? He follows a course that knows no bounds. He will sacrifice himself and anyone else to see his divinations realized."

"But they are the prophecies of the land, not the sorcerer. Besides," she challenged, "have you a better plan to save us from the destruction that Rathgar sends our way?"

"We had considered setting backfires to trap Rathgar and the Scots and to contain the blazes already alight," Branoc said. "And a good rainstorm would help," he added and studied the horizon, "but the skies are remarkably clear today. Even the fog and smoke have flown in the face of what is to come." His expression darkened like the clouds he yearned for. "At least we now know of the east entrance leading to the catacombs. Were you eventually going to enlighten me regarding that little discovery?"

Another bout of guilt afflicted her. She could not meet his gaze. He was correct, she should have informed him of the secret passageway. It was a breech of their defenses and could afford the enemy an entrance had they known of its existence. "I was afraid to tell you," she admitted, "afraid you would try to stop me."

"Did it not occur to you that I might aid you in your endeavor? Even if I do not believe in your cause, I believe in you."

Her heart ached at the beauty of his words. Here was a man who offered unconditional love such as she had not seen since the death of her parents.

Branoc gripped her upper arms and held her tight. "I believe that you had nothing to do with Rathgar's schemes or the false marriage decree," he proclaimed.

"We stand on the brink of destruction," she said, taken aback by his statement, "and you think to discuss such matters?"

"There is no time left for anything but truth," Branoc said.

"Yes," she agreed, and reached up to stroke his cheek. "You are correct. From this moment onward nothing but truth between us. And faith. Let this day be a new beginning for both of us, as well as for the land." She glanced at the pinnacle then back at Branoc. "I must usher the dragon home," she said. "Will you wait for me here?"

****

Branoc pondered her words as he stared down at the girl and the statue she held.

Then he recalled the declaration he had recklessly thrown in the face of his Lord the day he was knighted. *"Neither God nor man shall deliver unto this earth a dragon more formidable than the one known as Valtaigne."* Was today the reckoning of such an impudent challenge?

He studied the stony monument and the unnatural path that led to its base. His covenant of old had been made in anger, and if it now called forth retribution or danger, he should be the one to face it not the woman he loved and cherished.

"No," he said and tightened his hold upon her. "I will not risk the one thing that gives purpose to my life, especially not to fulfill the needs of a sly old wizard. He serves only himself and an ancient calling which is apparently best left unrevealed to us mere mortals. No," he repeated, "I will not allow it."

"But what could you possibly fear to lose? Martanzia asked. "The castle, the land, the power that allows you to rule this little province on the outcast northern borders? You told me once that you feared nothing, and I believed you. What is it you value so highly that you would fear to face life without it? What could you possibly desire so desperately?"

Branoc shook his head in wonder. How could she not divine the answer to her own question? "Why 'tis you, Martanzia," he said and gently chucked her under the chin, "'tis you."

Chapter 27

Branoc's words melted through Tanzie, leaving her breathless in the face of his love for her. She reached for his hand and caressed it to her cheek.

She was no longer alone in the world. She had a man of honor and valour to champion her cause. A man who loved her without question. She bathed in the glow of this most spectacular revelation. Then for once, she felt Morcar's presence prior to his unannounced arrival. Turning in the circle of Branoc's arms, they both watched his approach, Ealgith at their side.

Like a specter newly formed, the old Druid materialized on the shore. Glancing neither left nor right, he walked the pebbled beach, his purposeful stride never faltering. His unadorned white robe was cut simple as a hermit's, and his sandals were of plain leather, yet a kingly aura radiated from his face, and his eyes burned with a luminous power that seemed to emanate from deep within him. He carried a scepter of silver in one hand, and an orb of gold in the other, and his long gray hair and full beard mingled with the folds of his ordinary garb giving him an outline much larger than life.

Morcar paused before them, and studied first Branoc's face and then hers. "She must go," he said, "alone."

Branoc stiffened at the words and stepped between her and the sorcerer. "She is not obliged to do your bidding," he defended.

"No and neither are you Valtaigne, yet you will. You have both been chosen. The girl will be safe enough," he reassured, "and you are needed here."

Leofric appeared on the horizon following the same path as the conjurer. Morcar seemed to be the only one not surprised at his unexpected arrival.

Ealgith ran to Leofric and threw herself into his arms, nearly upsetting him backwards over a jumble of rocks. "Rathgar and the Bishop of Durham are here," Leofric reported as he gently disentangled Ealgith from around his neck and gained their side.

"Do they bring an offer of peace?" Branoc asked.

"On the contrary. They called at the front gate bold as you please waving the king's writ and declaring that you must give up Martanzia and the old man." Morcar flinched at Leofric's unflattering description, but held his tongue.

"Whose seal is upon the document?" Branoc asked.

"William Rufus's."

A look of consternation passed between Branoc and Leofric. "You said the king was dead," Branoc challenged Morcar.

"And so he is," the crystal-gazer reaffirmed. He appeared pleased as a child at the fair as he watched the events around him unfolding.

Tanzie was dumbfounded by the news of William Rufus's death. Fancy that no one had seen fit to tell her of such an occurrence. Even Morcar had withheld the information. But then after all she was just the good faith hostage, what business was it of hers.

Her irritation ignited and flamed, and then swiftly burned itself out. Isolated here in the middle of nowhere it mattered more what the men before her were about to do, rather than whom occupied the throne many miles away. It mattered more that Branoc had come to rescue and help her.

"Our guests refused to wait until you could be summoned back to the castle," Leofric continued. "I sent them the long way around and came ahead to warn you of their approach. Legal or not, as they carried a king's warrant, we dared not detain them without your word."

"They came alone?" Branoc asked the surprise evident in his voice.

"They made a great show of pretending such, but the Scots and the mercenaries watch the castle from the weald, and a full compliment of Saxon renegades hide beyond yon hill."

"We must not be caught out in the open," Branoc warned, attempting to usher them toward the hidden passage.

"It is too late for retreat," Morcar countered and held his ground. Tanzie peered around Branoc in the direction Morcar indicated.

As if enjoying an afternoon stroll, Rathgar and the Bishop sauntered along the shore. State and church nearly arm in arm and in this case the worst of both worlds.

The two men halted a short distance away. Close enough to talk conveniently; far enough back to draw sword or take cover should the negotiations go other than in their favor.

"I'm sure the good Leofric has informed you of our purpose here," Rathgar said, and held out the rolled parchment.

Branoc did not reach for the document. "I have no room in the scriptorium for more of your forgeries," he said. "Especially those signed by the hand of a dead king."

Flambard started in surprise. Rathgar gave a knowing smile. "How did you find out?" he asked, and tossed the parchment to the ground.

"The old Druid is good for some practical uses," Branoc said.

"Many enchantments roam the woods of the New Forest," Morcar put in brightly indicating he knew the precise location of the king's final hours, "and many horrors."

The words of the sorcerer enraged Bishop Flambard. His face reddened and his eyes burned with the glint of a zealot turned loose upon an unrepentant sinner. "You perverted monstrosity. You heathen spawn of Lucifer. What more do you know of this? Perhaps it was your power that turned the arrow in the king's direction."

Unperturbed Morcar gave a shrug. "'Tis an old custom for a sovereign to be sacrificed to the land. William Rufus is not the first king to die a violent death close to the cross-quarter days. Besides he was more of a threat to you and this kingdom than I could ever be."

Flambard howled with anger. "Hold your tongue, you unclean pagan."

The old Druid shook his head in pity. "You know as well as I, Flambard, that it is not a matter of pagan or pious only right and wrong. Now watch and see what your misguided intentions have wrought."

Morcar glanced at Tanzie and nodded. "Set the dragon free," he ordered.

Misinterpreting Morcar's words, Rathgar gave a burst of mocking laughter. "So, Valtaigne, your reputation has followed you across the channel. Yet, I doubt even the Dragon of Normandy can win against these odds." He raised his arm over his head and waved it back in forth in a great arch. The enemy that Leofric had warned of rose up and crested the far hill. The wail of the pipes sounded as well. No doubt, a signal to the other men waiting near the castle.

Understanding Morcar's true meaning Tanzie gently eased away from Branoc's side. It was now or never. While the men were occupied with their warring and politics, she slipped away. This was the reason she had come to Northumbria, this was the reason that the three people she had loved most in this world had sacrificed their lives. She pivoted, gained her footing and sprinted down the path toward the stone pinnacle.

"Oh, lady," her handmaiden wailed.

Poor Ealgith, Tanzie thought as she dashed onward, this time I have asked too much of her. Then she smiled at the sound of her friend's footfalls scrunching in the wet sand behind her.

Reaching the base of the towering stone, Tanzie observed the forbidding structure more closely. Several feet up the side of the monolith, there was a ledge with a niche that resembled a small grotto. It appeared empty and incomplete, as if it waited to be filled. That was surely where the little dragon belonged.

She glanced at Ealgith. No words did they speak. The love and faithfulness in her friend's eyes said enough. Snagging the end of the leather bag between her teeth, that she might use both hands for climbing, Tanzie reached for a handhold.

"The ascent to the right looks the less formidable," Ealgith encouraged and gave her a boost.

Tanzie clung to the wet stony surface and an image of the Keepers near blinded her mind's eye. With infinite detail, she saw the face of each unsung stalwart paladin that had preceded her, including her mother. The voices of the past called to her and their belief in saving the future urged her onward. Her efforts today would ensure that the trials and sacrifices of her ancestors had not been in vain and with fortitude stoked to a fevered pitch, she hauled herself upward and onto the stony outcropping. Spitting the end of the bag from her mouth, she reached inside the leather wrappings and liberated the last dragon on earth.

An unusual warmth emanated from the statue.

She stared at the creature's face and realized the ancient carving was all she had left of her mother and this too she must relinquish. Uninvited a wish to possess and control the dragon washed over Tanzie, and she fiercely clasped the image to her chest. The dragon and she had been together for a long time.

Cradling the statue like a child's doll the frivolous longing in her heart became covetous desire. Now she knew that the beast could be used to acquire great fortunes or to rule the land. Thousands would do her bidding. She could have everything she had ever wanted. But at what sacrifice? She would lose all sense of purpose and honor. She could even lose her soul as her mother had, but with no chance for redemption. She would surely lose Branoc.

Frightened by the temptations that assaulted her brain, Tanzie recited the promise she had made when the statue had first been given to her, and her mind was freed from the dark thoughts.

The little beast quivered in her hands, but she was not afraid. She understood the dragon's desire to be free. After hundreds of years of bondage in stony immobility, his spirit yearned to soar once more.

She traced her finger along the beautiful knot work carved around the base of the stone relic. The expression upon the face of the beast now seemed mischievous as well as majestic. She gave the dragon a quick hug and placed it in the waiting nook. Slowly she glided her hands along the smooth surface of his body. It would be the last time she would ever touch him. Then kneeling before the little dragon with whom she had shared so much of her life, Tanzie crossed her hands upon her breast and gazed skyward. The wind blew her hair back from her face, and she closed her eyes and chanted the words that Morcar said only a Keeper had the power to invoke.

"Staenen draca, eftarisan.

Stone dragon rise again.

Rihtan meoring et aliesend minnisc.

Rebuke the danger and redeem mankind.

Meord, draca dor.

Your reward, shall be the dragon gate."

In the ensuing silence, she opened her eyes and glanced around. Should the words have been spoken in Celtic rather than Saxon? She was not fluent in the ancient tongue, and Morcar had assured her it would make no difference. Just as she considered repeating the phrases, a fearful rumbling ensued. The solid rock beneath her shuddered and jerked, and she felt like a flea clinging to the back of a shaking hound. A convulsion quaked through the monolith. She lost her hand hold and backslid toward the ground.

Ealgith broke her fall and they landed in a wool swathed tangle of arms and legs.

Groaning in pain Tanzie righted herself. "Bless you Ealgith," she gasped. "I could not have succeeded without you."

Wide-eyed and speechless, Ealgith just nodded and sagged against her.

Struggling to her feet, she prodded Ealgith to rise and follow, and they ran along the narrow strip of land to joined the others waiting along the shore.

"The spirit of the dragon lives," Morcar grandly proclaimed.

The Bishop of Durham yowled and fell on his knees, and the enemy troops stood staring in disbelief.

Chapter 28

Morcar raised the golden orb as if offering it to the gods.

The breeze turned fierce and untamed, but the maelstrom did not affect the old Druid. The elements halted just short of contact with him, as if they feared to distract him as he called long-forgotten chants into the wind.

Thunder shook heaven and earth. The moon crossed directly into the path of the noonday sun, and like a shadow cast by the wing of an angel, a gentle darkness settled over the land. The enemy soldiers broke rank, their weapons and foul intent forgotten.

Then on the far horizon where the ocean met the darkened sky a billowing cloud began to form. It fumed and swirled in the dull canopy of air and as it drew near it took shape and form.

Tanzie watched in awe. It was the spirit of the dragon. Illusive as a dream or a child's fantasy, the promises and hopes of a people long forgotten took on the semblance of life. It was real, yet not of true substance. Animated, yet ghostly in its apparition.

"Do you see it, Ealgith?" she whispered, then wondered what answer she preferred to hear. No— indicating only she were hallucinating or yes— meaning the whole world had gone mad.

"I see it lady. But I would not admit it to anyone but you."

As the soaring image of the dragon drew closer, the wind whipped the sea into a foaming fury and breakers surged landward like small tidal waves.

Her little dragon had contained the essence of a spectacular creature.

Recovered from his initial shock, Ranulph Flambard grappled upright. "You shall not win, Druid," he screeched, like a mad man. "I rule this northern territory and all who enter here." Spittle flew from his lips as he cursed Morcar. The Bishop grabbed up the bejeweled crucifix that hung from a chain around his neck, and holding it out in front of him like a shield, he ranted and raved in Latin. But the louder he clamored, the more the wind did blow. It pummeled him like physical blows, as it filled his mouth with sand and tore his words asunder. Reduced to apoplectic rage Flambard cowered in the rocks and covered his head.

Morcar stood unmoving, an expression of might and expectation etched upon his face.

The wind abruptly ceased and a dead calm descended. The thunderhead shaped like a dragon hung in the muted atmosphere above them. Then they communed, the old Druid and the spirit of the ancient beast. And though no words could be heard, the silent commiseration was almost tangible in the space that separated them. The land seemed to come alive with a remembered exuberance. Misty shadows wavered upon the rocks and trees, and lacy illusions tumbled and pirouetted across the sand covered hills.

The hair on the nape of Tanzie's neck prickled, and a shiver raced down her spine, and she reached for Branoc's hand. It seemed as if everything around her suddenly had a disposition of its own. The shore grass whispered into the waiting ears of the seashells, and the driftwood leaned closer to the pulsing jagged rock.

The vibrations flowed around Branoc and through Tanzie, encapsulating them as one. It pounded in her temples and drifted the length of her. Growing ever stronger, it reminded her of making love and of how alive she felt cozened in Branoc's arms.

Rathgar drew his sword and severed the spell of wonderment. "Enough sorcery," he growled at the old Druid. "You and the girl are to come with us."

"But the dragon," Flambard sputtered and pointed toward the sky.

"Valtaigne is the only dragon that interests me," said Rathgar, "and his failure to defend the borderland and the crown's good faith hostage will no doubt be what interests the new king."

Tanzie glanced at Branoc. He appeared unmoved by Rathgar's insults and threats. But Rathgar was not their only concern. The renegades, having come to their senses, once more began the advance.

It couldn't end like this she thought. Morcar had promised that the dragon would save them. Yet they were severely out numbered, and the cloud-beast, though impressive, seemed more bluster than might. They needed something else...someone else to even the odds.

As the thought flittered through Tanzie's mind, the lady in white appeared. This too Morcar had predicted.

At the sight of the apparition, the Saxon renegades, born and raised on the legends that surrounded the North County, fled from the beach in terror. The wail of the pipes sounded again, and the Scots near the castle took to the woods as well.

Tanzie cried out in happiness. Beorce appeared exactly as Tanzie remembered her, and when she spoke the aura of light surrounding her softly glimmered. "You have made me very proud, Martanzia. I could not have wished for anything more in my life other than greater time to spend with you and your father."

348

The brilliance that radiated from her mother's face was remarkable to gaze upon. The tendrils of her hair were shot through with strands of gold, and a glittering like spun glass sparkled from the tips of her fingers. But even as her image was restored in full, it began to fade.

"Mother, please stay," Tanzie begged, though in her heart she knew it could never be.

Beorce extended her hand in Tanzie's direction. "My darling precious daughter. If the law of nature would so permit, I would gladly remain. But I cannot. Until we meet again in the Summerland, know that I loved you always."

A white mist gathered in a vortex around Beorce. "Remember me," she said softly. Her form blurred and disappeared, and a dove rose from the fading nebula. The white bird swooped downward once, then joyously spiraled upward to disappear into the heavens.

Tanzie reached out trying to hold on to the ethereal image of her mother. If only once more she could touch her hand, her cheek. She could not breathe for the pain that filled her chest. She wished to die, and follow her mother beyond this plain of earthly existence. To be torn a second time from her side was more than she could bear.

"I am sorry you had to lose her twice," Morcar said, recognizing her anguish. "With the quickening of the dragon's spirit her transformation is complete. We must let her find her peace. Your father has long awaited her coming. They deserve to be together."

Morcar was correct. It was time for Tanzie to let go. Tears and self-pity would only impede her mother on her final journey, and even if she could stay another hour, another day, it would never be long enough. A great sense of understanding and release overcame Tanzie and she felt dizzy. Her world spun dangerously out of control until Branoc gathered her into his arms.

She buried her face in his compassionate embrace, and her tears fell upon the cold iron rings of the corselet he wore. She savored the pain as the metal bit into her cheek, distracting her from the misery that gripped her heart. Her mind reeled with all that she had just witnessed. She had seen sights with her own eyes too marvelous to be believed. No wonder the likes of such magic could no longer be sustained on the face of the earth. It would take more faith than humans now possessed to keep it alive.

Branoc stroked her hair, and gently rocked her to and fro. The closeness they had shared last evening enveloped her once again, and his caresses told her that he shared her pain as well as her joy.

"Domlic draca, magister cignes." Morcar suddenly called out demanding the attention of the nebulous creature they had all but forgotten. "Quench the fires and renew the land," he directed. A battle of wills seemed to ensue between the old Druid and the spirit of the dragon, but willing or not the ancient beast would serve mankind one last time.

Lightning forked across the murky sky, and thunder growled all around them. Rain fell from the beast-cloud drenching the village. Torrents of water rushed through the streets, dousing the burning buildings and the smoldering crops. Steam rose upward where fires once burned. The hot thirsty earth absorbed the moisture as quickly as it appeared, and plants and trees once shriveled by the heat uncurled to reach skyward.

The land would survive.

"'Tis time to usher the last dragon home," Morcar said, quietly.

She glanced at the old Druid. A bittersweet smile twitched upon his lips, but his eyes remained as bright as two blue diamonds, and his resolve never faltered.

Morcar gazed into the orb he held. "The moment for which I have waited a lifetime is finally about to be realized," he added, his voice choked with emotion.

"Your time has come indeed, heretic."

Surprisingly agile for his cumbersome size, the bishop lunged forward and dashed the sphere from Morcar's hand. The orb shattered upon the rocks. Splinters of gold danced through the air, and there was a sound like that of fairy wings breaking.

As if struck a savage blow Morcar gasped, stumbled backward, and slumped to the ground.

A haunting resonance echoed down from the dragon-cloud.

Tanzie ran to Morcar and knelt by his side. The wizard sat up by his own volition but the fierceness had left his face, and his eyes momentarily dulled. "Without the orb," he said, and grabbed her arm for support, "the specter of the beast is beyond my control."

\*\*\*\*

The spirit of the dragon flew haphazardly about the sky. He was free, he lived once more. Spurred on by long stifled needs and desires, he remembered the way it once had been, when magic ruled the land and his kind were both honored and feared. He was the last and there would never be another.

As his spirit grew stronger, he glanced down from above, but no compassion did he feel for the pitiful humans below. He owed these present-day mortals no loyalty. There was no reason to be bound by promises of old.

After all, he was the greatest creature that had ever existed upon the earth.

Chapter 29

Morcar gained his feet. "You are a fool, Flambard," he chastised and brushed the sand from his robe. "In your attempt to further your own glory, you may very well have doomed mankind."

"I have doomed you perhaps," the Bishop replied, with a self-righteous sneer, "but I doubt one heathen more or less will greatly affect the course of human events."

Morcar marveled at the Bishop's audacious stupidity. "To dare to measure the worth of another man's life is a great responsibility," he said.

Stepping forward, Morcar intently studied Rathgar's face. "The goodness inherent in humans," he added, "often comes from the most surprising sources." Then his gaze shifted back to the Bishop. "And it is often found lacking in the most expected avenues. The old ways must run their course Flambard. They will be gone soon enough. Then whom shall you blame for your failures and inadequacies? You were better off with me as your scapegoat. When I am gone, you will have only mortal men to castigate."

"Infidels abound like the plague, blasphemer, they will suit. I shall remain busy for many years to come."

"No doubt you are correct. Your kind will wage untold wars all in the name of religion. But your victories shall be hollow, and you will be the loser until you learn to conquer your enemies through tolerance rather than combat. It is a hard lesson to learn."

The Bishop snarled and took a menacing step forward.

Morcar raised his scepter.

A small burst of lightning forked down from above, striking the ground dangerously near the Bishop. The priest's hair stood on end, and he swore like a common herdsman.

"I must admit," Morcar said with a chuckle, "there are times when even I find peaceful coexistence a difficult truism to employ."

With an exclamation of fury, Flambard slapped at his expensive robes and fretted over the bits of smoldering velvet ignited by the spattering of sparks.

It was clear to Morcar that the Bishop possessed a very dark and tortured soul. "You are more concerned with living in the image of a god, rather than living by the word of your God," he said. "But then it is all of your own making. Your God is what your need for religion has made of Him. And I am what your fear of failing that God has made of me."

As the two men glared at one another, thunder again grumbled deep and menacing. The dragon spirit seemed to have grown bored listening to the tribulations of Man, and the vaporous image roiled and billowed into the heavens growing darker and more omnipotent. The image of outstretched wings now spanned the dark horizon and the great cloud-mouth opened wide as if the beast wished to devour the universe.

Morcar calmly observed the creature made of mist and fog. It was to be expected. The dragon had forgotten the promise. Left unchecked he would become a fearsome tempest raging out of control, bending nature to fit his fury, destroying all who dared to cross his path. All but one. He glanced around. Only Branoc could save them, one dragon to lead another.

"Your time has come, Valtaigne," he said.

\*\*\*\*

Branoc glared at the old Druid then studied the sky. What was he suppose to do, wrestle a cloud, subdue a nebulous creature who's very existence mocked sane thinking even as it kindled childhood fears?

"Stand fast, Valtaigne," Rathgar said. "We've still a personal score to settle. You can play the hero later...if you survive."

Leofric broke away from Ealgith and strode forward to stand at Branoc's side.

The cloud-beast forgotten, Branoc drew his weapon and motioned Leofric back. Here was a confrontation a warrior could understand. No magic and no political intrigue and if he knew Rathgar no rules. Here was a confrontation he had dreaded for years and could no longer avoid. Today would be the death of the rivalry they shared and most likely the death of one of them as well.

With the instinct of wolves, the two warriors drew together and circled one another, and a lifetime of memories seemed to pass between them. Branoc stared with regret at the man before him. This was not the Rathgar who had been by his side as he had learned to sharpen a sword or play chess. This was not the Rathgar who had been with him secretly watching a serving wench from the chateau next door, as she swam naked in the lake in Ponthieu. The Rathgar before him was a stranger. His eyes were cold, with nothing of the boy left in the man.

Yet sadly, he knew there was no way to temper Rathgar's revenge. If given the opportunity Rathgar would slit his belly from groin to chest with no more concern than if he slaughtered a hog. And worse than the thought of his own death was the knowledge that Rathgar would have Martanzia.

Branoc hazarded a glance in her direction, and

he silently declared his love for her. No questions, no conditions. As if reading Branoc's mind, Rathgar growled and leapt forward. Fighting for Martanzia as well as for himself, Branoc met the lunging attack.

The clash of cold steel rang like a death knell across the empty beach. After a few experimental thrusts and parries the true ordeal began, and Rathgar attacked without pause, blow after jarring blow. The hollow clanking echoed across the darkened landscape, a litany that lent a deadly cadence to the dim primordial scene.

Branoc's sword seemed twice its normal weight, as he wielded it again, and again, and again. The unhealed wound on his thigh throbbed, and he felt a trickle of blood run down his leg where he assumed the stitches had broken.

With a glancing blow, Rathgar nicked Branoc, above the right temple. The blood mingled with his sweat and stung his eye even as it obscured his vision. He shook his head and swiped at the wound with the back of his wrist. His strength was waning. He was still not fully recovered from his encounter with Rathgar's arsenic. But this was the final hour. He could not fail. Everything he had ever fought for in his life paled in comparison to what he fought for at this moment. This was life, as he knew it...goodness fighting to triumph over wickedness, and love-inspired honor conquering the darkest of fears.

"Give it up Valtaigne," Rathgar jeered, "and I will kill you swiftly and painlessly."

His weapon held high Rathgar rushed forward on Branoc's blind side. At the last moment, Branoc saw the blade and twisted out of harm's way. As Rathgar's great sword came down the deadly blade struck rock and the steel shattered.

"By the Rood," Rathgar swore, and threw aside

the useless cross-piece. He unsheathed his short sword, lowered his head, and charged Branoc like a bull. Both men tumbled to the ground. Sand and pebbles flew from beneath their twisting bodies. They wrestled over jagged rock, and the pointed ends of driftwood dug into Branoc's back and thighs. They rolled and grappled, each man seeking the upper hand. Rathgar grasped Branoc's wrist and slammed his hand back against a stone. He lost his grip on the broadsword, and the smaller blade that hung at his side was beyond his reach.

Pinned to the ground with Rathgar astride him Branoc stared transfixed at the weapon that Rathgar held poised in the air. The silent symbol of death stood out brightly against the black sky. Confused thoughts jumbled through his mind and he felt suspended in time. Then Branoc thought again of Martanzia, the one thing that fate had seen fit to bless him with. The one thing that made his life worth living.

Fortified by his thoughts for the girl who loved roses, Branoc clawed at the sand seeking a weapon. His fingers closed around his opponent's discarded sword grip. Striking upward, he hit Rathgar in the face with the heavy pommel. Branoc felt and heard a sickening crunch as the metal made contact with the side of Rathgar's head. Blood flowed from Rathgar's nose and mouth, and he groaned and slumped sideways to the ground. Gaining his feet Branoc retrieved his sword and held the blade to Rathgar's throat as his opponent remained sprawled in the sand.

"It is finished Relentes," he said leaning closer. Both men fought for air in great shuddering gasps. Blood dripped from the cut over Branoc's eye to mingle with that which flowed from Rathgar's temple. They were blood brothers at last, but now it was too late.

Rathgar laughed up at Branoc. "The devil and I shall await your arrival in hell, Valtaigne."

Branoc tightened his grip on the blade, the urge to mete out final justice bunched the muscles in his forearm. Then he relented and stood to his full height. "You will not burn in the flames so quickly," he said. "The Weeper has finished the tower. You and Flambard shall have the honor of being the first state prisoners housed there."

As if overwhelmed by such a dreadful thought, the Bishop babbled to himself as if he'd gone addlebrained. He would offer no further trouble or resistance.

But not so for Rathgar. His eyes shone bright betraying his fear. "Kill me now and be done with it," he snarled. "I will go mad confined to one of Gundulf's cells."

For one tormented moment, Branoc thought of fulfilling Rathgar's request for death. It would certainly simplify his own life. But that was exactly why he knew it was the wrong choice. It was the easy way out, and he would not yield now and become the very thing he fought against. Searching his heart, he found pity for what Rathgar had become and with a shake of his head he sheathed his weapon.

Leofric stepped forward, grabbed Rathgar by his hauberk, and hauled him to his feet. "I'll see to our old friend," he said. "Just like old times, eh Rathgar. The three of us together again."

Martanzia rushed to Branoc's side.

The fire in his blood ran high from battle but it rose to a new glory as he held her to his chest and returned her kisses. She tasted salty and fresh like the sea, her rose perfume but a velvet memory upon her skin. If they had been alone, he would have lowered her to the sand and made love to her right there and then.

"We've no time now for your ardor," Morcar interrupted. "The spirit of the dragon must still be reclaimed and sent to the other side."

Branoc tore himself from Martanzia's warm embrace to question Morcar's meaning. "I thought you could not order the creature without the orb."

"That is so. I cannot. Now man must finish what man has begun." The old Druid held up a large gold disk suspended by a leather thong. It was carved with the rendering of a dragon. Then he nodded over his shoulder toward the stone monument that towered up out of the sand. "The spirit of the last dragon must return from whence he came. I cannot control him, but someone of great valour can. Someone with courage equal to the beast. Someone like you, Valtaigne."

Branoc passed his hand before his eyes. This nightmare of mythical trials and tribulations was never ending. He didn't even believe in these ancient curses and gods. Yet, he respected Morcar's dedication to the lost arts, more than Flambard's merciless rendering of Christianity. All he knew for sure was that he believed in the order of the universe and the triumph of the soul. And the Saints help him, he now believed in love.

Morcar swirled his scepter in the air and tossed the medallion to Branoc.

Instinctively he caught it, then he held his sword aloft in challenge to his ethereal adversary.

A roaring wind howled across the land and the cloud-beast was illuminated from within by an iridescent red glow. Words and images flooded Branoc's mind and for a brief moment, he was one with the dragon-spirit. He felt the glory of the creature that hung in the sky above them. The dragon possessed the power to reign supreme over the world, but he lacked the desire to rule with compassion. Was this then the quality that separated man from beast? No, he thought, compassion was too often lacking in Man as well.

A mournful howl rode the wind and the cloud writhed as if in pain. Branoc recognized the beast's profound loneliness, for this was an emotion he knew only too well. It was a crushing agony worse than any physical pain. It was a torment not cured by balm or time. It was the key to the heart of the dragon.

"Come old friend," Branoc called, "they await you. To be the last of your kind is a difficult duty. Alone you will grow bitter and hollow and angry. Go now while you are still in your prime. 'Tis an honorable choice and in the end that is all that truly matters."

Thunder cracked like a thousand whips and the dragon heaved and twisted. Then the moon left the arms of the sun's embrace and the smudgy darkness surrounding them melted into light.

In a burst of glory, shafts of sunlight speared through the thunderhead, turning the dragon-cloud a luminous pink. And as the image of the beast thinned and dissolved into nothingness, a great force funneled downward from above. The raw energy pounded through Branoc, excruciating yet exhilarating. It tore at him and pulled him in a thousand directions, even as it energized the very core of his being. The extraordinary force flowed collectively into the medallion he held, and the ancient rendering grew warmer and warmer until his hand felt on fire.

The roar of the dragon echoed once more through the countryside. Branoc clutched the pendant to his chest and for the second time in his life, he felt an odd sympathy for the beast under whose symbol he had lived and fought. "You were more than just an illusion after all," he said, awed by the spectacle just witnessed. "Your memory shall live on."

He slumped in relief. It was over he thought, as he delivered the golden ornament into the hands of the sorcerer. The land was reclaimed, Rathgar was captured, and all was right with the world.

"Branoc Valtaigne," Morcar said, with great pageantry, "you have conquered the last dragon on earth." A look of great peace enhanced the old Druid's expression. "I have worried over that beast for far too many centuries. He has made me old before my time."

"Perhaps", Branoc suggested, "you could spend the next few hundred years in the pursuit of less complicated endeavors."

"If only it could be so," Morcar agreed. The gravity of his voice annihilated the feeling of peace that had dared to set foot within Branoc. "The final task still remains," the enchanter declared. "Someone must deliver the medallion across the barrier and the gate must be closed."

Chapter 30

Tanzie stiffened to attention as the meaning of Morcar's words became clear to her. "What will happen to the one who performs this task?" she asked, her voice mere above a whisper.

"He will be lost forever," Morcar admitted. "Once closed, this gate will never be opened again."

Her glance slid sideways to the mountainous rock of which he spoke. It seemed to transform from solid stone to a wavering black void. It held a depth greater than the sea, and within that pitch darkness, a force stronger than the turning tide could be felt. "What if we do not close it?" she asked, desperately seeking an alternative to what she feared was about to happen.

"The dragons will eventually find a way to come back to us along with the other creatures that dwell there. We cannot allow a passage to another universe to stand wide open. Any number of unsuspecting animals and humans could wander through it never to be seen again."

Branoc made to step forward.

Cold dread filled Tanzie's heart. "No," she cried and grabbed his arm. "You have done enough."

"There seems little choice," he said softly. "Would you rather I lived on in fear and shame?"

"I would rather you lived, regardless of the cost. Without you I have nothing."

Even as she spoke Tanzie realized her words were in vain. Branoc would do what was honorable. It was the only way he knew.

Maybe she could be the one to close the rift. The

knowledge that Branoc still existed safely in this world would sustain her. "I will do it," she declared.

Branoc gazed at her his expression a combination of pride and affection. "You are willful even unto the end," he chided, and smiled down at her. "You will not do it. I am the one sworn to protect God, king, and country. For me 'twill be just another knightly adventure." He added the last with a half-hearted smile, as if he thought a mere jest could ease the terror that gripped her. Then she realized that no matter whose will won out they would both lose. Fate crossed them again coldly and cruelly.

"We could go together," she said. "Yes that is the answer. Better to face the unknown together than to remain here without you."

Branoc didn't reply, but rather he crooked his finger beneath her chin and kissed her lightly, his lips a silent prayer upon hers. Then he studied her face as if he memorized it for all time. "My most precious Martanzia. Either by my own foolish pride or by fate's sinister humor, I seem destined to be separated from you."

"But I love you, and you will be lost for ever."

"I love you too," he declared, "and I shall not be lost. You shall be my immortality."

Abruptly he turned away to reclaim the disk from Morcar's outstretched hand.

Tanzie recalled Branoc's face with their last kiss still warm upon his lips. Was this to be her final memory of the man she loved? Hopelessness overwhelmed her as Branoc strode closer to the monument of stone. This could not be happening. She could not let him go. Desperately she searched her mind for the words that would turn him from his final quest.

"Morcar," she cried out, "do something."

Why didn't he stop this insanity? Why didn't he close the gate himself? But the old Druid wore an inscrutable expression, and he made no move to alter the tragedy unfolding before her.

"Always the hero. You are so predictable Valtaigne."

The sound of Rathgar's voice startled Tanzie and halted Branoc in his tracks.

"Release him," Morcar commanded as Leofric struggled to keep Rathgar in place. "Each man has the right to choose his own path."

Rathgar sauntered forward and grabbed the medallion from Branoc. "And so insufferably noble," Rathgar added. "I refuse to once again be bested by you. You vanquished the damnable dragon, or whatever it was, but I shall take this through to the other side."

Benevolence was not Rathgar's strong suit. Did he plan more treachery? Tanzie ran forward and stood beside the two men.

Rathgar gently touched her cheek. "You shall be my salvation after all," he said, and for a fleeting moment, she saw sincerity and goodness in Rathgar's dark eyes. Then his familiar sarcastic smile returned, and his raised brow crowded out the look of sentimentality.

"Take special care of her, Valtaigne," Rathgar said. "She is even too good for the chivalrous likes of you."

An understanding seemed to pass between the two men, and in a show of fealty, they clasped one another's forearm. Rathgar strode forward to stand before the wavering portal. Legs braced, the pendant dangling from his hand, he gazed over at her one last time and gave a crooked smile. "The marriage document is forged," he called to Branoc.

"I know," Branoc replied, and eased his arm around her shoulders. "All shall hear of your final glory," Branoc promised. "You have won the day and the field." He tossed his sword to his old friend.

Rathgar neatly caught the weapon in his right hand. "I may not have lived well," he declared, "but a Relentes always dies well."

True affection flooded Tanzie's senses. What Rathgar was about to do was a sacrifice beyond measure or expectation. She prayed he would find peace in the kingdom that awaited him.

Rathgar appeared younger, and an aura of true valour overcame the anger and cynicism so deeply etched upon his features. Shoulders squared, he raised the weapon aloft, and his battle cry pierced the air as well as Tanzie's heart. Before the haunting wail died away, he ran forward into the great black void, and as he crossed the barrier, his form shimmered like a reflection in water. Then his image seemed to shatter and disappear leaving only the memory of his existence.

A rustling in the nearby underbrush made Tanzie jump.

Wiglaf scampered forward into the open. "Wait for me master," he cried, as he followed his lord into the beyond.

Rathgar's voice reverberated back from the other side. "Wiglaf...you faithful fool. Get thee here and let me tell you of my plans for ruling this new universe." His laughter deep and robust rang out then faded away and complete silence blanketed the shore.

The looming monument returned to solid rock, and it shuddered and shook and began to sink down into the sand and water. As the tip of the monolith slipped beneath the ocean a froth of seawater swirled briefly where the gate had once stood. Then the water grew calm and placid as if the rock had never been.

Gentle waves lapped against the beach, and they felt the warmth of the sun upon their shoulders.

Wonder and sorrow filled Tanzie's heart as she shifted her gaze to Morcar.

The old wizard appeared serene. "There are many worlds and many gates," he said, gently, "filled with beings beyond our imagining. Rathgar redeemed himself by his last act of courage, and he will live with the unicorns as well as the dragons. Perhaps his final doom is also his reward."

Branoc's arm tightened around her shoulder. His expression was distant as he stared out toward the sea, and his eyes were as cold as the gray waters he gazed upon. He had been through so much. And although Rathgar had been his enemy, he had once been his companion. "I'm sorry it ended thus," she said.

"There was no other way for it," Branoc admitted. "Today I regained the boyhood friend lost to me for many years, and in the end Rathgar proved himself a worthy comrade and an honorable man."

Leofric came to stand at their side. Wide-eyed and pale as a ghost, Ealgith clung to his arm and nervously chewed on the dried fruit she'd stashed in a knotted fold of her shawl.

Branoc glanced questioningly at Morcar.

"Yes," the old Druid reassured, "it is over. Except for the wedding," he added with a smug smile.

"I suppose you saw that in still water as well," Branoc growled.

"No indeed," Morcar said, as he scrutinized Branoc and her, "I saw it in your eyes."

Leofric gave a hoot of laughter and slapped Branoc on the back.

"Do not laugh too heartily," Branoc warned, "I intend to see that a double ceremony is arranged."

Ealgith blushed like a virgin, and Leofric grinned like a smitten young swan.

Epilogue
*Castle Bamburgh: September, 1100 A.D.*

"Good eventide, my lady," Branoc whispered in her ear. "Shall we continue to lie abed, or arise and greet our first moonlit night together as man and wife?"

Tanzie smiled, opened her eyes, and came face to face with her reason for living. "Abed awhile longer, husband, if you please," she murmured.

Beneath the covers, she ran her hand slowly down Branoc's naked chest and abdomen, her fingertips coming to rest upon the part of him that she now claimed as her own.

He groaned and pressed against her hand. He wanted her again, just as she wanted him, the passion they had shared only hours earlier having whetted their desire rather than slaking it.

Boldly, she draped one leg across his thighs. Then she arched closer to rain kisses upon his neck, his cheek, his mouth. She was thrilled by the new and wondrous delights they shared, and she heartily sought more of the carnal confection that she had quickly come to crave.

Branoc slid his hand downward, over the curve of her bottom. Then with a growl of impatient need, he rolled her onto her back, covered her body with his, plundered her mouth, and took her in one hard swift motion.

The feel of him inside of her sent her senses reeling, and the weight of his body pressing down upon her left her feeling both conquered and protected. He thrust harder, driving deeper, and she gave herself over to the aching desire and pounding rhythm that seemed to come so naturally to them.

Lost to his ministrations, she quickly crossed beyond mere longing to near full blown satisfaction, and what she experienced felt so good she thought it might be fatal.

"You are so beautiful, Martanzia" he crooned. "And mine to cherish forever."

His words excited her near as much as his touch and she moaned and writhed against him, diving headfirst into the waves of pleasure that washed through her entire body.

She held him close, her warrior knight, and felt his body shudder as he spilled his seed inside of her. It added to her enjoyment knowing that she satisfied his hunger, as equally as he satisfied hers.

Spent and contented, they lay side by side trying to catch their breath.

She levered upward on one arm, and gazed at her lover, her husband, her friend. "Now," she said with a grin, "I think we might arise. At least for a short duration."

****

They stood at the west wall. The light of a full moon bathed the land in an ethereal glow and Branoc was awed by the display. Or perhaps he felt so overwhelmed because his new bride of this morning stood beside him in the midst of God's artistry.

He moved to stand directly behind Martanzia, and enfolding her within the circle of his arms he rested his chin atop her head. Then he nuzzled her ear, and the fragrance of roses emanated from her soft skin. A rush of desire pooled again in his belly as he recalled the passion they had just experienced. Now such delight would be theirs to share often and forever.

"Would you have me if I were still a knight

errant?" he asked, knowing now there was no need to worry on that account.

Martanzia sighed and nestled her head back against his shoulder. "I would have no choice, my lord," she replied, "regardless of circumstance you shall always hold my heart hostage."

Branoc smiled. The new king, Henry Beauclerc, had formally granted him, in writing, lordship of castle Bamburgh. And Martanzia had received a large measure of coinage for her part in saving the North Country. The chateau in Flanders was also safely in their charge, and Uncle Malbourne had been reduced to living above the stable which he was ordered by royal decree to clean on a daily basis. They would want for nothing, as they journeyed into the future together.

Martanzia held out her hand and admired the little ring that encircled her finger with roses of gold. Although it did not flash with jewels, Branoc knew she cherished the dainty band. He had caught the expression of happiness in her eyes when she had first seen the ring during their nuptials.

"Castle Gray Scorn and Shining Hope are no more," he declared. "The skies are clear, and our hopes have been fulfilled."

"Then what shall we call our new home, husband?" Martanzia asked.

"We shall call it Briar Rose. You being the rose of course and I the briar. Someday the entire western slope will be covered with the beauty of roses, and the air will be heavy with their perfume."

Together they peered over the castle wall at the three hundred scraggly rose bushes that fought for a foothold upon the rocky terrain far down below. Branoc had ordered the rose cuttings from the castle at Lillebonne as well as from her garden in Flanders. The local villagers had helped to plant them, and even Morcar had postponed his trip home to Wales to lend a hand. The original rose bush that they had both championed stood out amongst the rest, its one small delicate white rose glowing in the celestial light. The flower had bloomed this morning as he and Martanzia had exchanged their vows.

Straightening to his full height, he sifted his gaze and contemplated his new tunic, and the unaccustomed hue of cerulean blue caught and tantalized his senses. The Dragon of Normandy was now embellished with the colors of Valtaigne. What had happened to the dreary gray and black trappings he had so carefully laid out in preparation of his wedding?

Wrapped in manly dreams of his wife-to-be, he had slept too soundly last night. He had not heard the intruder as the switch had been made. Intruder indeed, why not name the vixen, for Martanzia Verheire it had been. Branoc knew this as surely as he knew that the sun would rise tomorrow to brighten his world.

Fate had brought Martanzia to his side, dispelling the darkness in which he had lived for far too many years, and this was just another example of her thoughtfulness to honor and cherish him; this time in front of all those who had gathered to see them wed.

Tightening his embrace around Martanzia, Branoc savored the feeling of joy and contentment. Today should have been the most glorious day of his life—and it was.

# Historical Note

Regarding my heroine's use of a hairbrush: I could not prove nor disprove the possibility that the hairbrush was routinely available in the year 1100 A.D. However, in one form or another, such personal items were known to be employed by the ancient Greeks and Romans as well as the Vikings. I think it is possible that Tanzie could have had such a beauty aid at her disposal. I'm sure if they existed Ealgith, her handmaiden, would have procured a beautifully wrought silver one for her.

In 1095, Robert de Mowbray was not captured by William II during the siege of Bamburgh but rather he was taken prisoner outside the castle when for some unknown reason Mowbray left with a contingent of men and traveled to Tynemouth. His wife continued to hold the castle until the besiegers threatened to blind her captured husband.

King William II truly did meet his end in a hunting "accident" very near the day of Lammas. To my knowledge the assasin was never named nor caught, although the arrow that caused the king's death was similar to the arrows carried that day by Walter Tyrell (or Tirel). William's two brothers, Henry and Robert, were not officially implicated.

Ranulph Flambard, the Bishop of Durham, was the first political prisoner to occupy the Tower of London, and he is also the first prisoner to escape the fortification. He fled to Normandy and allied himself with Robert against Henry, the new king.

**From the author...**

I live and play in Colorado, where the moon rises over the prairie and the sun sets behind the Rocky Mountains. When I am not reading or writing, I'm taking care of my Noah's Ark of animals including ducks, geese, goats, donkeys, and cats.

Wherever it is that you live and play, I thank you for taking the time to read *The Dragon and The Rose* and I hope you will watch for *Lady Gallant*, a Victorian romance, available in the future from the Wild Rose Press. An excerpt for *Lady Gallant* is available now at www.ginirifkin.com

May all your ever afters be happy ones.

Thank you for purchasing
this Wild Rose Press publication.
For other wonderful stories of romance,
please visit our on-line bookstore at
www.thewildrosepress.com.

For questions or more information,
contact us at info@thewildrosepress.com.

The Wild Rose Press
www.TheWildRosePress.com

## Other Historical Roses to enjoy
## from The Wild Rose Press

### *from English Tea Rose:*
HIGHLAND MOONLIGHT by Teresa Reasor. Seduced by the warrior to whom she is betrothed, Lady Mary flees to sanctuary. But she is forced to wed him, to save him from the executioner. Was her dream as elusive as Highland Moonlight?

THE RESURRECTION OF LADY SOMERSET by Nicola Beaumont. An age-old mystery, a risky assignment, a marriage devised to suppress a secret... Lark has been hidden most of her life. With the death of her mentor comes the command to marry the new Lord Somerset. Without this marriage, the estate falls to his wastrel brother. Can either suitor satisfy the lady?

### *from Vintage Rose:*
DON'T CALL ME DARLIN' by Fleeta Cunningham: In Texas, 1957, Carole the librarian faces censorship. Will the County Judge who's dating her protect or accuse her?

SOURDOUGH RED by Pinkie Paranya: At the end of the Klondike gold rush, Jen and her younger brother search for her twin, lost and threatened in Alaskan wilderness.

### *from Cactus Rose:*
OUTLAW IN PETTICOATS by Paty Jager. Maeve had her heart crushed; it won't happen again. Zeke has wanted Maeve since he first set eyes on her...

SECRETS IN THE SHADOWS by Sheridon Smythe. Lovely widow Lacy had taken in two young children—and the rambunctious little angels wasted no time getting her into trouble with Shadow City's new sheriff...

### *from American Rose:*
EXPEDITION OF LOVE by Jo Barrett. An up-and-coming scientist in the world of paleontology collides heart first with an unconventional suffragette who has no desire to marry. Can they resolve their differences?

WHERE THE HEART IS by Sheridon Smythe. Orphan Natalie Polk steps into the shoes of the errant orphanage house mother. The new owner not only accepts her as capable of running the home but falls in love with her, with obstacles galore. How can they have a future?

www.ingramcontent.com/pod-product-compliance
Lightning Source LLC
Chambersburg PA
CBHW071646260626
47170CB00001B/259